The Forces of Bay House

a novel of suspense

Bess Paterson Shipe
& Susan Shipe Calfee

Wordwhittler Books
Ponte Vedra Beach, Florida

Interior and Cover Design by Oscar Senn

Editor, Lynn Skapyak Harlin

ISBN: 978-0-9895487-6-2 (paperback)

ISBN: 978-0-9895487-7-9 (ebook)

Library of Congress Catalog Number: 2024913965

Wordwhittler Books
3073 Cypress Creek Drive N.
Ponte Vedra Beach, Florida 32082

Printed and bound in the United States of America

First Edition

For my beloved sisters

Ann Cooper and Carolyn TenEyck,

my best friends on the journey of life

Prologue

It was an April evening in the year of our Lord, 1770. The Reverend Russell Witherspoon heard someone knocking on the door of his modest parsonage on Kent Island in the Chesapeake Bay. He opened the door cautiously, for this rural isle, a part of the colony of Maryland, was still strange to him even after ten years of service. He was relieved to be packing for the return trip by frigate to his dear England.

When he saw who was outside, he was astounded. Young Will Collington, the son of one of his land-owning parishioners, stood on the doorstep holding an Indian girl by the hand.

For a moment, there was a voiceless confrontation. No sound but the piping of tree toads from the forest across the creek. The moist, earthy aroma of first spring scented the dusk.

Then Will seemed to prime himself to speak, in a voice unnaturally loud.

"Reverend Witherspoon, Sir, we were thinking … we are thinking of asking you, Sir, if you could, please … marry us tonight?"

The Reverend stood motionless a moment longer. Moral issues such as this he was not prepared for, especially this night, and he rebelled against the burden of it. He and his family were already exhausted by the flurry of preparations in their small household.

"Sir," Will went on, "Reverend Witherspoon, we know you'll be leaving on the *Constance* in the morning. My father says it will be maybe a year before the *Constance* returns with the new rector. I was twenty-one last February, Sir, and I'm old enough to know my own mind."

The Reverend scrutinized Will's companion, who was dressed in deerskin.

"Are you with child, child?" he blurted. He chided himself for the awkward question he would not have put to a young English lady under any circumstances.

The girl's voice was soft, low, almost a whisper. She spoke English with the accent of the Matapeakes. "No, Reverend. I am not." She gazed up at Will, clutched his hand and stood as straight and graceful as a small, perfect tree.

"We'll have a child when Ellen Smalldeer is my wife," said Will. "We'll have no hiding it and will gladly take a grandchild to my father. Then all will be well."

Within Russell Witherspoon's meaty chest there beat a heart that had more than once gotten him into trouble with his superiors, and which led him into the ministry in the first place. Looking at the two in front of him he had no doubt that if he denied them the marriage rites they asked for so earnestly, with eyes so young, so innocent still, so hopeful, they would surely sin. The moon was already out, full and silver. The breeze was gentle from the bay, stirring the scent of pine needles, clean and sweet and wild.

"You will excuse me, please, a moment," he said. "Wait here."

He turned inside to the small room where he kept his few precious books, his Bible, and all the records of the church. He knelt, praying in silence, his hands clasped in supplication.

Father, forgive me for abetting this fine lad to deceive his parents, who will be sorely vexed. In so doing I may prevent a still more grievous wrong. Gracious Lord, send me guidance.

After he prayed, he tuned his mind to listen for the Lord. He felt no sense of reprimand, only a kind of peace. If there was any unrest it was for his daughter, Lucy. He knew she hoped to marry Will one day. But that, he reminded himself, was nothing but the girl's own daydream. Her ailing mother was right glad to be taking their daughter home with them to England.

About the possible reaction of the Indians, the good Rector could only speculate. There was but a small tribe of them left living in the woodland near the creek, although in times past they were reported to have paddled their way to church in their canoes. They were as anonymous to him as the deer and the foxes.

If this was a hundred years or more before, the story might have been a different one. The Matapeakes inhabited a large village once, on land now owned by the Collingtons, but they were peaceful even then. Not like the fierce Susquehannocks, or the Wicomeeses, who were their brutal enemies before any white man sailed up the wide, empty Chesapeake Bay to this green island of Kent.

The Reverend Witherspoon sighed, shaking his large head. This isle in the bay was a place of great, though alien, beauty to him. The history of man's struggle against man to possess it saddened him. Sometimes he had a dark foreboding from the trend of things he observed that more struggles would come between these colonies and the mother country herself.

"Ah, well." He roused his mind back to the moment and bade the young couple to come in. He lit two more candles placing them on a little table, which would have to do for an altar. He then stood behind it and faced the young pair.

Candlelight flickered on Will's strong, English features and blonde hair. On the straight black cascade that fell almost to the girl's waist, the tawny smooth skin of her face with its finely molded high cheekbones. And, the Reverend almost gasped in his surprise, sky blue eyes.

For some reason this made Witherspoon feel better still. Right or wrong, there was already a mixing of the blood in this new land.

He called his wife and Emma Hollins, their elderly maidservant, to be witnesses.

He performed the marriage ceremony from the Book of Prayer, pronounced Ellen Smalldeer and William Collington man and wife, and recorded the event in the *Marriage Book* reserved for such solemnities. He then admonished the young couple to tell the family of each what was done.

Of course, he had no assurance they would carry out this last instruction, but he was a man who did his duty as he saw it. Finally, he bade Emma Hollins hold her peace until all parties involved had time to adjust to this new turn of events. Having done all he could, he wished the pair Godspeed and turned them out into the starry night.

All might have been well, in the long run, save for one small act of evil that changed the tide of the future for six generations yet unborn.

The Reverend's sixteen-year-old daughter hid in the shadows, listening from the stairs. Never in her short life had she felt any emotion like the jealousy that seared her now. Just last Sunday, her last one here in America, she wore her new peach-colored frock to church, shiny ribbons in her curls. She dawdled so that Will would have to catch up with her after the service, her heart rising and sinking with hope and fear. Surely, she willed it, he would speak before she was on that ship, gone forever, and tell her he loved her. Then he did catch up. He looked so happy, so dressed up, clean and fine. He was whistling.

But all he said was, "Godspeed, Lucy. Have a safe trip. Don't get seasick. And don't break all the hearts in London."

So. This was why. This half-breed girl. This little savage. Lucy saw her sometimes, working in the kitchen of Gray's Inheritance, though Miss Lucy Witherspoon didn't usually bother to stop and speak to a servant. It seemed a long time since Lucy was twelve or so when she went to visit the Collingtons. Sometimes she was allowed to play with Will, his sister Mercy and their friend Richard Gray just outside the gate.

The Indian children who lived in the woods nearby played with them, too. Lucy only vaguely remembered the little blue-eyed Indian girl who ran so swift and silent they never could catch her in games. Lucy always tagged after young Will, four years older than her. He was tall, splendid, patient with the younger children. Only Will was important. Now, suddenly, she realized why Will rode right past the parsonage so often on his chestnut gelding. Only waving, never stopping. She supposed he was going to visit his friend, Richard Gray, when she watched him turn into the lane of Gray's Inheritance. But she was wrong. Now she knew Will was courting this lowly heathen instead.

Lucy's fury made the pain of jealousy more bearable. Her young heart turned to stone. Her Christian conscience ignited and burned to ash. When at last her parents were asleep, she stole into the room where the church records were kept. By the half-light of the banked fire, she opened the *Marriage Book* and stared at the last entry in her father's firm, florid script.

Her impulse was to throw the book into the fire. Stopping short of that, she cast about in the room for a hiding place. Quickly, lest she be heard or seen, she pried open the old wooden tobacco barrel packed with her father's treasured books that were so hard to come by in this new world. These were meant to be left for the next rector. She buried the leather-bound registry deep inside, under the heavy heap of tattered volumes.

"Let them search for it forever," she whispered into the darkness.

"And let Will suffer then as I am suffering now."

Of course, Lucy could not know that the loyal heart of Emma Hollins would give out long before the new minister arrived. Or that Sally Briggs, who could not read a single word, was due to come clean and scour for the welcoming committee. Sally had no use for books, hated trash and clutter, and would send that useless old hogshead off to the tobacco warehouse miles away.

1

June 3, 1965

Escape. It was not a conscious thought. The need to escape was a demon chasing us through the night. We hurtled down the dark highway. I trembled but kept my foot mashed to the gas pedal. My hands were sweaty claws clamped to the wheel I struggled to steer. I felt my eyes stretched wide as I stared at the road ahead and darted glances at the rear-view mirror.

My mouth was open and dry. I gasped in breaths too ragged to control. Matt could already be following. I knew he would never willingly let us go. Yet mixed with the terror was the smallest seed of elation. There was at last a chance, if I could master my shaking self, we could escape to something I dreamed of all my life.

The first traces of dawn were bleaching the black out of the sky. The morning air was chilly although it was early June, the days already hot and summery. With my left hand I rolled up the window, praying the fake wooden panels on our old station wagon wouldn't make us easier to spot. Even this small effort made my upper arm throb where purple bruises seemed to have penetrated all the way to the bone. My head hurt, too, from the tight cap where I stuffed my long dark hair. I was drained, and so terribly tired. But I had to keep driving. Keep straining to read road signs that flew by. Keep racing to beat the rising sun.
We skirted Baltimore, passed through the Tunnel. There were about forty miles to go on Interstate 95 before we reached the outskirts of

Washington. With my right hand I groped on the front seat for the map.

"Mommy." A rustling noise, then Benjie's little face was just behind my ear.

"Get down. Get down," I said. "You must lie down, Benjie."

"I'm tired of lying down and I'm not sleepy anymore." His voice was still high and piping. Although he just turned five, he was beginning to perceive everything I tried to spare him.

"Get down," I said. "This instant. Or I'm going to stop the car and come back there." *I hated the hiss that sounded as I spat out the command. And the threat.*

He started to cry but flopped back on the seat.

"This game isn't fun anymore," he said between sobs. "I don't wanna play I'm a stupid girl and I hate this stupid ribbon. I'm taking it off. And, Mommy, why do you want to look like a boy?"

Dear God, this child doesn't need any more grief from me. Please help me to hang on. I trembled, remembering the terror of our frantic getaway from New York, only hours ago. Still staring ahead, I fought to measure my words, control the shrill edge in my voice.

"Benjie, sweetheart, I'm sorry. You're not in trouble. I just really need you to lie down. It's very, very important for nobody to notice us. You can keep the bow off until we get to the city. Then we'll play the game again. Just one more time. OK?"

He sniffled, slumped lower, laid his head on his pillow. "OK, but I'm hungry, Mommy. And I have to go to the bathroom. How long 'til we get there?"

"Not long, Benj. Not long at all." I tried to focus my mind away from the fear onto some distraction. "Let's see. I'll tell you a story. You keep down, just lie still, and I'll tell you a story."

A car came even with us on the left with a man's silhouette hunched over the wheel the way Matt did when he was raging. My heart lurched, but the car roared on by.

"I really have to go to the bathroom, Mommy."

I twisted my right arm back between the seats, fingers fumbling to soothe my frightened child. But my hand could not reach him. Only my words could make us both brave.

"Once upon a time—this is an exciting story, Benj. Once upon a time there was a little girl named Abby."

"Was that you?"

"Yes, that was me. When I was just a little bit older than you. There was a little girl named Abigail Collington, and she went for a walk with her father in the woods."

"Was there bears in the woods?"

"No bears."

I paused to concentrate, raced past a truck, my heart racing, too. I had to keep watching the mirror.

"Um, this was a nice woods. A beautiful woods. Nothing scary. There were very tall trees not too close together, so bits of sunlight came through between them. There was moss on the ground in places, and little wildflowers."

"What are wildflowers? Like merry-goles?"

"No, these are tiny and they grow in the shade, so you have to know about them and look hard to find them. My father knew all about them."

I had to raise my voice so he could hear me since I couldn't turn my head. This memory was steadying me a little.

"These were like violets, and columbine. I don't think you've ever seen columbine, Benj. It's pink. It grows on a stalk and has blossoms like little bells. They smell sweet, just like you."

Half-hearted little kicks landed against my seat back. "This isn't a exciting story. This is a yukky story."

"We're coming to the exciting part."

I snatched another glance in the mirror. *I'd have to slow down. It was almost morning, the slate sky dappled with pearl. How long did it take to identify a license plate? I wrenched my weary mind back to my tale.*

"Well, there was a stream. The water was very clean and clear. There were rocks in the stream, a little waterfall rushed over them. We took off our shoes and socks, then we waded in the water. It felt all cool and squishy and swirly. There was a log from one side of the stream to the other. It wasn't very wide, but it was long and mossy. My father said, 'Hey, Abby-girl, do you want to play I dare you to walk across the stream on that log?'"

My toes wiggled in my sneakers, a flick of warmth touched my heart. "I remember, Benj. I really do remember how I felt. Happy. Free. And I was sure I could do it. So, I said, 'Daddy, I dare you to walk across that log without your shoes on.' Then he smiled and hugged me and said, 'I dare you back.' And we both did it."

"I could do that," Benjie murmured, sounding sleepy again.

"Anyway, we sat down on the other side of the stream with our feet in the water, my father and me. 'You're a plucky little kid, Abby-girl,' my father told me. 'Someday I'm going to take you back to Bay House, where I grew up. That's our real home, and part of it belongs to us. Don't let anybody ever make you believe that it doesn't.'"

"Not even," he said, "your beautiful mother."

I didn't repeat that last part to Benjie. The remains of my beautiful mother had just been interred in a small cemetery in Southampton near my father, who died when I was ten.

Silence from the back seat. With vast relief I stopped talking. I switched on the radio, trying again to fight the fear tightening like a hand around my throat. Music without melody blared in a jumble as I dialed, my eyes locked on the highway. In disjointed crackles a man's excited voice sputtered about NASA. Gemini IV. The second manned mission ever launched, putting June 3, 1965 in history books forever. And with it, the first space walk by an American. I was dimly aware that this momentous news might interest a little boy more than my jabbering about blossoms and a stream. But in the next instant we were engulfed by snarling traffic, squealing brakes, honking horns. I was ripped back to my own desperate flight.

We were approaching the outskirts of D. C. *I had to hang on. If I was alone in the car I would have screamed. But I had my son to care for. I could see by the clock on the dashboard that it was 5:15 if the old clock was right. Day was dawning with streaks of light. If only Benjie would sleep until I could find where we were going.*

As cars passed, I could distinguish faces, which meant, of course, people could distinguish mine. I clutched the wheel, my stomach churning. *Could I possibly look like a young beardless male in my low-slung cap and denim shirt, instead of a twenty-seven-year-old woman? Would Matt already have alerted the police? Could I already be a missing person?*

"Mom-mee." That heart-breaking whimper from the back seat. "Why was Daddy so mean to us? Why did we have to run away and play the game?"

Damn. How could I have been so stupid? How could I have talked about my father with all that love seeping through when Benjie's own father had just shaken him as a dog might shake a rabbit?

I shuddered, reliving the scene with Matt. Winced at the welts and bruises left by his hands. Saw Benjie's eyes, sunken circles of shock in his small white face. I fought the urge to sob, pound the steering wheel with my fists. I longed to stop the car and take my child into my arms.

But I said, "Daddy is sick, Benj. He didn't know what he was doing. We'll talk about it tomorrow. I want you to put that hair ribbon on and get ready to play the game one more time."

I found the street I was looking for. I knew I could find my way now to the women's shelter, St. Katherine's House of Grace. The creased and ragged news clipping I kept hidden for so long within the lining of my purse said its doors were open twenty-four hours a day.

2

The building was a four-story Victorian. Red brick painted gray long before and needing paint again. I drove by slowly, spotting the St. Katherine's sign on the shiny, geranium-red door. That door gave me hope. The place looked like a somewhat shoddy fortress with bars on the lower windows, but the door was fresh and bright. It was a beacon.

The neighborhood also looked dubious. This place was not what I pictured in my fantasy of escape, but what could I do but go on? I found a parking space on the street about three blocks away, possibly because it was still so early. People were stirring though, walking, waiting at bus stops, sitting on front steps. Cars went by. We trudged the three blocks, Benjie and I, looking straight ahead. Hopefully I appeared as a tall boy in a cap, work shirt and jeans, holding a little blond girl by the hand. A little girl with a pretty pink bow in her hair. Perhaps Benjie didn't feel my hand trembling.

Then we were on the doorstep, and I was knocking.

Someone peered at us through a small, screened window in that red door. Then we heard a bolt being sidled out.

"Oh, no," said the woman who opened the door. "When will you girls learn we can't take children here?"

I stared at her, too stunned to speak.

"You could try the Salvation Army," she said. "I can give you their address. They have more facilities than we do."

She was tall, lean, with a strong jaw. The sallow face wore no makeup. The gray eyes matched the color of her jacket and skirt and looked as if they had seen too much of a sad world.

I kept staring. I was so tired.

Benjie's feet made little marching steps. "Mommy. I have to go to the bathroom."

To the end of my days, I'll be grateful for those eight words.

The woman laughed. She doubled over and slapped her knee.

"I guess you'll have to come in then. And take off that hair ribbon, son. I bet you're sick of it."

Motioning us in, she bolted the door behind us. Thankfully, we were alone in the entryway.

She shrugged. Stuck out a firm hand and shook mine. "What the hell. After the night we've had here, I guess we can break a few more rules."

I managed to mumble my name, and Benjie's, though my voice seemed to come from somewhere other than my body.

"Well, hello there, Abby. I'm not a Sister," she said, although that seemed clear enough. "I'm Helen Barker, a volunteer. I went down this road a couple years ago, now I help out when we're busy."

Helen reached for Benjie's hand like they were old pals.

"I'll take him to the bathroom," she said, "then for some treats we have stashed back in the kitchen." She eyed me from head to toe. "You better sit down before you fall down."

Benjie looked back at me anxiously, his face as pinched as my mother often told me mine was. I knew he was afraid to leave me.

I hugged him, smoothed his hair, slid the pink ribbon off into my hand. "It's OK, Benj," I whispered.

It was hard to speak as I aimed a weak smile at Helen. "Thank you," was all I could say.

I sat on a lumpy sofa in the hall on the safe side of that bolted door, longing to hide here and never leave. It never occurred to me in my fantasies that some shelters couldn't keep children. I wanted to shout, "It's not fair!" But I felt like a suppliant. Something that crawled in from under a rock. I would have to persuade this Helen to let us stay longer, long enough for me to rally my forces. I was so very tired, slumped there holding my upper arms, trying to get my bearings.

This must have been an elegant house once, long ago, and it probably was many things since. Now it was clean and plain. The high-ceilinged walls had fresh off-white paint over cracked plaster. On one side was an empty Victorian parlor with long, deep-set windows and carved moldings, made into a TV lounge. On the other side was an office. I heard a clock ticking. A phone rang twice, then stopped. Upstairs, somewhere, faintly, someone was crying.

Helen came back with Benjie. He held a glass of milk and a donut. His mouth was trimmed with powdered sugar, but his eyes were still round and solemn.

In Helen's hand was a tray with two donuts, two cups of hot coffee. One, clearly, for me. The feel of the warm china, the steamy, normal morning smell of the brew were so comforting I felt tears starting. If the woman noticed she pretended not to.

She waved me into the office, plunked down at a desk, began sorting papers, nodding at the straight-backed chair opposite.

"You'll have to fill in these forms before I can let you go upstairs and get some sleep." She pointed to a worn wooden staircase leading up from the hall.

"How long ..." I began, but she interrupted as if I hadn't spoken.

She winked at Benjie. "Why don't you run on back and bring us that box of donuts?"

Benjie's face lifted in a sugary grin as he trotted toward the kitchen.

Helen leaned forward across the desk. "I'm dead on my feet myself. What a night. One of the girls who came here a couple days ago decided to go home after her husband tracked her down. Sent her a dozen red roses with a big bow and a card that said, 'My Love is Like a Red, Red Rose.' It's a poem, but from him it was garbage." She sighed, her gaze fixed on the barred window above my head. "So, what does she do? Goes back to the creep. Then at 3:00 a.m. this morning she's back here pounding on our door with two black eyes nearly swollen shut and her gums bleeding. That gorilla started drinking again, broke her nose and knocked out her front teeth. The Sisters don't approve of what I really want to call him. We had to get the cops, record and photo the injury before Sister Florence Katherine could take her to the emergency room."

Helen handed me a form entitled, "Admissions."

"Why don't you take off that cap?" she said, tapping her head.

I had forgotten. I pulled off the cap. My long dark hair fell straight to my shoulders.

I bent over the form and found myself putting my life down on paper. My hand trembled and it was hard to hold the pen.

Name: Abigail Collington Wells

Age: 27

Marital Status: I checked "Mrs.," but I wanted to write, "OVER."

I knew I would never go back to Matt unless he forced me somehow, with Benjie as a pawn in the game. I could hardly remember what it was like to love him.

Name of Husband, Ex-husband, Companion: John Matthew Wells.

I tried not to picture him lying on the floor of our bedroom. I had listened to his heart, and it was beating.

Address: 10 W. 82nd Street, Apt. 103, N.Y., N.Y.

Our tall, grim building. Our anonymous little apartment.

Next of Kin:

Oh, Fran. Oh, Mother. If only you could sail through that door right now with all your flags flying, I'd be so glad to let you help me. Then I felt a twist of longing for my father. "Parents Deceased," I wrote.

Children: Benjamin Collington Wells. Age 5.

Legal Counsel, (if any):

I didn't want to involve Mr. Dangerfield, our old family lawyer and friend. I didn't want anyone to know where I was. All I wanted to do was to find out how long I could hide here, then go to sleep.

I looked up at Helen. “Please. Can’t you tell me how long a person can stay here with a child? I mean, if it’s against the rules, is it necessary to fill out these forms?”

“Ha. That was only the first round,” she said.

Benjie was back, he and Helen were both munching donuts. “I didn’t even give you the whole passel. There’s medical and financial and police and family court. We won’t bother with those. Just hurry up with the basics and we’ll see if we get lucky.”

I forced my attention back to the form.

Legal Counsel, (if any):

I would have to call him, but I hated the thought. Benjie and I would need money. I wrote: “Mr. Arthur Dangerfield,” and the address of his New York law firm which I knew by heart. *Since my father died my mother was always saying, “We’ll get in touch with Arthur. He’ll take care of it.” That dear little man, whose face reminded me of a Bassett hound. I think he loved my mother. But then, she charmed everyone. When she wanted to. Since my childhood she’d always seemed like two different people. Especially to me. I never understood why her warmth shone, then cooled, like clouds passing over the sun. Those times when she was remote and distant, I played a game, calling her Fran, as if she was a character in a play, stealing the role of Mother. The duality stuck. I was confused, hurt by her indifference. But time passed, I stopped looking for explanations. Fran and Mother were synonymous, but I never knew why.*

There were other questions. I did the best I could with them, though sometimes the paper seemed a little blurry.

I gave the forms to Helen and she handed me a little packet. Through plastic wrap I could see soap, a washcloth, toothpaste, toothbrush, a comb. She smiled at me with unexpected sweetness, showing her large teeth.

"Go wash your pretty face," she said, "and try to get some sleep. I'll show you where."

She took Benjie's hand, leading us up the uncarpeted steps to a room on the second floor.

"Please, I still don't know, and I have to think." I came out with it. My voice wobbled and rose to an unfamiliar pitch. "How long can I stay here with Benjie?"

"I'm not supposed to have kept you here now, since you're asking. I told you already, we don't have facilities for kids. No day-care. Not enough funding, all kinds of legal hassles. But I'm in for it anyway, I guess. Who do you think was the idiot who accepted those roses for Nancy? I thought I'd let you grab a few winks until Sister comes back on duty. She can tell you about other services. We have wake-up at seven and breakfast at seven-thirty. So, if you want to avoid the rush, you'd better pull down the blinds and go beddy-bye right now."

The room was as clean and stark as the downstairs except for a little basket of yellow plastic flowers on the dresser. On the off-white wall between the two iron beds was a wooden crucifix. When Benjie was settled in one bed, I lay in the other, giving thanks, waiting for sleep at last. The crucifix on the wall made me feel safer.

I closed my eyes, but sleep didn't come. I kept seeing Matt as I left him, lying on our bedroom floor.

He started drinking early in the morning, just yesterday, though now it seemed eons ago. We were due at the memorial service for my mother at the church near her home on Long Island at 1:00. Before noon, I took Benjie upstairs to stay with Mrs. Trimble, a quasi-grandmother who understood my unpredictability. I managed to keep Benjie away from his father during the bad times. It looked as if this was going to be a very bad time.

All mother's cronies were there. Many of our own friends, too, although we stopped socializing since Matt's drinking got so hopeless and he was eased out of his job at Banks & Stevens. When the service was over people lingered outside.

Matt and I found ourselves manning a receiving line on the church steps in the sunny early afternoon. There was no one else to do it. Mr. Dangerfield hovered in the background, grim-faced, adjusting and re-adjusting his tie.

A queue of sleek, darkly dressed friends and admirers like a line-up of crows waited to say hello. Many of them teary, longing to tell us how they missed Fran after her stroke. Her eye, her energy, her contributions. At the garden club, country club, at this or that benefit over which she would have presided. At the committee meetings of her various charities, which she always made grand events. Now they would miss her always, and terribly.

People hugged me and told me how much I looked like my mother, except for my dark hair. Of course, I knew I would never be as lovely as she was. The blue of her eyes was darker than mine. Almost violet sometimes. My features lacked the classic proportions of hers. My cheekbones were higher, my mouth a little less tenderly bowed. The black silk sheath I wore hung more loosely on me, where Fran's natural curves would have rounded it out.

I stopped thinking about how I looked when I started thinking about survival.

Everyone was polite to Matt. Polite, but remote. Even our own friends kept their distance. Asked no questions about why they hadn't seen us, or how things were in the stock market.

After the service, on the way back to my mother's house in Southampton, I felt him begin to fume.

He pummeled the steering wheel, muttered through clenched teeth. "Screw 'em all."

"It just wasn't the time to talk about us, Matt. You're imagining things."

"Like everyone thinks I'm a lush," he said. Then he was red-faced, sullen.

I knew all the signals. My hands felt clammy as they always did when I began to be afraid. Matt reeked of Scotch. I knew he must have a bottle somewhere in the car. I was not about to mention it.

We turned down the country lane that led to my mother's house. The fact that she would not be there was unbearably real to me for the first time.

Mr. Dangerfield was waiting outside the beautiful old salt box that was once the summer home of my mother's parents. With his typical gentle courtesy, he allowed Matt and me to enter first, although he had a key.

We went inside. The long beige and white living room was perfect but still. Through the French doors with which my mother's magic touch transformed the staid old house, we could see the flagstone patio. White wicker furniture around the pool. Pale pink and purple azaleas. Rhododendron with lavender blossoms banked against the tall fence that closed out the rest of the world. The white marble bird bath was empty. No seed in the bird feeders. No sound, no movement. No life.

I began to sob. Mr. Dangerfield stood beside me, patting my shoulder, wiping his eyes, blowing his nose.

Matt disappeared into the kitchen, banging the white shuttered doors behind him.

After a pause Mr. Dangerfield gave a final blow and collected himself. He turned to me, his deep-set eyes two pools of sadness.

"My dear child. I asked you to come back here so we could have a quiet little talk. There are some things I'm going to have to tell you immediately."

Matt stomped out of the kitchen, slapping the shutter doors out of the way. His gait was heavy, crooked. A fresh wave of Scotch wafted before him.

We sat on the L-shaped couch. I edged as far as I could from Matt without seeming too obvious. Our lawyer perched in the middle, his feet just touching the floor.

His news was not good. Naturally, I inherited everything, but there was not much money left that wasn't needed for the expenses of the estate. During Fran's illness the past year he had to delve into the principal. Now there was the matter of her diminished finances. He coughed behind his small, fluttering hand. "Abigail, there are bills, inheritance taxes, estate taxes, etc. This house must be sold, hopefully for a sizeable sum in this exclusive community. But I must warn you." He darted quick sideways glances at Matt and me. "These things take time."

Our beautiful house. Everything that was my mother. Strange, distant, but still beloved.

Mr. Dangerfield produced a thick folder and proceeded to go into meticulous detail.

Matt became more and more restless and agitated. He caught my eye, jerked his head toward the door. He had heard more than he wanted to know.

The meeting was not really over, but I stood to make our apologies. I couldn't afford to incite Matt further.

Mr. Dangerfield avoided Matt's stare as one avoids the eye of a mean dog. "It might be wise for Abigail to stay here for a few days. She'll have to make decisions."

I knew he was trying to help. But I could not stay. To leave Benjie with Matt in the city when his father was in such a mood was not an option.

I stammered a rude, abrupt goodbye and followed Matt to the door. We started home.

It's hard to explain how Fran was the buffer between me and Matt's rages. It was her presence. Somebody once called that presence her Commando Charm. Even that wasn't an accurate description. She simply refused to accept as reality the fact that her own daughter could not handle this boy-next-door who became a monster of self-loathing and anger when he drank. "Like a werewolf in the glimmer of a full moon," she said once.

When I came home to visit she pampered me, put me to bed, found baby-sitters for Benjie and doctors or psychiatrists for Matt. Twice, she managed to send him to a small, expensive, very private rehab hospital. Nothing ever helped for long. Everything was always hush-hush, tiny changes never lasted.

"Matt has an excellent background," she vowed. "Blood always tells. He will straighten out, Abby, and he is Benjie's father. We must hold our heads high."

She never answered my questions about my own father or his childhood home.

Even Matt was overpowered by Fran when he wasn't drinking. Besides beauty and charm, she had all that money.

Now there was no money and no Fran.

On the way back on the Long Island Freeway Matt drove in that furious, hunched-over way of his. Morose, silent, with the old canvas porkpie hat he wore in college jammed on his head. I tried to stay calm, to avoid doing anything that might make him angrier.

We crossed the George Washington Bridge. Matt burrowed our old blue station wagon recklessly through the traffic. I turned on the radio to fill in his furious silence. "Goldfinger" was playing, followed by an ad for the movie. *I pictured how James Bond would've handled this scene. The racket of Manhattan, cars, people, taxis, horns, made my head pound. Matt reached forward and bashed the radio to silence with his fist. His eyes slid to meet mine while that fist lay clenched between us. I felt trapped, small and helpless on these narrow, clogged streets between giant buildings. I longed to open the door and run.* When we finally reached our apartment, Matt lurched ahead inside, weaving as he walked.

I rushed upstairs to the floor above to get Benjie from Mrs. Trimble. He was little, eager, warm, glad to see me. So comforting. He made me feel stronger.

"Thank you so much for keeping Benjie … safe. I'm going to be out at my mother's house this week," I said. "I'm going right back there and taking him with me." *Saying it out loud made it seem matter-of-fact and logical. This was a lie of course, but I knew then what I must do. I would find the car keys and then make some pretext about a short errand. A run to the deli for pizza. That, Matt might welcome, as a chance for more silent drinking. There was always this quiet, liquid build-up before the storm broke. The latest psychiatrist had warned me.*

I carried Benjie piggy-back down to our door. Everything should seem normal. Benjie was laughing his high little giggle. But we were too late. We walked into the eye of the storm.

Matt stood in the bedroom, weaving, next to the bed. Made no pretense of hiding the bottle he gripped. Whiskey spilled down the front of his suit.

"So now you're teaching my son to laugh at me." He never touched Benjie before. Never let out the full violence of his wrath when our child was present.

He grabbed both of my forearms with such force that I shrieked. Somehow, I held on to Benjie, perched on my shoulders.

"Shut up," Matt yelled. "Shut up, both of you."

Though by this time we were both mute.

Matt yanked Benjie off my shoulders and shook him.

Benjie's shocked, terrified screams came out in breathless jolts.

I put my arms around Benjie from the back. I think I was screaming, too. For endless seconds I tried to wrestle the child out of Matt's grasp, then, in desperation, I started kicking at Matt's legs. He had no control of balance. As he fell, I clutched Benjie against my chest.

Matt lay on the floor without moving. I knelt, realized he must have hit his head on the wooden bed post. I put my ear to his ribs, although the feel and scent of his body made me shudder. He was not conscious, but he was breathing, and his heartbeat sounded strong.

In twenty minutes, Benjie and I were in the car careening through Manhattan. He on the back seat with a pillow, blanket, a pink hair ribbon tied in a bow. My quilted bag was beside me stuffed with random things I grabbed from a drawer. I prayed my whimpering child would stay still.

I had more than a fantasy. I had a full-fledged scenario in my head, far more final than a brief escape to St. Katherine's.

Where it would lead us, I could not know.

3

I awakened in shock, realizing I slept after all in a small iron bed in a shelter for battered women, and I just had the dream again.

The dream was always the same.

In it I am very small. I am walking between my mother, lovely, soft and young as I only remember her in the dream, and my tall young father, whom I remember always. I am holding a hand of each, strolling on a sandy shore. In front of us is a huge expanse of gentle, brilliant blue-green water. No crashing waves, like the ocean. A smooth sparkling flow with white gulls swooping above. Behind us across a lawn is a large, lovely sprawling house reaching toward the sky, opening its arms in welcome. As I turn to look at the house, I wake up. The feeling that lingers after the dream is like a warm comforter. Until reality rips it off.

"Mommy, I'm awake."

The reality was Benjie, wrenching me out of my childhood and back to his.

I knew the house of my dream was the house where my father grew up. I knew it was somewhere on the Chesapeake Bay. I remembered my father telling me stories about it when my mother wasn't with us. Since I could not remember ever going there, I did not know whether the house in the dream was real or imaginary. It was just called Bay House. It could be anywhere on the eastern or western side of the Chesapeake Bay, in Maryland or Virginia.

In my scenario, I naively assumed I could stay in the protection of St. Katherine's while I got my bearings. I would slip out in the daytime to search for old maps, historic homes, books on genealogy in the Library of Congress my father told me about. I would find his family name, Collington. I would locate Bay House—if it still existed. Of course, it would still exist. Benjie and I would go there, somehow, and be safe.

Now I had to brace myself to go downstairs and confront the Sister in charge.

I tiptoed down the bare steps, Benjie trailing behind me. A group of women sat circled in the lounge, murmuring in low tones. A therapy session, I assumed. I wondered if those women gave each other courage. I knew I could not open myself to anyone.

A stout lady wearing a plain beige suit sat at a table in the hall, stacking brochures. She smiled up at us with deep blue eyes etched with crinkles, though her cheeks were rosy and unlined. She stood, took both my cold hands in her warm ones, radiating compassion and authority. I couldn't guess her age. She looked young and old all at once.

"I'm Sister Florence Katherine. You must be Abigail Wells. Helen told me you were upstairs. We keep hoping to provide facilities for children in addition to this space someday. But, as you know now, that just hasn't been possible. I'm trying to find another shelter for you and your son." She shook her head topped with short gray curls and reached for the telephone buried in pamphlets.

"Thank you," I said. *I tried not to show my disappointment. Despite my plan, I couldn't bear the thought of being on the outside of St. Katherine's strong door.*

"You and Benjie could wait in my office." She pointed at the room to the right of the hall. Of course, it was all too familiar from last night, Helen the volunteer, and multiple donuts.

Benjie and I sat there for a while, playing tic-tac-toe. We could hear the Sister's voice rise and fall, making call after call. I began to realize I was probably going to have to take care of my son myself. It was clear there weren't enough safe havens for abused mothers with children who came knocking on doors.

I checked my purse, found $12.57 in my wallet and a $50 bill in the lining, where I hid the clipping about St. Katherine's House of Grace in Washington, D. C.

I leaned into the hall, reluctant to interrupt my protector, and whispered. "May I please use your office phone?"

She nodded.

I picked up the receiver and placed a collect call to the office of Mr. Arthur Dangerfield.

"Abigail, my dear child," Mr. Dangerfield said. His voice held a hint of a tremor. "Where are you? Are you all right? And Benjamin?"

"We're in Washington. And we're all right. Benjie's had a hard time, but I think he's OK. We can't stay where we are, though, and I'm, well, honestly, I'm nervous about leaving. Have you heard anything about Matt?"

"Your husband was just here, in my office." The voice was definitely trembling. "He searched your mother's house on Long Island first. If we weren't in a public place I believe he would have become violent. He demanded I tell him where you are. I told him I did not know and," there was some pride in that voice, "if I knew, I certainly wouldn't have shared this information."

"Thank you, thank you." My own voice rose higher in my throat. I overreacted but I couldn't help it. "Of course you won't tell anyone, especially Matt. Benjie and I are going to disappear for a while. But also, could you please ..."

"Wait, Abigail. There are some extremely urgent matters to discuss."

What else could possibly be more important? "What urgent matters? We must hurry."

"Number one. A legal concern. Your station wagon is registered in Matthew's name only. Now be calm, Abigail. He has alerted the police. Technically, you are driving a stolen vehicle."

I felt physically ill. As if I'd been punched in the stomach. For a moment my knees almost buckled. But I was not surprised. This action was mean and calculated. Typical of Matt. Had I reached the end of my great escape so soon?

The clipped, precise voice at the other end of the line went on. "Number two, Abigail, are you listening? Earlier this morning I got an urgent phone call, and I have taken a great liberty. I hope I haven't acted against the wishes of your mother. First, my dear child, where are you? Where in Washington?"

I glanced at Benjie, slid the pencil out of his hand. He was starting to scribble on Sister Florence Katherine's desk. I was starting to feel a little hysterical.

"I'm not sure. Somewhere downtown. We can't stay here much longer." There was no point in asking him to send money when I didn't have an address. "Just, please, tell me about the urgent call and then I must …"

"All right, Abigail. Do not panic. This may be good news. The phone call was from a Mr. William Collington Buford. He saw your mother's obituary in *The New York Times.* He is your father's relative who now lives in a place you may have heard of long ago, though not from your dear mother. It's called Bay House, on Kent Island, which I believe is somewhere in the middle of the Chesapeake Bay."

I didn't know whether he heard me gasp.

"I took the liberty, the great liberty, of telling him your predicament. Now, my dear child, I realize this may be extremely embarrassing to you, but he was insistent. He wants to get in touch with you. He gave me his number for you to call as soon as I was able to contact you. Abigail, are you still there? Did you hear me?"

I felt weak. "I heard you," I said.

"My advice to you would be to call him," Mr. Dangerfield concluded, giving me the number. "I believe he wants to be helpful. Mr. Buford said he never knew Fran had a grandson. You must keep me informed, though, Abigail. You can't go wandering around with that young boy and no one knowing where you are. You must be very, very careful."

It was difficult to speak. I managed to stammer, "Thank … thank you.

I will be careful."

The day took on the surrealistic quality of a dream.

My hand was unsteady as I dialed the number.

Sometimes a person reaches a momentous point quietly. Turns a corner unaware of its significance, and only sees it looking back. This was not the case with me as I waited for someone to answer, in the home of my father's youth. I felt as if I had been waiting to turn this corner all my life.

Still, I was confused. I was searching for Collingtons. Who were the Bufords?

The man who answered the telephone sounded casual, cheery and totally in charge. He insisted Benjie and I come straight away to Maryland's Kent Island, then gave me instructions as if we were already engaged in some sort of mutual adventure. I found a scrap of paper, scribbled directions. I was to drive east an hour out of Washington to Annapolis on Route 50, leave the car at a garage called Hoyt's on Center Street, then meet him at the city dock at 5:00 that afternoon. His name was William Buford and he would be arriving on his boat, the *Queen Anne*, to pick us up. That's all he said, and I was too numb to ask more.

Before we left the House of Grace, Benjie and I received more kindness. Helen Barker cut my hair. She picked up my shorn locks, waved them in the air, yelling, "Freedom!" I felt myself smiling for the first time since my mother died. Helen was quite a pro at cutting hair. She made me look as much as possible like a tall beardless male instead of my thin, motherly self.

From our temporary barber shop on the second floor, I could hear laughing, sobbing, occasional screams, a hum of low, steady voices. Women passed the door without intruding. I could not help noticing one limping, with glazed eyes and an arm in a cast. I was not ready to relate to any of these people. Yet from this group Helen procured for me a small, worn blouse to complete Benjie's disguise. Faded pink, dotted with daisies. Even a dog-eared coloring book and box of crayons.

Sister Florence Katherine did not require a fee, but I left my $10 bill on the corner of her desk. I had lived a long time without undemanding generosity.

And now, like a miracle, I was found by a relative named William Buford, who lived in a place that was no longer a myth. I questioned nothing.

Following William's directions, I drove my stolen car carefully at 55, in the right lane, another hour east of Washington to the turn-off for Annapolis. Blood pounded in my ears every time a police car passed, but nothing happened. Benjie was still and quiet, possibly in shock, I worried, from the trauma of the last two days. He slept or colored, asking no questions.

We found Hoyt's garage and walked away from the car. A bit before five, we were on the city dock, trying to blend into the crowd. People strolled about watching the gulls, and the boats coming in and out. Some sat on the sea wall eating, chatting, eyeing groups of Naval Academy midshipmen in their summer whites. I bought Benjie a chocolate ice cream cone. He began to chirp again, in the usual way of a five-year-old. I could see that this town was quaint and charming, but I was on fire to leave it. I kept watching anxiously for a boat called the *Queen Anne.* Any minute, I expected to feel someone grab me from behind, to turn and meet Matt's fury or the eyes of a policeman.

At 5:00 a magnificent sailboat came gliding in, under power, sails down. The *Queen Anne.* I looked up with a hand at my brow, shading my gaze from the slanting sun. For a moment it cast a golden glow on the captain at the helm as he maneuvered the boat with ease against the dock. Benjie stopped licking his cone, holding it in midair. *Was it my imagination, or did the conversations around me cease for a tiny tick of time, as everyone looked up?*

A dock hand in overalls, red kerchief knotted at his neck, leaned against a tall piling. Smiling, he raised a quick salute to greet the captain. "Good to see you, Skipper. The winds are fair today, sir." He leaned forward to catch the bow line the captain tossed. The gilded sky turned blue again. Gulls swooped and squawked above the chatter of people enjoying the show.

The captain yelled over the sound of the engine. "Thanks, Jimmy. This time just hold 'er, don't tie up. I'm picking up my family."

This was my cue, though I had no idea how I knew it. I stepped forward, holding Benjie's hand. The captain did not change expression, as if we had rehearsed this scene from a spy thriller. He pointed to the walkway slanting up from the dock. "OK, you two. Climb aboard," he said.

Up we stepped, Benjie and I, as if we'd done it a hundred times.

"Thanks, bud," our rescuer called to the man holding the rope. "Let 'er go."

Slowly, he eased the *Queen Anne* out of the narrow slip, while a line-up of spectators watched a tall boy and his little sister go off with their father.

On board, nobody spoke. I doubt I could have. Benjie's mouth hung wide open, his chirping ceased.

Once outside the marina, our captain turned the boat to the wind and headed for a huge expanse of brilliant blue-green. The channel markers announced our heading: Chesapeake Bay.

Then he let his laughter out. Chuckled. Roared. Slapped his thighs. "I thought I was rescuing a beautiful lady in distress." He cocked his head, eyeing my disguise. "I didn't know I was just getting my handsome son and little daughter. We were great, weren't we?"

Benjie's hands flew to the daisies on his ridiculous shirt. He grinned, his eyes showing their sparkle again. "You were playing the game too, huh?" He hollered into the wind, his normal, chatty self again.

"The game? Well, yes, I guess I was," the man said. "Though I knew you right away. Come here, Sprout. I want to look at you." He pulled Benjie into his arms and hugged him as if they were long-lost friends. "You're all Collington, that's for sure. But this hair ribbon has got to go." One flick of his wrist sent the pink bow overboard to disappear in seconds.

For the first time, I began to feel a sense of belonging.

"Welcome aboard." He yelled back to me. "You're the most gorgeous boy I've ever seen, Mr. Abigail. Now sit down and hang on to your hat. I'm going to make you forget all your troubles."

That's a tall order, I thought, as I strapped life preservers on my child and me.

"Watch, Sprout. I'm putting the boat on automatic pilot, so I can hoist the mainsail."

Then he was back at the wheel again. "Feel it? We're getting wind. We'll tack against it, and I think we'll be sailing." He winked, giving me a little mock salute. "William Buford at your service, ma'am. Sit back and relax, and I'll have you in the Land of Pleasant Living in about five miles. Nautical miles, that is. The wind's with us so it'll be a perfect ride. It's the only way to travel. You'll see."

We zigzagged across the bay with the wind blowing spray in our faces, the boat over on its side, flying. Blue water. Blue sky. Freedom. Glorious. *I had forgotten what it was like to feel free. I even forgot to speak, introduce myself, ask questions. Or, I chided myself, observe details.*

"Neato," Benjie yelled. "This is neato." Benjie hopped up and down, a stranger to sailboats and hugs from a man named Skipper who called him Sprout. I pulled him into my lap where, lulled by the whispering wind, the sun on our faces, we sat in silent awe. Fear loosened its grip, time ceased to matter.

When the boat circled in a gentle arc and slowed down, I wasn't ready.

"Here we are. We're coming in. Coming home. Just call me William, Abigail. I'm kind of a kissing cousin."

There was that playful, commanding telephone voice from yesterday. Now I paid attention. I realized this William was older than I thought at first glance when we boarded. His body was tan and muscled against his white shorts and shirt, his hair golden blond. Longish, curling just above his collar, blowing freely in the wind. But I was not interested in him as a man. I was sure I would never be interested in any man again.

He represented safety, family I hadn't known I had, and hope of salvation.

"Best way to see any of these old places." William spoke as if narrating from a script. "From the water. See?" He pointed ahead with pride in his voice as if his whole heart was in his words. "To us, this is really the front, you know."

I was looking at the house in my dream.

4

There is a certain moment in late afternoon when sunlight slants against the earth making everything in its gilded path luminous. This was the moment, near sunset, that I first saw Bay House. The fairy-tale place of my father's stories. And my mother's silence.

I sat on the deck of the *Queen Anne* transfixed, grasping Benjie's hand. I was still in shock to think we were rescued by a distant cousin of my father, Ben Collington. A relative I didn't know existed. This golden man at the helm.

Now he lowered the sails, threw over the anchor. There was no sound except water lapping against the hull of the boat as we slowed, then stopped. No sense of time. Only the feeling of floating, my heart pounding in my chest. *I forgot I was exhausted, terrified, my arms bruised and aching.* The water shimmered turquoise in the shallows. It stretched from the rocking boat to a long, narrow dock above a patch of amber sand. A green-gold lawn met the dock gently at its own level. A creek, lined with glinting, feathery brown fronds of marsh grass, curved inward from the bay along the left side of the house.

Bay House. It stood back from the glistening water, just as it did in the recurring dream I had since I was ten. That was the year my father, the only person who called me "Abby-girl," instead of "Abigail" or "Abby," died, leaving me glowing stories, memories of his childhood home somewhere on the Chesapeake.

In the dream, I was never able to look at the house. Now, I looked. The rectangular structure was three stories tall, made of rose-colored bricks, brightened in the radiance. Long windows in the two stories below and dormer windows above seemed to catch fire. The wings on either side were not symmetrical. I could see, even in those first dazzled moments, this building was not a classical masterpiece. This home was added to in different centuries, a stately manor house just a bit awry.

Perhaps I should have felt a presentiment, right there in the beginning, that nothing used by man is immune to the forces of good and evil. Not the magnificent bay we just sailed across, not even this beautiful house. But I didn't. Benjie and I were in need of sanctuary, and here it was. Matt could soon be following. He already reported me to the police as a missing person, driving a stolen car.

William glanced at his watch. "That was a quick run, the wind was with us. It's almost a straight shot over from Annapolis. You're looking at Kent Island's western shore, by the way. And straight ahead is Bay House. People call it iconic, historic. All true. But, to me it's just home. See?" His arms flung wide as if embracing sea, land and sky.

Of course, I saw. I was already memorizing each blade of grass, every brick and windowpane. I became aware of William appraising me as I sat, incapable of speech.

"I know the feeling," he said. "I never come in, as many times as I've done it since I was a kid, that I don't see how great this place is."

Oh, no. There's no way you can understand how I feel.

For the last five years I lived with a kind of chronic fear that deadens all other sensations. I was a statistic. One of millions of trapped, abused, often battered, sometimes raped, even murdered wives. Such ugliness, grief, self-doubt. After dreaming, hoping, not even knowing whether this place still existed, I was here. I was so accustomed to stifling my emotions I couldn't tell this man how everything was shining. I knew this moment would be held in my heart for the rest of my life. No matter what else might happen.

"To me it's just home." *This man's words rang with authority, entitlement. Were they a warning? Although my father always swore to our inheritance, I felt like an outsider. How would I begin to stake a claim to William's piece of earth and sky?*

"I ... I don't know how to thank you," I said.

"Don't try. No problem. We're kinfolks, aren't we?" He flashed a boyish grin. His hair glinted gold, eyes swept the bay as if he owned it.

His kindness pushed my doubts away. I was over-tired, over-wrought, overwhelmed.

A motor started, back in the creek, and a small boat puttered toward us.

"Old Noah is coming to take you ashore," William said. "He's my Jack-of-all-everything. I have to take the *Queen* to the marina. Can't tie up here. Not deep enough, as you can see."

There was stillness while we waited. I'm not sure I took a breath. Gulls swooped and soared. Lines snapped, sails dripped onto the deck. I licked salt spray from my lips and wiped it from my face.

William winked at Benjie as if they were fellow conspirators. "We were great, Sprout, weren't we, back at the dock?"

Benjie nodded. His eyes popped wide with delight.

William turned to me again.

"After I talked to your lawyer in New York, I assumed I was coming to save a beautiful lady in distress. Then, when you called me from that God-forsaken place in D.C. …"

"St. Katherine's House of Grace for …"

"Never mind."

He was sparing me.

"We were still playing the game, weren't we?" Benjie said.

"Absolutely. We were stars, and we fooled everybody on the dock. With you in that ridiculous get-up, I could have sworn you were a girl. And your mother is the most gorgeous boy I've ever seen."

He studied Benjie from head to toe, then shot me a teasing glance from his blue-green eyes.

This was no game, of course, although I tried to make it seem like one to Benjie. William appeared to be enjoying the role he was playing, as if he didn't understand that, either. No matter. I was still floating in sunshine again.

"I'm never ever gonna wear another gross pink bow," Benjie said. He held up his hand and stretched out his little fingers. "I'm five, and I'm not a girl."

"Of course not," said William. He frowned, looking down on the top of Benjie's small head. It shone just a shade blonder than his own. He knelt on the deck, gripped Benjie's small shoulders. His voice dropped, the humor in it was gone. "You're all boy, son, and you are Benjamin Collington."

Don't forget, his last name, our last name, is Wells. But in my happy haze I let go of the thought.

A weathered skiff with an outboard motor reached us. The old man at the tiller angled the small boat alongside, downwind of us.

William stood, gave Benjie a playful poke, stiffened his back and saluted. "I'll see you later, Sprout. You take care of your mother."

I couldn't help noticing his changeable behavior.

"Thank you, again, I do thank you." I groped for better words but failed.

I climbed down into the smaller boat, feeling awkward, sensing something that could have been scorn in the narrow brown eyes of Old Noah. He steadied me with his strong right arm. His left hand held the skiff against the *Queen*.

"Take her up to the house, Benjie, and find your Aunt Harriet." William lowered him down to Noah. "She'll be looking for you."

The old man said nothing. His face was creased by wind and weather, tanned walnut by the sun, in contrast to his shock of white hair. His stony expression did not change when Benjie slid down into the grip of his skinny, sinewy right arm. I was glad to see Benjie's face without that pinched look, and he did not seem to be afraid. This short ride in the small bouncing boat was another adventure.

He's a plucky little kid. My heart turned over. How did I lose that plucky little kid who was Abigail Collington?

The boat touched sand and I scrambled out, carrying Benjie so he wouldn't get his shoes wet. Our one small tote bag swung from my shoulder.

"Thank you." Two small words which held such emotion.

Noah bobbed his head in acknowledgment and backed the boat off, heading for the creek.

So here I was, walking on the sandy shore. This was no dream. This was real. Benjie and I were alone and free.

As if I was coming out of shock, I began to realize the enormity of what I had done. My arms ached, and I was bone tired.

5

The golden moment was gone. Bay House seemed more modest now. Less resplendent. The brick a paler rose, window reflections not as fiery. It appeared more home-like than fable, shaded by towering trees arched over its roof, as if it belonged rooted where it stood. I noticed a winding pathway, old and well-worn from the look of it. Moss grew between the bricks which led to a sprawling terrace. Black wrought iron chairs with faded flowered cushions were grouped facing west across the bay. The sun was beginning to set, tracking rose and gold across the water.

Benjie and I stumbled past the dock, up the sloping grounds and onto the patio. I felt lost again and exposed. A trespasser, a voyeur, staring at doors and windows, wondering where to look or knock. I hesitated, but when no one appeared, I took Benjie's hand and edged along the pathway that seemed to lead around to what I assumed was the actual front, since we crossed a circular drive where cars were parked. Deep steps led up to a porch which ran the width of the house, and to the massive front door, shining with black paint and heavy antique brass hardware.

Before I found the courage to knock, the door opened. A tall, striking, dark-haired woman stood looking at Benjie and me. She eyed us as she might view a pair of wayward tourists seeking a room.

"So here you are," she said. Not a flicker of recognition crossed her face.

"Are you Aunt Harriet?" said Benjie. He tilted his head to stare up at the lady dressed in a navy shirtwaist.

The woman frowned, brows knitted together in a straight line. "Aunt Harriet?"

"The man in the boat said we should go up to the house and find Aunt Harriet," Benjie said. Then he beamed, puffing out his little chest. "The nice man named Skipper brought us here and called me Sprout, and his boat whooshed through the water just like my boats in the bathtub."

The woman smiled with a curl of her lips though her eyes remained inscrutable dark pools. She held out her hand and took mine. "You're Abigail. And this must be Benjie. Of course, then, I am Aunt Harriet. Do come in." She held the door for us. "I'm Harriet Buford, William's wife," she said. She gave a surprising little clap. "I'm not sure what our relationship is, it was all so long ago, you know, but I'd love to be an aunt."

When we were inside, she stooped down to examine my child.

"So," she said. "This is Benjamin Collington Wells. My goodness, what a big name for a little boy."

Straightening, she looked at me.

"We didn't even know there was a Benjie until we saw your mother's obituary in *The New York Times*. I'm so sorry, Abigail, about her passing."

"Thank you," I said. My throat tightened at the memory of my mother. "Mr. Dangerfield told me that was how you knew. Still, I was amazed that your husband thought to call him."

It seemed like mental telepathy at the time although I knew there must be a practical explanation. Or is it also possible that people communicate in times of crisis on some wordless level, deeper than they understand? Could presences in houses do this? At the same time I was hoping desperately to find Bay House, Bay House, through the Bufords, found me. It was wonderful, it was logical, though it still felt a bit bizarre.

"We realized it was too late to send flowers," Harriet said, "but we wanted to express our sympathy somehow. William had your family lawyer's office number in New York, so he called there to find out how to get in touch with you."

"That must have been right after I called Mr. Dangerfield from Washington. To find out if Matt, my husband, had been there looking for me. And he had. I'm sure he was … very hard to deal with."

"Apparently." Harriet's brief dry smile indicated she gathered this was an understatement. "Your Mr. Dangerfield seemed very upset, William said. At first, he insisted he couldn't give out information about you to anyone. Then he realized who William was. Finally, he told William in confidence where you were and asked him to help you. His voice was quivering. He said he feels responsible for your welfare, and Benjie's."

I had trouble controlling my own voice. "I can never tell you how much it meant when Mr. Dangerfield said some relatives were trying to reach me."

"I can imagine," said Harriet. *She eyed me with sympathy, though somehow I felt her judging me at the same time.*

"Well, that part's over now. We couldn't let you two stay in that place when we're so close, and we have all this room." Her arm swept across the wide, high-ceilinged hall where we stood. "And, Abigail, don't feel you're imposing on William." Now her eyes softened, her smile was warm. "He's never really grown out of play-acting. He loved coming to get you in the *Queen Anne.* Actually, it was his brainstorm to rescue you by boat so you could leave your car in Annapolis. We can have a driver take it back to New York."

She laid her hand on my arm. I tried not to wince.

"It was outrageous of your husband to report you to the police for driving a stolen car, just because it's registered in his name. You do look as if you've had a hard time."

I was suddenly conscious of how I must appear in my old jeans, baggy shirt, my hair cropped like a boy's, with no makeup. And Benjie still wore his absurd daisy blouse. I felt like an imposter. The disguises I'd concocted for our escape to the women's shelter seemed like a brilliant life-saving idea at the time. Now they made me feel even more out of place in this gracious manor house.

The hall smelled of furniture polish, flowers and a faint, musty antiquity. In a gilt-framed mirror above a mahogany table I caught a glimpse of my reflection and Harriet's. Next to William's wife I was small, pale, disheveled, compared to her tanned, coiffed elegance. *I felt my confidence shrinking. In all my plans of escaping to my father's home I never thought about other people who might live there. It seemed important to establish a bond, a right to be here, at this first meeting.*

Something more than gratitude.

I grabbed Benjie's hand again. *I was amazed by his patience during my conversation with Harriet. Everything was so strange and new to him. The warmth of his little fingers in mine made me stronger. I was going to have to learn how to be bold, for both of us.*

I began a piece of my story. "My father always told me that Bay House was our real home. That I'd understand this someday. For years I've dreamed of coming back here to find out."

Harriet brushed this aside with a flick of her hand, making her gold bracelets jangle.

"Let's not worry about any of that right now. My word, you've had a rotten time, but I'm sure things will straighten out for you." She smoothed the pendant that dangled at her throat. Now I'm going to show you where you'll be staying. Benjie, do you want to see where you're going to sleep?"

She started up the broad wooden staircase that creaked even under soft carpeting.

I felt the loving arms of the old house enfold us. Here were safety and home. I would have to find out why, and understand, and make Harriet understand.

Benjie scurried ahead, already exploring.

Reaching the second floor, I had a quick impression of a hallway with dark, wide-planked polished flooring. Oriental scatter rugs of mellowed reds, blues, gold.

Harriet climbed ahead of me up the next flight of stairs, her footsteps light and quick.

"Mommy, Mommy, lookit the toys." Benjie's voice rose with excitement. He sat cross-legged on the floor of a third-story room nestled under the eaves just left of the steps. A narrower hall had doorways opening into other small rooms.

"This is the old nursery," Harriet said. "I thought Benjie might like to sleep here. There's an adjoining room for you, Abigail."

She opened a door in the hall. I glimpsed flowery wallpaper, more eaves, long double windows. A single bed covered with a yellow quilt mounded with snowy pillows.

"Make yourselves comfortable," Harriet went on. "There's a bathroom across the hall. We'll be ready for dinner when you come down." *She must have sensed my embarrassment at our lack of clean clothes, or any clothes at all other than what we were wearing. I saw her eye the small bag dangling from my arm when we made our introductions.* "Your closet is full of items for our church rummage sale, all clean and in good repair. Please help yourselves to anything you'd like to wear," she said. "You, too Benjie, dear."

She bent over and kissed him abruptly, in the first awkward motion she had made, then left us. I could hear her footsteps going down the two flights of stairs.

I stood watching Benjie.

He was surrounded by wonderful old toys. A box of red-white-

and-blue tin soldiers, a drum, a horse-drawn fire-cart, dusty stacks of children's books. A doll in a cradle, a toy musket, tiny dishes on a small pine table, a child-sized rocker.

He smiled up at me with that sudden brightness of children's smiles.

"Mommy, I like this place. Can we stay here?"

"I hope so, Benj." It was all I could say as my throat closed with unshed tears.

I was suddenly awash with an inexplicable feeling of sadness. This was not my fear of Matt, though fear was still in my bones. This was not grief for my mother, though grief was still in my heart. This sadness came from outside of me. I sensed it for no reason. Perhaps it was just the knowledge so many children, now gone, must have played in this room.

Downstairs, I heard the front door slam, a man's footsteps, then William's voice, cheerful and commanding. "Harriet, did you tell Noah he'd be helping out tonight?" A delicious aroma wafted its way up the stairwell, which I now realized carried scent as well as sound. We were keeping William and Harriet from their dinner.

"Come, Benj," I said. "We have to wash hands and see what we can find in the closet to put on." *I was mortified, feeling like a beggar at the thought of dressing in hand-me-downs, though it was a practical solution to an obvious need. And I was certain Harriet meant only kindness.*

When we marched down the steps twenty minutes later, we were still anything but an impressive pair. Benjie was at least a semi-clean little boy in a Superman tee shirt, no daisies. I wore a simple long-sleeved white blouse, denim skirt, and pink lipstick from an unopened tube. I saw in the bathroom mirror as I swiped it on, the tired blue of my eyes was like the gray shadows beneath them. *I was numb. Exhausted. It was impossible to believe that I'd taken my son and fled our apartment in Manhattan. Was that truly only yesterday?*

I added one more thing, for courage. My most prized possession, grabbed at the last minute in its little velvet pouch. I clasped on my great-grandmother's pearls. *I'm a Collington, too. I must tell them. Benjie and I belong here. My father told me this is true.*

The scene was beyond perfection. Through long windows on the bay side, the lights of passing ships flickered in the twilight. On the opposite side of the room, more windows opened onto a garden where fireflies blinked among the blossoms. Portraits hung on the walls. The table was set with a crystal bowl of pale pink dahlias, lighted candles in silver candelabras. A white linen cloth that one obviously did not drip-dry, and delicate china edged with gold.

I, who was raised by Fran Collington, was no stranger to elegance, but this was different. Bay House, that night, was like the rare woman who is more striking in her old age because of the character that shines from her face, the structure of her bones, her lineage.

Harriet sat at one end of the table. Imperial in white slacks, a white, softly knit sleeveless pullover sweater, with turquoise earrings dangling. Her chestnut hair was pulled back in a simple twist. William, at the other end, wore finely pressed khaki shorts, a crisp white sport shirt. His thick blond hair caught gleams from the candlelight.

He sprang from his chair and pulled one out for me. This William, even in shorts, the ultimate country gentleman.

"You're right over there across the table, Sprout," he said. I held my breath as Benjie trudged, wide-eyed but silent, around to his place.

Please remember your manners, son.

William reached in his shirt pocket as we seated ourselves. He beamed at me, leaning over to place a hand-drawn map on top of my plate. For an instant I studied his thick lashes, breathed in his spicy aftershave.

"Welcome to The Land of Pleasant Living. I'm no great artist but I thought this might help you get your bearings, since you've only seen our watery driveway." He winked at Benjie across the table. "Remember our boat ride, Sprout? I've made this really easy to understand."

He tapped the map.

"Here's Kent Island." His finger traced the edges of an oblong outline in the center of the page. He stopped at a place about one-third of the way from the top, on the left-hand side of the island, marked with a star. "Here's Kentlands, our tiny old town. A little further north is Stevensville." His gaze wandered up through the open windows, where moonlight poured on the blue velvet bay. "And in between, is Bay House." His finger rested on the star.

Lengthwise down both margins were two squiggly columns, filled in with *X*s.

"Left column's the Western Shore. Washington, Annapolis, Baltimore. All that mess." Then he touched the right side of the page. "And this is the Eastern Shore. St. Michael's, Easton, Oxford. Ah …" he sighed. He closed his eyes, trailing his finger back to the center. "But here, on Kent Island, is the land of our fathers, their fathers, and their fathers. This is where we are, now and forever. Bay House. Built in 1762, and here to stay."

Amazingly, his finger landed on a tiny nub of shoreline jutting out ever so slightly into the white remainder of the map labeled simply, "The Bay." When he opened his eyes, he stared straight into mine. I realized I'd been holding my breath.

Harriet gave a slight cough, then cleared her throat. "Oh, William, Abby doesn't need a geography lesson tonight."

William raised his chin. "Well, some of us are proud of these facts. Some of us are proud we're still here on land that our ancestors fought for."

I felt so nervous. Sometimes I had trouble containing Benjie, even at McDonald's. So far, he was handling this. But how long could he sit still and not interrupt? How could I begin to ask the questions which would unravel the old mystery of my belonging here, of my inheriting a portion of this house and this land?

There was a sudden whack on a swinging door I hadn't noticed. Noah appeared in a starched white coat carrying a silver tray with plates of glistening orange-colored melon. He had the same unruly thatch of white hair and dour expression he wore only an hour before, when he helped us out of the small boat wearing tattered trousers reeking of fish.

Benjie's little mouth dropped wide open. "Hi, Noah. You sure look diff'ernt," he said.

I could not control the look of astonishment that must have rearranged my face. Or the surprising, irresistible urge to giggle. William caught my glance at that moment and in those blue-green eyes of his there was an unmistakable twinkle. That glance flicked between us for just a moment while I struggled to control myself. Looking away, I saw that Harriet was aware of this exchange. She was not amused.

Dear God, what is the matter with me? I'm much more out of control than Benjie. I sat in silent embarrassment while Noah placed the cantaloupe slices before us.

"There's really nothing like an Eastern Shore 'lope," said William. He sprang around the table to cut Benjie's into small eatable bites.

"We're going to make a real Marylander out of you, Benjie. Do you like soft-shell crabs?" *I thought I would never again consider cantaloupe or crab anything other than the highest form of Epicurean delights.*

Benjie wrinkled his nose. "Eww. You mean those things that crawl on the sand and pinch you? I don't think so." He shook his head until his hair flipped side to side.

"Well, that answers the question about hard crabs." William went on, sitting again. "Don't worry, Sprout. All you need's a long pole with a net and a little boat like Noah's that I'll let you steer. Or you can lie on the dock and dip 'em up the same way. We'll do it together. Catch 'em, clean 'em and eat 'em. You'll love it. Don't you think so, Harriet?"

Harriet smiled as I watched Benjie's face grow pink with elation. William seemed to know exactly how to make my traumatized child feel safe and special.

"Of course," Harriet said. "And we're having something else tonight I know little boys like."

The door whacked open again and Noah appeared with an overflowing platter of fried chicken. It tilted wildly as he placed it in front of William, who never changed his expression. I stared at my plate.

"Yum-mee. That looks better than McDonald's, huh, Mom? C'un I have a drumstick, um, please?" said Benjie.

My child said "please" with perfect timing. *The band around my middle finally released. All was right with the world.*

The chicken was moist, crispy and delicious. It was dipped in egg batter and flour, then fried golden brown in peanut oil and delivered, Harriet explained, by a neighbor who made it her specialty.

Then there were butter beans, simmered with bacon. Not exactly a New York thing but my mouth watered at the smell. Summer squash, fat red tomato slices, all from right here on the farm. Potato salad tangy with mustard. Maryland beaten biscuits with sweet butter and Harriet's strawberry jam. Benjie behaved like a small saint, not even asking why the biscuits were so hard.

William picked up his chicken, nodding at Benjie to do the same. All the while William and Harriet kept up an easy chatter. *I realized how hungry I was. How earthy-fresh everything smelled and tasted. Slowly, I began to relax. By the time Noah cleared the table and brought in vanilla ice cream with hot fudge sauce, I felt so comfortable, so pleasantly drowsy, so safe, I wished I could stay in this lovely cocoon. But I knew I couldn't. Nothing was said about the future, or my father and the past.*

"This has been such a wonderful dinner," I said. *It was time to speak my piece, though I didn't know quite how to begin.* "And such kindness to Benjie and me. You know, my father used to tell me stories about Bay House. I always knew how much he loved it. I knew I'd love it, too."

"And we are so happy to have you," said Harriet. She folded her napkin and laid it on the table. "Let's take our coffee out on the terrace, shall we? William and I like to sit out there in the evening. You can see the lights from huge cargo ships that travel on the bay at night. Do we have a few more minutes before Benjie has to go to bed?"

She did not wait for an answer. She stood straight up from her chair and led us from the dining room as we carried our cups.

Benjie chased fireflies. We watched the ships pass on the water. The Bay Bridge, off to the right, connecting both shorelines, showed us twinkling strings of light against the darkening sky. The summer evening had cooled, a soft breeze moved across the lawn from the bay. Stars were appearing as if lit by flame.

Did Harriet change the subject deliberately? Why couldn't I ask a simple question that must have a simple yes or no answer? Did I have to live in awe of Harriet and William? They were only people, certainly not more than 20 years older than I was. And I was a Collington. Their name was Buford.

I touched the necklace my father left me. The pearls felt smooth and real beneath my fingers.

I shifted in my chair. "I've been wanting to ask you, and wondering about this for a long time now. Did my father inherit a portion of Bay House?"

Crickets chirped. A boat horn sounded far off in the channel.

"Abigail," Harriet said, "let's talk about this in the morning. Really. You've had a long, rotten day and I know it must be Benjie's bedtime."

William jumped to his feet and was off chasing Benjie through the dusk.

"I bet I can beat you upstairs, Sprout."

"Bet you can't ..."

Benjie giggled, raced into the house, banged the screen door, with William pounding behind.

Dismissed, like a child. You blew it, Abigail.

It was rude, abrupt, but I rose from my chair, standing straight and tall beside it.

"Goodnight, then," I said to Harriet. "Thanks again for your kindness." *My dear deceased mother would have thought me unmannerly, although social graces were the last things on my mind.* I hurried into the house to put Benjie to bed. Harriet breezed past me. For a moment we stood together in the front hall before I turned to the stairs to follow my child.

Harriet smiled at me from the bottom of the steps. It was strange, unreadable. Her lips curled but her eyes were cold, unblinking.

William passed me coming down as I went up. He was flushed, chuckling.

"Good night, Abby. Sleep tight. And don't worry. We've got a good strong lock on that old door."

He shot me a look from those blue-green eyes. *I was sure he knew what I was thinking.*

I forced my heavy legs up one step at a time to the third floor, almost as exhausted as when I reached St. Katherine's just yesterday. *Could that be right? Could so much have changed, yet not changed, in a day? At this moment I was beyond caring.*

I heard William snap the double bolt on the front door. Our protector, I thought, with silent thanks.

I would try to put Matthew Wells out of my mind, and sleep. William and Harriet would have to answer my questions in the morning.

6

"Hi, Mommy. I'm hungry." Benjie was jumping on my bed, churning the sheets into a white froth. Sunlight spilled into the room. I looked at my watch on the bedside table. 10:00.

Damn. I overslept. With all my questions still to ask, and whatever forces I need to rally today still dangling.

And here was my little dynamo ready for action. "I need a hug, Benj," I said. "Then we'll get going." He leaped into my arms. I lifted him up and carried him to the window.

What a day. Blue, white, green, gold. *Will I ever get used to that constantly changing expanse of bay?* This morning it was ruffled with little whitecaps.

We wandered out into the hall, listening. All was quiet downstairs except for the creakings and rustlings that seemed to be normal for this house. A clock chimed ten somewhere, a little late.

When we were dressed, we went down to the first-floor hall. My fears were confirmed. The house was empty.

A scrawled note lay on the hall table beside a bowl of purple zinnias:

William had to go to Baltimore on business. I have errands. Back soon. Do have breakfast.

Aunt Harriet

P.S. Please don't let Benjie get into anything.

A surge of anger shot through me. Surprising, foreign. I'd been too anxious, tired, and afraid to feel much of anything else for a long time now. However, I was a grown woman and a family member. I felt the sting of Harriet's insulting P.S. I was not about to let Benjie "get into anything." Meaning, make a mess. Break something. Besides, Harriet said they would answer my questions in the morning. I absolutely had to know where I stood. Furthermore, where were our protectors now? Matt was not stupid. Quite the opposite. When he was not drunk he was crafty, a master manipulator. How long would it take him to trace a family named Buford living near the Chesapeake Bay in an old homestead called Bay House? How long to figure out this is where I would be? How long to get here, drunk or sober?

"Mommy, I told you, I'm hungry."

Benjie was not always a five-year-old saint. Now he was beginning to whine.

"Let's look for the kitchen, Benj. It must be right through here." I pointed to the dining room. *I remembered Noah banging in and out of a door with trays during last night's dinner. Also, William mentioned some old brick steps Noah had to climb balancing all those platters. The same steps that slaves climbed 150 years ago. This would be a history lesson for both Benjie and me. What other lessons this house held I was only beginning to guess.*

My intuition proved correct. We pushed on a heavy door next to a carved buffet. The door swung open in slow motion. We looked down into the kitchen from the top of those steps.

Across an uneven brick floor was a huge black iron gas range I assumed might be restaurant-quality from its size, burners and ovens. Next to it an ancient fireplace, once used for cooking, spanned the rest of the wall. Benjie ran to stand in it, waving his arms above his head. Set into the two opposing walls, on the bay and garden sides, were long windows with deep sills filled with African violets. A round pine table with four chairs sat in front of the fireplace. It was set with placemats decorated with flying geese, a pitcher of orange juice, a box of cereal, glasses, bowls, spoons. A dish brimming with luscious blueberries. A basket of cinnamon buns. A pot of coffee was plugged in and steaming on the counter below one of the windows. The bay flowed beyond like azure silk.

I felt my anger fade away with my sense of foreboding. This place was too disarming. It was home.

While Benjie worked on his second bowl of cereal, I went to the phone in the hall and dialed Mr. Dangerfield's office in New York. His secretary put me through to him immediately.

"Abigail, my dear child." The tremulous voice was as anxious as ever. "I was hoping you'd call. Are you all right?"

"Yes, I'm fine," I said. "Really. This place is beautiful. I'm at Bay House."

"And your father's relatives," he went on, "the Bufords. Are they … are they hospitable?"

"Yes, very." *I ignored any reservations.* "They're being wonderful to Benjie. And to me. But I'm going to need some money very soon. I'm going to have to find a divorce attorney." My heart sank in my chest. I lowered my voice, which felt stuck in my throat. "I know I'm going to have to fight Matt for custody."

Without warning, I began to cry. Mr. Dangerfield was the only link to my mother and my old security.

"I'm never going to let him hurt Benjie again," I said when I could speak. *Matt's abuse, my terror, my panic for the safety of my child, were dangers I knew Arthur would respect but never comprehend.*

"Now, now," he said. "There, there. Oh my, Abigail, my dear child. I'm working on Fran's estate right now. We're putting the house on the market immediately. I'm seeing the insurance people today. I'll let you know as soon as I can when we have some figures. In the meantime, whatever you need, I'll be glad to send a personal check."

"Oh, no," I said. "Oh, no, Mr. Dangerfield. I'll just wait. Thank you. That might be another way to trace me, too. I believe we can stay here for a while at least. I feel safe here. After all, it was my father's home, though I wish he told me more about the ownership of it. Do you have any information there, Mr. Dangerfield? Could there be anything in my mother's papers explaining why he believed it belonged to us?"

"It certainly is regrettable, but I can't help you. She never discussed your father and disposed of all his documents including background about Bay House shortly after he died. She was very angry that he left an annuity for some part of the taxes. I've sent a check every year, but I never had any other dealings with the place. She, Fran, was quite firm about that."

I could imagine how firm she was. The old question echoed in my head. Why, why, why?

"One thing more, Mr. Dangerfield. Could you try to confirm that our car was returned? I left it at Hoyt's garage in Annapolis the day I came here. Mrs. Buford arranged for it to be picked up by a driver and taken back to New York." My fingers twisted the phone cord around and around. "I guess I'm still a missing person, but at least I'm not driving a stolen car."

"Uh," the voice hesitated, then went bravely on. "Of course. I will. I'll try to double-check on that."

"Thank you," I said. "You'll never know how I appreciate your help."

I put the phone down, feeling very much alone.

But I have Benjie. I will hang in for Benjie. I wiped my eyes and went back into the kitchen.

"I don't have anybody to play with," Benjie said. He sat slumped at the table and mumbled, swinging his feet, banging them on the chair legs. He made little towers of Cheerios, then knocked them over with his spoon.

"You have me."

He gave me a mopey face. "Well, what'll we play? We didn't bring my soccer ball. I want my soccer ball, Mommy."

"Let's go exploring. We haven't begun to see this whole place yet. Outside, I mean."

I longed to investigate every corner of this empty, inviting old house but it didn't seem appropriate with Harriet and William away. Besides, Benjie might have been a disaster in the house at that point. He was ready for action.

"Come on, Benj. Do you know that your grandfather played all around here when he was your age? He was adventurous and very brave. Just like you."

That perked him up. "OK. Can we take peanut butter and jelly samwiches like a picnic?" I assembled his request along with two apples and a thermos of milk packed in a brown paper bag from under the sink.

We banged out of the screen door and across the patio. Noah was riding a high, ancient tractor, zigzagging across the front lawn, cutting grass. The pipe clenched in his teeth scented the breeze with tobacco and honey. He didn't glance in our direction though his presence made me feel safer. Matt was forty years younger, or more, but he was flabby now and sadly unsteady. Noah was old, but I knew those skinny, sinewy arms were strong. I wondered if Noah would go out of his way to protect a child.

Benjie loped across the lawn, down the steps onto the beach, full speed ahead. It was all I could do to keep up with him. My shoulders and arms throbbed with any kind of movement.

The tide was low. We kicked off our shoes so we could splash in the foam. The beach was separated from the lawn by a small cliff, no more than eight feet high, I supposed. We couldn't see the house from this beach, only an endless supply of wonders to entice a small boy.

Flat stones, fish bones, sea glass, driftwood of all shapes and sizes, cans and bottle tops. We threw stones and made ripples. Tossed wood into the water to watch it float. The water was clear here in the shallows. Through it we saw swirls in the sand, waving weeds, clam and oyster shells. A school of tiny fish flashed by. Benjie splashed through the water and tried to catch them in his cupped hands.

The day became hotter, nearing noon. I shucked my long-sleeved tee shirt since nobody was around, knotting it at my waist. I wore a halter top underneath with my short jeans skirt. With my hair so short from the hasty cut I received at the women's shelter, the sun's warmth soothed my neck, shoulders, bruised arms. Fear loosened its grip, I began to relax. Benjie's delight and fascination were therapy I had needed for a long time.

I burrowed in the sand, drowsy, content, watching him play. Breathed in the salty brine scenting the breeze, listened to the cries of swooping gulls. A parade of ships cruised by out in the bay. A pair of mallards honked and paddled past us followed by a procession of little gray ducklings. The parents flipped their heads and yellow bills into the water, looking for food, with only their feathery V-shaped rumps above the surface.

"What are they doing, Mommy?"

"They're looking for their lunch."

"Cool," he said. "That's cool. I'm hungry, too. Maybe they want to share our picnic." He giggled, hopping knee-deep in the water.

"That would be super cool," I said. *Sometimes I can't believe the words my five-year-old picks up. I pray he will soon forget words like disguise. Escape. Abuse.*

Lunch didn't take long. Benjie marched and splashed, munching his sandwich. Then he was bored again. He pulled at my hand, ready for more action, as I promised him.

"Let's go see what's around there. Want to?"

He pointed to the turn where the bay spilled into the creek. We could see the start of a narrow path leading along the side of the creek through waving cattails and sea oats. It was not really a pathway, but a narrow trail where the thick growth was trodden enough to pass through. A backdrop of tall willows separated us from the house.

I had seen Noah bringing the dinghy from a mooring down this creek. I thought it would be fun for Benjie to discover this boat. We could sit in it, pretend we were off on another journey. We could be pirates, maybe, or Indians.

We started into the undergrowth. I put my finger to my lips and whispered. "Look. Quickly."

A green heron stood poised on one leg at the edge of the creek. Startled, sensing our presence, it rose, flapped its wings and took off, soaring over the marsh grass on the other side of the creek. Benjie's eyes were round. He had never seen a bird so large.

I was carrying our shoes. "We'd better put them on," I said. The going was rough now, under our city feet.

We stopped. I knelt on the path to untangle his shoelaces. There was a small sound. A rustling in the undergrowth ahead of us. A bird, perhaps, or a rabbit. Or my imagination.

I realized Benjie and I were completely surrounded by dense weeds and saplings. It was very quiet. From far away I could hear the faint wheezing of Noah's tractor.

I heard the rustling again. Creeping footsteps. Then a trembling of the sea oats ahead of us. *Please God, no. Don't let it be Matt.*

My heart beat wildly. I sprang to my feet grabbing Benjie's shirt. *How could I have let down my guard like this? Our safety, perhaps our lives, depended on the web of secrets I had woven to keep me and my child invisible.*

"Let's run, Benj." But he was nose down, digging in the sandy pathway with his hands, enthralled with fun and freedom.

The weeds parted. *We're trapped ... Oh, God ...*

Before we could move, a small pair of bright blue eyes emerged, staring at us. Then a tousled head and freckled nose belonging to a little boy who looked no older than Benjie. Another boy, a little taller, pushed aside the growth to the right of us. On the other side, the creek side, we saw a pair of dirty sneakers thrusting aside the tall grass, and a third boy appeared. He held the hand of a little girl with a chocolate-smudged face.

There was no reason for fear, though my heart was still racing. My mind could not process what my eyes beheld. All I could do was blink. What did I tell Benjie about being brave, like his grandfather? My knees almost buckled under me, the perfect model of courage.

"Hey, you guys. Get back here. This minute." A husky female voice boomed through the thicket. A head bobbed toward us, just a little higher than the grasses. The voice barked, getting closer, louder. "I said stop. And I mean now."

I could make out a small, compact young woman with shiny bronze hair tromping through the weeds, looking side to side. A chubby baby was clamped to her hip.

"One minute you want cupcakes, next minute you …"

A child shouted. "Hey, Mamma. Over here. Look what we found."

Four kids emerged from the brush, circling Benjie and me on the path. They shared varying degrees of curly red hair and toothy grins. The next moment a petite young woman appeared, wearing overalls dusted white in places, and an auburn ponytail. Without question the mother of this crew, smiling at us without surprise, nodding at her circle of children.

"Good grief," she said. "So this is what started you playin' *I Spy* out here. Sure hope you didn't scare these folks to death."

She turned to me with a sunny smile that seemed to light up the creek, marsh, trees, the birds tweeting and flitting against the sky.

"Hey. We're the Tomisons. This is my tribe." Her children stood motionless, staring down at their shoes. "These guys," she said, "are Josh, Jess and Jake." She pointed from oldest to youngest. "They're 12, 8 and 5. Burleigh, their daddy, runs the farming at Bay House. I'm Sarah Jane, but everybody calls me S.J.," she said. Her ponytail swung as she bounced the baby on her hip.

"We decided to give the girls the prettiest names we could think of, so they grow up feelin' beautiful. This one's our six-year-old, Cynthia." She gave the older one a playful pat. "And baby Melinda's 18 months. But somehow these got shortened to Cindy and Mindy." S.J. nuzzled the baby's cheek. "So that's us."

I felt weak with relief. I could only gape at her, wondering how someone so small could sound so big. My legs turned to rubber, then folded under me. I landed on a cushion of weeds. Benjie, overcome by kids materializing from the woods, plopped into my lap, yanking my arms around in front of him like a shield. Pain shot from my wrists to my neck. I shuddered, wincing, for all eyes to see, as they stared at my fiercely purpled bruises.

S.J. dropped next to me on the path. Her children sat, too, as if on cue. She laid a gentle hand on my knee. I could see the crinkled edges of her deep-set amber eyes, freckles and smile lines in her cheeks. She seemed competent, kind, not much older than me. "That's right. You just sit and catch your breath. Good grief, girl. I know you must be Abigail and Benjie, the Bufords' relatives. But what happened to you?"

"I … I had an accident." *I could only stammer. I was not ready to complete this information. How could this woman know who we were?*

"My Daddy did it," Benjie said. "He hurt Mommy then he tried to hurt me."

Too late, I resisted the temptation to press my hand over my little boy's mouth.

The warmth in S.J.'s eyes was genuine. She shook her head. "You poor kid," she said.

Her sympathy was disarming but I could not accept it. I was still Fran Collington's daughter. I was not about to be anybody's "poor kid."

I had the right to be here, "in hiding." But why on earth did William and Harriet keep these neighboring children a secret? It never occurred to me to hope for kids for Benjie to befriend, much less someone near my own age to relate to. My cousins were a total enigma, though kind in their way. Who knew what they would do?

I sat straighter, struggling to regain some dignity. *Though I hated to admit it, I still felt comforted sitting on the wooded path with this woman and her children, and no one knowing where I was. Especially, for some nagging reason that made no sense, William and Harriet.*

"Yes. We are staying at Bay House for a few days. But that is an absolute secret." I wanted to tell her more, but I was too drained to continue my intricate story.

"OK. I see," S.J. said. Her voice became quiet and calm. "Meanwhile, what're you going to do about those arms?" Then, with her mom-bark, sent the kids off to play hide-and-seek where I can see you. Benjie hopped up to join the copper tops. His high little laugh mingled with theirs.

I was glad for someone to take charge, and glad that someone was her. I couldn't get over this tiny, feisty fireball. She didn't sound so loud now. Just upbeat and firm. I liked her. I trusted her.

"Like … what?" I said. *What could I possibly do about my arms? Consumed with so many other worries I let myself push the sick reality of Matt's abuse to some dark corner. Now I knew it was time to face the damages.*

"What should I do?"

"Report it. You know, show the police, or a doctor, or somebody, so you can prove it later. Besides, I know it hurts like hell. What if something's broken, or torn? You didn't exactly walk into a wall. How long can you keep pretending?"

Forever.

"A doctor," I said. "I'll go to a doctor but not the police. And I must be very careful. I don't want anyone to see me." *A contradiction in concepts, but there it was.*

"You need a plan." S.J. stood, brushed off her bottom, shook a few leaves from her hair.

She shouted into the woods. "Come on, guys, time to go home and finish those cupcakes. Quick, quick. We've been out here long enough."

She stepped behind me, bent down, joined her arms carefully around my waist and murmured in my ear. "I'm going to get you up without destroying what's left of you. Just push with your legs when I say go."

Then we were standing together, counting kids.

"So. I know you don't have a car, since nobody's but William and Harriet's or a workman or two have gone down the lane to Bay House lately. We share it, the lane, just the Bufords and us. It's long, twisty and dusty. But William says it keeps everything authentic, like the old carriage drive it used to be." She shrugged, throwing her hands up. "So that's that. But it takes you to the main road to Kentlands, then on to Stevensville." She frowned, wrinkling her nose. "I'm guessing you won't want to ask Harriet to take you to town. Or borrow her car."

Transportation. To find help, away from here. I had thought nothing about this. Now I dreaded the idea. And moments ago, I was almost rude to her. Cold, for certain. What was wrong with me?

"So. You're going to take my car. Tomorrow. Doc's office is close by. He's a bit short on bedside manners but he's patched up my kids fifty times each. William and Harriet are always off doing something. You'll have plenty of time."

How could she know it was not time I feared? Or only my husband's abuse. My future, my entire existence depended on what I knew I would never find. Proof. That I belonged to Bay House, and it belonged to me. Without that proof, who and what would I be?

Terror gripped me like a vice. My face felt frozen, my jaw clenched shut.

"Don't worry. He's easy to find. I'll set you up, write down the directions. They're good about taking walk-ins. Which is usually one of mine." She laughed, rolling her eyes skyward. "You can't see our house from the lane with the cornfields so high and the barns in the way. Just turn in at the white mailbox and knock on the door whenever you're ready."

But that was the trouble. I wasn't ready. I was alone, homeless, in hiding. And a complete coward.

7

I awoke in darkness to howling wind. A summer squall attacked the bay. Thunder and lightning clashed in a cacophony like a foreign language. I felt even more a stranger in a strange new land. This was no New York City storm. Rain beat in torrents against the high old windows of my third-floor room. Stabs of light pierced its shadowed eaves. In the distance I heard crashing breakers barreling down on our shore.

A bolt of lightning tore the sky above my head and shook the house. Benjie ran through the door and dove into my bed. I held his trembling body to me under my quilt, stroking his cheeks until his breathing slowed and his eyelids closed.

The clock read only 1:00 a.m. I tossed and turned as time crept by, unable to sleep. Waiting for morning, the doctor's visit in S.J.'s car. Praying this sudden deluge would end with sunrise and not keep William and Harriet from their appointments.

They have to leave so we can escape to town.

I watched my child sleeping peacefully through the storm. Little arms thrown behind his head, lips apart, breath soft and slow. I held him close. "I love you, sweet boy." Somehow the warmth of him, his small solid body, his soapy scent, gave me a surge of strength. I would do whatever I had to do to protect this child. Tomorrow would bring another chance. His hair on my cheek felt like silk, his breathing even, hypnotic …

Then it was morning. The storm had passed.

Now I could finally act on the plan arranged by S.J. The doctor would squeeze me in, courtesy of Mrs. Sarah Jane Tomison, and send her the bill. I was a friend, just passing through.

I dressed, crept to the second floor listening for voices, footsteps, the screen door banging. Nothing. Downstairs, through the rain-spattered study windows, I saw the empty circle where William and Harriet left their cars by day. I ran back upstairs, hustled a sleepy Benjie into shorts, his Superman tee shirt, feeding him bits of jelly toast I made for his breakfast while perusing the first floor. We slipped out and picked our way down the lane that led to S.J.'s. And beyond that, to the outside world I knew I needed but was terrified to re-enter.

The air was sodden. Thick with salt, as if it should be rinsed and hung out to dry. The bay lay still and gray. The sky dulled to pewter by low-hanging clouds, though the rain had stopped. Flowers drooped in clusters, tree branches bent and dripped.

William's authentic carriage lane was a muddy strip of pebbles and puddles. I squeezed Benjie's hand to keep him from playing leapfrog, splashing us both.

"Mommy. This is not a fun day. This is a yukky day." He tried to pry his fingers from mine. "I want to play with those kids. Not go to the dumb doctor. Why do we have to go there, anyway?"

I lacked an answer.

We trudged on in silence until we reached the white mailbox. It took only a minute or so, but it felt like lightyears. Here it was. The

Tomison farmhouse. A giant red tractor on high black tires, bikes and balls strewn across the front yard. A long porch layered with toys. Baseball bats, a rusted doll's buggy, stuffed animals missing stuffing. Its roof sagged a bit, giving it the look of an old gray hat pulled down at one corner. Wide steps led to the black-hinged front door split across the middle. Open at the top, closed at the bottom. A battered green pick-up truck was parked in front, behind the tractor.

S.J. waved at us, hollering from the porch in her loud clear bark.

"Change of plan. I'm taking you to town. No arguments." She bounded down the stairs as we approached, wearing jeans with a yellow tank top half tucked in at her narrow waist. "Burleigh can stay with the kids today. No one will look twice at his truck passin' through. You've got to stay hidden, at least till you get to Doc's office. I'm makin' sure that happens. So hop in and sit tight. Yep, Benjie. That means you, too." She tickled his neck, ruffled his hair, but got only a stony face in return.

S.J. was in charge, which seemed natural. Suddenly Benjie and I were high up, bouncing along the ruts. When we stopped to turn left onto the main road, I slid lower on the front seat.

"It's only about 10 minutes to our little village. Kentlands, I mean. That's closest. More of a crossroads and very old. I mean really old," S.J. said. She stretched out the word really far beyond two syllables. "Like, founded in the 1600s old. Beyond that is Stevensville, an actual town. But we're not goin' that far."

She looked over at me cowering next to her. "Seems like I've known you for ages. I forget it's only been a few days and you know nothing about where you are. Stay down, you won't be missin' much. Cornfields, soybeans, more cornfields. Lots more old places like Bay House down lanes you can't even see."

Benjie laid his head on my lap humming a random, sing-song tune. Like those he murmured on our frightening drive from Washington to Annapolis, where William rescued us. We both drowsed.

I felt a hand on my shoulder and flinched, bolting straight up. Of course, it was only S.J., but my heart thumped, my stomach knotted. "We're here," she said. "Kentlands." She pointed at the historical marker staked below what appeared to be the only traffic light.

We crept down the main street of a tiny crossroads that looked like the twentieth century almost passed it by. We rolled by several dusty-windowed antique shops, a corner grocery, Betty's Boutique, The Kent Isle Café. A few people strolled along the narrow sidewalks. Even fewer entering or leaving the stores.

S.J. peered ahead through the steering wheel. "There's a marina about two blocks down. My kids love to come here and look at the boats."

I couldn't think of beauty or boats or the bay. Only my fear and misery. My shoulders and arms were burning. I was beginning to worry they would never feel normal again.

We pulled up beside a weathered gray house that seemed to sprout from the sidewalk. No tufts of grass, no row of bushes to separate it from the cement. A small brass sign on the door read, "Dr. Peter Carpenter."

S.J. rocked the truck to a halt. "This is it. I'll be right here waitin' 'til you're done." She jumped down from her seat and came around to open our door. "I know everything hurts." She helped Benjie and me slide to the ground. "Be brave," she said. "And remember who you are."

I dragged Benjie inside with me, wondering just who that was. My child was sleepy and not at all compliant.

The receptionist reminded me she would squeeze us in since I didn't have an appointment. When I gave her my name and referenced S.J., she looked up to study me, cupping her chin in her hand. I guessed everyone knew, and possibly gossiped about, everyone in town. Benjie and I were new grist for the mill.

We sat huddled in a corner, well away from the windows. I was draped in a green flannel shirt belonging to S.J.'s husband, which covered my halter top like a tent. *It occurred to me that I really did look like a homeless waif. I wondered again if this was who I really was.*

I stared at the walls of this small, sterile house-turned-office smelling of new paint. Large black and white photographs hung everywhere. Wild geese flying, Native American Indians, bare trees against the sky. Nothing else. No magazines, no kids' toys, though this was the town's main practitioner, who treated patients of all ages.

The inner door opened. An elderly man in overalls shuffled out paying no attention to us. Behind him was a gray-haired nurse, starched white cap bobby-pinned to her head. "Come in, Mrs. Wells," she said.

I stood, pressing my fingers into Benjie's shoulder. Bending down I looked him straight in the eye. "I want you to follow me, sit where I say and do not move. Understand?"

The doctor did not look old, comfortable, or fatherly and understanding, as I hoped. He looked young, lean, harassed. He had the square shoulders and long arms of a tennis player, even in his white coat. But he didn't look like a man who played games. There was a sparseness about him. Closely cut brown hair, except for an unruly wave falling across his brow, no excess meat on his bones. No room for mischief in the serious brown eyes behind horn-rimmed glasses. No time for pleasantries on the long, plain face. He might have been attractive if he allowed the lines in his cheeks to crease into a smile.

I steered my son to a high-backed metal chair.

The doctor motioned for me to sit on the edge of the examining table. "Well," he said, "what can I do for you?"

I sat paralyzed with embarrassment.

He looked at the notes the nurse gave him. "You have an injury, on your arms? Why don't you just undo that?" He pointed to Burleigh's enormous shirt, sagging down my shoulders.

I unbuttoned it and let it fall. Sat, cold and shivering in my halter top. Exposed. Mortified.

He stared at my arms and let out a long, slow whistle. Shook his head as if to deny what he saw. The marks that were strawberry red under the skin streaked from purple to almost black from my shoulders to my elbows on both sides. The deepest, darkest blazes still showed the imprints of fingers.

The doctor bent toward me, starting his exam at my wrists. He felt along each arm, rotated my elbows in and out, ending with the joints where they attached to my shoulders. I squeezed my eyes closed as pain fired through me. He kept saying, "Sorry, sorry," each time I winced. But I felt no empathy, no true sorrow, as he examined me.

"How long ago did this happen?" His brown eyes bored into mine.

I looked away. "Three days ago."

He frowned. "Might have helped if you came in sooner. I don't think any bones are broken, maybe some ligaments pulled. But I doubt if you have a whole capillary left intact anywhere in your upper arms. It's going to take a long time for those contusions to heal. Lie down as much as you can. Use ice packs. I can give you something for the pain."

As if I could lounge in bed with a young child to look after. I doubted he even saw Benjie as more than a shadow in the corner. I could no longer stifle my impatience. "What I need is, I mean, could you, would you, give me some kind of statement, some description …"

"You want a description of the injury?"

I forced the words out. "I'm going to need evidence. So I can sue for divorce and get custody of my son." *There. I said it.*

Dr. Carpenter pushed his glasses higher up on his nose as if to examine a specimen more closely. I felt like a worm in a petri dish.

"You are stating that your husband caused this condition?"

I nodded, looking away. *This is what my mother tried to protect me from with all her cover-ups. This humiliation. This shame.*

For the first time he glanced at Benjie, looking him up and down. He turned back to me, red-faced, clenching and unclenching his fists.

"Is this the first incident of abuse?"

"No."

"Any abuse of the child?"

"No." *Wait. Surely shaking counts.* "Well, yes. Once. He shook our son but did not strike him." Tears stung my eyes. My voice came out in jagged breaths. "That was ... the day I left him."

He stood so fast his stool teetered and spun. With one long stride he reached Benjie sitting hunched in the corner. Pulled a metal scope from his breast pocket and shined it in Benjie's eyes. "OK, now watch my finger." Benjie moved his eyes from side to side. "What's your name, son?" he asked without a trace of warmth. I could barely hear my child mumble it. "OK. Does your head hurt?"

"Uh-uh," Benjie whispered.

He turned to me and spoke in the same cold voice. "The boy looks fine." Then he sighed as if the weight of his words came at a great cost. "How long has this been going on with you?"

"Four years, maybe five."

"Good God." He rummaged through a desk drawer, brought out a folder and slammed the drawer shut. "Here are some forms. I've seen similar situations, but they mostly come in on Monday mornings." He handed me a pen and a clipboard to write on. "You fill in these pages giving the necessary details. Then I'll describe the injury and sign it."

He was silent, chewing his lip, observing me as I wrote. When I finished writing he read in silence, leaned on his desk and scrawled across the document's last line.

Then he wheeled around, lunged forward on his seat. Lips clamped almost closed. Eyes blazing with scorn. "I know there are many psychological and economic reasons why women put up with abuse." He spoke as if he would burst. "But they're nothing but psychological and economic reasons for stupidity. Nobody in this country has to put up with abuse." He took a deep breath and seemed to will himself into neutrality. "However, as your injuries are so severe, you will heal more quickly if we reduce your pain for daily functioning." He scribbled on a pad and slapped a prescription on top of the document he signed.

Then he rubbed his forehead and spoke slowly, in a voice that had lost its zeal. He pulled some pamphlets from his desk and laid them next to me on the exam table. "Here's some information that might help. Read them. Come back if you have any questions."

I grabbed the shirt I arrived in, pulled the long sleeves over my arms, buttoned it as fast as I could with shaking fingers. I snatched both slips of paper, the pamphlets, took Benjie's hand and fled.

S.J. was waiting. We scrambled into Burleigh's truck and slammed the door. Tears rolled down my cheeks but I was too angry to care.

S.J. shot the old green truck away from the curb. "That one's not exactly Dr. Charm, right?"

I could only nod. She reached over and patted my hand.

"Let's face it, most men might be good at whatever they're good at, but when it comes to another person's feelings, they don't know their ass from a hole in the ground. He probably acted like it was all your fault, gettin' those bruises. Like you wanted it or deserved it or somethin'."

Another speechless nod.

S.J. eyed the papers I held. "Oh, well, you got what you needed, I see."

I stopped crying and looked at this Sarah Jane Tomison. *She was right. I didn't deserve any of this, much less my innocent child. Again, she went to the heart of the matter and skimmed off the chaff. I felt better. As a matter of fact, I felt alive. Buoyant. Strange as it was, we shared a bond. It was silent, unspoken. But I knew she felt it, too. For the first time in a long time, I had a friend.*

8

"So sorry." S.J. turned to me, the corners of her mouth pulled down. "There's one more detour before we head home. We've got to use the pharmacy in Stevensville. It's the only one we have. It's only ten more minutes. Then we'll be on our way back to Bay House. I promise."

Benjie, at the end of his five-year-old rope, broke into sobs. "No, Mommy. My tummy hurts. I wanna go play with my toys." He wailed as he hadn't since the nightmare in New York when his father, in a drunken rage, shook him like a rag doll. And assaulted his mother. *Guilt settled upon me like a shroud as I held his quivering little body. I was still terrified of being seen.*

We both sat dazed as S.J. sped on through streets I barely saw. Darted in and out of the drug store, hopped back in the truck clutching a small white bag.

She tapped Benjie's shoulder and pushed his hair from his tear-streaked face. "Hey, Benj. Look what I found." From the bag she pulled out a Superman comic book, grinning as his eyes popped with surprise. "You can be our superhero," she said. "Oh, yeah. Here's one more thing. Hope you like strawberry as much as my kids do." She winked and dropped a popsicle in his lap.

S.J. to the rescue again. I took the bag, felt the small bottle with its clinking pills. Closed it in my purse. My child sat straight up and began to flip pages. He licked his treat and offered me sweet frozen bites.

When we left Stevensville, we had to cross a twentieth-century highway where cars roared by in an endless line. I peered down the road. I could see a shopping center, gas stations, a large neon arrow pointing to a seafood restaurant.

"Traffic's like this all day every summer," S.J. said. "People trying to get to Ocean City, 'bout fifty miles east. You wouldn't believe it on Friday afternoons." She shook her head, ponytail bobbing. "Sometimes cars line up like a million ants waitin' to cross over the Bay Bridge from Baltimore and D.C. to get here. There's always a bottleneck at the little bridge at Kent Narrows. You've got to cross it to get to the Eastern Shore or go on to the coast, all the way up to the Delaware beaches. Bethany and Rehoboth. Sunday afternoons and evenings, they're all lined up the other way, tryin' to get back."

The comfort I longed to feel drained away. This noisy modern world so close to Bay House alarmed me. Approaching Bay House from the water, Benjie and I were safe and secret. But this part of the island was no sanctuary. I hunched down into the front seat. Matt could be anywhere. Or would he have a police car looking for us?

I must have held my breath for miles, until we reached the road that wound south out of Stevensville, to Kentlands. *This was the road S.J. wouldn't let me see on the way to the doctor. The road my father always described as if it was a magic carpet leading to a gilded castle. Our home.*

Now I gulped clean, salty air, stole glances when I dared, surveying this sliver of Kent Island at last.

Kent Island. It was a land of fable to me. From my father's stories. From the belief in his voice, the love in his eyes as he spoke of it. A mythical, poetic Greek Isle steeped in history and sunshine. With blue-green water lapping at its edges.

The narrow road curved through woods, acres of corn, small farms and hidden lanes leading off to houses that must face the bay. We could hear birds singing in the trees, smell turned earth, ripening crops. *I fancied we were back in another time.*

We turned into our lane at the sign that said, "Bay House–Circa 1740."

The lane was long and tree-lined. Sunlit fields half-hid a rambling red barn, smaller outbuildings clustered amid waving cornfields. It became a circular drive dotted with blossoms leading to what I now knew was the back of the house with its center hallway, chimneys, porches and stairs. Beyond it, shimmered the Chesapeake Bay, flashing in the distance under a storybook sky.

This, I saw with a sinking heart, was where peace, fantasy and anonymity ended.

"Lookit all the cars, Mommy." Benjie's voice was high and shrill with excitement. A sign of his full recovery from our trip to Dr. Carpenter. Revived by his hero's comic book and popsicle's sugar, he knelt with his palms and nose pressed to the truck's window.

The circle was full of cars. Women in bright-colored summer dresses clustered nearby in the garden or lounged in white Adirondack chairs scattered about the lawn.

S.J. wheeled off the lane onto the dirt track that led behind the big barn. A route I didn't know existed.

I pulled Benjie back into my lap, crouched again as low as I could. "Keep your head down, just a minute more." *As we tossed and jostled unseen I was reminded again of S.J.'s expertise in the workings of Bay House. How blessed I was to have found such an ally.*

"It's got to be the church ladies, getting ready for the Open-to-the-Public," she said. "Harriet's probably telling them how to show off her flowers and every blade of grass. If you make a run for it, you can get in the patio door and up the steps before they go inside."

She stopped the truck behind the barn. We slid out in silence.

Benjie and I ran as if the devil was behind us instead of a group of church women. We eased through the screen door without a sound and were on the second-floor landing when we heard Harriet's voice. She let an entire group merge into the main hallway that led straight through the house from the back, sending the sweet-blended scent of many toiletries up the stairwell.

I whispered to Benjie. "Tiptoe upstairs. Be very quiet. You can play with the toys." He crept up the steps. The toys were still a novelty, and the running and tiptoeing were fun.

We were both hot and sweaty from our long morning, the house was fragrant and cool. I longed for quiet and a nap. The pain pill S.J. insisted I take made me drowsy.

I stood at the second-floor railing. *This was not fair. Harriet should have told me our sanctuary was about to be invaded. But still, this was a chance to hear what I had been longing to hear, the true story of this house. When the women reached the second floor, I would take Benjie in the bathroom on the third floor, turn on the water and hook the door before they came any higher. I was beginning to think like a fugitive but at least I was able to think, sleepy or not.*

"On the wall to the right," Harriet said, "is the earliest portrait." Her crisp descriptions were easy to hear, even from the floor above. "I'll explain for any of you who aren't already familiar with the history. This is a rare one, unusual for Kent Island in those times, in terms of color and perspective. It is William Henry Collington, the original builder. His wife was Maude, they had two children. A son, called Young Will, only eight at the time, and a daughter, Mercy, just a toddler. This family portrait is believed to have been painted in 1758 by an English artist visiting in Virginia.

Harriet continued as if reading from a script. *You'd never know she was talking about William's family.*

"William Collington came from Virginia to Kent Island in 1740. He purchased a large parcel of land, some 600 acres. The small cottage still standing on it belonged to a Collington ancestor who came with William Claibourne's original English settlers in the 1630s." She droned on. "William Henry Collington added the present rectangular structure to what we now call the Old Cabin, with bricks brought from England. At that time, it was a kitchen and slave quarters. This was a thriving tobacco farm then. The so-called new kitchen in the wing on the other side was added in 1850. It's been modernized through the years and is the one we use now." She paused. "Are there any questions?"

Feet shuffled, someone coughed. A strong voice drifted upwards. "This may be off the subject, Harriet. Just a suggestion, mind you. Maybe we ought to make all this history a little more, ah, colorful, or something, as we go along. What about the ghost? Isn't Bay House supposed to have a ghost?"

"Ghost," the voice said. My hands froze to the railing. I must have misunderstood, with the ladies' gasps and rising chatter.

"Honestly, Rosemary," said Harriet. "This is history, not salacious tales. I've lived here for fifteen years, and I've never seen a ghost." I pictured her reaching to pat her perfect French twist in place.

"There's a lot of stuff in the town library. I came across it the other day." Here was a lively young voice this time. "The Collington Papers. If anyone wants to do serious research, there's a whole pile to dig through."

"Well, let's go on, can't we?" This voice was older, slower. "I want to see this lovely place before my knees give out on me." There was a ripple of laughter.

These women were friends. I wished I could stop hiding. Just be a normal person. But I could imagine what would happen if Rosemary got even a glimmer of my juicy tale.

Harriet began lecturing again. "Here is young Will Collington on his big bay gelding when he was 21, painted by an unknown local artist.

Quite good, don't you think? And his sister, Mercy, just before she married. Now, on the other side of the wall are later portraits."

I strained to hear. *What about my father, Benjamin Henry Collington?*

Harriet must have turned her back, and the group faced the other way. I couldn't hear so clearly now. I caught the name Buford several times before Harriet led them off into the other rooms.

Benjie was too quiet. I crept up the last flight hoping this wasn't an ominous sign of mischief. But my son was sound asleep on the nursery floor, the firewagon in his hands. I picked him up and laid him on the bed, still sleeping.

I went out into the hall and listened. The women were swooping up to the second floor.

"There are three bedrooms on this level," said Harriet, "furnished with some excellent old pieces, some newer. Ask about anything you think people might want to know. One thing I do want to caution you about." Her voice notched higher, louder than normal. To me, it sounded strained. "Attention, please, ladies." She clapped her hands until everyone was silent. "You may certainly show the master bedroom. Just know that the small door in the wall on the right is locked and bolted. For security. It leads directly into the upper section of the Old Cabin, which we're doing over, you know. There's no flooring where the loft was. So, there's a very dangerous drop." She paused, asked if anyone had a question. No one spoke a word.

She continued. "The little room at the end of the hall was made into a bathroom as you can see. Just take your time, wander around. We won't go to the third floor today. That's really not ready for display yet."

Did she say that especially loud, so I could hear?

I ducked back out of sight and hovered in the shadows of the third-floor hallway, well away from the stair railing. I listened for what seemed a long time. The chatter turned away from history. I caught words and phrases now and then, about a Hepplewhite desk, something crystal, the lace-trimmed canopy on a poster bed. I could see why Harriet was worried about Benjie "getting into things."

The group started downstairs. I could hear steps creaking, voices drifting downward. Relieved, I stepped forward to peer over the railing to be sure they were gone. Two women stopped just below me.

The clear young voice I noticed before spoke up. "What I don't understand is what happened to all the Collingtons. You don't see or hear about any of them after Young Will. He must have been so young in 1760, or was it '62? Anyway, everybody here seems to know a lot more about this than I do because nobody asks questions. Of course, I've only been here for six months, but ..."

Rosemary's voice was quick to answer. "Honestly, it's no secret, believe me. Everybody around here knows about the Collingtons. But it's like family. You don't have to tell everything to strangers who'll be going through the house."

"It must have been something tragic, then." The young voice persisted. "You see Bufords, and Dunlops, and names like Calhoun and Livingston in the archives. I don't know how I remembered that. But whatever happened to the Collingtons?"

Above them, I stopped breathing to listen with all my senses.

"They lived here for many years, my dear. The last was Ben Collington. He left when his wife refused to stay any longer. They had a little girl if I remember right. They were in their 30s, I think? They didn't own a single bit of Bay House, or the land. It all went to the earliest daughter's descendants, Mercy. You saw her portrait downstairs."

Rosemary's voice softened. "We do have to hurry on," she said. "They'll be wondering where we are. But, yes, there was a tragedy involved. A strange story, if it's true. Young Will's only child, a son, was illegitimate. Naturally, of course, Will didn't inherit.

"You mean the child was cut off, and all of his family after him? Yet they continued to live here? That's really weird."

"Well, dear, you know what the *Bible* says about the sins of the fathers."

The two women started downstairs, their voices drifting off.

I slid down onto the hall floor, gripping the banister.

So, this is the terrible secret. A tragic old scandal and no inheritance. No home for Benjie and me. The end of the dream. Except that my father said, "Don't believe it." I remember his exact words. "Someday I'm going to take you back again to Bay House where I grew up. That's our real home and part of it belongs to us. Don't let anybody ever make you believe that it doesn't." He must have had a reason. Even after 17 years I remember how fine and brave he made me feel, and how I trusted him.

Right then, I made a decision. I still would.

"Mommy, why are you sitting on the floor?" Here was Benjie. Hot and tousled from his nap.

"A very good question, Benj."

I was too tired to get up. I was drained, and my arms ached. It occurred to me that if Dr. Peter Carpenter was the mother of a five-year-old he might have some idea how impossible it was to stay in bed with ice packs on one's arms. I hated taking the pain pills which made me sleepy. I needed, above all else, to stay alert.

"Oh, Abigail." Now it was Harriet calling up the steps. "Everyone's gone. You and Benjie come on down to lunch."

I was not ready to face Harriet. I felt an urgent need to think, rest, be alone. None of which were possible, of course.

Hoping to stall for time, I called down to her. "Do we have a minute to clean up first?"

"It's only us. Just cold chicken and potato salad. I have a golf date in half an hour."

She obviously was not for waiting. I shrugged on my long-sleeved blouse. We washed our hands and went down, though I couldn't imagine my child being hungry after the stress of the doctor's visit topped off by a huge popsicle. My stomach was in knots and food was the farthest thing from my mind.

We sat at Harriet's kitchen table where she had laid out a simple cold lunch, as promised. Benjie was pale and subdued from this morning's outing. He yawned while he picked at a chicken leg. I sipped at a glass of iced tea and toyed with my napkin, feeling ill-prepared for the conversation to come. Harriet managed to look elegant and put together in a beige golf shirt and matching skirt which showed off her long, tanned legs. *My mother would have loved it, but Harriet made me feel I was shrinking.*

"Where on earth did you go earlier?"

I gave her a brief version of our morning.

"I can't believe you went off with Sarah Jane Tomison."

"She was really very kind."

"I saw you, you know, as you dashed behind the house."

"I do thank you for not letting anybody up to our—up to the third floor."

"Well, we have a lot of work to do before the house is open for the bazaar in the week before Thanksgiving. We'll have to include the nursery then. The house tour and bazaar benefit our church, you know. Then after that, well, there may be a lot of changes."

She glanced at the clock. "You must not go into town again if you want to stay in hiding, Abigail. At the moment, no one knows you're here except Noah. He doesn't talk to anybody. And the Tomisons." Her hand flew to her cheek as she shook her head. "I hope Sarah Jane can keep those children quiet."

"There's the doctor," I said. "Don't worry, I won't be going back to him. But doctors are not supposed to talk about their patients, are they?"

"Of course not." Harriet looked amused. "Besides, I've heard Peter Carpenter's not exactly chatty. He's a strange duck."

I sensed a lecture coming. Or perhaps her calling me Abigail was a way of distancing herself from an unpleasant topic.

"When he first came here, he was in medical school in, I don't know, somewhere out west, I think." Harriet gave a flip of her hand, dismissing every institution which wasn't Johns Hopkins University in nearby Baltimore. "Anyway, he came to visit Dr. Sommerville's son, Buddy, who for some strange reason was in the same medical school. Apparently, they became friends, which is why Carpenter came to visit here one long summer weekend. Fourth of July, I think it was. You know how everybody talks in this place. People wanted to hear all about him. The young girls were all excited. He wouldn't be bad looking if he ever relaxed, but he always seems reserved, distant. Plus, he has this thing about Indian history. Spends his free time writing articles on ancient Indian medical practices."

"I remember," I managed to say. "There were blown-up photographs of Indian faces all over his waiting room. I didn't pay too much attention to them. I was too nervous."

"I've never been in that office," Harriet said. She busied herself brushing the table of imaginary crumbs. "We always go to Dr. Sommerville. He's a love. He won the sailing trophy for years, too. But getting back to Peter Carpenter. The story is that his father was a government doctor on some Indian reservation in Arizona, and Peter grew up there. Even though he decided to become a doctor too, he never got over his obsession with championing the cause of the original Americans. Or something noble like that."

She continued as if by memory. "Then Buddy Sommerville dropped out of medical school and went into insurance in Baltimore. Old Doc invited Peter Carpenter to come here after his internship and take a place in his practice. So, Carpenter arrived about three years ago and opened a separate office. He does take a load off our dear old friend, but he is definitely not famous for his bedside manner."

I gave a small nod. *I did not want to think about cold, curt, impatient Peter Carpenter, much less discuss my visit with Harriet.*

She glanced at the clock again. "All this about the doctors is beside the point," she said. "I'm getting side-tracked. I was trying to talk to you about this secrecy. If you must hide, then stay here, right here on the property. But you know it can't go on indefinitely, Abigail. You're going to have to face up to someone, sooner or later, you know." She eyed Benjie, who was pushing potato chips around his plate.

I felt myself shudder. My hands automatically crossed at my chest and slid up to my shoulders. "I can't," I said. "Not yet. You don't know what it's like."

I looked away to avoid the disapproval in her dark stare. *It seemed hopeless to try to explain to someone as in control as Harriet, the trap in which I was caught. Yet, if Benjie and I were going to be allowed to stay here she was going to have to understand.*

I put down my fork and slid my chair forward. "Harriet," I said, trying to sound forceful. "Matt hurt me. Physically. Not only emotionally. I was lucky I escaped before he put me in the hospital." Of course, she could see this. Everyone could.

Benjie was in another imaginary world playing war with the salt and pepper shakers. I pressed on.

I tried to tell her why I left, starting with the ride home from my mother's house on the day of her funeral. To make Harriet see it, as I couldn't erase it from behind my closed eyes. *Matt hunched over the wheel as if he wanted to crush the road. That stupid pork pie hat jammed so low on his forehead. That menacing silence. His fist on the seat between us. The reek of Scotch, the building tension.*

Harriet cut me off, holding up her hand. Her jangling bracelets made me want to scream.

"I don't need to hear any more. Of course, you'll stay here till you're stronger. I just meant that sooner or later ..."

"I know," I said, between clamped teeth. "I will. But, please, not yet. There's something else I've been trying to ask you. I heard what some of those women were saying today." I forced myself to look straight into her eyes. "That there's some sad old story about young Will Collington. But all of that must have happened more than two hundred years ago. I was led to believe, and I've always dreamed ..."

Harriet clasped her hands together and leaned toward me across the table. "Abigail." She stopped me again. "I'm beginning to realize what you've been led to believe, what you've hoped. I know it's going to seem simply rotten to you, but you might as well know the truth. You have no legal right to Bay House at all. You and Benjie are guests."

I looked back at her, unblinking. "My father didn't believe that. Why?"

"Your father was a dreamer."

"You knew him?"

"Only briefly, when I was a child. We lived down the road, you know, on the old Parker place. The Sellmans own it now, from New York. I was only about fourteen when your parents left here, with you."

I dropped my hands on the table to steady myself. "Would I have been about four?"

"Possibly." She begrudged that admission of our age difference, perhaps, but I didn't care. I jumped up, ecstatic.

"Then I was here. I did remember. My dream was true."

Harriet stared at me as if for the first time she saw a real person. "It's too bad, Abigail, but dreams don't count. Facts do."

"This one matters to me," I said.

We heard the crunch of a car in the turnaround. A horn honked.

"Oh, dear. That's my friend for golf. Excuse me, I must run. Don't worry about cleaning up. Bye, bye, Benjie." She dropped a kiss on the top of his head and was gone. I had a feeling she was glad to escape.

I was left in fury and frustration, full of unanswered questions, for a long afternoon. I cleaned up the lunch dishes, then had to get out of the house. I raced Benjie to the beach, surprising us both.

"Mommy, you're fast." Benjie gaped at me as I caught my breath.

"When I have to be," I said.

S.J. was perched on the sand watching her crew splash in the shallows. Just who Benjie and I both needed. She grinned at me and patted the spot next to her. "The girls are down for naps and Burleigh's workin' on the tractor, so I'm catchin' a break."

"Lookit, Mom. The guys are here." Benjie was ecstatic. He kicked off his shoes and ran to join them. Every once in a while, there would be a shriek when one of them spotted a stinging jellyfish. Soon Benjie was digging sandcastles with Jake, while Josh and Jess stood deeper in the breakers, skimming rocks.

We lay on our stomachs, facing the boys. The sand made warm hollows that cradled our bodies. I rolled up my sleeves to let the sun bake my arms and pulled up my skirt. So much time in the sun was turning my skin to a dark bronze.

We watched the children. We watched the water. We told each other funny things about our kids. Sometimes we didn't talk at all. After what seemed a long time, I said, "S.J."

"Huh?"

"Do you know the story about young Will Collington? The one in that early portrait, on his horse?"

"Sure. Everybody around here does."

"Will you tell me?"

"You're not going to like it."

"Please. Tell me anyway."

S.J. shifted onto her side, propped herself on her elbow. "Well, according to legend, Young Will ran off in the woods with an Indian girl. And they had a child. A little boy. Will brought the baby home to his parents, brought the girl, too. Claimed they were married, but nobody believed them."

I sat straight up. I could picture my proud mother hearing this story. "So, what happened?"

"William Collington, Young Will's father, said they'd keep the baby. But he didn't want any part of the Indian girl."

"So, what happened to her?"

"She ran away. And then, somehow, she drowned."

"She drowned? But how? That's so sad," I said. "So terribly sad. Is that all?"

S.J. hesitated. "Yeah, that's about all," she said. "I told you weren't going to like it."

For a few minutes, we were both quiet.

"Abby," she said. "People tell a lot of tales in a place like this. It's a small town and a good many folks have lived here all their lives. They remember things. It just seems kind of funny, now that I'm lyin' here looking at you." She began drawing circles in the sand. "They say that Indian girl had black hair and sky-blue eyes. Just like yours."

9

The week that followed began peacefully.

Harriet avoided conversation about the past with her casual shrugs, her busyness, her changes of subject. I studied the portraits in the house, especially William Collington and his wife, Maude. Handsome and fair-haired, with their blond children, Young Will and Mercy. I looked at my own little tow-headed son and thought I saw a resemblance. I examined myself in the mirror and saw what I always thought was my father's dark hair, my mother's blue eyes. I still looked like a plucked chicken, with my shorn locks and skinny frame. The tan helped, though. The hollowed eyes were not so deep.

The household seemed low-key, with William still away on business. Harriet, Benjie and I ate at the kitchen table, even for dinner. Some evenings we could hear the putt-putt of the small dinghy in the twilight when Noah went trolling, as Harriet explained, for rockfish. We would have them for dinner the next night. Fillets salted and peppered, seared in butter until they were slightly crisp, then baked with lemon slices, capers and white wine. Harriet was an excellent cook. I was beginning to realize she worked hard and constantly, with the house, gardens, meals. All the while creating the illusion she had nothing to do but keep up with her friends, golf and committee meetings. I tried to help as much as I could and still keep Benjie out of trouble.

This place and the way of life here had a lulling effect. They seemed to be working some kind of healing in me. The fact that William decreed I must not leave the grounds was justification for drifting. There was the heat of late June, the beach, S.J. and the children. The family of ducks that were our friends to visit every day. The cool shelter of the house. New York seemed a continent away.

Then Mr. Dangerfield called, and the peace was shattered. "Abigail, dear. I have, uh, some rather unsettling news. I checked with the garage attendant and your car is not there."

My pulse quickened as I gripped the telephone. "Have you heard anything about Matt?"

"I tried again and again but I could never reach him. Your building superintendent said he hadn't seen him going in or out, so I must tell you that I asked for a passkey." He spoke with his usual tremble. "I checked the apartment, and, my dear child, it looks as if Matthew hasn't been there for days. There were newspapers and mail stacked up, unwashed dishes in the kitchen, uh, that sort of thing."

I could not imagine Mr. Dangerfield doing anything so daring, possibly dangerous. It occurred to me the tremor in his voice was not just because he was nervous. Mr. Dangerfield was getting old.

He looked old to me seventeen years ago, when my father died. And my mother started saying with such carelessness, "We'll get in touch with Arthur. He'll take care of it."

I think I grew up another notch just then. It was a cold and lonely feeling. I was not surprised Matt was gone from the apartment, because I was sure he was looking for Benjie and me. But I was not going to burden Arthur about it again. He had taken care of me long enough.

All I said was, "Thank you. Thank you so much. You've been wonderful. I'm sure you've done all anybody could do."

"I'm sending you some papers to sign, Abigail. And soon there may be a small check. Just try to sit tight, as it were, with those good people who've taken you in. Try not to worry. You can depend on me to do my best for you, just as your mother would have wished."

"I know," I said. "Don't you worry, either. Benjie and I are fine here. Just fine."

As I hung up the phone, I knew what I had to do. Time was running out and the respite was over. I had to get to town to the library while William was still gone, and before Matt caught up with me. Whether Harriet liked it or not I would find that stack of Collington papers.

"There's a lot of stuff there," the girl's voice said.

If I was going to fight for my father's belief about Bay House, I better start doing it. I knew Harriet was not about to lend me her car, so I would have to wait until she was out and borrow S.J.'s. Again, I counted my blessings my ally was just down the lane.

And then, as so often happens with best-laid plans, everything changed. It rained.

Benjie and I stood just outside the screen door. He had his red sand bucket. I was holding the thermos and a paper bag of lunch. S.J. and I agreed I would come take her car as soon as Harriet left for her golf game.

The storm whipped up suddenly, as I now knew storms on the bay often do. First, the wind. It slammed into us, bringing the smell of a salty deluge. Waves beat against the shore. The sky and water darkened to slate, making Benjie's little bucket stand out like vermillion, sending clouds scudding toward our beach.

"My word," said Harriet. She stood at the door, hands on her hips, scowling at the weather which dared to ruin her plans. "Look at that thunderhead. We're in for it, Abby, when the wind comes out of the northwest like this. It happens every year around the last week or two of June."

Then the rain came. Pounding, slanting from the bay side.

"Come in, come in," said Harriet. "The floor's getting wet."

We ducked inside while Benjie shrieked with excitement.

"His hair's sopping wet," she said. She brushed his bangs from Benjie's eyes, slid her hand across his cheek in a gentle caress. *I sensed a strangeness in her attitude toward Benjie. She didn't seem to want him in the house, yet she seemed drawn to him almost against her will.*

The phone rang. "That will be Alice, canceling." There was no golf that day or the next.

Harriet started a major cleaning, getting ready for the Open House, making use of indoor time. I offered to help, but she called in Noah and shooed Benjie and me up to the third floor. We were trapped.

We stared out the dormer window of the nursery at the wall of rain. Small boats scuttled to shore. The wind made weird, keening noises through the gutter spouts. We were so high, I almost felt the house sway a little, like the mast of a ship.

Benjie climbed into my lap as we sat and watched nature's fury. "Is this scary?" he asked.

"Well, sure. A little," I said. "It looks scary and it feels scary, doesn't it? And it sounds scary. But it's just a storm that'll be over soon. You'll see."

"Oh, well, nothing bad's going to happen way up here, right?" He pulled my arms around him, while I determined not to flinch. "I guess it's fun scary. So c'un I have Jake over? There's nothin' to do."

"Not in all this rain," I said. "We'll think of something."

I did not know what on earth it was going to be. I was bursting with frustration, myself. The prospect of entertaining Benjie in this one room all afternoon, delaying my plan, was maddening.

I knew he would whine in protest. "But Jake's my best friend."

"I said no, Benj. You have all these toys to play with. I'll be right next door in my room. You can play by yourself for a while, and that's final."

He kicked the firewagon, rolling it across the old floorboards without enthusiasm or sound effects.

Something must have caught his imagination. He started talking in a soft, high-pitched voice, began lining the toy soldiers in parade formation. I knew he would be all right for a while. He was good at playing pretend games alone, though not for long.

I would use this time to start drafting a statement about Matt's abuse to show a lawyer, along with the evidence of the arrogant Dr. Carpenter.

As soon as I had some money.

Stuck here in the rain as I was, the memory of my visit to the doctor's office flooded back. Again, I felt sick with shame. Shame and anger. The man did not need to humiliate me. He could have signed the forms and let me go without the benefit of his personal belief about my "psychological or economic reasons for stupidity." He knew nothing of my life, my marriage or my husband. Or what it is to be a woman in a trap. He judged only that I had submitted to abuse.

It was clear he was some sort of crusader, full of opinionated righteousness. Probably the boring kind of man some of my friends married after Matt and his pals passed them by. I could think of several. Inspired by intellect, social conscience. Blind to any corporate or social ladder. They became Little League coaches, attended PTA meetings and never thought of beating their lovely, capable wives.

Peter Carpenter must have thought I was the dregs of the earth. Sudden tears stung my eyes, slid down my cheeks in unison with the rain on the windowpanes. Freedom, Abby, I reminded myself.

What did freedom even look like? I pictured the Statue of Liberty. Waving hair aloft, torch ablaze. It doesn't matter what anybody else thinks about you. It's what you think about yourself that counts. You're not the dregs unless you believe you are. "Oh, come off it, Abby," I said out loud. Dregs was a bit too much, even to me.

I grabbed a tissue, wiped my face and eyes, glad that Benjie was not watching his emotional mother. Now I would get busy on that statement.

It was time for me to take control of my own life. I settled against my pillows and began to write.

For a while I was engrossed in putting plain words to the painful truth of the past five years. I supposed this was a kind of therapy.

As I was re-reading, I happened to glance into the hall. The door to the room across from the nursery was wide open. That door was shut when we came up the steps. I was sure of it.

There were three doors on each side of the narrow third-floor hallway. Each leading, I assumed, into a small room with one of the dormer windows one could see on the outside of the house. The nursery, my room, and the renovated bath were the only rooms in use now, as Harriet explained to her troop of volunteers. The others were used throughout the years for older children, indentured servants. Slaves who were nurses to the children, or spinster relatives. Now they were used for storage. Those three doors had not been opened since Benjie and I arrived.

I went out into the hall and peered at the entrance to the opposite room. How could that door have opened? The wind? Rain drummed on the roof as I stood there wondering. Could there be that much draft through the hall in a storm?

Of course, I went in.

This seemed to be a typical attic storage room filled with what one would expect to find in a house of this age and location. Old trunks, old books, old clothes. A big-wheeled pram with fraying wicker. Dolls with faded faces, yellowed dresses. Ancient crab nets fallen to tatters. A

Revolutionary-era sword and sheath dangling high on a hook. Portraits, paintings and photographs. Stacked on shelves, leaning against the walls, piled against the chimney bricks. Here were dark-haired people, gazing at me through films of dust. The Collingtons, I thought. The banished Collingtons.

I don't know how long I stayed there.

My heartbeats kicked up a notch. This was buried treasure. Something has to be here that will help me. I couldn't examine things fast enough.

Back in a corner, I found a bit of gold. I didn't know what, if anything, it would prove, but I hugged it to my heart. It was a photograph of my father as a young man, maybe 17 or 18. But unmistakably Ben Collington, standing with his arm around an elderly lady who was wearing my pearls.

"Abigail." Harriet's voice was shrill and strident.

I didn't hear Harriet come up the steps. She stood in the doorway holding two glasses of lemonade, looking as if her tan was suddenly bleached. "How did you get in there?"

I stood up, brushing the dust off my clothes. "The door was open."

"It couldn't have been open. It was locked. It's always locked."

I shook my head as I answered her. "No. The door was just standing open. I thought it was strange because I'm sure it was closed when Benjie and I came upstairs."

Harriet stared at me while the rain beat on the roof, so close to our heads, and the wind whined and rattled the gutter spouts. I resented her accusatory silence.

"It must have been the wind," I said. "Maybe somebody forgot to lock the door."

"What is Benjie doing? Quickly. We must find him," Harriet said.

She seemed flustered, not at all herself. We both peered into the nursery.

Benjie was sitting on the floor talking in the voice he used for pretending. Content and safe. Toys spread all around him.

I felt ridiculous, defensive. As if I had ignored my parental duties. "He's been terribly good. So good." I stumbled over my words. "He's been playing by himself for a long time. He's just learning to do that."

"Come downstairs," said Harriet. "Come downstairs at once. Both of you. There's a stack of children's books in the study. You can read to him."

She was being inconsistent, but I didn't bring that up.

For the first time, I felt there was something eerie about that third floor. I knew Harriet felt it, too, and understood it better than I did.

Benjie tried to protest but I tickled him into submission, and we followed her downstairs. For some reason, I didn't discuss the photographs.

The rain beat down, the afternoon wore on.

Through the long, narrow windows of the study, Benjie and I saw the taller blossoms in the garden being lashed and drooping. We could hear Noah in the entrance hall, polishing brass, humming a wordless tune. And the occasional clink of china as Harriet worked in the dining room across the hall. The hominess of the cleaning sounds was reassuring.

One wall of the study was lined with shelves full of books. The lower shelf was stacked with books for children. I recognized some old friends: *Little Women, Little Men,* all the Alcott books. *Hans Brinker and the Silver Skates, Winnie-the-Pooh, Peter Pan, Treasure Island,* the *Oz* books. And poetry–Longfellow, Eugene Fields, Robert Louis Stevenson. Many of these my father read to me after our Saturday afternoon trips to the library.

So, this room must be another part of the world Ben Collington came from. I understood better than ever his preoccupation with his writing and with old volumes. Did he curl up on this same worn leather couch between the two long windows on rainy afternoons, as we were doing now, when he was small? Was there somebody who read to him here?

I let Benjie choose a book, the *Just So Stories* of Kipling. I was not sure I could evoke the magic of the old classics, as my father had. Benjie was a little young, and he had the contrast of TV. Yet I managed fairly well. After a while, he forgot to be restless and I forgot to be frustrated.

"Now, I choose," I said, as one story ended. I had an urge to read him some poetry. Something with lilt and melody in the sound of it, but something not too grown up for a five-year-old.

My eyes were attracted by some lines in a volume of illustrated poetry for children:

> Up the airy mountain.
> Down the rushy glen,
> We daren't go a-hunting
> For fear of little men …

I remembered the inexplicable shivers I felt when Daddy read that to me. No. We'd better not read anything frightening on this gloomy afternoon.

I never forgot how I crawled up under his arm as he held me close and read to me. His soft shirt, his deep, resonant voice I could feel rumbling through his tweed jacket. The thin pungent plume of tobacco from his pipe. But most of all, I remembered his kisses, as he let me turn each page.

I gathered my child to me, kissed his cheeks and hair.

Now, Benjie turned the pages. Here were beautiful pastel illustrations from "Hiawatha," and excerpts from that long poem.

"Benjie," I said, "I choose this one. It's about Indians. You know, I'll bet Indians used to live right here. Near this bay and in these woods, long ago before this house was even built."

He looked up at me, wide-eyed. "Real Indians?"

"Sure. This is a poem about a little Indian boy named Hiawatha."

"I wanna color." He banged his heels on the sofa cushions.

"'On the shores of Gitchee-Gumie' … that was a lake," I began, loving this, myself. "'By the shining Big-Sea-Water, stood the wigwam of Nakomis …'"

"I don't like it," said Benjie. He tried to squirm out from under my arm.

"Come on, Benj. You're going to love it. It has a beat, like music. How 'bout this part?"

> Then the little Hiawatha
> Learned of every bird its language,
> Learned their names and all their secrets,
> How they built their nests in Summer,
> Where they hid themselves in Winter,

> Talked with them whene'er he met them,
> Called them Hiawatha's chickens.

Benjie gave me a little grin on that one, but I could feel his attention span running out. It was going to be a long time till bedtime.

I turned the page. Here was Minnehaha, "Laughing Water," the pretty Indian maiden, walking in the forest. Without question, I thought, not Benjie's cup of tea. There was a small television in the corner half-hidden by a lovely knitted shawl and a pot of trailing ivy. Any minute he would discover it and beg for something like *The Flintstones.*

I started to close the book.

"Don't," said Benjie. He lunged forward, tapping the page. "There she is. The girl."

"What girl?"

"The girl who comes to see me. Upstairs in my room. Does she live here?"

What happened to the Indian girl? She ran away, and then, somehow, she drowned. Isn't Bay House supposed to have a ghost?

There was a prickling at the base of my scalp.

"Sweetie," I said. I prayed something else would come out of my mouth. "That's just a picture of a pretend Indian girl who lived long ago. Nobody comes to see you."

"Uh-huh," said Benjie. "Yes, she does. I told you. She's my friend."

Suddenly, Noah was standing in front of the couch, glaring down at us with a fierce, unreadable face. I had not noticed when he stopped humming and started listening. "Get off the Island," he said. "Go back to New York City. You and the boy don't belong here."

I tried to put Noah's words out of my mind. I could not afford to speculate on frightening things I didn't understand. I could not, would not leave Bay House until I knew whether we had a right to be there. Besides, we had no safe place to go.

10

By late afternoon the next day the rain stopped as suddenly as it started. The dull sky looked as if it might clear. The wind gentled, the air turned warm and sweet. The grass was an emerald carpet.

Benjie burst outside barefooted. Jumped in puddles on the lawn, letting off his pent-up energy. Tree toads chorused. Birds sang. Small boats darted out from shore. I stood watching my son. Everything safe, sane, normal. I loved this Bay House with a depth I had never felt for any place before.

The ground was too soggy for golf for several days, so Harriet stayed intent on her cleaning. I had to bide my time. It was not until the week's end that I got a break. Benjie and I came inside in the late afternoon and heard Harriet talking on the phone, offering to pick up a friend on the church board at 6:00.

She scribbled notes on a pad by the phone. Looked at us, frowning and tight-lipped as we trooped into the front hall. I knew she was thinking of muddy floors. Something else to clean up.

Her words were clipped, abrupt. "I'm going out unexpectedly, to a meeting, and will be back after dinner. You can look in the refrigerator and see what you might like to have."

I nodded, aiming a smile at her. "Certainly," I said. After she went upstairs to dress, I picked up the phone and, called S.J.

We trotted to the Tomisons fifteen minutes after Harriet drove off.

Benjie and I were that tall boy and little girl again. He looked sturdier, browner. Much less like a female in the battered little pink daisy blouse. He complained right away, in no mood for the game.

"The kids'll laugh at me," he said. "I'm not letting Jake see this stupid bow." In an old sewing box in the attic, I found a ball of pink yarn. I tied several loops around Benjie's head, replacing the ribbon William threw overboard the day he rescued us.

S.J. was waiting by the mailbox next to her ancient green sedan and handed me the key. I had warned her about our dubious disguises. She didn't look twice at my ridiculous cap.

Benjie dove into the car without a word. Lay flat on the back seat, hands covering his head, face buried in the worn upholstery.

Nevertheless, off we went. My heart was racing. It was nearly 6:30 as we rattled into town. The library closed at 9:00, S.J. said, as she gave me directions. It was still light when we reached the building. No one paid any attention to us.

A few people were sitting at tables, bent over books or newspapers. One or two stood at the shelves, browsing. A petite young woman with wire-rimmed glasses and dangling name tag darted back and forth behind the main check-out desk. Boxes of books surrounded her on the desktop, on the floor, on tables behind her.

The main reading room was freshly painted. Bright white walls with woodwork and molding done in a soft moss green, colonial fashion. Wall-to-wall carpeting matched the trim. It seemed pleasant, inviting.

Safe. Except the room was oppressively hot. The storm must have knocked out the air-conditioning.

I went straight to the main desk. Benjie dragged along behind me, kicking at the rug.

I hated this charade. Tight jeans, baggy sweater, slicked-back boyish hair. Benjie's humiliating pink bow. I kept my voice low and quiet, in disbelief that I was reduced again to my absurd disguise.

"I'd like to see the Collington papers, please."

The girl at the desk seemed as deflated as I was. She pointed to a doorway on the right. "In there," she said. "The Reference Room. All the Maryland history's in there. Local history is on the last two shelves in the back. I'm afraid you'll have to dig around for it. There's nobody on duty in there tonight and I've got a deadline for an inventory of children's books."

She glanced up with a weak smile, ignoring my appearance. I already recognized the clear young voice I heard in the hall at Bay House.

She sighed, brushed her hair from her face. "Don't ever try to move a library. We just did it and I don't think we'll get this place straight for the rest of our natural lives."

Hot as it was in the main room, the Reference Room was stifling. It was smaller, crammed floor to ceiling with horizontal rows of shelves. Stacks of books, encyclopedias, magazines, newspaper clippings. Cartons of files teetered in non-sensical piles. A fat *World Atlas* stuck sideways atop volumes of *Horticultural Digest. Birds of North America* stuffed between bins of *National Geographic* and *Seventeen Magazine.*

I plunged toward the back of the room.

"It's boiling in here," Benjie said. My poor child was red-faced and angry, with sweat beading on his forehead.

I took crayons and a Superman coloring book out of my duffel bag. "Look what I brought, Benj. You can sit right on the floor here and color 'til I find what I'm looking for. And if you will just cooperate, we'll be through in a jiffy."

I made a beeline for the last two shelves. My hands were trembling. For the moment there was a blessed quiet.

What to look for? Probably not hardbacks. Nothing was cataloged yet or arranged in order back here, either. I would have to go through box after box of papers.

I wiped damp palms on my jeans and glanced at the child at my feet. He was busy with his crayons.

I started through the boxes, steeling myself for a fruitless search. When, suddenly, there it was as if I had willed it to appear. On the front of the third box, neatly pasted, was a photograph of Bay House. In the background, above the beach, a man and woman walked hand in hand with a small girl. These were my parents. And me. This was not a dream. It was real. A moment I remembered, engraved upon my heart.

I slid down on the floor beside Benjie. My fingers were shaking. It was hard to breathe.

The box was a large cardboard filing drawer. In the front, on the first divider, printed in bold letters, was a title: *The Collington Papers.*

My fingers trembled as I began to leaf through the As, staring, unbelieving, at pictures of myself as a baby.

A as in Abigail. These were my father's papers. These were what he had collected, poured over, written about. These were the papers my mother disposed of after Ben Collington died. It was so like her, complex and inscrutable, to get them out of her life and mine. But not destroy them, because they were a part of my father. And to send them here.

"Mommy, I'm finished. Can we go now? I'm burning hot." Benjie tugged at my arm though I could not move.

"Just a few more minutes," I said. "I found something very important."

Where to start? Why did my father believe the Collingtons still inherited? Maybe under F. F for Family.

I flipped the files open to that section. On the *F* divider was printed in bold, inch-high letters, the word, "FORCES." There was a thick typed manuscript stuffed in next. With fingers still trembling, I pulled it out.

I forgot where I was. I forgot everything except what I was reading.

THE FORCES OF BAY HOUSE

by Henry Benjamin Collington

The land and the water lie here together, it began, innocent and beautiful. The house stands as it has for more than 200 years where it can see both. The winds blow through the house and around it, and spring comes and summer and fall and winter, and then spring comes again, and each season has its own kind of glory. It is only man, who has struggled

for possession of the land and the water and the house, who has created cycles of good and evil amid the beauty. Do these forces remain in a place that has felt them so strongly?

In the beginning there was only the forest and the bay. The fish, oysters, crabs, deer, beavers, otters, possum. The rabbits, foxes, bears, and all the birds. A kind of Eden, perhaps.

There is no written history to tell us when the first Indians came. The Matapeakes. There is mute, eloquent evidence for a child with a shovel or a farmer with a plow, that these Indians once inhabited the area in and around the site where the house now stands. Stone ax heads, shards of primitive pottery. A necklace of wampum once upturned in a cornfield. When Henry Collington had his slaves dig out the old icehouse by the creek, they found razor edged arrowheads, of a kind made by one of the fiercer tribes to the North that were known to attack the peaceful Matapeakes...

"Mommy," Benjie yanked at my sleeve. "Come on. Let's go. I'm too hot in here. C'un I go get a drink?"

"Five more minutes, Benj. Just sit still for five minutes. You cannot leave here without me, and that's final."

"Well, I'm not staying here and that's final." Benjie's small face was flushed and sweaty. He jumped up, stamped his foot, scowling at me in defiance. "I'm not wearing a hair thing ever again and that's final." He pulled off the yarn and hurled it toward the aisle between the shelves. The yarn caught around the toe of a large, wide sneaker. It belonged on the leg of a man I was too engrossed to hear as he entered the room.

I sat on the floor, turned stony for a split second, unable to look up. If this should be Matt, we were trapped, Benjie and I, in this stuffy little room with no other exit, with my son in revolt.

My eyes traveled up that leg that was long, tan, lean. Not like Matt's I knew too well was chunky from calf to thigh. Past the khaki shorts and rumpled tee shirt stamped Maryland is for Crabs, into the stern, brown-eyed gaze of Dr. Peter Carpenter.

"What on earth are you doing here," he said, "skulking around on the floor?"

I scrambled to my feet. My whole face felt on fire.

"I'm not skulking," I snatched the cap from my head and held it behind my back. "I'm doing vital research which doesn't concern you in any way."

"Except that your son just lassoed my foot with his hair bow."

He bent down and removed the pink circle from his shoe and handed it to me. "When are you going to stop hiding? Are you under the remotest illusion that this child looks like a girl? Are you lost in some perverse version of early Halloween?"

"I'm a girl and Mommy's a boy," said Benjie. "It's a game."

He stared at Benjie, then at me, as I stood there looking like Huckleberry Finn's big sister. He began to laugh. A grin came first, then a surprised chuckle, then the kind of helpless chortling that brings tears to the eyes and bends you over.

I turned, clutching the manuscript, pulling Benjie by the hand. Be calm, show some pride, I told myself. I would escape with my head high, not an easy thing to do while dragging a five-year-old.

Somehow, we made our way to the check-out desk. "I'd like to take this out," I said. I spoke to the young librarian, who, along with the few remaining patrons, was now studying us with curiosity. Dr. Carpenter's guffaws no doubt preceded us. "Could I have a temporary card please?"

"I'm really sorry," she said. "That manuscript, anything like it from Reference, doesn't go out. It's the only copy we have."

I glanced toward the doorway, hoping Peter Carpenter would not emerge.

"I'll have to copy it then, very quickly. Can I use your machine?"

"I am sorry. Some of our fuses blew. The copier's not working. Anyway, we're almost closing. Could you come back tomorrow sometime?"

"But I need it so badly." *I wanted to shout I was Benjamin Collington's daughter but managed to control myself.*

The girl shook her head. "Listen," she said, "I'll keep it right here at the desk. If you come tomorrow you won't even have to look for it."

There was nothing to do but hurry away in angry frustration. At least we could avoid the insufferable Dr. Carpenter. We had to get back before Harriet came home from her meeting.

I didn't bother Benjie with the bow. It was stuffed in my pocket. I crammed that cap into the trashcan as we pushed through doors and fled to the car. Luckily the parking lot was lighted because it was almost dark.

I jammed the key in the ignition. S.J.'s old clunker sputtered a bit, but it started.

We pulled out of the parking lot. A car started up behind us, out of the shadows. I glanced in the rear-view mirror. It was a blue, paneled station wagon, exactly like Matt's and mine. I didn't pause to check further. I pressed the pedal to the floor and shot out of the lot, grateful that no cars were passing at that time of night and made for the highway.

It couldn't be Matt, I told myself. It was just a coincidence.

When we reached the main road, cars were coming and going, headlights beaming. I felt less fearful. It was not Matt. I left that old wagon in Annapolis.

I had to pause at the stoplight at the intersection where the narrow road toward Bay House veered off to the left. The light turned green. When I turned, the wagon pulled close behind and followed. As its headlights flashed in my mirror, I saw the driver hunched over the wheel, wearing a porkpie hat.

I reacted as a person who jumps into the ocean from a boat already sinking. I drove as fast as I dared, hoping someone else would come along that dark, tree-lined country road.

"Why are you going so fast? You're going too fast, Mommy."

"Hush, Benjie. Don't talk. We have got to get home. Sit back. Sit back. Push down the little button that locks the door."

The road was still slick from the storm. Wet leaves and small branches littered the way as our headlights shone on the pavement in front of us.

The car behind crowded me to go faster. Its high beams boring into the rear-view mirror blinded my eyes to the darkness around me. Was he trying to pass? That was insanity at such speed on this narrow road. Yet I dared not slow down. My hands were locked on the wheel. Each bend in the road took every bit of my will and strength.

When the car skidded, I had no more control than if it was on roller skates. We slid to the left the moment I moved into a curve. Slithered across the opposite side of the road, plowed into the shoulder and halted in soggy grass. The headlights pointed straight at the broad trunk of a tree.

In that same instant, as S.J.'s old car moved out of its path, the one behind us roared on. I sat, unable to breathe, with the car doors locked, waiting for that car to turn and come back. We crouched there, frozen, until the sound of its frantic motor died away. All we heard were drops of water dripping from the trees.

It occurred to me then I should try to see if we could still move. It was either move this car or walk. The engine started. I tried to roll forward a few inches, but no luck. I put the car in reverse and ground back just a little, enough to give me some hope. Again. The wheels spun in the muddy grass but moved a bit more. Again. Rocking back and forward now. Once again, and S.J.'s old clunker pulled itself out.

I had to watch every shadow as I drove ahead, terrified Matt was hidden somewhere along the road, waiting. I swallowed fear and panic. Allowed myself no thought but to steer until at last we reached our lane and turned right. Puddles and pebbles in the headlights meant home and safety. I realized I was holding my breath. Released it, felt my ribs expand, my heart stop pounding. At the white mailbox I turned into the Tomisons' drive. S.J. was there to meet me. From here we could both see the big house. All the downstairs lights were blazing. In the circle were Harriet's Chevy and William's Mercedes. So much for my secret mission, I thought with a sinking heart. William was back from his trip. They were both home. I had prayed to slip upstairs with Benjie, unseen, crawl into bed, and pull the covers over my head.

Now there would be hell to pay.

I handed S.J. her keys, kissed her cheek. Whispered, "Thank you."

"Stand tough. Remember who you are," was all she said.

I carried Benjie back to Bay House. He was too exhausted to walk.

When we reached the front door, Harriet and William stood like angry, anxious parents whose children stayed out too late. I should have explained, with dignity, that I wanted to see the Collington papers. But I was too drained for dignity.

"Matt followed us," I said. "I'm sure it was Matt. We almost hit a tree." Against my will my voice trembled.

They both started forward. Harriet took Benjie, holding him against her shoulder. William put his arm around me as if I were a child, too. For a moment I could have put my head on his shoulder and wept, but something in Harriet's expression stopped me.

"Come," she said. "I'll help you get Benjie tucked in. We'll talk in the morning."

William's voice burst out loud and commanding. "But hear me well, Abigail. You are not to go off this property again until you have legal protection. Is that clear?"

"Yes, William," I said. I started up the stairs, almost too weary to lift my legs.

I hadn't reached the second floor when I turned back again, tired and shaken though I was. *I knew I mustn't slip into the luxury of letting William take care of me. I knew I was going to find a way to read Ben Collington's story, no matter what.*

William was still standing there, feet planted on the majestic hall rug, fixing me with his intense blue-green stare.

Freedom, Abby. Don't let it go. I spoke with all the dignity I could muster. "I need your help right now and I appreciate your kindness. I do. But I am not a child, and I don't expect to take orders like a child."

He continued to gaze up at me. Was there a hint of a lift to one corner of his mouth? "Consider it a request then, Cousin. For Benjie's sake," he said. "And believe me, I am quite aware you are not a child."

There was a silent pause between us. The stairs creaked. The sea wind moaned through the maze of hallways as the house settled around us.

I felt I had scored a point as I said goodnight and dragged myself up the steps. But I had a feeling he was still watching. Like a predator studies its prey. Sizing me up. Like he was the spider, and I was the fly.

Silly. It was only the fatigue hitting me. I just needed to sleep.

11

"It was Matt," I said. "I know it was. He's found us and he's here somewhere trying to frighten us. He wants to punish me for running away and taking Benjie. It's exactly the kind of thing he would do."

Sunday morning. Clear, still, beautiful. Harriet and William and I were settled in chairs on the terrace, facing the bay. Benjie was still asleep upstairs. Harriet refilled our coffee cups.

"Nonsense." William put down the Financial Section of *The New York Times*. "It was probably some local hotshot entertaining himself on Saturday night."

"It was Matt," I said. "It was our car."

"Then why didn't he stop?" asked William, not waiting for me to answer. "You're being melodramatic, Abby. You've got nothing to worry about here with us in," his arms opened wide, "the Land of Pleasant Living."

Harriet would have sniffed, I think, if she was the sniffing type.

"I'd worry if I were Abby," she said.

William cast her a sideward glance. "But then, Dear," he said, "you are a worrier, aren't you?" There was laughter in his eyes but his mouth was a grim stern line.

He turned back to me.

"Just sit tight. If you hadn't gone off on that wild goose chase last night you would have been fine. Matt's not going to come in here and attack you on my property. And we sure as hell know he'd better not lay a hand on Benjie again. It's just going to take some time to work this thing out."

He stood up and made a little half-bow. "Excuse me, ladies. I've got to see to the plantation."

Harriet looked puzzled. "But William …"

He held up his hand. "Sorry," he said, "no church today. I've got things I have to check out with Burleigh Tomison." Then he was gone.

Harriet glanced at me, smiling like an indulgent mother. "The Lord of the Manor. He's only play-acting that he's play-acting, you know."

We sat in silence, sipping our coffee. My mind whirled with conflicting thoughts. *"My property," William said as if it was an accepted fact. What if I didn't intend to accept it?*

When the doorbell rang, we both jumped. That bell seldom rang. Most callers said, "Hoo-hoo, Harriet," or "Hey, William," walked right in, or came around to the terrace.

Harriet and I stared at each other. *Matthew Wells?*

"I'll go," she said. "You're not here."

I held my breath.

She hurried through the hall. I heard her say, "Oh, it's you." Then she was back, leading a very short, shiny-faced visitor.

It was Jake Tomison, scrubbed so he gleamed, wearing long blue pants, white shirt, and a red bow tie.

"I told him you were busy, but he says he has to speak to you," said Harriet. She eyed him with one eyebrow arched.

"Why, Jake. Aren't you looking handsome today." I had to smile. "What a nice surprise. What is it?"

"Well ... see ... um ... tomorrow's my birthday. I'm gonna be six and we're having a crab feast and my mom said I could ask Benjie to come at 5:30 and nobody else is coming except our family so it'll be safe."

He paused for breath, grinned up at me, gawking at Bay House's grandeur I knew was so different from the Tomisons' happy, messy sprawl. "You can come, too," he said. "And besides, my birthday's the fourth of July. We get to have sparklers 'n stuff."

What was wrong with me? How could I have forgotten the date and the fun of fireworks?

Harriet gave me a disapproving look, her brow rising higher as if she read my mind.

"I'll have to see, honey. Thank you, though. And tell your mother thanks."

Jake trudged to the door and shot off for home.

Harriet stood ramrod straight with her hands clasped in front of her. "Honestly, Abby, I'd think you could see Sarah Jane Tomison's wild tribe are no fit companions for Benjie. Or that Sarah Jane is no fit mother. She's as wild as they are. Why, that girl murders the King's English. They all look like savages except on Sunday, when she makes a big to-do about taking them to Mass in that ancient jalopy." Harriet frowned and shook her head as if what she described was a sacrilege. "If Burleigh wasn't such a good farmer, I'm sure William wouldn't keep him on. That family lives practically rent-free, but they still let the old farmhouse run down like a shack. How you could take Benjie into town in that rattletrap, when William asked you not to leave here, for your own protection, is beyond my comprehension." She glared at me, her fists balled at her hips.

I gathered this was Harriet's sermon for the day.

A few minutes later she left for church. I could hear her car's motor as she drove down the lane, then the sound faded.

I went inside through the gleaming kitchen, the fragrant hallway, up to the third floor. The house was still, except for the small noises it made if you stopped to listen. I found Benjie lying awake in his bed in the nursery.

I put my hand to his forehead. It was cool. "Are you feeling all right, Benj?"

"I guess so," he said. He made no move to get up, which was unlike this child. He looked pale, sleepy and, as my mother would have said, "peaked."

"Let's go have some breakfast."

"I'm not very hungry."

"What about happy-face pancakes?"

"OK."

"What's the matter, sweetie?"

"Nothin'."

"Come on, Benj." I brushed blond wisps from his forehead. "Tell me what's wrong."

He sat up, looked at me with worried eyes. That look pierced my soul. "Was that Daddy," he said, "last night? Was that our car? Did Daddy try to hurt us again?"

Oh, how I loathed myself at that moment. What a stupid, immature idiot I was to blurt out more fear of Matt in front of Benjie. I folded my arms around him.

"No, Benj. I was wrong. William says he's sure that was just some crazy teenager hot-rodding to show off. Your Daddy's far away in New York City. Maybe he isn't even sick anymore." I took his little hands in mine. "I think your tummy needs something yummy. I want you to hoppy-toad right off that bed and we'll go eat breakfast."

We each had two happy-face pancakes. Raisin eyes and noses, smiles made with half-slices of banana. I gave them silly-sounding names: Hortense and Adonijah. Drew mustaches, curls, and eyeglasses with chocolate syrup, which always guaranteed giggles. Today nothing was funny. Benjie's face was rosier under his new tan, but his expression was still pinched.

After we cleaned up, the house seemed quieter than ever. Sunlight poured through the windows and lay golden on the kitchen table. I did not intend to say it, but I was afraid to go outside alone. Maybe Benjie was afraid, too, because he wasn't begging for the beach.

We wandered into the study. Harriet had placed a basket of toys from upstairs in the corner. Benjie dumped them all out on the rug. I didn't have the heart to stop him. He lay on his stomach, chin cupped in one hand, pushing cars and blocks around with the other, listless and withdrawn.

I picked up a small journal half hidden by newspapers and magazines scattered on the coffee table. Feeling just as listless as my child, I sat on the old leather couch and opened the cover. *The Kent Island Chronicle* was light and entertaining. Part *Farmer's Almanac* mixed with local events. The feature article was more serious and railed about the pollution of the bay.

I glanced at Benjie, now sprawled asleep among his playthings. One more tidbit, I told myself, then out we'd go into the sunshine. When I turned the page, I caught my breath at the full-size black and white photo so brimming with life it seemed to leap from the paper.

I gazed into the lively, capricious eyes of a face I'd seen. But where? His smile was both warm and wise despite his youth, perhaps beyond it. A boyish tilt to his head hinted at laughter about to spill from his lips. Feathers were tucked into his long black braid. Beneath the picture in bold print were these words:

In Loving Memory of James Wohali Adams
June 1933–June 1945, Window Rock, Arizona
My "Eagle" brother, soaring forever

The author of this tribute was a name I knew but was so unexpected I had to read it twice.

Peter M. Carpenter, M.D.

I remembered Harriet describing his interest in Indian lore, but beyond this my head was spinning. This could not be the same curt, cold clinician who examined my damaged arms with such disdain that day in his office. If he had any softness in him, he certainly hid it well. And this wasn't lore. This was a boy who had lived and died.

"Mommy, I'm bored." Benjie was bouncing beside me, tossing

magazines into piles, knocking them down, adding his best explosive sound effects. I was so intent on Dr. Carpenter's photo I didn't hear my son awaken. He hopped up and down waving a magazine above his head. "Lookit, Mom. It's a house with a dock like ours." I glimpsed the shiny cover showing a tree-sheltered home with a long pier jutting into the bay. I knew every house along the shoreline had versions of the same thing, lined with boats and crab traps.

It was time for serious diversion. "OK, Benj. We're going outside and have a race to the beach. First, we're going to straighten up this mess you made. Hand me that last magazine, please."

The front door banged open. Benjie and I froze.

There were loud footsteps, William's voice booming. "Hey, Sprout. Hey, Cousin Abigail."

Benjie jumped to his feet, squealing with delight. "Here we are."

William burst through the doorway, larger than life as he seemed sometimes, in his white shorts and sea-blue tee shirt, with the rest of him long and tan. He strode over to me and pulled the magazine from my hands.

"What are you two doing inside on a day like today? Fair goes the wind for France, Lass, and we are off for Brittany."

"I beg your pardon?" *I intended to sound stiff and remote, although I could feel a ridiculous smile creeping across my face.* "I don't think you're making any sense."

"I am making much more sense than you are, wasting this glorious morning. Come on, Sprout, we're going fishing. You, too, Cousin Abigail. No arguments."

"Won't Harriet miss us when she comes back?" Breaking any of her unspoken though severe house rules made me nervous. "Maybe we should wait until after church."

William dismissed his wife with a flip of his hand. "She'll be busy going to a pre-church meeting, then the service. There's usually a post-church meeting that turns into a gabfest. Harriet's chairman of the Christmas Bazaar, didn't you know? She and her cohorts are on a non-stop marathon from now 'til middle of November." He winked at me over Benjie's head. "Anyway, there's one little Collington here who needs a sunny day."

I was not so sure about Harriet, but I tried to stifle my uneasiness. There was no question William was right about Benjie. So, once again, I ignored his misuse of our last name.

He swung Benjie onto his shoulders, marched off toward the kitchen. I could hear them chattering, banging around, I guessed packing a lunch.

I ran upstairs, combed my hair, put on lipstick. I was already wearing a long-sleeved tee shirt and old blue shorts, things I had taken from the stack in my closet. It's time to go shopping, whispered a strange voice in my head. I let the thought skim by, grabbed an extra shirt for Benjie, and rushed down to find the fishermen.

Twenty minutes later we were buckled in life jackets, putt-putting along the creek toward the bay in Noah's weather-beaten skiff. Benjie was perched on a small board that served as a seat in the bow. I sat in the middle, a picnic basket at my feet. William lolled on the seat in the stern, one hand on the tiller of the outboard motor.

I glanced back at William. He smiled, blue-green eyes sparkling.

"Neato," Benjie yelled. He bounced on his seat, feet dancing on the boat's floor.

I knelt forward, careful to keep my balance. "You've got to sit still, Benj," I said. *I was glad to be busy and avoid looking into William's eyes. Something in his glance today was like too-bright sunlight.*

For a while no one spoke. The air was warm and soft against our bodies. It smelled clean, briny. All around us blue water shimmered, reflecting the sky. The bay was polka-dotted with white sails this morning. A ship with a foreign flag plowed along far out in the channel on its way to Baltimore. I had heard much about the pollution of the bay since I arrived on Kent Island, but at the moment, I didn't want to believe it.

As the shoreline receded, so did my mood of fear and depression.

Matt could not reach me here. I closed my eyes, gave myself over to feeling relief, freedom, the touch of the sunny southwest breeze that gentled across this Chesapeake Bay.

The motor stopped. I opened my eyes. William threw over the anchor, the boat weaved and tugged a little, then came to rest.

"OK," said William. "All hands alert. We will now study the fine art of fishing for rockfish. Finest fish in the bay." He handed Benjie a small rod. "Benjamin Collington Wells, you are about to be initiated."

Now I felt William reading the correct script. As Harriet said earlier that morning, he was only play-acting at play-acting. There was something intense and serious going on. I had no idea what it could be.

"My father gave this rod to me," William said, "when I was a sprout about your size. I've been waiting for some little boy to come along who fits it. I think maybe that just might be you."

Benjie clutched that stubby little rod as if he was an acolyte bearing the Holy Grail. His eyes were wide and bright, glued on William's every move. His cheeks were already turning peachy with sun and wind. There was no sign of that peaked little fellow who didn't want to get up this morning.

"Now, Benjie, if you want to be a real Collington, you've got to understand this bay. Plus," William tapped his forehead, "you've got to learn to understand the fish to be a real waterman. Not just some landlubber who comes for the weekend and tears around stirring up the water with no clue what he's doing. Because then," William gave a firm nod of his head, "the fish know it, too."

Collington, again. What happened to Wells?

William went on instructing Benjie, man to man. I doubted he'd ever had a more rapt audience.

"Now, this is the bait box." William pointed to a small wooden crate behind his seat. "It's full of peelers we're going to cut up for bait. Let's you and I change places, Cousin Abigail."

"What's a peeler?" asked Benjie.

William opened the box so Benjie could look inside. His eyes locked on the crabs scrabbling and scratching on top of each other.

"Good question, Sprout," William said. "It's a crab. It's just called a peeler because its hard shell has peeled off leaving a softer shell underneath. Peelin' gives a crab a chance to grow. When it's time to bait your hook, you throw 'em down hard to make 'em numb. Then you peel off the shell, claws and flippers, pick out the claw meat for bait. You end up with six or eight little pieces from the body for bait, too."

"C'un I do some, please William?" Benjie's eyes were shining with wonder.

My squeamishness out-matched Benjie's fascination, though I remained silent.

"Next time, Sprout. First, you're going to learn to cast. Now, watch everything I do."

William picked up his own rod, stood up in the boat. He moved his right arm behind him, then swung it forward in a graceful arc. At the same time, he released the line so it spun off the reel ahead of the rod tip in a neat straight line. The sinker at the far end plunked into the water and disappeared.

"Neato," yelled Benjie.

William looked around, grinning. He put his fingers to his lips. "We have to remember to be quiet," he said. "We don't want the fish to know we're here."

It was touching that he was so pleased by one little boy's admiration.

William was a glorious specimen of a male in his prime and could not have helped knowing it. For some reason, I shuddered. Perhaps because those live peelers were struggling around in the bait box.

William didn't notice. He showed Benjie how to work the reel on his small rod. How to put his thumb on the reel to stop the line. Send that line soaring, again and again.

"You've got to think about this a little bit, Sprout. We're practicing first with this cork on, because if you sling that line around with a bare hook on it you might just snag something besides a fish." He shot me a look and a laugh. "You wouldn't want to do anything to hurt your pretty mommy."

My brave boy stuck out his chest. "No way."

"Well, then, you're going to release the catch on the reel. You're going to snub that line with your thumb because you're not ready to let it go yet. You're going to fling that rod forward, just like I did, and while you do, you slowly let that line out. Then you let it drop into the water where those fish are down there just waiting for a good dinner to come along. You tighten your catch on the reel again, so it can't play out anymore unless you want it to, and boy, you're fishin'."

Benjie squared his small shoulders, pressed his lips together. My heart flooded with love for my plucky, determined child.

William crouched behind him, circling Benjie's forearm with his strong fingers, guiding his arm as he cast the rod forward. Benjie was too late to snub his thumb on the line. It flew from the reel in a crazy ball before William reached over Benjie's little shoulder and caught it.

"Good try, good try, Sprout," said William. "Never saw anybody in my life who got it the first time. You're going to get it," said William. "You're a Collington."

Benjie looked over his shoulder at me as if for help.

"Maybe this is too much coordination to expect from somebody who's five," I said.

"Nonsense," said William. "This boy is beautifully coordinated. It just takes a little practice."

He got it on the tenth try. He cast that little rod and snubbed the line with his sore thumb as the sinker dropped gently into the water.

"Neato, I did it," yelled Benjie.

"Yay, Benjie," William and I shouted. We forgot all about not scaring the fish.

Maybe we did scare them because we didn't get any that day. We sat for a long time with lines in the water, the boat bobbing gently up and down, the water softly slapping the sides.

Benjie sighed. "I'm tired of hearing those peelers. And I'm hungry."

"Come to think of it, so am I," said William. "What about you, Cousin Abigail?"

"Me, too."

"Well, then, if you'll just trade places with me, Cousin, we will dine alfresco on yonder island." He stood in the middle of the boat, turning to me back by the tiller. "Watch your balance, now, pretty lady." Our bodies touched as we side-stepped, switching benches. I studied my feet, the coiled anchor rope, the bait box, careful to avoid his bright blue gaze.

"OK now, got your seat? Hold tight."

He let out the throttle, sending the boat skipping across the water. There was indeed a small island, not too far from our shore. A curve of sandy beach, overgrown with stubby trees and brush. I never thought of it before as anything but part of the scenery. Now William beached the skiff, taking my hand to help me out, although I was in no need of assistance. Benjie jumped ashore in his bare feet, agog over this new adventure.

William grabbed our lunch basket, shook out a red and white checked tablecloth and spread it on the sand.

"Please, have a seat," he said. "You here on this corner, Cousin, and Sprout, you're over there." He pointed across the cloth with a playful nod. "I'll sit right on this side and we'll put our feast in the middle. Hmm. What have we here?" He unwrapped thick sandwiches cut into triangles. "Here's one for you, Benjie. And one for your sweet mother. Ahhh. This one's for me. I think it's breast of guinea hen with artichokes and mushrooms."

"Mine's peanut butter and jelly," said Benjie, already stowing his away.

"Well," I said, "you sure fooled me. Mine looks like peanut butter and jelly, too."

"That's very strange. Let's see what mine is. Well, I'll be darned, I think it's sliced hippopotamus."

"Mine's elephant," said Benjie, catching on and beginning to giggle. "I have an elephant samwich."

"Tusk, tusk," said William.

"That's the worst pun I have ever heard in my life," I said. I couldn't help chuckling, too. William's daredevil mood was infectious, disarming. I forgot about keeping my guard up.

"I can't believe it," William said, "the lady's laughing. I didn't know she could."

"Oh, sure she can. She laughs a lot of times. Like when we make happy-face pancakes. Stuff like that," said Benjie.

"I'd like to try some of those sometime," said William. He cocked his head, smiling at me.

I was conscious I must look a mess. Hot, sweaty, scrawny in my long-sleeved shirt and faded blue shorts. Hair ragged and blown. I backed off a little farther on my corner of the tablecloth.

"OK," said Benjie. "How 'bout tomorrow morning?"

"Sounds great, Sprout. But let's see here. We must have something along to wet our whistles."

He rummaged in the basket producing, with a flourish, one can of Coke, which he presented to Benjie. Next, he pulled out two plastic cups and a bottle of red wine. He jumped to his feet, draped a napkin over his forearm. Formal as any waiter, he bowed to me. Brought an opener from his pocket and unscrewed the cork.

"Madame." William loomed above me, handed me an over-flowing cup, all traces of play-acting wiped from his face. He dropped to one knee. Leaned forward to brush hair from my cheek, trailed his fingers along my jaw, pausing just below my lips. "Cheers," he said.

Nausea hit me like a wave. I felt physically ill, hot and cold at the same time. It was more than the heat, the jarring implication of wine. *Fear rose like bile and with it came a black swirl of memories. The helpless, hopeless outrage of abuse I thought I escaped.* I thrust my head between my knees to keep from fainting.

William treated me like a pawn in a sick game. And he knew it. Worst of all, I was his kin and he, my protector. This lovely outing had turned sick and insane.

I managed to speak. "I'm sorry. I don't feel well at all. Let's just go home."

"Home?" said William.

How could his voice sound so astonished? So innocent.

"Well, sure, of course, if you're ill."

Benjie patted my shoulder, wanting to help. William packed up the basket in silence.

As we cut back across the bay the wind was brisk against my cheeks. I began to feel less nauseated. Only tired and weak.

Harriet stood on the lawn in her turquoise suit, waving to us as we neared the mouth of the creek. For a little while I had almost forgotten Matthew Wells. But I had completely forgotten Harriet.

12

I escaped up the two flights of stairs to my room taking Benjie with me for a nap, pleading my sick headache. I could hear William explaining to Harriet how he hurried through his farm problems with Burleigh in order to get Benjie out for some fun in the sunshine. Benjie, he said, must not live in fear of his no-good father. I could not have agreed with him more, but it still hurt me to hear those words spoken with such contempt, out loud, after all the years of my mother's genteel concealment.

I had an uneasy feeling the morning's adventure was not planned with only Benjie in mind. It did not seem that way on the island, but then my emotions there suffered a kind of wild confusion, making me ill. I was glad Benjie ran upstairs ahead of me and couldn't hear the conversation below.

I took some aspirin, made Benjie lie down on the bed beside me, blanked out my mind, and fell asleep.

I must have slept several hours. When I awoke, the room was steeped in July heat. Late afternoon sun slanted in low through the dormer window leaving shadowy corners. I felt hot and sticky. I longed for a shower and fresh clothes. June was over. Summer was slipping by and, instead of answers, my mind was filled with even more shadowy questions. Angry and frustrated, I turned to check on my child. He was gone.

I jumped up to look in the nursery next door. He was not there. The bed was not rumpled. I had a panicky feeling he might have gone down to the beach alone.

I ran out into the hall bathroom. Empty. The door of the storage room was locked, as usual. I flew down the first flight of steps on my way outside, when a small sound made me pause on the landing and peer into the entrance of William and Harriet's bedroom.

Benjie had wandered a few steps in and stopped. The normally padlocked door in the wall of that room was wide open. I heard the eerie echo of Harriet's warning to the church ladies about it being unsafe and off-limits. Now Benjie was leaning into the black opening, staring down at whatever was below.

I wanted to cry out, "Stop!" but realized I might startle him into falling. I crept forward in silence, heart pounding in my chest. In my panic I didn't hear the steps rushing from behind. Harriet lunged around me, grabbed my child and pulled him backward to safety.

She wheeled him around to face me and William who was marching down the hall carrying a roll of blueprints.

Harriet was shaking, her face drained of color. Her clear brown eyes, always so cool and self-confident, were wide with anger and fright. She kept a firm grasp on Benjie's shoulders.

Benjie looked frightened too, and defiant.

"Benjie." My voice sounded weak, distant. I was trembling. "You know that …"

Harriet cut me off. "Of course, he knows. He was deliberately disobedient. He had no right to be prowling around this part of the house, much less opening this door which he's been warned is dangerous."

"I wasn't pwowling," said Benjie. "The door was open. It's so hot and Mommy was asleep. I was just lookin' for William. There wasn't anything to do."

"He should be put to bed with no books or toys, or sympathy." Harriet blurted on. "He needs discipline. You cater to him too much, Abby. And William, you never should have left that door open. How could you be so careless?"

William didn't do anything by accident. Why, indeed, did he forget to lock that door?

Benjie's brows knitted together in defiance. "I don't even care about that stupid old door. "There's nothin' down there and I wasn't going to fall. Anyway, I wanna go to Jake's house. There's nothin' to do here."

"If I have anything to do with it," said Harriet, "you're going to stay away from that whole tribe from now on." She pointed a finger at Benjie and shook it.

Benjie stamped his foot and began to wail. "I wanna go to Jake's house."

"Now, look, Benjie," said William. He knelt, dropped the blueprints, and took Benjie's hands. "You're not going anywhere right now. Except upstairs to stay in your room awhile."

He turned to Harriet, a scowl creasing his forehead. "We don't have to make a federal case out of this. The boy was just exploring. But he does have to learn to respect authority."

"Son," he said. "You and I are going upstairs to talk this over. Then maybe you can think about it some more." He led Benjie, still sniffling, up the steps while I watched like a voiceless statue.

Neither William nor Harriet gave me the slightest glance.

When I turned to face Harriet, expecting a tirade, she was still staring after the two of them. Her eyes brimmed with tears, her face slack, colorless. Without a word she turned, snapped the lock shut, whirled from the room and disappeared downstairs.

I huddled in the shadows feeling like a fool. No one seemed to realize my right to discipline my own son had been preempted. Like I wasn't even there. I was about to storm upstairs, then I thought about the tears. Harriet and William must have wanted children. Maybe William and Benjie were good for each other. Maybe Benjie needed a father figure, not just me hovering over his every move. Everything seemed so confusing. I felt pulled in so many ways in this house. There was nothing to do but wander downstairs.

I ambled out to the terrace. The sun was setting across the bay, working its magic, rouging the sky, caressing the tide with soft beams of rose and gold. I felt the familiar rush of emotion that caught me each time I saw this scene. No matter how often I looked, my heart filled with a sudden quickening throb, like someone meeting a lover. I knew I belonged here. Somehow, I would find a way to prove it. There must be room on all this land for Benjie and me.

There were still so many unexplained puzzles. Why was reconstruction in the old section going to be so dangerous? If it was being restored, why didn't any building go on in there? I hadn't seen or heard any activity within that small dark wing which clung to the south side of the house. Why had I never even looked inside, as fascinated as I was with all the history around me?

Curious, I strolled between the fragrant boxwoods that lined the terrace. I never thought to explore beyond the shrubs that bordered it, though now I noticed in the shadows an uneven, grass-covered path. It wound beyond the hedge like a maze. As if magnetized, I followed it, picked my way through the tangled undergrowth, and found myself standing at the door of the Old Cabin.

Peeling white wooden panels sagged from rough black hinges with an ancient-looking rusted doorknob to match. Cobwebs draped above the door like a border of old lace. Twisted vines and a gloomy thicket of blighted maples hid most of it, though on one side I thought I saw a hint of glass. My hand crept forward to turn the knob, but I pulled it back, suddenly feeling like a trespasser.

Stop it. You're being ridiculous. You belong here.

Standing on tiptoe, I could see in one of the small windows. The fading light pierced nothing but stillness. Dusty emptiness, like a tomb. The gulls ceased their swooping and calling, and in the lonely silence my imagination sprang to life.

What would it have been like to live here, so long ago, more than 200 years ago? With nothing but this small room, the bay, fields, and woods. Or was anything else here then? A fort? A trading post? Indians, surely.

Were there other settlers nearby? Were they friends of my ancestors?

Someone put arms around my waist. I gasped. "You want a boost, Cousin Abigail?" said William.

Frightened and furious, I whirled around to face his burning gaze. "No thanks." I backed away. "No thank you." I heard myself say, "Don't ever creep up on me like that again. You should know I have a feeling that Matt's always right behind me."

And how your fear tactics affect me. What about your behavior just this morning on that bizarre picnic? Did you think I would forgive and forget how you trapped and manipulated me?

William raised his eyebrows, pursed his lips. "Well, well," he said. "The lady has a temper, after all. You just might be coming to life again, Cousin. Look, I'm sorry. I didn't realize you didn't hear me coming," he said. "I wanted to tell you Benjie and I had a good talk about rules and he's going to stay in his room until supper. Case closed." He flashed me a smile as if I'd thanked him for handling my own child. "I guess you are kind of curious about this old part of the house, but, believe me, there's nothing much in there to see."

"Maybe so, but I'd like to look around anyway. You know I'm not just snooping. I have a right to be here. This was my father's home. The people who built this place were my ancestors as well as yours. I am definitely going to see inside." I crossed my arms and stood motionless before him. "Then I'll go tell Benjie when he can come down. It's my job to discipline him, you know."

I felt William's blue-green stare mocking me. I expected him to cheer, "Bravo." Instead, he remained silent, the stare replaced by his teasing grin. "Well, you're in luck, since the key's right here."

As I listened to the crickets' twilight shrilling, William stepped sideways into the brush and kicked over a moss-covered rock. Under it lay a large rusty key. He jiggled it in the lock. With a shower of dirt and debris, the old door swung open as its hinges creaked and groaned in protest. William stood aside for me to enter.

The air was dank and musty. I could almost taste the dust motes quivering in the slanting light from the two small windows on the bay side. There were two similar windows on the opposite side of the room, smothered by overgrown shrubs clinging to them from the garden. To my right, on the south end of the room, I could make out remnants of a huge gaping fireplace that added a hint of old, dead ashes to the stale air.

I knew I did not like this place, just as I knew I loved the big house the moment I walked in the door.

"Not much to see, is there?" said William. "This wing never did have electricity or heat, of course, except for the fireplace. Way too old. Or any allure, in my opinion." He shrugged as his eyes scanned the emptiness. "Harriet won't let me pull it down, though I'd like to. We used it for storage ages ago, still patch the roof and exterior walls to keep the rain out. Enough owners over the ages shored up the main structure to keep it standing. But it hasn't been lived in for years. Ha." His laugh was an empty echo. "Make that for centuries."

He produced a flashlight, aimed it around the stained yellowed walls. There was nothing in this space but stacks of lumber and heaps of large, jagged flagstones.

I started to shiver. "It's strangely cold in here, for summer. I suppose that's because the walls are so thick?"

William beamed the light above us. I could see the uneven flooring of what must have once been an attic. Boards were missing from the center, rotted out, I guessed, leaving splintered edges and a hole half the width of the room. Through which I could look up at the ceiling rafters.

"This lower floor had two rooms, originally," said William, "and the loft was used for sleeping. Children, I guess, first, then the slaves who worked in the kitchen when the original Bay House was built and attached to the cabin. There used to be a ladder on the wall by the hearth. Harriet wants to rip out what's left of the second floor and re-make the loft. Then re-do the fireplace and the stone floor for authenticity's sake, she says. From there, who knows what. She's going wild, of course, making plans. And she can be very persuasive." He rolled his eyes and seemed eager to change the subject. "But, Abby, I want to show you something." He nudged me forward, his fingers tight on my elbow. I winced and took a sharp breath as pain shot up my arm, though he didn't seem to notice. Or care. "Watch where you step. Flagstone is razor sharp until it's cut and laid properly. Don't trip."

He steered me to the center of the room and shined the flashlight straight up. "Take a look at this," he said. My eyes followed the light to where it landed on a doorway in the wall of the main house. The door was closed.

Suddenly I knew I was looking at the padlocked door in the wall of the master bedroom. "William, is that the door where Benjie …? It couldn't be. It looks so small."

"When our ancestors built this place, Cousin, it was ancient history, like 1630-something. This so-called Old Cabin was only a story and a half high. Later, when the big house was built and joined to it, the floor of the old loft was lower than the floor of the new second story." He reached up, traced a square against the gloom. "So, to get from the master bedroom into the loft, you had to go through that small door, jump down and duck, because the roof wasn't that tall. We always keep that door padlocked now, except today, when I was looking at plans. Besides, Benjie didn't get hurt, so let's not worry about it."

Not worry? How could William give such absurd, unrealistic advice? Especially since it was he who forgot to lock the door.

My apprehensions were only increasing. There was something disturbing about being in this shadowy secret place with William. I shivered again and hoped he didn't notice.

"Sweet Abigail, we can't have you freezing through your first tour." His arm snaked around my shoulders and pulled me to him. His strength was frightening.

I remembered the picnic. The panic. His hands on my face, his breath in my hair. He hadn't uttered a word of apology. Now I knew he never would. Fury boiled up inside me and overcame my fear. I would collect myself and refuse his attempts at intimidation.

I turned my back to him, edged away and changed the subject. "William, what is the mark on that beam up above? I just noticed it. "It looks like a Roman numeral."

"Well, ah, yes, that's exactly what it is." He mumbled, as if numbed by my rejection, then reverted to his usual arrogance. "A lot of people around here who are really into restoring old homes would pay a big price for that beam. Carpenters used those numerals, carved them as markers in the 1700s. Didn't use modern numbers until along about 1810."

He came closer, pointed the flashlight directly above us. "Now, can you see better?"

I tilted my head and nodded.

"We don't want to make this place too authentic. Harriet just wants her own private spot. For reading, meetings, planning, whatever. I have no idea why." William sounded bored with his wife's dream. "It's always seemed kind of mournful in here to me. Kind of spooky. Especially when I was a kid. You know, a distant ancestor hung himself here."

I spun to face him so quickly my forehead bumped his chin. "What? I didn't know that. What … what are you saying?" *I was suddenly filled with a sense of hopeless terror, desolation.*

"I shouldn't have sprung it on you," William said. "This happened ages ago. Like maybe in the 1800s, and no one ever knew why." Then his arms were around me again.

For a second, I cowered there, paralyzed with helpless confusion. Then I was running, out of the old wing, around the path, across the terrace. The sun disappeared and the golden light was gone.

Our supper that night would be better forgotten, though Harriet made the perfect cool meal for a hot evening. Salad made from lumps of backfin crab meat right out of the bay. Green beans laced with butter and dill. Iced tea with lemon slices and mint from her garden, hot yeast rolls, sliced ripe tomatoes and cucumbers she grew near the mint. Benjie was subdued and sulky. Harriet was stony. I stayed silent. William chatted as if nothing happened.

Noah glowered at me as he banged in and out of the kitchen door. He had not spoken to me except in a perfunctory way since that day in the study during the storm. Those narrow brown eyes under that mop of shaggy white hair still seemed to resent my intrusion here. Those eyes seemed to say, "Didn't I tell you to leave?"

Why? Another unanswered question.

There was a full moon later that silvered the bay and the terrace, but I took Benjie upstairs for a bath and a story and did not stay for coffee. I lay awake a long time that night, confused and miserable.

Had Matt found us? Was he lurking about somewhere waiting for a chance to punish me for running away? Did I dare to stay here anyway, now that William had displayed his reckless intentions so clearly? I had not imagined it. But still … was this new William merely being attentive in his own teasing, overbearing way? "Play-acting," as Harriet called his tendencies to overdo? Benjie and I needed the security of Bay House, regardless of William's whims. I would steer clear of him without Harriet around. It was plain to see she centered her life around William and held her head high, as my mother would have said, when he was … elsewhere.

Besides, if I left now, where would I go? Didn't I have to protect Benjie? I couldn't abandon the hope of an inheritance that could make us truly free until I had finished the papers in the library. My father called them, *The Forces of Bay House.* As clearly as if he was speaking to me, I remembered his words:

> It is only man, who has struggled for possession of the land and the water and the house, who has created cycles of good and evil amid the beauty. Do these forces remain in a place that has felt them so strongly?

I had felt a force, this day, as inconceivable as it might seem. A force that terrorized me in the small, dark, empty place where a Collington ancestor met tragedy. I felt such a passionate longing now to read the rest of my father's words that it was a physical pain. In those writings I knew I would find answers, understanding, comfort. Perhaps, even, the strength not to be afraid.

Moonlight from the dormer struck me with a feeling of wonder as I sat straight up in bed. I had an idea. Of course. I would borrow S.J.'s car and go back to the library where those papers were waiting for me, while Benjie was at Jake's birthday party. I almost forgot the comical invitation that could be my salvation. Harriet might storm, and William might try to play the protector, but they really couldn't stop me from taking Benjie to that party. Benjie would be safe with the Tomisons.

If I ran into danger from Matt, at least I would be alone.

13

I awoke with the uneasy feeling I had overslept and dreamed. Then, with a sickening knot in my stomach, realized I had not been dreaming. Benjie was sitting on the floor in the nursery playing with the firewagon, talking in the high small voice he used for pretending.

Though Benjie was hungry, I stalled for time. I made him pick up his clothes and line up the toys while I made and re-made my bed. When we couldn't dawdle any longer, Benjie danced downstairs first, begging me to make happy-face pancakes for William.

"Not today, son," I said, which meant that I meant it. "We have lots of other things to do."

What these other things would be was a mystery, but I was not about to make anything special for William in Harriet's kitchen. It would be all I could do to face William and get through the day.

Harriet sat on a straight chair pulled up to the phone in the hall, her long elegant legs crossed, a pile of papers in her lap.

"With you in a minute," she said. She waved her slim hand as she spoke. The church bazaar, of course, with its endless details.

When she came into the kitchen, she was brisk, unsmiling. William was gone again on one of his regular trips to Baltimore and Philadelphia. Something about stocks and investments. It was as if the electricity had gone out of the air.

Benjie was disappointed. I felt only relief. We sat at the kitchen table eating cereal, cantaloupe and Harriet's oven-warm cinnamon buns.

Harriet poured coffee and joined us. She stirred her cup in slow, rhythmic circles. "Abby," she said, "just what are your plans?"

My glance was casual, masking my fear. *Could she possibly have sensed what I was planning for tonight?*

"Don't look so alarmed, Abby. I know you must wait 'til your financial affairs are settled before you can start on divorce, custody and all that." She waved her hand like she was swatting a fly. "My word, I realize you're trapped here until you find out where somebody is and what that somebody intends to do. But, really, don't you think you ought to set some kind of time frame?"

"Benjie, run on into the study and play," I said. He obeyed without complaint. I wondered if he had spotted the television under the trailing ivy, surely only a matter of time.

As soon as he left, Harriet continued. "Remember, the house tour is scheduled for mid-November. Everybody will want to see the third floor. You'd be surprised how many people bring children when they know we have antique toys in the nursery. Of course, we're careful about them and have hostesses stationed everywhere keeping an eye on things." More slow stirring in her cup as she looked at me, unblinking. "Anyway, I've been thinking. It would be awfully uncomfortable for you to be here then, wouldn't it, with Benjie? The house will be open all-day Friday and we've been asked to hold the antique auction here on Friday afternoon. We're calling it A Day by the Bay, just so you know. There won't be room for it back at the church with the bazaar and luncheon going on. Everybody and his uncle will be here and going through this entire place."

"Yes. That would be awkward," I said. *Polite, agreeable, dispensable Abby. It was obvious I had outworn my welcome. Harriet made her point, tactful as always. I now had a deadline.*

She went on. "Actually, I'm not sure how safe Bay House is for you with William away. He has Noah and Burleigh Tomison alerted for any stranger who might try to trespass. I'm sure William believes they could hold off an army, but, think about it, Abby. There are two hundred acres here with trees, corn fields, the barns. Accessible shores, all kinds of high grass along the creek. A person who wanted to, in a drunken rage, as you seem to expect is your husband's perpetual state, could sneak in anywhere, even by water, onto the beach, at night. Then hide and wait."

Like an idiot, I shivered. I crossed my hands over my chest, hugged my upper arms.

"I truly think that you and Benjie might be safer if your Mr. Dangerfield could find you an apartment in a quiet neighborhood with a good security system."

No use talking to Harriet about my right to be here. From any other point of view except that one, she made a lot of sense.

I struggled to achieve her pragmatic tone. "Right now, everything hinges on the sale of my mother's house. I'm sure the real estate people are doing all they can to push it. I know I can't just let my life dangle indefinitely." I folded my hands together in my lap. "Mainly, I'm trying to do what's best for Benjie."

"Then I'm sure you're not planning to take him down to the Tomison's tonight."

My hands knotted into fists. I had given her the perfect opening,

"He's a child, Harriet. He needs other children to play with. And today's a holiday."

"Not those children. They'll only make him want to be as wild as they are."

"He's been through a terrible time," I said, looking down at the table. "You don't know what it's like. You have William." I looked up again and met the full power of her probing brown eyes. It was as if she was trying to penetrate my inner being. "Benjie needs fun. He needs other kids. He needs birthday parties. And surely you can see fireworks up and down the bay." Fumbling for words, I glanced away.

"Abigail," she began, "I'm sorry, but ..."

"Mommy." Benjie stood in the doorway. "Mommy, I can't find the book with the Heewatha girl."

"Well, never mind, Benj," I said. "Why don't you play with your trucks?"

"I want to see what she looks like again. She was here last night when you were sleeping. She stood right by the door and smiled at me, but when I wanted her to come in, she went away. Did she come to see you, too Aunt Harriet? Do Indians live in the woods near here?"

Harriet shot up from the table. "No, Benjie, she did not come to see me." She rushed to the doorway, knelt and gripped Benjie by the shoulders. "There are no Indians here now. All that was a long time ago. You were having a dream. It was only a dream."

"Oh," said Benjie. "I thought she was real." He was quiet for a minute or so as if he was trying to figure this out. "Then I must have dreamed about her a lot of times." He turned and wandered back into the hall.

Harriet faced me, thin-lipped, furious. "Honestly, Abigail. Someone's been filling that child full of ridiculous tales. It's criminal. He's been through enough. It must have been those Tomison kids. Not Noah. Surely Noah wouldn't want to frighten Benjie."

"Harriet, you know he's had that dream before." I kept my voice even, while under the table my fists opened and closed. "Now I think it's only fair to tell me about the ridiculous tales."

"Nonsense. I don't even want to discuss them. Every old house has stories, Abigail, you know that. It's part of the mystique of old houses. It's one of those things that makes people so fascinated about going through them. William has lived in this house all his life, and I've lived here with him for fifteen years. We should know what's true and what's not true."

Well, I will find out on my own, soon enough. "Maybe he's just pretending," I said. "He does that a lot because he plays by himself so much. Some kids have imaginary playmates when they're lonely."

Harriet started clearing the table. Dishes clattered in the sink.

"Abigail, I have a feeling under that helpless exterior of yours there may be a very stubborn person. OK, take Benjie to the Ramshackle Road Birthday Bash. If you can stand it, you're a stronger woman than I am. I'll have Noah drive you down there and Burleigh bring you back. But I'm afraid the day will come when you'll wish you had listened to me."

I have to block that warning out of my mind and go on.

Noah drove us down to the Tomisons' at 5:30. A short, silly trip he completed under orders. He looked sour, threatening, and didn't say a word.

S.J. appeared on the front porch and waved. Benjie flew out of the car, running to find the other children. I took my time, bracing myself for tonight's ordeal, carrying the marshmallow fudge we made for Jake since we had no way of buying him a present. I also held a can of worms for pole-fishing, which Benjie dug for Jake that afternoon with tender loving care.

I climbed the porch steps and laid our presents amongst the scattered toys. Leaned toward S.J. and lowered my voice. "S.J., please. Could you lend me your car again for just a short time while I leave Benjie here? You know it's important or I wouldn't ask."

"Oh. Abby, didn't you know? I can't do it. William came around first thing this morning and raised Cain because I let you have it Saturday night. Burleigh's s'posed to keep a real dead eye open, see you don't go off the place and see no strangers come on it."

I forced myself not to shake S.J. by her shoulders or scream, "But I absolutely have to."

She leaned forward and took my hands, her eyes full of regret. She started to speak but was interrupted by someone shouting her name with a voice like a bullhorn. We both looked up at the man who came loping around the side of the house.

Burleigh Tomison. I had never seen a bigger man. Not fat. Large as a tall, solid oak. The huge hand he extended was like a bear's paw. His smile was wide, disarming, white-toothed, with a mop of red hair blazing above.

"Hey, honey," S.J. said. "Finally, you get to meet my good friend, Abby." She aimed a thin smile from him to me before staring at her feet.

I knew I wasn't going anywhere. The disappointment was like a physical punch.

"Come on in and we'll go find the kids out back or wherever they are." Her words were rushed. She still hadn't looked me in the eye. I knew she hated being part of this forced collusion.

We wound through the house to the kitchen, a cluttered testimony to S.J.'s cavalier style of housekeeping.

"Don't mind the mess," she said, forcing cheer I knew she did not feel. "No sooner'n I get one meal cleaned up it's time for the next one, so I don't take it too much to heart."

"Pardon, ladies. Time to set up the table." Burleigh shouldered out through the back door carrying stacks of newspapers.

S.J. led me to a small front parlor. "I want to show you this before everything gets crazy. In here's different." The shades were drawn, the room was neat and spotless. It was furnished with a Victorian loveseat, a coffee table topped with a glass vase of artificial red roses, two matching Victorian chairs, and a glass-front cupboard full of flowered china. There was a black oval rug under the coffee table, hand-woven with more red roses.

"My mother's things," said S.J. with pride. "The kids don't play in here. I keep it nice so there's one place that's clean and pretty."

We followed Burleigh through the back door into the grassy backyard. The farmhouse sat on a small bank above the creek. *I recognized the woods and the narrow pathway where Benjie and I were discovered by all those little peering Tomison eyes. Somehow it seemed like a lifetime ago. I sighed at the simple beauty and peace of this home, wondering where home really was for my child and me. And if I would ever find it.*

At the edge of the bank a picnic table was covered with newspapers, strewn with wooden mallets and laden with piles of boiled hard crabs. They were strange looking. Bright orange and spikey shelled. Children were everywhere, laughing, running barefoot in the warm evening breeze, chasing fireflies.

Benjie's eyes sparkled. His face was aglow. Ecstatic. *My foiled plan ceased to matter.* S.J. marshaled everybody together around the table onto picnic benches.

Jake, the birthday boy, wore a paper crown glued with sequin swirls. He was seated at the head of the table with the rest of us surrounding him. Benjie was next to His Majesty, both smiling ear to ear. Mindy, the youngest, reached the table perched on a tower of old newspapers, telephone books and magazines.

Burleigh bowed his head. All the other heads went down. "Our Father who art in heaven," he said, "for the food we are about to eat we are truly thankful. Amen."

"Now everybody dig into these crabs," said S.J. "Josh, why don't you show Benjie's mom how to open 'em, crack 'em and all? That is if you don't know how to, Abby."

I remembered averting my eyes from the peeler lesson the day William took us out in the skiff and taught Benjie how to fish. This seemed all too similar.

It was messy. Josh, the eldest, showed me how to twist off the flippers and claws, put the flippers aside to crack and eat after the main job was done. Then he pried off the top shell, scraped out the inedible parts with a knife. He pointed these out like a young biologist: the devil fingers, the apron, the eyes and the mouth. I could imagine my well-groomed and always fragrant mother, taking a dim view of all this, once upon a time, but I tried to launch into the spirit of the occasion. Josh cut what was left of the crab into two equal parts through the middle. Then with a mallet he cracked away at the shelled pieces, so I could pick out bits of sweet tender white meat.

This was the prize, the famous lump, worth all the fighting for. What did it matter if my fingers were slimy with yellow, gooey crab fat? It was not quite dark yet, still and hot. The cuffs of my shirt were beginning to smell, so I took it off, glad I had worn the halter top underneath. I could see nobody noticed or cared about anything but this feast.

Jake showed Benjie the entire ritual. I let him alone, though I wondered if he would bash his own thumb or cut his fingers any minute.

He pounded and giggled, elbow-deep in bright orange crab pieces.

Bits of shell flew around the table as everybody hammered away, popped up and down, argued about which crab was the biggest and who caught it.

It was noisy. *"Sometimes you can hear those Tomison children yelling all the way up here at the house, long after bedtime," Harriet said to me once. I was sure she could hear us now.* I had the strange feeling I was on a kind of enforced holiday, in a make-believe world. I began to enjoy myself.

S.J. ducked in the house and brought out a platter of McDonald's hamburgers and French fries. Jess, the middle brother, explained this was Jake's very best favorite dinner and the crab feast was, too, but both together were super special, just for his birthday. The boys gathered up the newspapers with all the wrecked crab remains, rolling them in a ball on the ground. We all munched our burgers and fries, watching wide-eyed as Burleigh polished off the remains. S.J. carried Mindy up toward the house, laid her on the grass and changed her diaper.

Cindy, sitting cross-legged beside me, edged closer, crawling into my lap. I could smell the sweet scent of baby shampoo.

Maybe we should have another child, Matt, I said once. Maybe we'd have a little girl. I'd love to have a little girl. And Benjie ought to have a brother or a sister. He'd looked at me with that narrowing of his eyes. "You've got to be out of your mind, Abby. We're just getting free of one baby. No more. Ever. No ma'am. I don't want to hear about it again."

Cindy twined her skinny little arms around my neck. "I think you're pretty," she whispered. Then she slid off my lap and disappeared down the bank.

There were no kids left at the table. They were all thrashing and shrieking around in the tall grasses that lined the bank.

S.J. smiled at me. "Don't worry about Benjie. Those kids don't go anywhere after supper but right along the creek, or maybe over to the pond at the edge of the field. There's a little hollow where they like to look for frogs and tadpoles. Sometimes they just play games, like hide and seek, or Baby Moses in the Bulrushes. They made up that game one day after Sunday school."

Burleigh let out a deep, long chuckle that shook his whole body from his red curls to his muddy work boots. "They get in fights, sometimes nobody wants to be Baby Moses. Lord-a-mighty. The way they act it out, who would? Sarah Jane won't let 'em take Mindy yet."

"Let's let the kids play a little longer," said S.J. "Let it get darker before we bring out the cake. That way, it's more like fireworks when we light the candles. I've got the sparklers. I think everybody's forgotten this is the fourth of July."

We sat there together, the three of us at the table, with Mindy playing in the grass, tossing bits of clover into a stack of pink plastic teacups. The sun turned hazy, melting into the sky. Twilight settled around us like a soft blanket.

"What'd you do when you went in town today?" S.J. asked Burleigh.

"Nothin' much. Got some seed. Saw Buster Smith." Now Burleigh's voice was a low, easy rumble.

"How's Buster?"

"He's fine. His daddy's all crippled up with arthritis, though."

"Sally Beard was telling me about that."

I was so comfortable I could have nodded off.

"Good thing we got a little breeze workin'. Could've had a raft of mosquitoes tonight."

"Good thing," said S.J. "Well, I guess you could call the kids now. It's dark enough. I'll go get the cake when they're all around the table, so they'll get the whole bang of it."

The children thundered up the bank the moment after Burleigh gave three blasts from a whistle he pulled from his pocket.

"Sure got up here fast tonight," he said. "Somebody must be expectin' somethin' special. Better sit down now, all of you. Where's Benjie?"

I wondered the same thing as I counted the little heads bobbing through the dusk. The water, the darkness, turned games into danger. How could I have allowed myself to be so careless about his safety?

There was a scrambling sound down near the creek. My heart lurched, I held my breath. A clump of sea oats parted. Benjie appeared. His shorts soaked, his hair, face and body covered with mud. He was grinning from ear to ear, dragging a muddy laundry basket behind him.

"Guess what?" he said. He pulled grubby handfuls of weeds from his hair. "I got to be Baby Moses in the Bulrushes."

Burleigh bent double, slapping his knee.

S.J. pushed back from the table. "Goodness sakes, Mr. Moses. Why don't you and Jake get everybody back to their seats? I'll bring you a clean shirt. Abby, would you help the kids with these paper plates while I go get the C.A.K.E?" She laughed.

Everyone popped into place while stars appeared one by one.

Moments later the door of the farmhouse burst open. S.J. started down the porch steps, carrying a tray holding a giant chocolate sheet cake with six candles glowing in the dark like miniature torches.

Nobody had to be prompted. "Happy Birthday to you ..."

Then from a distance, there was the sound of a motor. A car was coming down the lane. Everyone stopped singing. S.J. stood poised with the cake, candles blazing.

If the car was going to the big house, it would pass the Tomisons' turn-off. It didn't.

We all ran to the front of the yard so we could see the lane and the headlights approaching. The car slowed at the Tomison's mailbox, turned, then crawled up the drive.

Burleigh's face lost its glow. "You boys," he said. "You do what I told you in case we have trouble." He spoke with a new note of command. "You girls, get on in the house. Benjie, go with your mother." We all obeyed.

S.J. and I stood, speechless, with the two little girls and Benjie, in the kitchen. She blew out the candles, still holding the cake with the wax dripping. My hands gripped Benjie's shoulders.

The night was very still, except for the constant high croaking of the tree toads. A car door slammed. We heard men's voices. Burleigh, and someone else. There were footsteps on the porch. Burleigh lumbered into the kitchen. He looked puzzled, but no longer ready for battle.

"It's that doctor fella from town. The young one. He says he has a package for Mrs. Wells at this address. Says it's important. You know what he's talkin' about, Abby?"

My relief swung into anger. "I certainly don't." *I had given him this address so he could send me a bill. That didn't give him the right to track me down. A doctor is not supposed to make you feel like a fool.* I stormed out to the porch. Burleigh tramped behind.

Dr. Peter Carpenter. Wearing a dark suit with a square-cut jacket, cuffed pants and thick-soled dress shoes. Next to Burleigh he looked like a rail. He was holding a brown manila envelope.

"Mrs. Wells," he said stiffly, "I think I owe you an apology. Both times I've seen you I acted ... unprofessionally." Looking awkward, he glanced down, then from Burleigh to S.J., and back to me. "I don't want to be known that way. I think I kept you from getting what you wanted the other night. You didn't know it, but I was looking for the same thing. So, here's an extra copy."

He handed me the envelope. I simply took it, staring down at the miracle in my hands. I felt stunned, voiceless. Far out in the bay a ship's bell pealed.

"Thank you. Oh, thank you." I could only stammer silly, empty words for what I was thinking was too good to comprehend.

In the light from the porch's overhead bulb I could see on Peter Carpenter's plain but mobile face the determined expression of a man completing a difficult but necessary task. He looked so decent, so responsible, so human. Everything Matt was not.

I was about to forgive him for condemning me in his office and laughing at me in the library. For one moment I almost forgot myself and threw my arms around his neck in gratitude.

The moment hovered between us. He spoiled it, of course.

He pulled horn-rimmed glasses from his pocket and pushed them onto his nose. Bent forward, wrinkled his forehead and studied my shoulders. Again, I felt like a specimen on a slide. Then he said, being professional, "Those contusions look better."

Embarrassment washed over me. I had forgotten my bare arms, the fading bruises, the marks of my humiliation. *The man is impossible.*

"Good night," I said, clutching my shoulders. "Thank you very much. Good night." I ducked inside.

I heard him stomp down the steps, slam his car door and drive off.

The rest of the evening couldn't pass quickly enough for me.

S.J. relit the cake. We ate in the kitchen and sang "Happy Birthday," drowning out the tree toads and the bullfrogs in the creek. Jake loaned Benjie a pair of dry jeans and received his presents like a king. Benjie's and mine were just right, fudge and worms.

Burleigh drove us home. In an instant, Benjie fell asleep on the front seat between us. I tried to thank this gentle giant.

"Benjie hasn't had so much fun for a long time," I said. "And you even have some sort of plan to protect us if, if somebody tries to come here when William's away? What was it you were telling the boys to be ready to do?"

He ran a hand through his curls and turned to face me. "Jess runs and gets my shotgun and shells, brings them to me while I stand watch. And calls the cops, if it seems like somebody's been drinking heavy. And Josh gets out the big tractor. I just taught him to drive it. You'd be surprised," he chuckled, "how a grown man'll turn around with a thing like that after him."

The mental image made me laugh out loud. How wonderful it was to laugh and to feel safe again.

"Goodnight, and thank you again, for everything." I woke Benjie, helped him slide out of the car and stumble into the house. We crept past the second-floor landing. Harriet's light was still on, but it flicked off when we reached the third floor. I put to bed one dirty, happy little boy.

And then, at last, I settled into my own bed, with a small lamp burning in the softly creaking night, opened the manila envelope, and pulled out *The Forces of Bay House.*

14

...**t**he fiercer tribes to the North who were known to attack the peaceful Matapeakes ...

I started where I left off, that night in the library.

I believe... my father wrote, and in the stillness of the night I remembered him poring over his books and papers in the small den of our long-ago home, his face earnest and intent. Often, he would glance up, his brown eyes serious and kind, acknowledging that I was there on the couch playing with my paper dolls, or reading a favorite book. The manuscript went on.

I believe the Matapeakes were a splinter group from the Nanticokes who were settled on the Nanticoke River not much more than twenty miles away. I write here of the Matapeakes because, as destiny played out its drama, the blood of this small and almost forgotten tribe would mingle with the blood of the Collington family who had owned land in Kent County, England, since 1545.

In the 1620s, while the Collingtons were living the life of landed gentry in England, the Matapeakes had been pushed by other harassing tribes to the southern tip of Kent Island. There they had a sizeable village. They also farmed and fished and tried to remain at peace.

The Matapeakes were a smaller people than the dreaded giant Susquehannocks. They had dark brown eyes, straight black hair and their skin was a rich ivory that tanned to a deep bronze. These were real people, we must remember, not myths. This was their place in the world. They saw the blue of the sky, the green of the land, the shadows of the tangled forests.

One can picture them going about their normal life on a fine spring day. Women would go to the fields to plant seeds for beans or corn or pumpkins, taking the young children with them. Men would be checking the traps for otters, or beaver, on the creek. Some would be making weirs, driving stakes into shallow water to form fences with narrow openings, through which fish swam and were trapped. Always, there would be the anxiety of possible attack, and the Matapeakes needed to be ready with their five foot bows and their edged arrowheads of bone, just as the white men, who came soon after, were ordered not to leave home without their guns in case of Indian attack.

Sometime in July of 1631, many pairs of dark brown eyes belonging to those Matapeakes must have been riveted upon the surging sails of a great canoe. It skimmed across the breadth of the Bay between Kent Point and what was already Virginia and landed white men somewhere on the southeastern tip of the point. These people brought possessions as if they meant to stay.

One of the company of 100 men who came with the Commander, William Claiborne, on the ship, Africa, out of England, was a young neighbor and adventurer named William Henry Collington. And so the story of the American

Collingtons and Bay House begins and is intertwined with the earliest tales of Kent Island.

Even after more than 300 years, Claiborne remains a controversial figure in the histories of Maryland and Virginia. In the reading of seemingly dry, dead documents, we discover potential tinder for the first bloodshed between Englishman and Englishman here in this beautiful water country that still sings of flying geese and peaceful sails.

Claiborne purchased the Isle of Kent from the Indians in what was considered fair trade. He had a royal license to establish a trading post and expected to be granted a charter to colonize.

The Matapeakes and probably another tribe, the Monoponsons, moved northward, to the central part of the island.

William Collington, who was still in his twenties, had some education, was a ready soldier and able sailor, became one of Claiborne's circle of most trusted men. These men were devoted to their charismatic leader. Under their guidance a fort was built, and the settlement became a farming and ship-building colony.

William married Janet Ware, whose father was a settler from Virginia, and Claiborne and some of his chief subalterns started their own farms. Claiborne established Crayford, to be his own plantation. To the north on the island's western shore, facing the water and the sunset, were the small house and vast lands of the first William Collington. He called his domain Bay House.

I felt a physical clutch at my heart. This was not just history. These were our shores, our lands. The original Old Cabin—preserved after all these years—and still part of our house.

The light bulb on the old lamp beside my bed flickered. I had lost track of time. I heard the mattress on Benjie's bed rustle as he turned over in his sleep. It was still very dark out. Good. I had all the rest of the night. I couldn't turn those pages fast enough, seeing my father's words bringing history to life.

It seemed that Claiborne's Eden was about to flower. Not so.

In 1634, the Ark and Dove sailed up a branch of the Potomac River on the western side of the bay flying the blue and gold emblem of Cecilius Calvert, Lord Baltimore, to a site that was christened St. Mary's. There another dauntless band of Englishmen planted the colony of Maryland. Lord Baltimore received a patent to colonize. Claiborne never did.

In the middle of the new Maryland proprietorship, on a vast watery, vulnerable stage, sat the Isle of Kent, which had been claimed by Virginia. What resulted was a small naval war.

Astonished, I made the instant connection. Here was the history of our glorious Kent Island. Yet I felt it was still a "vulnerable stage" on which the quest for my identity was being played out. My father's words blurred on the page. Written so long ago, how could they help me now?

Our Collington ancestor survived the gunshots and cannon fire that blasted the ancient stillness of the Chesapeake and brought death to the warships of both sides. Then the snake arrived in Eden, in the person of one George Evelin, or so it seemed to the men of Kent Island. Evelin came as a representative of Cloberry and Company, the London merchants who supported Claiborne's venture. Claiborne was ordered to go back to England to give an account to the company, leaving Evelin in charge of the fort and the settlement.

Evelin went over to the cause of Governor Calvert and the Maryland faction at St. Mary's. In fairness to the man in the hindsight of history, he may not have been the traitor he seemed. He may have been sent for this reason. In fact, whatever his motivation, he accepted a commission from Leonard Calvert to be commander of Kent Island.

Claiborne's high-spirited, outraged followers refused to accept Evelin. They were armed and not about to knuckle under. Eventually, Leonard Calvert, himself, sailed forth with an expedition of 30 choice musketeers to take the island by force for Maryland.

The light bulb flickered again, forcing me back to the present. Wild to read on, I leaned over and screwed it tighter without a thought to my singed fingertips. From out in the channel, in the night stillness, I recognized the heavy drone of a huge vessel, but I was seeing a time, three centuries before, when the only way to move across this bay was by sail.

This was the scene I have imagined over and over, that has affected me all my life.

Early in the morning, just before dawn, while Claiborne

was in London and while people in the settlement and within the fort were sleeping, that vessel large enough to hold those thirty men, and more, must have anchored off the southeastern side of the point and put out small boats to row ashore.

I know dawn very well at that site. I have fished there, man and boy, as they say, at daybreak. Gray water moves under a translucent gray sky, touched at the horizon with a promise of rosy light, yet there are still stars. The sounds are nature's sounds. The water laps the shore like a gentle ocean. Water birds are awake, beginning to feed, skimming the shallows near the shore. Land birds chorus as one never hears them later in the day. One can make out the two notes of the bobwhite, the four notes of the dove, among the chirping, lilting whistles. God's special time, I've often thought.

Three hundred years ago, at the edge of an unspoiled land, daybreak must have been even more lyrical. Yet, here came these small boats, the men rowing, dipping, pulling in grim silence. They would have been anxious, their faces taut. They stowed their boats and crept toward the fort, men and muskets like shadows, still unseen. The front gate facing the water was locked, but someone, possibly Evelin, says one historian, let them in at the back gate. The people in the fort, asleep in their beds, were surprised and overpowered. With the fort captured, the attackers moved on to seize the other leaders in their homes. Some protestors were taken as prisoners to St. Mary's. Some were hanged without trial.

Anyone reading this account may already know that William Collington was one of those taken from Kent Island who never returned.

So little Bay House was lost from the hands of the first

American Collingtons and stood empty for many years. The fertile land was used to grow tobacco. Kent Island had become a part of Maryland.

More than 100 years later, in 1740, a Collington returned from Virginia. We can see by the deed of purchase that he acquired the remains of the original dwelling and nine hundred acres around it. He built a larger house, a very fine house for those times, made of brick and three stories tall, and called it Bay House to honor its ancestor. He incorporated the first little Bay House, in comparison only a one room cabin, as a wing.

I sit here and wonder. Did he sense the grief, the evil that seemed to linger in that small space? Did he picture a man and his wife awakened in their bed? Ordered to arise, possibly wrenched apart? And what of the children? Did they stumble down the ladder from the loft and cling to their father in terror as he was dragged away? Was there any time to say goodbye?

Was the house silent after the man was taken? Or were there sounds of weeping as normal life and hope faded, then the eventual despair of departure, followed through the years by a bleak unending stillness?

Silent tears slid down my face as I sank deeper beneath the quilt, shivering, clutching the journal. I remembered that desolate cabin. The loft. The fireplace. The sorrow that hung in the air like the smell of old smoke.

There is no way, of course, to know these things. Only the sense of some tragic, evil force that lingers there, too strong to be destroyed. In any case, this William Henry Collington must have repaired the fireplace and rebuilt the rest to use as a kitchen only with sleeping quarters for servants in the loft. From his journal we know many things pertaining to his tenure, as well as the day by day condition of the weather and his crops. He had a son, his namesake. A daughter named Mercy, and a beautiful, though severe looking blonde lady for a wife. We know this from several family portraits which still exist. His was a prosperous tobacco farm with a stable full of horses, a fine view of the Bay, a sailing boat, and, apparently, good standing in the community.

In the year 1770 there was a gap of six months without a single entry in the journal. Then there appeared a specific reference to a document, a will. That will has been preserved and stands to this day as a legal document. In its way it tells the story that must have caused William Collington too much pain to record. A copy of this will follows here to make this tale complete.

That crazy old light bulb blinked again. On fire with hope and impatience I twisted it tighter, then replaced the shade, my heart marching. Why hadn't Harriet or William told me there was a will? Could the answer to my question be right here in my hands?

The paper trembled as I picked it up again.

15

Last Will and Testament of
William Henry Collington

January 16, 1785

I, William Henry Collington of Queen Anne's County in the State of Maryland, being a widower of advanced age, but of a sound, disposing mind, memory, and understanding, considering the certainty of death and the uncertainty of the time thereof and being desirous of settling my worldly affairs, do thereof make and publish this my last Will and Testament, in manner and form following. After my debts and funeral expenses are paid, I devise and bequeath:

1st to my daughter, Mercy Elizabeth Collington Buford, per stirpes, one half of Bay House Plantation, the 450 acres of land to the South of the house.

2nd to Benjamin Henry Collington, one half of Bay House Plantation, the 450 acres, more or less, of land North of the house, if it can be proved the said William Henry Collington the second was lawfully married to Ellen Smalldeer at the time Benjamin Henry Collington was born. Despite my enduring love and affection for Benjamin Henry (this grandchild) and with deep regret, I must decline to convey any property to him or his heirs in fee simple if his parents were not united in marriage by the sacraments of the Christian church. I cannot, in all consciousness, leave the property to an illegitimate child.

3rd if either my daughter, Mercy Elizabeth Collington Buford, or Benjamin Henry Collington, should die without a legal heir before the matter of Benjamin Henry Collington is resolved, their legacy shall lapse and be inherited by the legal heirs of the other.

4th, the house which rests on the properties described above is to be shared by my daughter, Mercy Elizabeth Collington Buford and Benjamin Henry Collington, and their heirs until the legitimacy of Benjamin Henry Collington is resolved, etc., etc.

So, here was the joker in the deck, the clinker. This is what gave Harriet and William their air of certainty, of innate pride, of belonging in a way that is bred in the bone. They viewed my claim to inheritance as a winsome, romantic ghost story. Nothing more. Yet, I was still my father's child. His hope was my hope. I believed in his truth, and I would follow it.

I flipped through the rest of the bequeaths until I came back to my father's writing.

Now I, Ben Collington, six generations later, two centuries removed from the signer of that will, am going to continue this tale as I heard it from my grandmother who told me this story as it had been told to her. I believed her then as now. This is the way history comes down in families, just as the stories of Abraham and Isaac were told and retold and memorized by generations until one day they were written down, becoming part of the Bible.

I, Abigail Collington Wells, realized this was the old lady in the picture in the locked room across the hall. The lady with the kind eyes, wearing my pearls. I felt I could reach back in time and touch her cheek. Warm and real as my father's love, and the legend that proved his unwavering belief that Bay House belonged to him. In detail, he repeated the story.

One winter evening in the year of 1770, young Will Collington asked his parents to be ready to receive a guest. When the elder Collingtons were seated in their parlor beside their blazing fire, he brought in an Indian girl called Ellen Smalldeer, who carried an infant in her arms, bundled in a blanket. He proudly claimed the girl as his wife and the newborn child, his son.

Will's mother was outraged. She had seen the girl working in the kitchen of a neighbor's plantation. She was vaguely aware that most of the small group of Matapeakes, who still lived in bark huts in the woods somewhere near the gates of Bay House, were also employed by wealthy landowners. Of course, the Indians were no longer a threat, in this year of 1770. The fiercer tribes had long since weakened or disappeared. Yet, this savage girl, brought into their midst by their own kin, shocked the wife of William Collington to her staunch, Anglican soul. This strange girl before them holding an infant, wore a long skirt and blouse of homespun, though she was wrapped in a cloak of skins and fur. She stood, graceful and straight as a small, perfect tree. Her skin was smooth and tan. Her hair, long, black, shining. Her astonishing eyes were blue, the color of the sky on a clear summer day. It was plain to see there had already been a tainting of English blood. Now, another desecration, by their one and only perfect son.

Will's father stormed. He had been planning a suitable marriage for Young Will, his beloved son and heir.

"I told you." Maude Collington, Will's mother, spoke in a sudden, harsh outburst to her husband. "I told you, Will Collington, we should not allow our children to play outside the gate."

William was startled out of his own angry speech, not following the train of thought that had brought this sudden rush of recall to his wife.

You said it would do no harm to let them play in the woods so near our home, the accusing voice went on. You said the Indian children were innocent, happy playmates. Do you remember Will's tenth birthday, the day he got his pony? This girl, this child, was there, with the other little savages out on the bridle path. I remember even now. Will asked you to lift the girl up and let her have a turn to ride. You did this, tho she was quite small. When I saw her face high upon that horse I thought, 'How very strange. Her eyes are blue.' We never should have let our children go beyond our own boundaries."

Will came to stand beside the girl. He took her left hand because her right arm cradled the baby.

Father spoke the truth, he said. We were innocent playmates. I was not allowed to venture into the woods often, you remember, but Ellen and I were friends. And then last April, we realized that we could not remain friends. We knew we loved each other as we would never love anyone else. I was twenty one, you know, he added, looking so proud, so young that it must have twisted his parents hearts. Old enough to know my own mind.

We were married in April of 1770. Will's declaration was bold, though perhaps his voice trembled a little. The last week of the full moon, as I remember clearly. It was the night before the Reverend Russell Witherspoon was leaving on the Constance to sail back to England. We went to the parsonage on Broad Creek.

Ben Collington interjected here, seeing with his poet's eye the scene of the family legend which he must have heard over and over.

I know what the waters of this island are like on April nights in the last week of the full moon. I've often imagined the night Will tried to tell about. How it must have been, with the first softness of spring in the air, with silver touching the creek, with the breeze from the forest picking up the pungency of pine needles, clean and sweet and wild, and two young people longing to be together.

We knocked on the door, Will said. The Reverend answered it himself. We asked him straight away to marry us then, that night, because he was leaving for England. We knew it could take a year for another parson to make passage from London.

At first, he did hesitate, then he bid us come in. He married us there in his parlor, with his wife and their servant, Emma Hollins in her nightcap, for witnesses. I signed the book, the *Marriage Book* that lay on the table he used for an altar between two lighted candles. Ellen signed, too, as I had taught her.

The room was crowded, for all the goods of the household were packed up ready for leaving the next morning. There were wooden crates and old tobacco barrels standing about, so it was a strange sight for a wedding. Not what you would have wished for me, but we were happy.

Ellen Smalldeer Collington spoke once, in soft, halting English with the accent of the Matapeakes. I was not . . . I give my word . . . with child on that night.

She stopped then for she could sense what Will could not.

The Native Americans were also a race of great pride, which must not be forgotten.

"I thought," said Will, "if we were married by the minister of the Church, and if after we had a young one, you would accept the marriage for your grandchild's sake."

"Russell Witherspoon was a fool," William Collington sputtered. "I always thought he had too soft a heart for life in that wilderness. But he was not that great a fool. He would not have dared perform the act you suggest."

Will realized then that his parents saw this child as the result of a young man's indiscretion in the forest, a scandal he was trying to avoid with his tale of marriage. It was inconceivable to them that a Collington would take this Indian, Ellen Smalldeer, for a wife.

He pleaded with them to go to the church where they would find the legal ceremony recorded in the *Marriage Book*, which listed the parish members, births, deaths as well as marriages. In their distress, the family called for their carriage to be brought around despite the late hour, the snow flying fast and thick against the inky sky. Bundled in blankets they ventured into the cold night, leaving the Indian girl by the hearth fire with the infant.

They searched the church, but the book was not to be found. They went to the parsonage where a new maidservant greeted them, all in a flurry, for she had already locked up. The house was tidy, bare and swept, ready for the new minister's arrival. The *Marriage Book*, as she hastily named it, was missing from the table between the two brass candlesticks where Will swore he and Ellen both signed it. The young maid apologized for knowing nothing about the old furnishings. She had been settled in only a fortnight before, after her ma's dear old auntie, Emma Hollins, passed away in her sleep.

Will could not let the matter rest. He begged his parents to go on. They stopped at the home of the first alderman, a landed neighbor, who was startled by the knock on his door at this late hour. He could see the Collingtons were in a state of unnatural frenzy but informed them with regret that the book they sought and a number of other valuable tomes, left by Witherspoon for his successor, had been mysteriously missing since April.

Father, mother and son rode home in stony silence, chilled to the bone. The coachman's boy had to hold two lanterns, so the horses could make their way on the narrow, rutted country road crusted with snow.

When they reached their own warm parlor, Ellen was still waiting by the fire with the sleeping baby wrapped in her arms.

Will's strict and proper parents, bound to the conventions of their class, could not accept the girl, but they loved their son. They didn't doubt that the child was his, for the skin was light and there was a clear resemblance. This mite, they believed, was flesh of their flesh, though their son was lying about its legitimacy. They vowed to keep and accept the child. But not the girl. Ever.

Flushed and furious, Will refused this cruel verdict, but

the girl handed him the baby in silence. While he paced, clutching the child, the family railed and argued. Ellen slipped out unseen into the frigid, windy night. When the fire had turned to embers, his parents pale and mute in their chairs, Will saw with horror that she was gone. He rushed out after her. Hannah, the family servant who had been a nurse to Will and Mercy, whisked the baby upstairs to the old nursery. She found their dusty old cradle and laid him in it.

Next morning, Will returned, ashen and shaking with cold. He had not found Ellen. He took brandy, heavier clothing, and went back out to search for her.

In the drowsy early afternoon, Hannah dozed in the rocker, keeping an eye from time to time on the sleeping infant. Suddenly, she let out a chilling scream, heard by everyone in the house, and pounded down the wooden steps from the third floor. She awoke to see the Indian girl, who had appeared from nowhere, bending over the infant.

When the whole household raced back upstairs, the baby was still asleep. The Indian girl had vanished.

Next day, it was reported by a lad who was fishing along the shore, that he had seen the last of the Matapeakes leaving in their canoes, heading west across the bay.

The body of an Indian girl was found a few days later, washed ashore, lying in a bed of reeds.

Hannah insisted she saw the spirit of that girl saying goodbye to her son as she left this world. Through the years, other servants, relatives, guests, and Collingtons, claimed to have seen her, too. Always in the nursery. Always when a child was ill or in danger.

I jolted straight up in my bed. Then, suddenly, that flickering bulb gave out and I was in darkness.

I stumbled to the nursery to look at Benjie. To assure myself he was safe. My eyes adapted to the dark. There was always a slice of light that shone through the windows from that canopy of open sky above the bay.

Benjie lay on his back, breathing quietly, eyes closed, mouth open a little, his expression wiped clean of everything but his innocence. I pulled the bedspread higher around his chest, bent forward to kiss his soft cheek.

The urge to discover what happened to Young Will and the child who slept in this very room was irresistible. Everything felt surreal. As if I were being drawn back and forth between the poles of two centuries.

I would tiptoe downstairs and get a new light bulb from the kitchen.

By now I was familiar with the steps that creaked. I padded down along the sides in silence. There was no sound from William and Harriet's room as I passed the second-floor landing. No light shone from beneath their door. The stairs were eerie in the darkness. Once down, I would grope my way through the long back hall to the kitchen, where its light could not reach the second floor, and take a bulb from the pantry.

My bare feet skimmed the carpet as I reached the bottom step. Midway across the hall I heard the click of a key turning in the lock of the back door. I froze in the dark, flooded with adrenalin, wondering whether to bolt for the steps or the telephone.

The back door creaked open. A tall shadow with a familiar cut to the shoulders hovered there for a moment. Then the door closed, and I knew William was coming toward me. *If I move, he'll think I'm an intruder.*

"William, it's me, Abby. Here, by the dining room," I whispered.

"What? What on earth?"

Then his arms were around me, his mouth crushing mine.

I flung my hands behind me. Wrenched his arms apart. Pushed against his chest with all my strength. Darted through the half-light of the dining room, the swinging door into the kitchen, snapped on the light.

William lunged, gripped my shoulders. Then his lips were hot against my neck. "Abby, I can't believe, this. You were waiting for me. How did you know I was coming home tonight?"

"No, William." I turned, palms against his chest, forcing him back. I wanted to scream. "Oh, no. I didn't dream you were coming home just now. How could I? Get away from me. I only came downstairs to get a new light bulb."

He laughed out loud, his eyes blazing with a brilliance I did not recognize. "Come on, Cousin Abigail, do you expect me to believe that?"

"Yes. Of course, I do," I struggled to keep my voice low, although it was hard to speak at all. *My God, if Harriet should awaken, follow our voices and enter this scene ...* "What is wrong with you? It's true. I was reading, upstairs, and the light bulb burned out."

"At 4:00 a.m.?" His eyes seemed to change to a darker blue, like deep uncharted water. "Abby. Darling. Don't back off now. You know you feel what I feel. You must have been waiting for me, here in the dark."

He inched close again. Caught my hands in a vice-like grip. His lips pressed my ear. "Let's go down to the beach. It's magnificent down there just before dawn."

Just before dawn. The words rang in my mind like an echo. The body of an Indian girl was seen a few days later, washed ashore, lying in a bed of reeds.

"No, William. Not now. Not ever." I wrenched my head back, shook free of his grasp, sprinted through the hall, up the steps to my little fortress.

My son still slept safely. I bolted his door and mine. Shaking, leaning against it, taking ragged gulps of air. I waited, listening for William's stealthy tread, but heard only the creaks and groans of a house filled with danger.

I lay in my bed, frozen with fear, heart pounding against my ribs. The sky turned light, but I could neither sleep, nor read, nor quiet my soul. Let's go down to the beach, William taunted. It's magnificent down there just before dawn. God's special time, I've often thought, wrote my father. The forces of Bay House were no longer historic. They were real and powerful, and I was at the center of the battle.

16

The next day was not the one I hoped for. No chance to deal with William and his crazed advances. His every move seemed calculated. Designed to keep me off-balance and in the dark. Was it coincidence, or did he plan it that way?

He left the house before I was up, to race in a sailing regatta. When Benjie and I shuffled down to breakfast, Harriet was all composure and I was all guilt, though I knew I was being unfair to myself. *What did she hear in the night? What must she think of me? What of William? I knew she loved William as the center of her life under that efficient, elegant, calm. I couldn't tell her about the light bulb. It would be foolish to defend myself when I wasn't accused.*

Even so, I couldn't look her in the eye. I chattered to Benjie, quizzing him on the alphabet letters blazed across his cereal box.

She left early to watch the races, cool and commanding in cream-colored shorts and matching top that emphasized her tan. Her perfect chestnut twist gleamed under a beige visor, making her pearl stud earrings stand out like stars.

At last Benjie and I were alone at the kitchen table. He slurped his cereal without the reprimand of Harriet's raised eyebrow. I slurped my coffee in solidarity, staring out at the leafless flagstone terrace lined with ranks of her pink geraniums in perfect bloom. *I wonder if the blue and boundless Chesapeake Bay, rippling along the manicured shoreline, does so at her command. I wonder if William ever dares to defy or frighten her as he terrified me last night. In the light of day, I am certain this would not be possible, though I catch myself wondering how any woman could handle William.*

I will handle him like a mature adult. Earlier, sometime around sunrise, I fought down my fear and the impulse to bolt. I escaped Matt's wrath to get here. I will not turn back until I have exhausted all hope that we belong here. William Buford will not change my mind.

"Mommy," said Benjie, "there's nothin' to do." He slouched on his elbows stacking Cheerios into soggy leaning towers. "C'un I go to Jake's?"

My spoon clinked in my coffee cup. "He's in school, Benj." I was too preoccupied to lecture him about manners.

"No, he's not. This is Saturday, 'member? William races his boat on Saturday. Why don't we go watch him?"

I don't want to say we are hiding. Still hiding. Always hiding. I am getting so tired of hiding.

"Let's go to the beach. Maybe we could see the boats from there."

Benjie's hands flew up, his voice rose in protest. "We went down there already. William said they wouldn't sail up this far. An' the jellyfish are bad today. I could see 'em. There's nothin' to do. Please, c'un I go to Jake's?"

"Son." I placed my spoon on the saucer. "Look at me. William took you to the beach?"

It's magnificent down there, just before dawn.

"Yeah. We checked the crab pots, too, out on the dock. It was neato, but he's a grown-up. I wanna play with Jake an' catch frogs."

I was over-tired. The sun was shining, the sky was blue, and my adventurous five-year-old was bored. Of course, he should be allowed to play with his buddy.

The prospect of being on my own in Bay House took a sudden turn. My pulse quickened at the thought of a few golden moments to continue reading the Forces again in private.

"On second thought, catching frogs sounds like a great idea. Sure, you can go. I'll walk with you and we'll see if they're home."

Benjie beat me getting dressed, even tying his own shoelaces as I was teaching him to do. When we banged through the screen door he took off, almost dancing down our lane.

Jake ran to meet Benjie as we reached the Tomisons' mailbox. The children were all out in the front yard, the girls with their dolls and tea sets. Josh was driving the tractor, cutting grass, with Jess standing on the back.

S.J. waved from the porch as we walked up the short drive.

I waved back. "Can Benjie play awhile? I would have called you, but I needed the exercise."

"Sure. We're here. I'm baking cupcakes and everybody can take turns with the icing."

She laughed in her deep-throated way. "That'll be fun." She smiled at me with the wide, encompassing grin that made my world feel younger.

"Come on up on the porch a minute, Abby. I have somethin' to tell you."

"What is it?" I was anxious to get back to the *Forces* but I went up the steps. "I'll just stay a minute." *I was tempted to tell her about last night's strange encounter with William but kept silent.* A warm breeze ruffled the clean sheets hung to dry in the sun. The kids' squeals of laughter joined the seagulls calling and swooping. My story, even if half-imagined, did not belong in this moment.

"I think that doctor's sweet on you."

I could only blink at her. It seemed like eons since I'd thought of him, though it was just two days ago that he crashed Jake's party. "Oh, for heaven's sake, don't be ridiculous. That's preposterous. It's the exact opposite of the truth." I couldn't sputter the words fast enough.

S.J. continued to look impish and wise. "Sorry, but I really think so." Her ponytail swung as she nodded.

"You're wrong. He thinks I'm stupid, weak and spineless."

"In other words, a wimp," she said. "Come on, Abby, let me ask you something. Would a guy like that who's never been known to pay any mind to anybody but sick people come all the way out here where nobody's sick?" She took a deep breath. "At night, on his own, with whatever it was he brought you? Just to prove that he's, what did he say? Professional?"

"He might," I said. "He's stiff-necked and proud, and that intrusion was hardly professional. It was downright nosey. When I went to his office for help, you know how he lost his temper. Then when he saw Benjie and me in the library, he couldn't stop laughing."

"I remember. Truth is I might have cracked up a little myself when

Benjie tore off his hair ribbon and lassoed the fella's shoe. And with you dressed up in some kind of baggy boy-disguise, who wouldn't laugh?"

I went on, ignoring her question. "Then, right here at the birthday party, he stepped way out of line. That was no professional visit, and he had no right to call attention to my bruises."

"Yep," said S.J. "He sure was un-pro-fessional." She shrugged, rolled her eyes upwards. "I saw the way he looked at you while you were too steamed up to notice. He just acted like a natural man."

"And he's just naturally made me feel humiliated every time I've seen him."

"Sounds like you've been thinkin' a lot about those times you've seen him, girl."

"I'm leaving." I stood and tromped down the porch steps two at a time. "You can go on with your fantasy. Thanks for keeping Benjie," I said over my shoulder. "I'll be back for him in an hour or so."

"OK. Whatever you say." I didn't need to see her face to know she winked. "We'll save you a cupcake."

I marched up the lane back to the big house, but for an instant the girl I once was wanted to skip. It was the thought of freedom, of course. Some adult time to be alone. Peter Carpenter had nothing to do with it. S.J. was just trying to boost my morale. If she was only slightly correct, that doctor fella was the world's worst communicator. I reminded myself he was a crusader, according to Harriet, on the subject of injustice to Indians. I knew he labeled me victim of abuse. Took pity on me, determined to do the right thing by bringing me the precious papers. The man was insulting. Infuriating. Self-righteous and obnoxious. Our dreams could not have been farther apart.

Then I was alone in the front hall of Bay House, wrapped in its peaceful silence. I ran upstairs. *The Forces of Bay House* lay under my pillow just as I left it. Freedom. Wonderful freedom. Time to read the rest of *The Forces* uninterrupted. My chance to find out the truth of my father's unshaken belief that we inherited. I would find out and I would not give up until I proved he was right.

Nestled on the leather couch in the study I felt close to the boy who lived in this house long ago. Bees hummed in the gardens outside the open windows facing the long, empty driveway. Then even that sound slipped away, and I was back again in the past, lost in my father's words.

> Will Collington was never Young Will again after Ellen's body was found. He became a man overnight and a sad and sober one, wracked with guilt at the age of 22.
>
> He had his son christened by the new minister in the empty church on a Sunday afternoon, not at morning worship, to spare his mother who was still ashamed of the cloud on the child's birth. He named the baby Benjamin Henry Collington, not wanting to impose a William Henry Collington III on an unwilling grandfather. He chose the name Benjamin from the Bible, and in some way was comforted. That other Benjamin was the youngest son of Isaac, was his father's favorite because Isaac had loved Benjamin's mother, who died

in childbirth.

Hannah was an excellent nurse, and Will made the toddler his daily companion on the farm. Little Benjamin was a beguiling child, sturdy and bright, and he began to warm the cold, unwilling hearts of his grandparents.

My hand flew to my heart. This was my own child's namesake. Born centuries apart yet so alike. I felt the past and present merge, woven together by my father's loving hand. I burned to know more.

Then, one clear, cloudless day in 1774, when he was not yet four, Little Ben stood with his grandfather at the edge of the lawn looking across the bay at a gleam of fire and smudge of smoke that seemed to be rising from a brig anchored off Annapolis. Ben's pa, Young Will, and Mercy, and Grandmother Collington came and watched, too.

Here was history, like a script, seen through my father's imaginative lens.

William Collington said solemnly, "Well, it's come to this then." His wife put her hand to her throat. "It frightens me, William," she said, "if that is truly Mr. Anthony Stewart burning his own ship."

"With 2,000 pounds of tea aboard," said Young Will. "What a bonfire. That'll show King George and all his Tories we are not about to pay his import taxes here in Maryland any more than they are in Boston."

"I understand that a vote was taken in a public meeting that only the tea was to be burned," worried the elder Collington. "Feeling must be running dangerously high."

"I used to wish you'd name a ship after me, Father," said Mercy, "like Mr. Stewart did for his daughter, Peggy. Sometimes I used to think how it would sound. The Mercy Collington. I wonder if Peggy Stewart is somewhere watching while her ship burns."

Young Will lifted little Benjamin up on his shoulders and gripped his hands. The whole family drew in closer together. They stood in shock and fear, watching the distant plumes of ominous smoke.

Shock and fear, I thought. I live with both. I shuddered, hugged my arms to my chest, fingers creeping to my newly healed forearms out of habit. I pictured flames leaping from a boat in the bay.

Feelings did indeed run dangerously higher and higher. In July of the next year, 1775, the Maryland Convention ordered that all able-bodied Freemen between the ages of 16 and 50 should enroll in a company of militia. Young Will enlisted in an independent company of the Continental Army made up largely of men from the Eastern Shore and his own island. Some of them he had grown up with, including his old friend, Richard Gray.

The Kent Islanders were anxious. There they sat on their water-surrounded stage, vulnerable to attack. Lord Dunsmore's pro-British fleet was in the lower Chesapeake. It was rumored that the British might invade the Eastern Shore where there were many Tory sympathizers and necessary provisions.

Will's new company and local militia, untrained boys readier to be sailors than soldiers, were in need of everything: weapons, food, water, clothing, housing. Blount's tobacco warehouse on a wide, navigable creek that wound through Great Neck Plantation, was quickly converted into quarters.

At Bay House, though daily household chores and work in the corn and tobacco fields went on, everyone waited with a feeling of mounting crisis. Nothing mattered greater than shreds of news passed from watermen just off their ships, or from neighboring planters on horseback.

"Where is my Pa?" Little Benjamin asked, over and over.

Benjie's voice, my little Benjamin's voice, echoed, trembling, in my head. "Why did Daddy try to hurt us, Mommy?" The memory tore at my heart, but I brushed tears from my eyes and read on.

"He's not far away," said his grandfather. "He'll be home soon. Any day, now, you'll see him riding up the lane on Chesty."

He was wrong.

In July of the next year, 1776, some gentlemen in Philadelphia signed a document that made a new version of the old struggle for dominion over the land inevitable.

Shortly afterward, a group of transport ships surged past the western shore of Kent Island and Bay House in full sail. The Collingtons saw the ships. But they did not know the Independent Company had been ordered to leave in haste, to be transported to the Head of Elk at the northern end of the Bay, to disembark and begin marching north to join General

George Washington's forces.

There was a long, agonizing period of waiting at Bay House. No word from Will, though the islanders soon knew that his company had departed. No shiny haired, sturdy young man came riding between the gateposts and up the lane.

Months later, the family heard the story of the Battle of Long Island, where two hundred fifty outnumbered Maryland men attacked the advancing British again and again, until the rest of Washington's army escaped in fog across a swamp. Out of the 250, only nine made it back to the American line. Young Will Collington was not among them.

It was Richard Gray who came, at last, to tell how bravely Will died. Richard brought two important documents. One was a citation from Major Mordecai Gist, himself, who had commanded the Maryland men in their forever-famous charge. The other was a letter, old and tattered, but still legible, which Will had asked his friend Richard to deliver, in case he reached home before Will did.

The elder William Collington took the letter with unsteady fingers and read it aloud to his wife, whose tearstained face crumpled in grief.

I tucked up my legs, sank deeper into the cushions, held my breath and turned the page.

17

The letter was written on a long strip of rag-edged paper. It began in Will's careful penmanship that was somehow still like that of a young schoolboy.

Dear Mother and Father,

I must tell you a remarkable truth and please believe me. I know you did not believe me in the past, for which I am to blame. I did not tell you when I first loved Ellen, or that we would have a child, because I knew you would not approve. But we were married, under God, as I told you, by the Reverend Russell Witherspoon.

I know now why the Marriage Book and the other books were missing, because tonight, while I was here in this barracks where I've come so often in the past to unload our tobacco, it seemed to me that I witnessed a miracle. I was leaning against an old hogshead, just waiting with nothing to take up the time, thinking about all of you, and my little Benjamin, and how things were coming on the farm. Most of the good barrels have been used and cleared out of here to make room, but a few older ones were too rotted out to bother with, I suppose, and just standing about holding rubbish. The ones I leaned against gave way, splitting wide open. I found myself falling backward into a crashing of old books and loose pages that made me sneeze. To my astonishment, there were those very missing books, some of them falling apart, with J. Russell Witherspoon, writ big, in his hand as I remember it, in the front of some of them.

I could see in my mind the parlor of the parsonage that night in spring as I stood there with Ellen holding tight onto my hand. She was small and shy, you know, but she was brave. She was part like us and part like the Matapeakes and the two together made her prettier than any other girl I ever saw, and something more. I just cannot find the words to write. I long so much for you to understand. Anyway, I remembered that small parlor the night the Reverend Witherspoon married us and all the crates and tobacco barrels standing there. It came to me like a thunder bolt. The books must have been packed up in one of those hogsheads, after the Reverend left, and sent off by mistake to the warehouse. So, I lit a candle, opened and turned over each one, with my hands shaking. The good Lord did reward and answer my endless prayer. I found the Marriage Book, with my own name and Ellen Smalldeer's writ there as I had taught her.

I was on my knees, scrambling about. The fellows here must have wondered what I was doing, but I *stayed on my knees and thanked God. If only I could ride home, right now, to show you, but we have orders not to leave the barracks.*

Here the careful writing changed to a slanting scrawl.

Time short now. Captain just reported. Rounded us all up we embark in the morning to catch up with General Washington. My beloved parents no choice but to go. Continental army needs reinforcements. I long to make you proud of me.

Sending Elijah from Great Neck to leave this precious book in the special place where this true story began, 'til I can come home and show it to you and see your happy faces for myself. Please believe me and forgive me and believe that I am always,

Your loving son,

Will

Tell Benjamin his Pa sends love.

I glanced from the letter through the window to the empty lane. Tears ran down my cheeks. I wiped them away with the palms of my hands and went back to reading my father's journal.

Young Will's "remarkable truth" remained unproven because the "special place" that held the "precious book" was never discovered. Yet now, six generations later, there is still the unmistakable ring of truth in Will's words.

William Collington believed his son at last, too late. He started a search that has continued through two centuries. Where was that special place?

Will's father rode immediately to find Elijah. What he found was disappointment and frustration. Old Elijah did not remember taking books to any special place. The old man did not remember anything, even his own name.

Perhaps the book had been moved to the old parsonage where the marriage was said to have happened. That building was searched, and the shed behind it, but nothing was found.

Letters were sent to the Reverend Witherspoon in London, but those letters were unanswered. The new minister was of the opinion that Witherspoon had retired and moved to the north of England.

The church was searched, Bay House itself, even the woods outside the gate where the empty bark huts of the Matapeakes still stood. The book was not recovered.

William, Will's father, rode back to the tobacco warehouse and found it bustling with soldiers in training. All the rotting hogsheads had long since been burned. Nobody remembered seeing any old books. One farmer who lived nearby said he saw a peddler driving around with a wagon full of junk, but another farmer said his friend had been drinking too much of late and his word should not be counted. If Will's miracle did happen, it was a tantalizing, inconclusive one.

The years wore on. Benjamin remained with his grandparents at Bay House, fished, farmed, loved the land,

> and grew into his father's place in his grandpa's heart. Mercy Collington, her proud mother's favorite, married a planter from Virginia and moved across the bay, producing a trio of tow-headed little boys, legal heirs to their grandfather's estate. Hence the strange will that William Collington made in his old age.
>
> Benjamin married a strong-minded girl from Talbot County who was not put off by the cloud on her husband's birth or strange tales of a gentle ghost at Bay House.

There followed in this journal a scholarly genealogy showing the descendants of Benjamin Collington and those of Mercy Collington Cross. I skimmed the names until I finished the list. When my eyes caught the next paragraph I shot forward in my seat.

> It was not until after the War Between the States that the mutual ownership of Bay House was contested, and the classic struggle began again.
>
> Mercy's children were not interested, after all, in the provincial farm in the middle of the Chesapeake Bay where the land was no longer so productive for the growing of tobacco. They established, or married into, plantations of their own in the South. Then came the Civil War and everything changed. Sons and husbands died and land was lost.
>
> One great-granddaughter, Mercy Collington Buford, survived with her youngest son to come back and claim their inheritance. This event occurred in 1871. Then that son died, leaving Mercy without an heir.

Now this account must take a more personal tone if it is to be a true history of Bay House, the conflicts in and around it.

The Buford descendants, according to William Collington's wishes, were the owners. The Collington descendants had the right to live in the house and use the land. Unless my ancestor Benjamin Henry's legitimacy was resolved and ownership reverted to him.

My head spun, my vision blurred from too many words. Bufords. Collingtons. William's threats. My father's truths. The secrets swirled around me, within me, were a part of me. I longed to push up from the leather, bang out through the back door and stand in the sun. I rubbed my weary eyes and kept reading.

When I was 15, I realized I was considered a poor relation at Bay House. I didn't care. I knew I belonged there. It was my side of the family who had remained, cared for the house, worked the land, kept up the boats and the constantly eroding bulkhead. We had always lived in that big house in a mixed generation family group, as they did in the old days.

It was my Collington grandmother who gave me Young Will's letter and told me about his remarkable truth and all the rest of the story. She was my source of strength when my parents died. My Aunt and Uncle Buford were good to me in their way, though they were busy with their social life. They were glad to let me manage the farm by the time I was out of school, and I loved that. And then I met Fran.

This was a jolt back to the present. My mother, Fran. My dream, the three of us walking on the sand in front of Bay House. Was I finally going to find out what happened? Faces floated before me … who held the answer? William, Harriet, Peter, Benjie? I looked at the clock, hating to tear myself away. I would phone S.J. and beg for more time.

She answered after the first ring. "Don't worry. Benjie's right as rain. We just came in for cupcakes and he's covered in chocolate. Just walk down when you're done."

I was already back in the past, longing for the truth about my mother. My usually reticent father went on.

> Fran was the most beautiful young woman that could have been created. As perfect in every physical detail as a young, fair-haired goddess. Also possessing a warmth of gaiety, charm, and a certain self-assurance that magnetized all of us lesser mortals into helpless followers. She came from New York to visit friends on the island and all of us young people here, who were well-locked into our own small, not too exciting circle, were blinded by her presence.
>
> I loved her right away and I knew it. What staggered me was that she loved me, too. We were married after knowing each other only two months, without a lot of fuss, which I found out later was not like Fran and had not pleased her wealthy family. We were in love that summer. We thought of nothing except each other.
>
> Fran simply stayed with me at Bay House. I never doubted that she felt the same way about the place that I did. I

fully expected to live happily ever after right there in that beautiful spot. When our daughter, Abigail, was born, my cup of joy brimmed over. My little Abby-girl was the image of her mother except that, although she had Fran's blue eyes, her hair was black, like mine. Then one evening I came in from the farm's twilight to find Fran packing. Abby, about four years old at the time, was slumped and sobbing on the poster bed, watching her mother, crying tears which streamed down her little face.

To repeat here, word for word, the conversation that ensued, would be unnecessarily personal and painful. It may suffice to say that it centered around the word, B.A.S.T.A.R.D. Spelled out so that the word need not be said in our daughter's hearing.

I should have anticipated gossip reaching Fran. Scandal, even old scandal, lingers like the sour scent of mildew in a closed and empty room.

She naturally assumed I was the young scion of the illustrious Collington-Buford family, future heir to the estate. God knows, and I say it reverently, I did not deliberately deceive her. I didn't think my legal status mattered, or my heredity, or old and outworn prejudice. And then, of course, I believed in Young Will Collington's remarkable unprovable truth.

It was not that Fran didn't love me. Loving was not the issue. The fact was she couldn't exist anywhere in what she considered to be second-class status.

We went back to New York to live. Fran will never return to Kent Island. She wants our daughter to have the past of Bay House removed from her life as if it never existed. What I want for my daughter is proof of that remarkable truth, so that she will someday come into what is rightfully her own. This is my dream, and the reason I am putting this tale down on paper. For Abby.

Somewhere, there may still exist that special place where Will Collington left the *Marriage Book.* Where? In what condition could a book be after 200 years? These are questions I have pursued for the past five years and which I will continue to pursue while I have life and breath.

According to the experts at the Rare Book Room in the Library of Congress in Washington, D.C., books do last, sometimes for centuries if they are kept airtight and dry. They're not necessarily affected by heat and cold. For one thing, the paper was made from rag bond at first, not from wood pulp, as it is today.

I have been heartened, from time to time, by reading bits of information here and there about old books that have turned up in unlikely places.

Several years ago I was reading a child's book about Maryland history, wondering whether it was too soon to start telling my Abby-girl about the heritage of her birthplace, when I came across a short paragraph describing letters from Leonard Calvert, the first Governor of Maryland, to his brother, Cecilius, in London. Letters in which the problems of

William Claiborne were undoubtedly mentioned.

"For a long time, nothing was known of these letters," I am quoting directly, "but a few years ago they were discovered packed away in an old chest in the home of an English gentleman. For more than 200 years they had lain there forgotten."

My heart hammered when I read this, I remember. Old letters that had survived for 200 years! It was not impossible, then, that the *Marriage Book* could have survived.

I began writing to second hand stores in Baltimore and Annapolis and places on Maryland's Eastern Shore. I was rewarded. Last April I received a package from Annapolis that contained a tattered, somewhat disintegrated but once elegant leatherbound copy of Shakespeare's *The Tempest*. It was worth every cent of the high price I paid for it. There was a faded amber signature, perfectly legible, on the flyleaf in an opulent old script that dated it unmistakably: J. Russell Witherspoon.

How did the book get to Annapolis? Were there other volumes also found and sold or given away? Could Will never have sent the *Marriage Book* to that special place, as he intended? Could it have disappeared with the other books? Could it turn up some day in a dingy bookstore, in a library, an old church, a private antique collection? Is it still somewhere back on Kent Island? One day I will go home again and continue the search.

The journal stopped. That was all. My head spun with the questions, the legends, the people who fired my father's imagination and fueled his endless search. I had seldom felt closer to him, even when he was alive. I closed my eyes and rested my head on the back of the couch.

The stillness of that Saturday morning was suddenly shattered. A child's voice was screaming, "Missus Wells, Missus Wells." Bolting upright, I rushed to the windows. Jess Tomison, red-faced, wailing, was tearing up the lane. I knew something had happened to Benjie.

18

Dear God, let him be alive. I ran down the driveway. I saw Benjie sprawled on the ground behind the shattered gatepost and the tractor's huge black wheels. Josh was kneeling beside him.

I bent over the small still body of my son. His eyes were closed. His face was the color of the concrete bits strewn about, but he was breathing. I tasted my own tears as I felt for the pulse in his narrow wrist.

Josh was sobbing, gulping air while trying to speak, his face a mask of misery. "I'm sorry, Missus Wells. So sorry. We were just turnin' around. He wanted to ride on the back."

People were crowding us. S.J. was there now, and Noah, and the other children. S.J. took my hands. She was panting. "I phoned Dr. Sommerville. Carpenter is on call. He's on the way. He says don't move Benjie. He's sending an ambulance."

All the children were crying now. "You kids shut up. Get back from here. Give this boy some air." It was Noah, scowling as always, skinny arms waving and shooing the kids away. In an instant the children quieted and moved back.

Noah's shaggy white head brushed mine as he crouched beside me, very gently fingering Benjie's neck. Fear lurched through my body. Did he think his neck was broken?

"Oh, no." I shook my own head.

Noah stood up. For the first time those fierce brown eyes looked into mine with kindness. "I don't feel trouble there. The boy'll come 'round. You watch." But Benjie's eyes did not open.

From far off, down the narrow road from town, came the faint wail of a siren. The ambulance. We waited, a group of statues, for what seemed an endless time, while the sound of the siren grew louder. Then the ambulance was there in billows of dust and slamming doors. With it the blunt Doctor Carpenter, spouting the word concussion. Medics lifted Benjie onto a stretcher and into the back. The doctor sprang in behind, fingers clamped to Benjie's thin little wrist.

I climbed in beside my child. Gripped his free hand as we started the ride back down the road and through strange country I didn't see. Everything seemed unreal. I could only focus on Benjie's closed eyes in his small, gray face, under that tousle of silky hair.

Open your eyes, Benj, I pleaded in silence. But he did not. "Please open your eyes." I must have said it out loud that time.

"Mrs. Wells. Mrs. Wells." I jumped.

It was Dr. Carpenter, abrasive as ever, his stethoscope to Benjie's chest. "Mrs. Wells, I don't think your son hit his head on the bricks of that post. There would be an obvious injury. Much more swelling. Contusions. More bleeding. His vital signs are good. I think his head hit the ground when he fell off the tractor. This could be a relatively mild concussion."

I stared at him. And it could not be, I thought. *If only I had gotten to Benjie sooner. I would have ordered him to stay off the tractor. I hung my head in misery. This was my fault. My fault. My fault.* Trees passed the ambulance window in a blur. All I could hear was the siren's scream.

"Mrs. Wells." The doctor's voice seemed to come from far away. "We're here. This is the Emergency entrance of Stevensville Hospital. They'll be taking Benjie for x-rays right away."

I stayed with Benjie every minute I could, except when they wheeled him off down a long narrow hallway.

Minutes dragged by, flashed forward. I remember signing papers, steel elevator doors, then Benjie and I were in a room on an upper floor. A curtain hung between us and an empty bed.

Benjie still had not opened his eyes. A needle was taped to that little wrist and a tube led to the bag of intravenous fluids that hung by his head. Benjie lay sleeping. Too silent, too still. *Open your eyes, sweetie. Please, open your eyes.*

"Mrs. Wells. Mrs. Wells." It was the doctor, interrupting my prayers.

"What?" I spat out the word. I was furious at the world and rudeness was all I could produce.

"I'll be back. I have some other patients to see. I've been trying to tell you, Benjie's x-rays showed what we hoped. A blow, not a fracture."

So, a blow to a child's head is good news? "What? Then, he will be all right?"

"You're going to have to be patient. It may take some time and I can't promise, but there doesn't seem to be any internal bleeding and all his vitals are good. He'll probably be fine."

"Probably? Oh, just probably?"

He came closer and took me by the shoulders. I flinched at his touch. He flushed and dropped his hands but looked at me with steady confidence. "Think positive. Talk to your son. It may help him. I'll be back."

I was left alone with Benjie. Two echoing words were all that made sense. Help him, help him. Anger melted into acceptance. Acceptance into reality. I was his mother, on my own, caring for my child. And I would be strong.

Nurses came and went. A different doctor appeared, rattled off questions and checked Benjie's IV. And I talked. Oh, yes, I talked.

"Benjie, I'm right here. Benj. It's Mommy. You're in a nice, clean bed in the hospital and you're going to wake up any minute now and you'll see me sitting right here smiling at you and you'll say, "Hi, Mommy," and maybe tomorrow morning we'll go home, and I'll make happy-face pancakes."

I rambled on and on. Choked back tears and uttered nonsense, told stories, and watched my sleeping child. When did he lose his baby chubbiness, the dimples in his hands, and become a skinny little boy?

"Benjie, it's time to wake up now." I tried to sound stern. Felt ridiculous and apologized to thin air. I had no idea how long we had been there. A lamp was on. Darkness cloaked the window from outside.

A patient in the other bed behind the curtain coughed and let out a soft moan. It sounded like a young man. When did he arrive? Nurses bustled in and out. I did not want to disturb whoever was there, but I was afraid to stop talking.

I held Benjie's hand, kissed his forehead, whispered against his cheek. Felt love and strength flow between us. Everything else was endless and still. Time stopped. The only breaks were the visits of the vigilantes in their white uniforms. Each time I implored them for signs of improvement.

"Nothing negative, dear. Benjie's just the same." Then, again, endless stillness.

At some point, the heavy door swished open once more. I looked up, expecting nurse Nothing Negative. Dr. Carpenter brushed aside the curtain and stood in silence observing Benjie and me. He held a paper bag.

I moved from the chair where I was sitting to give him room.

He side-stepped along the bed and bent over Benjie. Then, straightening, he tried to hand me the bag. "You might as well eat something," he said. He laid the bag on the tray at the foot of the bed.

"Oh, I couldn't."

"But you should. It's 2:00 a.m." He pulled out a clear-wrapped sandwich stamped Ham and Cheese, and a lidded cup with the scent of coffee. I realized I needed that coffee. My fingers shook as I started to take the top off the cup and stir in sugar and creamer.

The doctor touched my arm. Not the medical probing I felt as his patient. This time, I felt a soft tenderness, a soothing comfort. Surprised, I looked at him. He pointed toward the bed.

"Mommy," said Benjie.

I rushed around to the opposite side, bumping the table, almost spilling the cup.

"Mommy, I'm hungry." Benjie rubbed his eyes, peered around the room, gave a little kick under his starched white covers. The band constricting my heart broke free and with it the tears I was holding back.

"I think maybe we can find this boy some ice cream somewhere," said Dr. Carpenter. "And I think," he said, handing me the coffee, "you're a very brave woman." He smiled deep into my eyes. I could not look away. He brushed at my tears with a lingering touch. *Not like a doctor. Like a man.* The rush of warmth that traveled up my neck had nothing to do with coffee.

19

I leaned my face into the early morning sunshine streaming through the window. I imagined the air would smell sweet, newly washed by the gentle breeze fluttering the leaves and blossoms in the parking lot below. Cars glinted red and green and blue and silver in the sunlight. I realized I was ready for breakfast as I turned back to gaze at my son.

"Nothing negative," Nurse Harrison said. She checked his IV and gave his shoulder an encouraging pat. "You'll probably be getting rid of this thing as soon as the doctor comes. We'll just keep it in a little longer, so you won't jump up and run away." Benjie rewarded her with a little giggle.

I felt a rush of love for this good, kind woman, as I did for all of life at the moment. My son was alive. Awake. Laughing. And the doctor would be coming soon to send us home. A familiar melody lilted within me.

> *Morning has broken like the first morning.*
> *Blackbird has spoken like the first bird.*

I could have hummed out loud or burst into song.

"I'm going off my shift now, Mrs. Wells. Good luck. Oh, by the way, your relatives will be coming up soon. I hear they've been downstairs storming the office for quite a while."

"Thank you," I said. "Benjie and I could never thank you enough." She waved her hand and disappeared behind the curtain.

William and Harriet. I had not given them a single thought.

I smoothed Benjie's covers and cleared an untouched cup of broth from his tray. I heard clinking as a breakfast cart rolled by in the hall, sending in whiffs of toast and coffee. But I was not as hungry as I thought.

A new nurse from the morning shift came, checked Benjie and stepped around the curtain. She spoke cheerfully to the young male patient, David, as he announced yesterday in a glum voice. Beyond simple introductions we had no further conversation. Now he talked in clear, rapid spurts, which made me think his condition, whatever it was, had improved. I was glad. This should be a day of happiness for everyone.

The door swished open again. "Oh, excuse us," I heard Harriet say to David.

"Over here." William, of course, commanding as ever. He burst around the curtain with his lithe, arrogant stride, hurried to the bed and dropped down beside Benjie. "Sprout," he said. "My little Sprout."

Harriet followed. Her eyes filled with tears as she watched William frown, trace the IV tube to the needle still taped into Benjie's wrist. She moved to the other side of the bed and took Benjie's hand.

"They won't let me have anything to eat," Benjie said. "I want a popsicle." Harriet clapped her hand to her mouth, laughed, and cried some more.

"Well, Sprout, we'll have to see about that," William said in his teasing way. Then he turned to me, folded into my chair in the corner. His eyes bored into mine with a sudden fury I could feel across the room. I was unprepared for the venom in his voice.

"They wouldn't let us up here. They wouldn't let us call the room last night when we got home. Said the switchboard was closed. Why didn't you contact us? You could have called, you know." His fist slammed the tray table. "And why did you let this child stand on a moving tractor? What kind of a mother are you?"

I felt myself shrink farther back into the corner, taking on my load of guilt.

"William, darling," said Harriet, "there's another patient here, remember?" She spoke as if choosing each word with great care. "And Abby looks as if she's been through a terrible night. Can't we talk later?"

William ducked his head, long fingers massaging his temples. When he looked up the anger was gone, his eyes were blank. His expression softened as if he was seeing me for the first time.

"Why don't you go and freshen up, Abby?" Harriet said. "We'll stay with Benjie while you take a break."

I didn't want to leave Benjie at all but realized I must look frightful. I knew all color was drained from my face. "I'll do that, thank you. I'm sorry I didn't think to call. I'll be right back, sweetie," I said, and blew Benjie a kiss.

In the haven of the women's restroom down the hall I tried to compose myself. My hands shook as I washed my face, combed my hair, put on lipstick from my handbag. I found a vending machine, downed a cup of black coffee, and tried to think.

William's eyes. They were as changeable as the bay itself. No matter.

My job was caring for my child.

When I hurried back to the room again, Harriet and William were stationed in the hall. William was fuming and pacing.

"Peter Carpenter is in with Benjie. I told the guy we'd like to bring in our own physician, Dr. Sommerville, for an opinion. But he says Doc's out of town. So, I guess we're stuck with this ... substitute. I sure as hell hope he knows what he's doing."

"He is abrasive," said Harriet, "but I remember someone telling me just recently that he relates to children even though he antagonizes their parents."

Peter stepped out of the room. There was a strained silence. I forced myself to cover it, as my mother would have done, with politeness. "Dr. Carpenter, these are my cousins, Mr. and Mrs. Buford."

Harriet gave him a tight smile. "Indeed. We meet at last. How is our little boy?"

"Benjie suffered a mild concussion, not a fracture." Peter did not blink. His voice was icy. "He seems fully recovered now, but we'll have to be sure there aren't any complications. He'll have to stay another 24 hours and remain quiet. No visitors." He nodded his head toward me. "His mother should stay. No one else."

My heart sank to think of another night imprisoned in that chair.

"Listen here." William's voice exploded. "It's extremely urgent we get them both out of this hospital. Now. There are personal reasons. We can hire a private ambulance to take them back to Bay House and keep

Benjie just as quiet at home. You could come to see him there just as well as here, couldn't you? Of course, the fee wouldn't be any problem."

Peter's face had the look of carved stone. "If Benjie is my patient until Dr. Sommerville returns, he stays in the hospital for 24 hours. Then I'll make a final diagnosis and a decision about his release. Excuse me." He turned and stormed down the hall.

Harriet shrugged. "He is arrogant, but he's probably a good doctor or Sommerville wouldn't trust him. William, it's only one more day. Benjie's father is not going to find him in such a short time. The accident just happened yesterday morning."

I could only stare at them. I never dreamed of Matt finding us here. My only thoughts were about Benjie. The corridor that seemed sheltering suddenly became dark and hostile. But of course, we had to stay. I felt faint but managed to speak. "I won't leave Benjie for a second."

"But you were up all night, Abigail," said Harriet.

"I dozed in the chair toward morning, after Benjie woke up. I was so relieved. I can nap there again if I get sleepy. The nurses are very kind, they keep checking. And Dr. Carpenter," I had to say this, "is a good doctor, William. He was here off and on all night. He is impossibly blunt a lot of the time, but I think he does care about us. About Benjie, I mean." *In the light of day, I had to wonder about the us, even though he had touched my cheek and defended me from William and Harriet's intrusion.*

"Abby, child, you are so naive." The hot steel melted from William's eyes. He looked at me with tenderness. "I wish I could take you both home right now."

"I wish I could stay here," said Harriet, "and spell you, but I simply cannot." She reached for her purse and slung it onto her shoulder. "I'm pushed to the wall with the upcoming bazaar and tour of Bay House. I need to be home to receive all the antiques for sale being delivered to the stable for the next three weeks. My word, I can't believe that's all the time we have left. And I must find a bricklayer to repair that post."

"Oh, Harriet, I'm so terribly sorry," I began. "I was ..."

She waved her hand to silence me. "No need, dear. I shouldn't have brought it up now. Forget the post. The big thing is for Benjie to get well. William, we're going to tell him goodbye now." They stood arm in arm at the end of the bed.

"Sprout, when you get home, I'm going to have a surprise for you," William said. He raised his arm and saluted. "You've earned it, and you're going to love it. Do everything Mommy says and you'll be home tomorrow." Benjie's eyes were huge and happy.

After William and Harriet left, I studied those eyes again. The pupils were not dilated. Thank God.

The day dragged on with a syrupy contentedness. I felt exposed and vulnerable in the hall, but our hidden half of that room behind the curtain was a cocoon. Sometimes I read to Benjie or told stories. We played tic-tac-toe, or he slept. Once in a while, I dozed. Nurses came and went. The house doctor stopped in. The IV was removed.

David had a visit from his parents. They sounded anxious, bossy, loving, and normal. *Ten years from now, this could have been Matt and me and Benjie. In another life. But never, now. Never ever to be again.*

At lunchtime Benjie ate chicken noodle soup, crackers and cherry Jell-O squares he jiggled on his spoon. I was served a tray ordered by the Bufords. Sliced roast beef with gravy, mashed potatoes, hospital peas and carrots and a chocolate sundae. No meal in one of New York's finest bistros could have tasted better.

At 4:00, Peter Carpenter checked back, the floor nurses clustered behind. He examined Benjie, his expression fixed and studious behind his horn-rimmed glasses. "You're looking good, young man," he said. "You've been a fine patient. I want you to keep it up. Stay quiet. You're going to get tired of this pretty soon and you're going to want to get up and start running around. But you can't do that if you want to get well. OK?"

"OK." Benjie wrinkled his nose and slid down deeper into the covers.

When the nurses left, Peter turned to me. "So," he said, "have you read *The Forces of Bay House*?"

This man was always thrusting at me with the unexpected. I was about to make an emotional speech of thanks.

"Have I what?"

"Your father's journal. You must have read it by now."

"I can't bear to think about it."

Peter's hands flew open. "Why not?"

"Because I was reading it when this happened to Benjie. He was at the Tomisons' playing with the children. I wasn't watching him."

“Well, what is he supposed to do? Never go out and play with kids? Stay locked up with you 24 hours a day?”

“Please,” I said, staring out the window. “I can’t talk about it.”

He dropped his hands. “Abby Wells,” he said, “I read it too, you know. Why do you think I was in the library that night, back in the stacks where you were?”

“You read it?” I whirled to look at him.

“I’m doing some moonlighting, research on Indian tribes of Tidewater Maryland and Virginia. I’m trying to find out how they survived here in the wilderness and along the bay and the creeks before the settlers came and brought the blessings of civilization. Like measles and typhoid and dysentery and whiskey.” His dark eyes turned darker, his lips tightened, pulling down at the corners. “Do you know why so many colonists died of malaria and the Indians didn’t? Do you know who taught us to plant and harvest corn?”

Peter didn’t expect answers to these questions, since he spat them out faster than I could reply. I felt his passion for the same piece of the past my father loved.

“It’s amazing how much information you can dig up here and there in bits and pieces. Those lost tribes, the Matapeakes, the Monoponsons, the ones your father wrote about and understood. They were highly civilized people in their way. Yet history gives them so little credit. But, listen, I haven’t got time for this now.”

I dropped my voice, sensing his frustration. “Peter. I saw what you wrote in the *Chronicle*. I saw your photo of that boy, your friend. His braid, the feathers, your tribute to his life and death. It was so sad. You must have been the same age."

He looked as if he might reach out to hold me. Instead, he stepped back and glanced at the boy in the bed. "I'll see you later, Benjie. Remember what I told you because I mean it."

"Abby. Come out in the hall for a minute," he said.

The hall did not look threatening with Peter there, straight and tall in his white coat, hornrims, stethoscope dangling from his broad shoulders. The nurses' station guarded one end. In the other direction it dead-ended in the sunny waiting room with lime green wicker furniture.

Peter stood facing me and seemed to deflate. His square shoulders drooped, his arms hung as if paralyzed. "Polio. He died of polio. We were twelve. My father was a doctor and even he couldn't save him. I still can't talk about it rationally."

I was about to start my speech of gratitude again. Now my heart flooded with sympathy as well. There was that moment, the night before, as Benjie opened his eyes, when the barrier between this man and me lifted. Now, standing so close to him I caught the scent of his aftershave, I was almost certain he was aware of the moment, too. He gazed at me softly, with no trace of his usual guarded glances. I wondered what he would say or do next.

"I just want to tell you," he murmured, "while those two Doberman Pincers aren't around, I think what your father believed about Bay House is true. You own half of it."

"What?" I was stunned, my tenderness turned to anger. "Are you talking about William and Harriet? Doberman Pincers? That's insulting. They've helped Benjie and me when they didn't have to. They're the only family I have." *I would banish every doubt about them and refuse to be disloyal. I pushed every clouded memory away.*

"I also wanted to tell you," he went on, ignoring my outburst, "I don't believe there's a chance in a million you can prove anything at this point or find that book. You must know it's too late for that. I wouldn't go back to Bay House if I were you, Abby." He looked down at his feet as if he wished they would carry him away. "You won't want to hear this either, but I think your so-called Cousin William is an arrogant ass, or worse. There's something wrong there, Abby. There's something more going on than just his protection from that SOB you're married to."

"Don't be ridiculous," I said. "Of course, I'm going back." *The man is impossible.*

"Won't you walk into my parlor said the spider to the fly?" He shot me a level look. Once again, I felt him judging me. Labeling me a helpless victim. He turned and stalked off toward the nurses' station. The remembered warmth from the moment in Benjie's room vaporized.

"You are totally …" I grasped for that one word he did not want to be called. "Totally unprofessional." I hurled it after him, so angry my voice quivered. I ran back behind the curtain, aghast that someone might have heard me.

Harriet popped in for a few moments that evening but did not linger. She brought changes of clothing and promised to pick Benjie and me up the next day at noon. We both assumed the doctor would dismiss Benjie in the morning. I thought she looked wan, not as fastidious as usual, which made her seem more human. William, she said, would be gone on one of his business trips and was counting on her to bring us safely home.

The early evening passed quickly. Benjie was allowed to get up and shuffle about the room. We could have wandered in the hall, but I was not about to come out of hiding and parade us up and down with the other ambulatory patients. At 8:00 Benjie protested going to bed, vowing he wasn't sleepy. He was out in 10 minutes. Heavenly, healthy Benjie.

The charge nurse offered me a cot in an empty room, but I stayed in my recliner dozing and waking. I watched the sleeping child, hugged my joy to myself, and tried to put all the crawling thoughts of guilt and anxiety out of my mind.

Sometime after midnight, I was awakened by a flurry of noise in the hall. Benjie slept on, but I sensed the nurses were dealing with an emergency. Soft, urgent voices, quick footsteps, the metallic clatter of stretcher wheels on the bare, polished floor. By the time quiet returned I was wide awake and sleep was impossible.

I stared at the walls of the dimly lit room and tried not to think. It must have been 45 minutes before I gave up, pulled aside my blanket, tucked in Benjie's covers, and tiptoed out. I would try to find something to read in the green wicker waiting room, then scurry back.

The area was bright but deserted and smelled of old cigarettes. The coffee maker was empty. I didn't dare take time to start a new pot. I looked for a magazine. Old and new, they were tumbled on the table where people had tossed them. One cover caught my attention because it looked familiar, though I couldn't think how. It showed a sprawling brick house half hidden by a canopy of trees. *Beautiful Homes*, a bit worn and thumb-marked now. Where did I see a copy of it brand new?

I started back down the hall with it clutched in my hands. Then it hit me. Of course. The day Benjie and I went fishing with William. We were huddled in the study, frightened and dejected, that Sunday morning in June. The magazine was strewn with others on the table.

I crept into Benjie's room. Settled back in my chair, draped the blanket over the lamp so I could distract myself reading until sleep came, and flipped pages without really seeing them.

Despite my noble speech about loyalty, I couldn't erase the memory of that horrifying island picnic, which I kept to myself. I did not want to think about William's mercurial eyes. Or Doberman Pincers, my son's rightful inheritance, finding another doctor. Or Matthew Wells.

Suddenly I found myself wide-eyed and sitting upright. I lifted the page closer to the light. The photo I was staring at looked so much like Bay House. It was an aerial view of a rose brick home, surrounding lands and outbuildings, bayfront, and creek. Amazingly similar. Too similar. It had to be a twin.

I read the bold print twice. It was for sale. For sale. There were the fields, the circular driveway, the flower beds surrounding it. The Tomisons' farmhouse, the barn and stable. The lane with its canopy of trees. Even the little cliff, and yes, I saw with shock and certainty, our dock and our beach. It was Bay House. On the market for a discreetly unlisted price. Described by a realtor down to the last dazzling detail.

"What are you doing inside on a day like this?" William had asked that Sunday morning. Then pulled the magazine from my hands and tossed it aside.

I thought nothing of it then, bedazzled by his bright and easy sunshine. What was the other ludicrous thing he said next? "Fair goes the wind for France, Lass, and we are off for Brittany." Yes, he said that. And poof. *Beautiful Homes* had disappeared. I did not sleep again that night, nor try to.

By the time an attendant brought Benjie's breakfast tray, I winnowed through my problems back to the major issue, my son's inheritance. Bay House was a magnet, and I was a small sliver of iron.

When Peter Carpenter arrived at 10:30, Benjie and I were both anxious to be on our way. His greeting was stiff, formal. My response was the same. I was not about to tell him I just discovered what everybody else on that small island must already know.

Peter examined Benjie with his usual creased brow and dark eyes flicking behind his hornrims. "OK, son," he said. "You can go now, with your mother. I want you to be quiet for about a week. And stay off tractors from now on." He did smile at the boy and gave me a few instructions.

"Thank you for helping Benjie, Dr. Carpenter," I said. He gave a curt nod and was gone. Benjie and I were free.

"Come on, Benj, let's get your clothes on. Aunt Harriet will be here at 12:00." I opened the suitcase Harriet brought and got out the small jeans and clean plaid shirt.

"William said I'm gonna get a surprise." Benjie was babbling. "What do you think it is?" One of the nurses sailed around the curtain, a brisk and cheery battleship in white.

"I hear you're going home, young man. You don't really want to leave us, do you? Mrs. Wells, you'll have to stop by the front desk and get release papers to be signed in the office downstairs before you go. And I believe there's a message for you."

My heart kicked up its beat. "Um, Benjie, get your shirt on. I'll be right back." *I hoped Harriet would not be delayed by one of the constant crises of the bazaar. I had to find out.* The nurse was happy to stay with Benjie while I ran downstairs.

"Oh yes, here it is," said the young aide at the reception desk. "Margaret took the message before she went off her shift. She said she didn't want to disturb you so early."

The slip of paper read: "Mr. Wells will be here at 11:30 to take his family home."

I gripped the counter to steady myself. The girl's large blue eyes swam in front of me like a fish's eyes in a tank. The nauseating, familiar rush of adrenaline shot through the pit of my stomach.

He was just a man, Matt Wells. Weak, selfish, alcoholic, sometimes vicious and brutal, but nevertheless, not a demon, just a man. And I was standing in broad daylight in the bustling lobby of a public hospital. Still, I whitened my knuckles at the edge of that counter until the world stopped weaving. Reason is one thing, but emotion, so very often, another.

I glanced at the clock on the wall. 11:00. "May I use your phone, please?"

"There's a booth right down the hall, Mrs. Wells."

"No, please. Couldn't I use this one? I haven't time."

"Well, go ahead then. Are you all right?"

I nodded, dialing Bay House. No answer. Harriet must have left.

I fought to keep my voice from shaking. "Are there, is there any taxi service in this town?"

"Yes, ma'am. Though they take ages to get here. Are you sure you're OK? Would you like to sit down?"

"An ambulance," I said. "Could I have an ambulance?"

Peter Carpenter entered the lobby from the far end of the corridor. The aide looked from me to him with alarm. "Doctor, could you come here a moment?" He walked to the desk, glanced at me without changing expression.

I handed him the note. He scanned it, raised his eyes to the ceiling and looked disgusted.

I was too frantic for pride. "Please, could you help to get an ambulance or borrow a car so Benjie and I can leave right now? Harriet isn't getting here until 12:00."

"You could tell him to get a lawyer, you know."

"Please, you just told me Benjie shouldn't be under any stress."

He shook his head. *I was obviously a hopeless, spineless imbecile.* "Would you call a wheelchair for Benjamin Wells," he said to the girl. Her eyes followed our exchange like someone watching a tennis match. "And see that he's brought straight down to the door."

Peter held out his glasses, squinted, rubbed each lens with his tie. "Abby. Get your things and meet me right here in ten minutes. I was just on my way back to the office. You can come with me." We drove away at 11:25, pulling out of the hospital parking lot just as I saw the old blue wagon roll in at the far end of the lot.

Benjie's high spirits filled the taut silence on the way back to town. He giggled. He jabbered. I kept looking behind to see if we were being followed. The road led between fields of corn and soybeans burnished with autumn sunlight, wooded stretches where the leaves were turning russet and gold. There were few other cars and no blue station wagon. Yet in the very ordinary daylight I could not stop trembling.

The car lurched to a halt. I twisted from the front seat to look out the rear window again. Benjie was in the back, but I could see above his head. "What is it?" I said. My heart raced, my palms began to sweat. "Please don't stop."

The expression on Benjie's face made me spin around. He was staring at something on the side of the road ahead, wide-eyed, mouth gaping. I glanced at Peter. His face wore the same rapt expression. They were both motionless, barely breathing.

Then I saw the two deer. They were poised in the grass along the side of the road just beyond a copse of pine trees. A doe and fawn, inert as statues. Heads held high, ears tilted forward. The golden tan of their hides blended into the sunny dappling of grass and trees.

From the opposite direction, approaching along the long flat road, barreled a black sedan. "Sit still," whispered Peter. "We don't want to scare them into running across the road."

"We can't let them," I said. Without thinking, I was out of the car racing toward the deer in the path of the oncoming car. The doe leaped with the most ravishing grace, hind legs soaring, and disappeared into the woods. Her young one followed in a flash of speed and beauty.

The driver of the black sedan, having missed seeing the deer, honked at me as if I had lost my senses, swerved around our car, and roared on by.

"Gosh, Mommy," said Benjie as I jumped back into the car. "You ran fast."

"Well, I'll be dammed," said Peter Carpenter.

I'm just as surprised as they are. I acted on sheer instinct. I didn't say much on the rest of the drive to Peter's office. Man and boy talked about the ways of the wild, deer in particular, and Bambi. I felt better than I had felt for a long time. I stopped trembling.

We reached Peter's building without further incident. Two patients were already waiting for the Doctor. Peter had left word at the hospital for Harriet to meet us in his waiting room. Benjie and I sat on the couch and looked at pictures labeled as a Navaho reservation in Arizona. *Now I knew this was where he grew up. Of course, I recognized his friend's young face. The smile, the braid, the feather.* No, the nurse had not seen Matt. But then, of course, she did not know what he looked like.

Benjie knelt on his chair and watched through the large window onto the street. "Aunt Harriet's here, Mom. Beat ya to the car." He ran to the door and was halfway down the sidewalk before I could grab his sleeve.

Harriet cast a solemn look at Benjie, ignoring me. "Young man. You may not run. Remember the doctor's orders. We're going to get you home and get you well, and that's final." Even Benjie rode back to Bay House without uttering a sound.

At last we reached our fortress on the third floor. Home. Sunlight flooded through the dormer, touching the wallpaper's faded cabbage roses with new bloom. Beyond the still-green lawn, the bay shimmered like blue silk. Two ships paraded up the channel. Smaller boats frisked nearer shore, bouncing over the swells made by the ships' wake, leaving frothy white Vs behind. A brown gull swooped past the window on his way to a perch on our roof.

Up through the resonant staircase, we could hear the house making its cozy, welcoming sounds. "I can't," I said out loud.

Benjie was already settled on my bed surrounded by toys. "Can't what, Mommy?"

"Can't believe you're home safe and sound." I leaned over and gave him a squeeze, but silently finished the sentence. *I can't let them sell it.*

20

"Benjie, please stop chattering, sweetie. I'm trying to think."

Harriet's brisk footsteps were climbing the stairs. No "Hoo-hoo, Abigail. Benjie, dear." Nothing but the relentless tread that made my heart beat louder with each approaching step.

Outside, the day held the bright warmth of late summer. Still, I shivered in my sweater, in our room high above the treetops. *Perhaps I had a premonition. It was as if something or someone was telling me everything I feared was converging upon me at once. It was like the children's game of hide-and-seek, when the one who is It, calls, "Ready or not, here I come." I was It, and I wasn't ready.*

"But William hasn't come home to give me my surprise." Benjie was already bored and beginning to whine.

Harriet leaned against the doorway. "Don't worry. He'll probably be along just when you don't expect him." She held a dish of chocolate ice cream, and a folded newspaper tucked under her arm.

"I know this is between meals but it's so hard for little boys to stay put all afternoon. I hope you don't mind." She handed Benjie the bowl, of course, without waiting to see if I did.

Freedom, Abby. He's your son. My inner battle cry sounded, but I did not protest out loud. This was not a matter of courage, or lack of it. Harriet's attitude toward Benjie moved me. Despite her cool self-possession, there was a tenderness when she touched him and a yearning softness in her eyes when she looked at him. Besides, I knew something more was coming. Here it was.

"How about saying thanks, Benj," I said.

"Yum. Thank you, Aunt Harriet." He dug in, the world's politest boy.

Harriet flashed Benjie a smile, then turned to me with a frosty stare. She tossed the newspaper onto the bed.

Bay House was front-page news. It featured a large color photograph of a familiar lane flanked with one tall brick gate post, another opposite, only half-standing, surrounded by a pile of broken bricks and concrete.

The caption underneath screamed out our whereabouts in bold letters. I glanced at her in dismay.

"So much," she said, "for secrecy."

> The venerable gate to Bay House, circa 1740, home of the Buford family, and originally, of the William Collingtons, was damaged in an accident on Saturday, which also injured Benjamin Wells, aged five, a guest.

A chill went through me. I looked up from the paper. I couldn't resist a New Yorker's sarcasm. "I see that the venerable gatepost was hotter news than not-so-venerable Benjie."

Harriet didn't appear amused.

"Of course, you know how upset I am about the post, and I intend to pay for the repairs, but it is kind of funny," I said.

"Read the rest of the article." Harriet's voice made me think of icicles.

> The accident was caused by children riding a farm tractor that went out of control and hit the post. The injured boy is recovering from a concussion at Stevensville Hospital. He is the son of Mrs. Matthew Wells of New York City, a relative of the Bufords. Mrs. Harriet Buford is currently serving as chairperson for the St. Mark's Episcopal Church "A Day on the Bay" Bazaar and House Tour.
>
> Bay House, located off Route 8, and its original gate posts, are among the few structures left standing on the island that date back as far as the 1740s and are on the National Historic Register.

I scanned back up to the color photo, studying the details I missed. The entrance to Bay House, with its proud sign hanging above the one remaining post. Our lane, the house, and the bay, blue and serene, in the background.

"After this," said Harriet, jabbing a finger at the article, "I doubt if a certain party would need any more information about your present address." She glanced at the child on the bed, slowing her words as if trying to choose the most damning ones. "But if he did, this is better than an engraved invitation."

I glanced at Benjie, too, and held up my hand to silence her.

"That's all I have to say," she said. "I've been saying the same thing all along. Grow up, Abigail. Face your problems. But not here. This ridiculous game, if that's what it is, has gone on long enough."

What about the game you're playing? I wanted to hurl out the words. Why didn't you tell me Bay House is for sale?

But Benjie was supposed to have healing time without stress.

"I have to get out to the stable," Harriet said. "People are starting to drop things off every day, and we're way behind in the cataloging and pricing. There's going to be a very public auction here, Abby. It's going to be a huge event, on the same day as the tour. The Open House. We should make enough money to start a fund for the new pipe organ the church needs so badly, as well as continue our mission projects. You have to accept the fact, this is not a place to hide anymore."

She started for the door, moving as she always did, gliding with that straight, taut carriage. She paused to send Benjie a flicker of a smile. "Fried chicken for dinner, Benjie," she said. "And a gingerbread man."

The woman was as changeable as the tides. And, lately, as unpredictable. We heard her on the stairs, and soon the front door opened, then closed.

"Mommy," said Benjie, "there's nothin' to do." I let out a huge breath, expecting him to ask about our hiding game.

"Why don't you play with your toy soldiers?"

"I already played with my toy soldiers."

"Well, put your puzzle together."

"That isn't any fun. I already know how it goes."

"Do something else then, please. I really have to think."

"Hey, how 'bout a fort? C'un I make a fort on your bed?"

"Great idea, Benj." My mind was far away. I plumped up my pillows, added an extra quilt from the closet. I think I would have let him cook hot dogs on my bed if I hadn't been afraid of the fire.

He made himself a tent and crawled under it with his soldiers and all the old cars and trucks and wagons.

Thank God. A little time to figure out what to do. Then, panic. The manuscript. The Forces of Bay House. I left it downstairs in plain sight when I bolted out to find Benjie lying on the ground, flung from the tractor. My heart began a frenzied beat. That was almost three days ago.

"Stay right where you are, son," I said. "I'll be right back." I flew down the steps from the third floor. Down to the second. Down to the first.

The front hall was quiet and mellow and beautiful as I rushed through it to the study. Sped to the couch. Spied the pages in their blue binder. They were there, just as I left them, though half hidden under several newspapers. Silly of me. Why was I worried they might not be?

I hurried back upstairs. Benjie was still in his tent, talking in his high little pretending voice. I sat down in the rocker and lost myself in those pages again. If there was any help for me it had to be here.

When the front door opened in the hall sometime later, I didn't hear the sound, but Benjie did. He sat up and kicked off the quilt, his eyes bright, expectant. "Maybe it's William."

William. I was not ready to cope with William. Footsteps pounded up toward us.

Then the doorway was filled with William, his whole face shining and brimming with delight. His hands were behind his back. "Surprise," he said. His booming voice sounded as excited as Benjie's did.

His arms came from behind him. In them was a sleeping puppy. A very small puppy with a stubby, baby-dog face, floppy ears and a coat of soft, curly, russet-brown hair.

Benjie gasped in pure, astonished joy. Then the puppy was in his lap, burrowing, wriggling and whimpering among the toys.

For a while, William and I could only smile and watch, like an ordinary fatuous couple, united by love for a child, and a puppy making a disaster of my bed. Except, we were not any kind of a couple.

"He's a Chesapeake Bay Retriever, of course. Finest dog in the world. And a purebred, just like you." William grinned and ruffled Benjie's hair. "This little guy's ten weeks old. I went and picked him out myself from all his brothers and sisters. I know a fella that breeds 'em. Went and got him and his papers and all this morning," said William.

I tried to collect myself. Tried to stop feeling giddy with the sudden splash of fun into the murky waters of my life. "Benjie, calm down. For your own sake and the puppy's. You have to remember he's only a baby." Benjie scratched the pup's round little belly and giggled as if it was his own being tickled.

"William, really, it's wonderful." *I meant to ask if he believed this unexpected gift would impress me. Or that I wouldn't see the strings attached. Instead, all I muttered was,* "It's so kind of you, but Benjie's supposed to be quiet."

"OK. We won't overdo it. I guess I better take him, Sprout. But he's your dog now, you know. I'm going to teach you to shoot someday, Benjie, and this little fella'll grow up big and strong and go hunting with us. These retrievers swim right out into the water and bring back your birds, while you're sitting there in the duck blind. I'll tell you about those later. Most importantly, what do you think we ought to name him?"

The sudden glory of being asked to name his own dog was almost too much for Benjie. He sat somber and still for a few moments as the puppy licked his face with a tiny pink tongue. "Is it OK if I think about it for a little bit?"

"Take all the time in the world, Sprout. He's yours."

"But we can't keep a puppy up here, William," I said. "He's not housebroken. I don't think …"

"Aunt Harriet would like it?" William finished my sentence. "You are one hundred percent correct. Noah's going to take care of him out back in the stable. In the old tack room. Or in the cottage back behind the cornfield, where he lives. He can stay in a crate in Noah's kitchen when winter comes and the nights get chilly. Besides, these dogs love cold weather. And Benjie can play with him outside as soon as he's well enough. You see, Mommy," he turned to me with that taunting grin, "I thought of everything."

"So, c'un I keep him?" Benjie's eyes were blue circles of anxiety, his little fingers lost in the puppy's soft fur.

No stress. William, what have you done? You've just handed me one more problem. A dog in a New York apartment, if Harriet is right? But you can't give a boy a puppy one minute, then take the puppy away.

"Of course, Benj," I said. "You can keep him as long as we're here. And then we'll see."

"But he's my dog, isn't he? Forever?"

Again, William has backed me into a corner. "All right. Yes. Forever." *What else can I say?*

Benjie sank back against the wreck of his fort, beaming. "I think his name is going to be Skipper."

"Skipper?" William and I repeated the word together.

"Well, Chesapeake is too long. And that other word, the kind of dog he is ..."

"Retriever," said William.

"Yeah. I couldn't remember. Ree-tree-ver. That's too long, too. And it kinda doesn't sound like a dog. But Skipper's a good name. We can call him that, easy. Here, Skipper. See?" The pup wiggled in Benjie's arms. "He already knows his name. I'm gonna call him Skipper 'cause that's what William is, mostly." Benjie looked up at William with shining eyes. "You know. Like a boat Captain. The man at the dock called you that. The day you rescued us. So, don't you think it's a good name, William?"

"Well, I'm honored, Sprout." He pulled his broad shoulders back and gave Benjie a crisp salute. "I think it's perfect," said William.

"So do I," I said.

We looked at each other. How could a five-year-old have come up with something so right? Or maybe so wrong.

"And now, little buddy," said William, "you're going to lie right there and have a nap, while I take Skipper out to Noah. You've had enough excitement for quite a while. And your mother's going downstairs with me for a few minutes because we have some things to talk over."

Benjie yawned, slumped into the pillows and rolled up in his covers. He looked exhausted. I leaned over, straightened the bed and kissed him.

William took the puppy in his arms and beckoned to me with his eyes. I followed him from the room, picking up *The Forces* in its blue binder as I went. Down the two flights of stairs, through the house and out to the terrace. The wind had changed. The sun began casting late afternoon shadows.

"Don't move, I'll be right back and tell you more about the dog," said William. "I'm taking him to Noah." *I did wonder about Noah sometimes. The loyal and secretive fellow who never seemed to leave the property. Now I knew why. He lived here.*

I stood waiting until William jogged back from the stable, breathless, and pointed to the sky. It had darkened to a smokier blue and clouds billowed across it like sails on a hard tack. There was a new nip in the air. The bay was restless.

I heard wild, stirring cries. A perfect *V* formation of geese winged its way below the clouds, followed by another, then another. The leader veered east and swooped lower. The others veered and swooped, following a pattern like aircraft on maneuvers until they were out of sight below the trees on the other side of our creek, where acres of corn fields lay in stubble.

"There'll be hundreds of them here soon. And swans. Flocks of wild, white swans drifting among geese and canvasbacks and mallards, back and forth along the shore, in the protected water. You won't believe how beautiful this place is in the winter."

So much for today. I sensed there would be no additional lecture about the care of canines. Again, I'd been tricked into being alone with William. It was deliberate. And intolerable. Now was my chance to turn the tables on him and demand the truth. Show him I wasn't afraid or fooled any longer.

I squared my shoulders and turned to face him. "William, how could you even think about selling Bay House?" There. I said it.

His green-blue eyes probed mine. "Because I didn't know about Benjie. Or you. It takes a lot of money to keep all of this going, Abby. You don't make it farming, not anymore. Harriet orchestrated the only practical solution."

I looked off toward the bay where gulls skimmed the shallows near the shore. The water was brown, cloudy. As low tide peeled it back, I saw the shifting sand underneath. The gulls were skimming and dipping, skimming and dipping.

"Why didn't you or Harriet tell me?"

"Come on, Abby. You weren't ready to hear the home you dreamed about all your life was for sale. You were scared out of your wits and you'd been through enough. All you wanted to do was hide. And I wanted to hide you. I had no intention of letting Matthew Wells get his hands on you, ever again. He has no right to consider himself your husband, or Benjie's father."

I made myself turn back to face him, to make myself say what I needed to say. I was still clutching the blue binder. I ran my thumb against its spine.

"I think it was more than that, William. I think you wanted to keep me in hiding so I wouldn't hear about the sale of the house until it was too late. You didn't want me to find my father's papers. Or realize Benjie and I have the right to live in Bay House as long as it stands. Even if we never find proof that we own half the property."

William dropped his hands to his waist and started to pace. I thought he was offended, but when he stopped, he was smiling. His eyes crinkled at the corners.

"You're wrong, Cousin Abigail. From the minute you and Benjie stepped off that pier in Annapolis into my boat, I knew what was going to happen. But I knew it was going to take some time until you could see it, too. So, I waited. Until now. I think you finally see what I see, and feel what I feel. You just won't let yourself admit it."

Through the house we heard the sharp slap of the screen door. "Hoo-hoo," trilled a woman's voice. "Hoo-hoo ... Harriet?" Footsteps tapped in the hall. "Oh, here she comes."

Another woman spoke. "She's on her way up from the stable. Maybe we should just wait here."

William grabbed my hand and pulled me along the edge of the terrace. I started to resist but knew I must prevent Harriet from catching the slightest hint of William's speech. Besides, the door of the Old Cabin was ajar and I wanted to see inside again. "Come see where the construction's started. I'm sure everybody heard the sawing yesterday."

We ducked inside, though he had to tug me into the gloom.

"Good God," he said. "Escape from the Hounds of Heaven. They'll be on our doorstep from now 'til the bazaar's over, and all in the name of the church."

"William, that's awful, and incredibly rude," I said. "I wish I could be free, and have a group of good friends, and be working out in the open for a cause. I'm so tired of hiding, William."

I felt more and more desolate as I spoke. Weary, lonely, chilled. The Old Cabin was much colder than the last time I was there, in the fullness of summer. The smell was danker. In the dim shadows I could see everything was just the same. Except where the carpenters had torn the loft flooring from the north side of the house. The door in the wall of the main house was completely exposed. What remained of the loft along the south wall was a sagging, narrow strip with no railing. The huge gaping fireplace was surrounded by stacks of jagged flagstone.

"Maybe you won't have to keep hiding too much longer. Now I'm going to finish making the speech I started weeks ago before we were so rudely interrupted." His voice was commanding, confident. "And you're going to listen."

"I'll go back to the beginning," he said. "When your father and gorgeous Fran shook the dust of this place off their feet, you were four years old. When I came home from school for the Christmas holidays that year, you were gone. I was half in love with your mother, like everyone else around here, and I was heartbroken. But I understood how she felt." *I couldn't fathom William having empathy for anyone, but I did not interrupt him.* "Nobody with any pride would hang on here because of a myth about an Indian girl, the will of a senile old man, and a tale about a missing marriage record. I mean, that's the stuff kids' mystery books are made of. *The Rover Boys and the Secret Panel, The Camp Fire Girls and the Moldy Old Trunk.*"

I didn't laugh, just gripped the *Forces* with my fingertips. "But, William, my father."

"Ben Collington, if you'll forgive me for saying so, Abby, was a fine man but he was a bit daft. He believed all that stuff because he wanted to believe it. He was, well, maybe kind of a mystic. He saw things differently from Fran."

"One time, I was a little tacker, knee high to a duck as they say down here, Ben had diphtheria. Of course, he was in his teens by then. They put him upstairs in the old nursery and sent me away to a friend of my mother's."

"When I came back, he scared the pants off me. He told me he actually saw her, that Indian girl. He even told me what she looked like. Everybody knew he was delirious, but I never forgot it. I never wanted to sleep up there again and I never did. He shouldn't have told that tale to a young kid, but he was strange. He liked her."

So does Benjie, I thought, and shivered again.

"Look," he said, "we're both getting cold. We'll sneak out of here in a minute, but that was a side track. I'm not finished. I don't know how you found your father's journal or heard about the house being for sale, or whatever, but it doesn't matter now because you and I are going to be together someday soon. I'm taking Bay House and all the land off the market and we're going to raise Benjie together to inherit this place. He'll be my heir. Benjamin Collington Buford."

"Oh, no. Oh, no, William. You don't mean that. What about Harriet? She adores you. You're her whole world."

He rushed on. "Don't you see how right this is, Abby? Harriet can't have children. She wouldn't deny this to me, and I know you love this place as much as I do. You'd own it with me. You and Benjie."

I stared at him, my heart beating so wildly I could feel the pressure drumming in my ears. "You're talking about two divorces. Mine and yours." I tried to sound reasonable, rational.

William kept ranting on in the same irrational way. "And custody of Benjie, and then another marriage. Ours. And happily ever after," he said. "Abby, don't you know we are part of the history, the future, of this house?"

"Oh, no, William. You don't mean any of this. You couldn't. I couldn't. It would be cruel."

Cruel. The word hung suspended in the dark atmosphere of the Old Cabin, echoing and reaching back through the years.

"Cruel? Abby, you are such a quaint child, I can't believe it. It's almost," he looked at me strangely, "as if you're from some other century. Divorces happen every day, you know. People change, and then they change partners."

He tried to pull me close to him. I stumbled, afraid to take my eyes from his face as I backed toward the door.

"We couldn't help it that this happened to us, Abby," he whispered into the dismal gloom as he crept closer. "It just happened."

"William, believe me." Now I felt anger rise in my voice. "Nothing. Has. Happened. There is no Us. And this conversation is madness."

A crack at the doorway let in one long sliver of sunlight. Through the opening we heard the sound of children's voices. William pushed the door open a bit more so we could see out. A small, curly head darted past, toward the terrace. Then Josh, Jess, Jake and S.J., wearing her green Sunday dress.

"Now, hush. All of you." S.J. instructed her flock, her voice low but clear. "And be polite. We'll go around and knock on the kitchen door and maybe Abby will hear us and not all those ladies."

I knew she had no idea William and I were hidden and listening just steps away. "They're coming to visit Benjie," I whispered to William. "They still feel …"

William shot out of the door. "Not one step further," he roared.

The Tomisons whirled together, startled, staring. Cindy burst into tears and ran behind her mother, clutching her legs.

I followed him out into the clean twilight breeze. *I could not stand mute in the face of William's sudden threat.* "What are you thinking?" I shouted. "You just made a six-year-old cry. These are only innocent children."

William advanced and shook a fist at Josh. "You could have killed Benjie. You know that, don't you? You're an irresponsible delinquent and none of you are to come around here looking for Benjie again. Do you understand? This house is off-limits. And any place Benjie is, ever, is off limits, too."

The frightened children moved back against S.J. She reached out her arms to gather them to her. She looked very beautiful at that moment and very proud, with her cheeks flushed and angry. Her auburn curls were carefully combed and her bright green dress was fastened with a round, girlish collar that made her look very young. The children clustered there, speechless, clean and scrubbed in their Sunday best.

"And you ..." William shook his finger in S.J.'s face. "You're not fit to take care of children. You're not fit to be a mother. I want you all gone. Now."

Suddenly, memories of Matt's abuse came flooding back. As if William's finger was Matt's fist. His voice full of Matt's drunken threats. His stance full of Matt's violence that once had the power to turn me to stone. But not today. Not anymore.

"Hold on, William." S.J. took a brave step closer to him. "You don't understand what this is. The kids came to tell Benjie they're sorry. They're his only friends."

"They don't need to tell Benjie anything." William's voice was a vicious growl. "Anyone can see what they are. Pure trash. Like you."

S.J. stalked past William as he stood in her path. The children followed in silence. Her car coughed to life then spun down the lane.

"You're wrong, William," I said. "And blind. S.J. has true courage. All you are is a coward in expensive suits."

I found myself staring at him. *Here was a total stranger. Just like Matt. Now I understood how the toothless, terrified Nancy appeared twice on the House of Grace's doorstep as Benjie and I took refuge there months ago. I had known abuse, suffered violence, but survived.*

Of course, he ignored me and said with a cheery smile, "Ha. Those Tomisons, Benjie's friends? That's why I got Benjie the puppy." Now he sounded casual. Chatty. "He's going to need a playmate for a while. Those ruffians could have killed him, you know. Don't worry, though, Abby. When he goes to school here, the right school, he'll make plenty of friends."

"No, William. Never."

Of course, William just grinned at me, the laughter crinkles back, as disarming as a college boy. "I think you'll change your mind."

I stumbled back to the house. Stumbled in fury. Not in fear. The ladies were in the study drinking tea, chatting to Harriet. I flew up the stairs, to Benjie and sanity.

21

I do not know a lot about psychic phenomena, although I understand much scientific research has been done on the subject. But I do believe there was a force sometimes on the third floor that helped us and related especially to children. Just as I knew the force in the Old Cabin wing was evil. It was only when I began to think like the children that I guessed what all the adults in previous generations failed to explore.

It started on the beach.

Benjie and Skipper and I walked miles on that beach and along the shore in the days that followed William's seductive proposal, the last golden days of September. Benjie was lonely without the Tomison children to play with, and the puppy was a godsend, as William planned.

He left abruptly on one of his business trips as if nothing extraordinary had happened. Harriet spent every possible moment at the church or in the stable. I tried to gather my strength and sanity, so Benjie and I could go back to New York and start life on our own, with all the problems that was going to bring.

We were on the way back from one of our long walks. I pondered my options while we splashed along the shoreline. Benjie threw bits of stones, sticks, and shells that were tossed up by the tide to little Skipper, who leaped and twisted in mid-air, never missing a mouthful. The pup wasn't so little anymore. His paws reached Benjie's shoulders when he jumped, which is all he seemed to do, after or during a daily swim. I was amused by their dance pose, Skipper's good-natured licks and barks. The spirited wiggling and tail-wagging seemingly in Benjie's command. I realized how right William was about the gift of this wonderful friend.

Our return to New York was no longer impossible, it seemed, at least not financially. Mr. Dangerfield called with news of a contract on my mother's house. He sounded gleeful over the telephone.

"Now, don't get too exuberant, Abigail. There is a contingency clause. The buyers must sell their house first, in Cleveland, but we've checked this out very thoroughly, and it's just a matter of time. So, keep your hat on, my dear child, and when I call again in a few days I may have very good news indeed."

Mr. Dangerfield's news only increased my impatience, though I made myself sound appreciative when we hung up. I could no longer hide here from Matt, whatever his game. I could no longer stay without being involved in what my father called the classic struggle for possession.

When did we come here? Was it only in June? It already seemed another lifetime ago. I was beyond naïve, assuming we belonged here. My right to beautiful old Bay House and all its land, waters, shore. My father's poetic prose in his tale of the past and Will Collington's remarkable truth—all of this I would remember and believe for the rest of my life. However, without proof, we must go. All I wanted was to claim what belonged to Benjie and me. If I took what was Harriet's, I would be part of the procession of people who were so beguiled by this place that they forced it away from somebody else.

And I could not remain at Bay House with William here, no matter the circumstances. Even Peter, the irascible Dr. Carpenter, the only person I knew who believed Will Collington, thought I must leave. There was no chance, he insisted, of finding legal proof in a book lost for two hundred years.

There was also that maddening quote of his. "Won't you walk into my parlor said the spider to the fly?" Did that make me a victim or willing prey? Of what? Or was he saying I was as ineffective as the fly?

I picked up a small branch and hurled it with all my might, out where the tide would catch it. Benjie eyed me with surprised approval. "Good one, Mom. And you know what? Your arms aren't that funny color anymore."

"Finally, yes, though it took long enough. Now it's your turn again."

"I'm tired of throwin' stuff. I wish I could play with Jake."

I wish you could, too, with all my heart. But I'm not about to risk provoking William where the Tomisons are concerned. His temper is too unpredictable. "Well, we just have to make the best of things for a few more days. People don't always get what they wish, son. Look, I'll race you down to where the creek starts. Last one there's a rotten egg."

We ended up in a tie, bent and panting, with Skipper leaping on both of us in the excitement. "I'm done, Benj. Whew! You two are some champion racers. I'm going to sit right here in the sunshine for a few more minutes. Then we'll go in and you can watch TV until dinner."

I dropped down on the driftwood log, bleached almost bone white and warmed by the late afternoon sun. Benjie burrowed in the sand at my feet, face flushed, hair curling at the edges from exertion. He hauled the puppy into his lap. Skipper sprawled himself across Benjie's legs, then flopped his head on Benjie's knees. For a moment, all was quiet except for his ragged panting. The tide was low, the wind was down. The water made soft lapping sounds that were lulling me to sleep.

Plop! Something hit the end of the log. I jumped, always expecting danger. I hated feeling hunted but couldn't stop my reaction. It was nothing but a stone sliding off the end.

I looked back again at the bay, stretching far in front of us to a faint green blur on the other shore. There were a few large boats in the channel, streaming towards Annapolis, but the whole expanse on our side was empty. No summer sailors, no water skiers. The bay belonged to Benjie and me.

Plop! Plop! Two more stones hit the end of the log. We both jumped and looked behind us. I reached for Benjie's hand. Skipper bounded from Benjie's arms, sniffing, circling, yipping.

The small sandy cliff that separated the beach from the lawn was just behind us, though lower where it sloped to the creek, and fringed with the sea oats and other marshy grasses that hid the path. As we stared upward, a larger stone crashed through the brush and landed in a hollow spot on the tip of the log. The sea oats waved. We heard scrambling and a child's snicker.

Benjie clapped a hand to his mouth. "What's going on, son?"

"You gotta promise you won't tell William."

"William doesn't have to know everything. You can tell me."

"Well, OK, if you don't ever tell anybody else."

Benjie inched close and whispered in my ear. "This is our secret hiding place. I thought Jake musta forgot. But he didn't."

He went to the end of the log and peered inside. He pulled out a piece of notebook paper, a candy bar, and one stick of bubble gum. From the look on his face it could have been gold doubloons and a casket of jewels. The message must have been written by Jess, who was in the third grade. "We are real sorry about the traktor. Sind something back."

I put to bed one happy boy that night. He fell asleep planning what he was going to "sind" back.

I kissed his cheek, still sticky with a pink streak of bubble gum, went into my own room, and took out *The Forces of Bay House*, as I did every night. Some passages I almost knew by heart. Curled up in my bed, I went over it again.

Yes, of course I was leaving this place with Benjie as soon as I could. That was the only sensible, logical, decent thing to do. And yet, my mind kept pursuing the dream, illogical though it was, that somewhere the *Marriage Book* was waiting to be found.

I kept turning back to the same place in the *Forces*. To the end of Young Will Collington's letter to his parents:

"I'll send Elijah to leave this precious book in that special place where all this true story began, 'til I can come home and show it to you and see your happy faces for myself."

There was something that tugged at me and wouldn't let go. Something stuck in my subconscious, tangible but elusive. A thought I tried to grasp but couldn't hold. It went beyond logic. Beyond a dream. It was something I knew in my heart and felt in my bones. But what? My mind ran back along all the blind alleys my father pursued.

The old parsonage, where the Reverend Witherspoon once lived, was gone centuries ago. Harriet told me this among other familial facts as if she was rattling off minutia about crop rotation. The church on Broad Creek burned to the ground in the 1800s. The land where Indian huts once sat in the sheltering emerald forest beyond the Bay House gate was now corn and soybean fields. Beyond lay a vast paved sprawl of tract housing.

Incredible, I mused, to think of Young Will as a boy, and his sister, Mercy, playing on their side of a gate, with Indian children living in the woods just beyond. How mysterious it must have seemed to the young towheaded Collingtons. How wondrous to learn the ways of the Matapeakes, to play and run together in that vast forest. If they weren't forbidden to venture outside that gate. If so, how did they manage it anyway, as history proved they had? What friendships would they have formed, in the way of all children who gravitate together?

When did Will first encounter Ellen Smalldeer, the graceful half-Indian girl with the sky-blue eyes? Would they have used a hiding place secret to themselves, like Benjie and Jake?

For no reason, I glanced down at the bedside table. The newspaper Harriet brought was there, as I suppose I left it, open to the color photo on the front page. And then, of course I knew, as surely as if someone shouted it.

Will's *"special place where it all began"* was in the gatepost. When or how the book got there I could only guess, but Will's letter was clear and convincing about sending his groom, Elijah, back to return it there for safekeeping.

I held my breath. Pulled the article almost to my nose. Among the bits of debris from the broken post, which should have consisted of nothing but shattered bricks and concrete, was something that looked like a bundle. Brownish, flat, half-buried. The photo angle obscured most of it and the quality was very grainy.

I sat on my bed feeling like Isaac Newton when that apple fell on his head. Then I went down on my knees and thanked God, like Young Will in the tobacco warehouse when the barrel fell apart behind him. How long I stayed there, I have no idea, but I remember jumping to my feet with a new sense of panic. That photo was taken over a week ago.

I grabbed my dark jacket, tied a navy scarf around my head, and checked my son. Aside from those few things, I had no thought of caution. Five minutes later I was outside, tearing through the night toward the gatepost.

I did not realize how much fog had seeped across the land from the bay as it so often did on cool, damp nights. The outline of the lane was hard to follow. The trees that flanked it moved like giant ghosts. I stumbled once or twice over ruts in the dirt but raced on. I reached the entrance and stood still to get my bearings. The road beyond the entrance was no help, it was unlighted.

One post stood firmly as it always had, blacker than the foggy night. I touched it. Worn bricks, crumbling concrete, wreathed in a blanket of moss and ivy. Almost up to my shoulders, with its little sign hanging above. On the opposite side of the lane, I could see nothing. I touched air. Knelt down to feel the spot where the matching gatepost must have stood. There was a jagged foundation, a neat stack of bricks. Nothing else. As my eyes adjusted to the mist, I reasoned that all the rough remains of the accident were cleared away.

I could have wept with frustration and disappointment. If only I wasn't so consumed with Benjie. I'd been back and forth right past that post when all the debris was there. And so had everybody else. Had no one realized? Had the trash been dumped or burned? Or did someone figure it out? Someone who did not intend to tell me.

I turned to grope back up the lane when the courage that propelled me to the entrance vanished. Fog. A faint wind. The moaning of a ship's horn on the bay. Ephemeral, deeper shadows. A long, long way to the safety of the house.

A silhouette moved to the right of me, just off the lane. A shape shorter than the trees. I began to run. The shape moved as I moved. Faster. I tried to go faster.

The shadow disappeared and I told myself as I ran it was the fog deceiving me. Then I saw the vague shape again, looming ahead. It emerged from the blending blackness of a tree trunk and waited.

I did not look. I flew past, on and on and on, until I reached the open patio door, which I left unlocked. Slid to the floor inside, bent over, hugged my knees, chest heaving. When I could stand and move again, I locked the door and crept upstairs. The house was silent and still, except for its creaky, old ship sounds. The light was still on in Harriet's room as it was when I left. I tried to avoid the dips in the stairs that sighed and groaned. Benjie slept soundly, entwined in his covers.

I tiptoed to the bathroom window across the hall, on the side of the house that faced the garden and the lane. I stared out, without turning on the light.

A vague dark presence stood on the path looking up. As I watched, it turned and moved off toward the stable. In the dim light that filtered from the second-floor hall window, light that must have shone down from William and Harriet's room, I could see the distinct outline of a shaggy head, like no other.

Noah. Why?

22

By morning the fog evaporated and so did my resolve to return to New York as soon as possible. Every instinct I possessed told me to stay. I had new hope, although I had new fear. One thing I was sure of, Noah not only acted as my warden. His attempts to frighten me were deliberate. And he showed no mercy when he must have seen how well he was succeeding. He never wanted Benjie and me to be here, not from the first moment when we climbed into the dinghy with him to be taken ashore from William's sloop. Well, God willing and giving me the courage, we were staying, regardless, until I found what had been hidden in the gatepost. The possibility that something was already found and destroyed was so disastrous I refused to consider it.

Somebody found that book. Somebody who didn't want me to know it. I was going to do my best to find out who that was, and nothing fog or fear could do was going to stop me.

The air floating through my open window was heavy with the familiar fall scent of burning leaves. Benjie and I got into jeans and old shirts and trotted down the steps. Noah was out in Harriet's garden, raking leaves from the chrysanthemum beds that were by now a bruised purple and a frowzy gold. A red sports car was parked in the turnaround, top down. A wire trash bin off to one side was smoldering. I could not resist a furtive glance to see what was in there, slowly burning. Leaves. Nothing but leaves.

Noah looked up from his raking and met my gaze, unblinking. His deep-set eyes were devoid of all expression. More alien than if he shot me one of his usual hostile glares.

"Good morning, Noah," I said. My voice did not tremble at all. "I've been wanting to thank whoever it was that cleared up after the accident. Was it you, Noah? I think I should help pay for the work and damages since Benjie was partly to blame."

Noah looked up again with the same blank stare. "You take the boy," he said. "Go back to New York City." He slung the rake over his shoulder and marched off. I felt as though I'd been punched.

"Why does Noah want us to leave, Mom? Why didn't he answer you?" Benjie wasn't as busy kicking leaves as I thought.

"I don't know, Benj."

"Why doesn't he like us? I don't think he likes us."

"I really don't know, Benjie." My mind was racing.

I stared after that old, sinuous back as Noah stalked away, feeling alone, forsaken, except for my small son. I had not felt this abandoned since I came to this place. Noah and Burleigh were supposed to be our protectors.

Something else was happening. Something different. I was beginning to be able to live with fear. Last night Noah was a terrifying shadow. Today he was still strange and frightening, but he was real. I would deal with reality, even though I had to do it by myself.

Freedom. There was a deeper dimension to the word. I had come a long way since Helen waved my shorn locks in that small upstairs room at the House of Grace. Freedom was not just a state of being. Freedom was also having the courage to act alone.

I said, "Next, we'll tackle Harriet, the lioness in her den."

"Huh?" Benjie was breathless, somersaulting across the grass. His arms circled the air, his face aglow like a pumpkin on Halloween. I was glad he only half heard his mother talking to herself.

The house was quiet. Harriet was nowhere inside. A circle of cars by the stable led me to assume she was there. Huddled with her committee members and whoever drove the red MG. I would have to wait. Benjie and I still avoided the stable when volunteers were around.

The telephone was ringing. Probably a bazaar volunteer needing Harriet's advice on setting up the buffet luncheon in the church parish hall. Or one of the workers assigned to help William with the auction at Bay House. Neither of them was back yet, and I was thinking about what I might find in the refrigerator to fix us all a light meal.

I answered the phone, unprepared for Mr. Dangerfield's voice. "Abigail, my dear child, I have excellent news." He was almost crowing.

"Oh, how nice." I had to sound noncommittal in case Noah was listening.

"Well," the lawyer said, "you may have some difficulty in believing this. You may, indeed. I know you've been under a great deal of stress and worry, but all that is over now. I have a surprise for you that I'm sure is exactly what your dear mother would have wanted."

Just get to the point, I pleaded silently. With the telephone cord in my right hand, I stretched back into the dining room for privacy but missed part of what Mr. Dangerfield was babbling so happily on the other end of the line.

"… so you can actually see it for yourself with your very own eyes. Remember, now. Perhaps you should jot it down. Do you have a pencil there, Abigail? It airs at 8:00, the channel is WQSV but I'm not sure, of course, what station that is for you down in Merryland." He chuckled at his own little pun.

"Now, don't ask me anymore. I'm not going to say another word. Just be sure to watch. And let little Benjamin stay up and watch, too."

"But wait," I said. "I didn't …"

"You'll see. You can start a whole new life now, Abigail." Then he added, "God bless you, child," and hung up. I stood there, staring at the telephone.

The contract on my mother's house must have come through. We would be solvent again. We could go home. So, what was there to watch on television? It must be something special to rate prime time on a Saturday night. Maybe a new concept of ultra-secure condo living. Elegant and near a good school if it was to be what my mother would have wanted for Benjie and me. And of course, it had to be in the state of New York. My legal battle would have to start there someday. Could he have already made a down payment? That couldn't be it. Maybe the show was about the pollution of the Chesapeake.

Early that morning we traipsed through the wet grass to free Skipper from his box in the tack room. We let him lope along the shore, barking and lunging, while we threw sticks for him to chase. There were no messages or childish treasures in the hollow end of the log. The sun went behind clouds and the air began to nip at us.

The day dragged and Benjie was whiny.

We went back inside, I made sandwiches. Egg salad stickmen with carrot-curl noses, hot chocolate topped with whipped cream. Benjie dumped his crayons and coloring books on the kitchen table with mopey eyes and a martyr's face. I sat, doodling, thinking I would be very cool and cunning. *I'll ask my casual questions about the gatepost, then watch the expression of the person I'm questioning, to see whether I can recognize the truth or detect a lie.*

It was 2:00 when Harriet came back from the stable. I heard her talking in the hall. It was not the voice she used to instruct volunteers. She sounded playful, amused by someone who must have gone into the study. Then her brisk footsteps were tapping toward us. She came into the kitchen carrying a tray with the remains of a picnic lunch she must have served the workers.

"Abby. Here you are," she said.

At the same time, I said, "Harriet, one quick question."

I knew I was abandoning my plan to be careful and patient, but I could not hold myself back. I jumped in before she could speak. "I'm so worried about the damage to the gatepost. I feel partly responsible, you know. If I had been watching Benjie the whole thing might not have happened. I want to pay my share of all costs. Who," I plunged on, "cleaned up after the accident?"

Harriet's glance was vague. She was putting dirty glasses in the sink. "Those Tomison children, of course. William gave Burleigh orders to make those little roughnecks clean up every bit of that debris. But Abby, that's not why I was looking for you."

She leaned against the counter and folded her arms. *I could see her mind was on whatever was coming next. I couldn't help wondering who she left waiting in the study.*

"Abigail, it's high time for you to know what's going on here and has been ever since the spring before you came. It was asinine to keep it from you and to let you dangle, hoping and dreaming like your father. But William wouldn't hear of telling you. Now even William says you have to know. So here it is. This whole place has been up for sale and we'll probably sign a contract with the buyers a week after the bazaar."

I felt my jaw drop. There was obviously a great deal William hadn't told Harriet, but with relief I realized he must have accepted my final no and settled back into truth and reality.

I tried not to think about William's fantasies. Those dark moments when, alone and hidden, he spun out his bizarre ideas about me, Benjie, him and Bay House. I decided he was play-acting some harmless daydream. Didn't Harriet excuse and explain away these occasional lapses with warmth and amusement? Like his first game, saving us with his sailboat?

Benjie's patience with crayons was over. He rolled them off the edge of the table, making his favorite mock explosion sounds as they hit the floor.

"Harriet, I've known the house was on the market for a while now." I was determined to keep my voice smooth and even. "In the hospital. It was advertised in a magazine ..."

Harriet's hand went up to silence my speech. "Never mind," she said. "That's over now."

I stood up, straight and tall behind my chair. "Well, if you're finished in the stable, I think Benjie and I'll get Skipper and go for a walk." I was on fire to talk to S.J. and ask her if the children found anything at the gatepost.

"Wait. You haven't heard the whole story." *How like Harriet to have the last word in any discussion.* "This is bigger and more exciting than anything you could have imagined. I want you to meet someone who's going to make this real to you. My college roommate, Vera Turner. She smokes too much, drives too fast, and may seem a bit strange, but don't be fooled. She has a degree in architecture from Georgetown and she's one of the most sought-after designers in D.C."

I pictured one of Harriet's more zealous cronies from the Historical Society. The ones who appeared with coke-bottle eyeglasses and bulging briefcases, to pour over crop reports from the 1800s.

"Benjie, I'm going to borrow your Mommy for just a few minutes." I permitted myself to be propelled into the study, more impatient than curious. I hoped the Playdough I added to Benjie's crayon pile would help keep him occupied.

"Abby, meet Vera," Harriet said.

Enthroned on the sofa was a movie queen. She appeared to be of medium height and built solely of curves. Her hair was silver-blonde, wavy and long. She wore a leopard-print jumpsuit, gold chains glinted from her plunging neckline. A black spiked heel jiggled from her foot as she lounged amidst the pillows, puffing plumes from a silver cigarette holder as if smoking added the ultimate ambiance to centuries-old Bay House.

The woman had perfect features. Sapphire eyes accentuated by hints of blue shadow on the upper lids, though the long black lashes could not have been real. Her lips were full, plump and crimson. She looked more actress than architect.

Vera eyed me from head to toe. "Love the tan. Who are you again? Pocahontas?"

"Vera. Honestly," said Harriet. A corner of her mouth curled as the two exchanged glances.

"Abby," she said, "we're dispensing with secrecy here. Vera knows your situation and after this discussion you will know mine. Now, Vera, please. Show and tell."

"I thought you'd never ask." Vera gave a low chuckle, pounced down on all fours, pulled a fat blueprint from a stack on the floor and spread it in front of the couch. It outlined the vast acreage of Bay House.

"My master plan," she announced. "Bay House Manor Club and Country Estates. Kneeling to one side of the blueprint, she used a yardstick for a pointer. "Golf course … private marina … tennis courts

… home sites."

I caught bits and pieces of her inspired vision while a storm howled in my head.

"Bay House will remain as the focal point. It's the clubhouse. Members only. Major renovations. New kitchen. The Old Cabin as you call it, that decrepit mess, completely rebuilt. Permanent residence for the Bufords, for as long as they live. William's had the blueprints for weeks. More on that later."

It hit me like a blow to my ribs. The memory of Benjie suspended before the gaping door in the master bedroom. William running to his defense with a roll of plans wedged under his arm.

Vera paused for breath, parted her lips in a wide crimson smile at Harriet, and rushed on. "Olympic-sized pool, here. Lighted tennis complex, here. The old farmhouse will have to go, of course, to make room for the marina."

I pictured with dread the Tomisons' cozy front porch being met by a bulldozer.

"Ta Da!" She smiled and batted her eyelashes. "Inspired, no?"

I stared at her in horror.

"What about the tadpoles?" I felt numb, stupid with shock. Trapped in a bad dream.

"What?" said Harriet and Vera together.

My mind veered off on an absurd and disconnected track. I saw children playing along the creek on summer evenings while fireflies lit their tiny lanterns in the trees and bullfrogs croaked. Saw the fields stretching out from road to bay, green and fertile with crops, a working, productive farm. The quiet shoreline, home to wild creatures, a natural playground for children and adults alike. I saw lights come on in Bay House, room by room, up to the third floor in the house that had been home to seven generations of a family. A house built on a site once torn by violence, and since regained, tended, cherished. My son's heritage.

Harriet and Vera Turner were still staring at me. It was difficult to speak. Words stuck in my throat, then almost refused to form at all. "I was thinking … about the creek … the natural ecology …"

"Ah. You're forgetting the mosquitoes," Harriet said, "and the bills. Abby, you don't have to sit there looking like a lost soul. If you want some kind of permanent space for yourself and Benjie, if you want to visit in the summer sometimes, perhaps, and use the third floor, or part of it, I suppose we can still throw a clause to that effect into the contract. That is your right, under that ridiculous will. But that is your only right. This deal will be going through within the month, surely. You're just going to have to face it."

I shook my head. "How can you do this? I don't see how you can."

"My word, it hasn't been easy for William and me. It's been terribly hard on him. All the business meetings, all the running back and forth between Baltimore and New York, Washington and Philadelphia. We had major investors interested, Abby, as soon as they learned it was on the market. There aren't many parcels of waterfront land left on the island, and there are tough laws that protect the bay."

I longed to stop her but all I could do was blink back tears.

Harriet droned on, proud of her enlightened stance. "Commercial developers can hardly build here anymore. It had to be something really big, an imaginative project on a grand scale, aimed at wealthy people with wealthy investors forming a corporation to create it. We had to be sure the offers were valid. Convince the county commissioners. Screen people with the help of lawyers and surveyors. It's been a frightful and expensive process. We were only too thrilled to enlist Vera's expertise."

Vera aimed another cigarette into the holder. "It was all quite simple, actually. I'm very good with numbers." She struck a match and narrowed her eyes with a sly smile as the smoke rose. "Commissioners, too."

"If you had the sense to see, Abigail, you'd realize everything on this place is running down and needs repair. Noah and Burleigh and I have barely been holding our fingers in the dike."

"William isn't a farmer, never will be." Her eyes softened with that indulgent, maternal tenderness I had seen before. "He's an eighteenth-century gentleman living in the wrong time. This way he'll still be Lord of the Manor. The best sailor, the best shot, the best fisherman. The finest, most charming sportsman and host. Now we won't always be in debt and we won't have to see Bay House go to seed before our eyes. It's the only way."

She paused, stared through the long study windows, twisted a curtain tassel round and round her finger. "Of course," she continued, "if we'd had children, things might have been different. William might have cared more. But there was no chance of that and we both knew it. William had an accident, years ago when he was only twenty, water skiing. He was injured ..." Her voice trailed off. When she spoke again her voice was hard and flat. "I have to think about William," she said.

Vera crouched forward, chains dangling, and pulled another blueprint from her bag.

"Look, Harry, there's no use in crying over spilled silt, or whatever. You are living in the sublime present." She slid her eyes toward me. "And about to make megabucks."

I was still reeling at the thought of anyone addressing Harriet as Harry.

Vera pinned her eyes on her friend's. "Now, you know I already created plans for the Old Cabin, which William has, and I'm sure you've seen. Small space, huge challenge, I must say."

"Light. Bay view. That mammoth fireplace. Those were the easy parts. Creating a canvas wiped clean of tales of death, doom, and disaster, that was a different story. Frankly, the place gives me the creeps. But we tear down to build back. That's the name of this game. And you asked for more details, so here they are."

"Voila," Vera boasted. Her lips made a smug scarlet curl. *The plan she unfurled was all too familiar. I didn't have the stomach to look. My hands felt like ice and the old, dank smoke I smelled did not come from cigarettes.* I jumped up and wandered along the bookshelves, trailing my fingers across the covers and down the spines. I blocked out my memories of the Old Cabin although I heard Harriet oohing and ahhing. Over the compact Pullman kitchen, the corner powder room, the graceful iron railing protecting the loft where skylights afforded romantic views of the moonlight.

"You and William can stare down into the fireplace flames, then see stars when you look up. So to speak," Vera said.

I remembered William's hot breath on my neck. The massive carved beam where an ancestor was hung.

Harriet crossed her legs. "My word, how you do go on. But you don't need to sell this plan. It's exactly what I wanted, only better. Vera, you are a genius."

"I know," Vera said. She scrambled to her feet, rolled up her blueprints and tossed them into Harriet's lap. "Now I must run. Dinner date. One of those crumbling joints in Annapolis." She winked. "It's about to get a facelift, and me a nice paycheck."

"Let me know," she paused at the door, "when you get the green light. I'll begin conferencing with the builders asap. It's been a pleasure, Abby." Then she was gone.

I stood. "Excuse me, Harriet. I have to see what Benjie's up to in the kitchen and let him get outside." I rescued my child from his crayons and Playdough. We banged out of the screen door and started running. It was 3:15 by the kitchen clock.

I knew very well all the Tomison children, except Mindy, got off the school bus at the end of the lane about 3:00. They took a shortcut across the cornfield to the farmhouse since most of the cattle corn was harvested and the rest was still standing in shocks. Once they were home, or out again to play, they had orders to steer clear of Benjie. But what could anyone say if they happened to meet us by accident on their way home?

I sent Benjie into the tack room to get Skipper. I was pacing in front of the stable when Josh, leading the others through the cornfield, emerged from a path between the rows. "Stay there, Benj," I called. "Wait 'til I come for you. I mean it. Do not come out."

I was sure Harriet couldn't see me from the house, but I never knew where Noah might be. Or Burleigh, or even S.J. I couldn't afford to trust anybody. Harriet's disclosures filled me with terror. Would I lose my inheritance just as I was about to prove it?

There was another layer of consciousness, of pain. Harriet revealed it in that last hour, arousing a reluctant sympathy in me. She was William's protector. Harriet, you don't really know him, I thought at the time. Although it was clear he lied to me about their reason for being childless, perhaps out of pride. William was not weak, or a daydreamer. He was something else, but I didn't have time to think about it now. I had to act.

I reminded myself to appear as normal as possible. "Hi, everybody." I spoke with fake, hollow cheer as Josh, Jess, Jake and Cindy each appeared, pushing their way through the dry, waving stalks.

They halted, nervous and unprepared to see me awaiting them, not knowing what to do. They were ready to bolt if they saw Benjie, I was sure, because Burleigh must have made the situation more than plain.

There was so much at stake. I tried to sound casual. "I have a question for you kids. Can you think back to the day of the accident?"

They nodded, four wary little copper tops. "That was a awful day," said Jake. I was surprised to see tears in his eyes.

"After we left in the ambulance, after Benjie and I went to the hospital, what happened? Who cleaned up the trash from the broken gatepost?"

Josh hung his head. He, I remembered, was driving the tractor. "Nobody," he said, wiping his nose on his sleeve.

"After a while," said Jess, "a man from the newspaper came and took pitchers. He had a big camera, just like on TV, but Mom wouldn't let us stay. We went home and got punished."

I studied the oldest brother. "Josh, somebody cleaned up. Didn't Mr. Buford tell your father you had to do it?"

"Yes ma'am," he said. "But we didn't do it then, that afternoon, 'cause we had to pick up our rooms and do chores. The next morning it was Saturday. We cleaned up then. Stacked up all the bricks that were left, the ones that weren't broken. Then we put the busted pieces in the wheelbarrow and dumped 'em back behind the stable."

I took two steps closer to the children, leaned forward, and made my voice sound like what I did not feel—carefree and casual. "Now, I'm going to ask you something else and I want you all to remember carefully. I know there were pieces of brick and cement. Was there anything else in that trash? Anything else you found?"

Josh looked up, biting his lip. He looked at Jess. He looked at Jake and Cindy. Nobody uttered a sound. He hung his head again. "No ma'am," he said in a muffled voice. They turned together and trudged toward the farmhouse, avoiding my eyes.

I didn't have to be a career psychiatrist, only a mother, to know the boy was lying.

23

I would have to talk to S.J. I would have to trust somebody and not let myself become paranoid. By late afternoon I was dying to see her, but no opportunity presented itself. I couldn't leave Benjie and I certainly couldn't take him to the farmhouse. Suspense was making me restless.

I offered to cook dinner. "That would be lovely," said Harriet, "really. I must check inventory in the stable. Why don't you just make hamburgers and salad? There are a few ears of corn in the fridge. William won't be coming home until later tonight so you and Benjie and I can eat in the kitchen."

As soon as she was out of the house, I made two phone calls. The first was to the local newspaper that published the picture of the damaged gatepost. I asked to speak to the photographer, and I was in luck. He was just checking in before leaving for the day. Did he notice anything unusual in the debris from the post that was shattered? Did he notice the children who were there picking anything up?

"I'm sorry, ma'am," he said. Exasperation edged out the professional courtesy in his voice. "I was just there to get a shot of the entrance. Yeah, there were some kids playing around, but I can't say I paid much attention except to tell 'em to back off so I could work."

Next, I called S.J. "Abby, I can't believe this. I've been wanting so much to talk to you, but I couldn't figure how to do it. What I have to tell you is real private, now, and I better not say it over the phone."

Hope leaped like a waning fire in a fresh draft. "S.J., you're a wonderful friend. Can you come to the stable this evening when Benjie and I go to put Skipper in the tack room?"

"Ah, all right, Sally," she said. She raised her voice a notch. "I'll be seein' you soon then." I knew Burleigh or one of the kids had come within earshot.

I worried about escaping Harriet's vigilance for this meeting, but I need not have. I volunteered to clean up, and Harriet left for town as soon as we finished our hamburgers.

Benjie and I headed for the stable. It was still early evening, but the water and sky were already blending into the same shade of pewter. The air had a nippy feel and a cold smell that made me think of burning logs and hot cider.

It was warmer in the tack room. I flipped on the light so I could see Skipper's crate in the corner. There was no sign of S.J. I lingered, letting Benjie play and tumble with the puppy.

The green plaid blanket in his box made a spot of color in that small room. There was an electric heater on the wall that must have just been turned off because the room was stuffy. The bare planks of the walls were covered with pictures of long-ago horses and riders. One large faded photo still captured the magic moment of a horse in flight over a high fence, the rider elegantly top-hatted, coattails flying. I studied it, trying to decide whether this man was a Buford or a Collington.

There were touching sepia images of children on ponies and another large shot of a group of people waving gaily from a buggy. Several ancient saddles still hung on one wall. The air was pungent with the aroma of old leather, old stable, and dust. I became sharply aware of all the life that once vibrated in this quiet place.

The only sign of present use was a battered oak desk and an old filing cabinet. This was Burleigh's office, I guessed since the desk was stacked neatly with papers and what looked like accounting books. Hence the heater, which would only be used in his presence.

But there was no S.J. I opened the inner door that led into the stable. Inside it was large and shadowy in the faint light from the tack room, and completely still. I had to know if anyone was in there. I switched on the light by the door and stood gaping.

The stable was transformed into a charming and imaginative antique shop. The walls were scrubbed down, the floor raked and strewn with a layer of fresh sawdust, giving the place a carnival atmosphere. A giant horseshoe of dried country flowers festooned with ribbon hung just inside the closed entrance doors. There were three stalls on either side of the wide aisle that once accommodated carriages or buggies. Signs in Old English lettering announced the contents of what were now overflowing booths. The first two held Antiques and Collectibles, an array of large and small furniture. Next was Jewelry, Baubles and Bangles. Then Knick Knacks and Bric-a-Brac, beside the booth marked Prints and Maps. Finally, like a rainbow's pot of gold, were Books and More Books.

Of course, my eyes were drawn straight to the bookstall. There were stacks, piles, shelves-full, and a long library table waiting to be filled. What if the *Marriage Book* was somewhere hidden in that massive collection?

"Abby." I jumped. S.J. was right behind me.

"Turn off the light. I don't want Burleigh to know where I am. He just left here and started down the lane to take the pickup to the shop. Noah's following to bring him back."

"Where can we talk?" I asked. I glanced at Benjie who was intent on the hopeless task of teaching Skipper to sit.

"Let's go over by the furniture. We can see enough if we leave the door open."

"Good idea. Benj," I said to him over my shoulder. "I'm going to look around inside for a few minutes with Jake's mother. You stay right there, son."

My heart began a quicker beat as I envisioned finding the book I prayed to find. "You're a dear to come, S.J.," I said, as my eyes adjusted to the half-light. To my surprise, I hugged my friend as I hadn't hugged anybody except Benjie since the last time I saw my mother. S.J. hugged me back and added a few squeezes.

"I had to," she said. "I've been wantin' to tell you somethin' but I couldn't get my nerve up." She stepped back so she could see my face. "You're going to think it's none of my business, maybe."

"I'm sure I won't think that," I said. "I knew the kids were keeping something from me. Did they find the book?"

"What book?"

"What book? Oh, uh ..." I said. *I was so sure. Now I don't know how to proceed.*

"Did they lose one of Benjie's books? I don't know but I'll sure ask 'em. That's not what I wanted to talk to you about, though, Abby."

"Then, what?" I felt my hope sinking.

"Honey," S.J. said, "I've got to tell you something I've never told anybody before and never meant to tell as long as I live." I waited, trying to stay calm and slow my breathing.

"Summer before last, two summers before you came, I mean, Burleigh had to go home. Over to his father's farm in St. Mary's County on the other side of the bay, for a couple of months. His dad took sick. He had a stroke, poor, dear man, and didn't recover. Burleigh stayed there and worked his place and stood by his mother and all until it was over. He got one of the Tyler boys from down near Snow Hill to come here and work this place for William 'til he got back. Arthur. It was Arthur Tyler. Things ran down a lot and Burleigh hasn't got it all caught up yet."

"I know the farm's not making money." *Where is this story going? I'm trying not to be impatient.*

"Well, no. Burleigh's a good farmer. He has a natural knack for it. He says he knows he could make this place more than pay for itself if William didn't spend up all the profits. William, well, he thinks you can get money out of a farm without putting anything into it, and it doesn't happen like that. William," she sighed, "William's a ... sport. He likes to spend money."

"I have to get Benjie ready for bed, S.J. Why don't you just tell me whatever is so hard? I won't tell anyone. I promise."

She looked away, even though the light was dim. "The other evenin'," she went on, "when I tried to bring the kids to see Benjie, I saw you were with William in the Old Cabin. I saw your face when you came out. I knew right then what was goin' on and I knew I had to warn you. Abby, he doesn't want you. He wants your son."

I stared at her, speechless. My breath caught in my throat.

"That summer," S.J. continued, peering at me closely now, "William started out by looking after us, me and the kids, with Burleigh gone. And then, somehow, he was looking out for me. We'd go down on the beach or out in the boat, the sailboat, and it was always for the kids, at first, of course. Mindy wasn't born yet. Then after a while it would be just me and William. He'd talk me into letting them go stay with one of my girlfriends in town. It was always when Harriet was at a meeting or was playing golf or something. Abby, you know as well as I do, that man can charm the birds off the trees. He has his little ways like it's only you in the whole world that makes the world mean anything, and everything around you is new and ... and beautiful. And he makes up a special name to call you by, that nobody else calls you. Like, Unplain. He called me Unplain Jane."

S.J. shook her head as if casting off the memory that still clung. "You wouldn't believe me, the mother of four young ones and with my own good man away, to be such a damn fool as I was. He'd give me a look out of those eyes with all that magic in them ..."

"He calls me Cousin Abigail," I said. "His kissing cousin."

"There's more," said S.J. "I found out I was pregnant. Oh, William wasn't the father, but it could have been close if I wasn't scared of facing Father Monahan when I went to confession. It was bad enough as it was. But do you know what he wanted, Abby? Do you know what he really wanted? He wanted to adopt my baby. And I know what else he wanted though he never came right out and said it. He wanted everybody to think it was his."

"I told him I could never give up a child. He said '$10,000.' For $10,000 he'd take the baby and give it everything, and Harriet would love it, too, and she'd understand. He said, after all that I had four children and from the looks of things I could have plenty more, and I'd be right here and I could watch the child grow up."

"So, I came to my senses then, and a good thing too. Burleigh came home and I never told him a word because I think he would have killed William. I really do. Burleigh seems easygoin' even though he's so big, but he has a temper that you don't want to fool with, I can tell you. Once in a great while, if something really riles him, look out."

"Anyway, when Mindy was born, William still didn't give up. I know he didn't. Mindy was sudden and quick, two weeks early, being the fifth, and all. Burleigh went over to help his mother. She was having to sell her place and she was all upset. William got to the hospital before anybody else came and it just so happened that the baby was in the room with me. I held her in my arms."

"I said, 'Meet my little girl, William,' and I think the word girl surprised him. Then he took a long look at the baby's red hair. Red, just like her daddy's."

"And I laughed. Abby, I couldn't help it, because I knew what he was thinking. And I was feeling giddy and light-headed and happy the way you do when your labor is over and your baby is born all whole and strong. But I shouldn't have done it. You don't laugh at William."

"He's got this grief thing inside about children. There's a story around here that it's his fault they don't have 'em, because of something that happened to him once. But believe me, I never brought it up."

"He's hated me ever since. You saw him turn on me and the kids that day and run us off like he was another person." She leaned closer, hand against her mouth, and stared at the ground. "I hate sayin' this again. But I've got to," she whispered in hoarse, ragged breaths. She looked up, clutched my arm with both hands and leaned even closer. "Because now I think he wants your Benjie."

"Benjie," I repeated. I ran to the door of the tack room to see if he was still there.

"Let's go, Mom." He was sounding whiny and tired. "Can't we go now?"

"Put Skipper in his box. I'll just be one more minute."

I turned back to S.J. terrified to hear more, terrified not to.

"Harriet hates me, too," she said. "Don't think she's blind to William's shenanigans."

For a moment reality was suspended. I couldn't think or speak. As if I'd been putting out fires but run out of water. "Thank you," I managed to mutter. "Thank you so much for telling me all this. You know, I don't have many friends." This might not have seemed to make sense, although it did.

We parted in silence. Benjie and I started for the big house as she started back to hers. I had found nothing about the *Marriage Book*. Only more wildly disturbing elements to absorb.

Benjie ran straight to the kitchen. "Mom, c'n you make some popcorn? C'un we turn on the TV?"

"Sure, Benj. Why don't you get the butter out of the fridge, then go upstairs and put your PJs on. I'll leave it here on the counter and you can meet me in the study."

I almost forgot Mr. Dangerfield's coy instructions to watch for a surprise on television tonight, but I was glad I didn't mention them to Harriet. Whatever plan that well-meaning little man had up his sleeve for Benjie and me, I was never again going to live in New York City. We had to go back to finish up our life there but someday, somehow, Benjie and I were coming back to Bay House.

I turned on the television. It was almost time to see Mr. Dangerfield's surprise. We'd watch this show, whatever it might be, although I really wasn't interested now in any plan he might be making for us. Then Benjie and I would go to sleep. I would need all my strength to face reality.

It was a little before eight. I switched to the correct channel. The special program was starting.

"... a program of interest to many Americans," the announcer was saying, "more than we realize. An experiment in living and learning and working together, rediscovering values ..."

What on earth was my well-meaning little advisor getting us into? And what could this topic have to do with Benjie?

The screen showed a tree-lined suburban street in a pleasant-looking town. The camera lingered on an open iron-grilled gate, then panned up a long driveway to the veranda of a large, rambling hotel-sized house.

"Welcome to Starting Over." A man with thinning white hair and glasses spoke with measured calm. Deep lines of care and concern were etched about his eyes and mouth. "Starting Over is not a hospital. This is a treatment center where people come to relearn how to live happy and productive lives."

There were groups of young to middle-aged men and women lounging about on the porch, some on the steps, some on the long white wicker sofa, or playing cards at a corner table. They were well-dressed and expectant-looking, like guests at a house party.

The speaker continued. "These folks don't shy away from using the words alcoholism and addiction. We use the words here, but we do not believe they need to brand any of us for life. Because of this," the man leaned forward as the camera zoomed to his face, "some men and women who have been patients, who have completed the 14-week rehabilitation program here, are willing to speak about it, to tell you how it works. These people are not actors. They are real and they will use their own names."

Matt mingled on the porch with the others, leaning against a shiny white pillar.

He turned, and I could see every angle of his face. He smiled as if on cue. The camera was doing close-ups of these brave, rehabilitated people.

For a moment, the focus was on Matt. The curve of his lips had no relation to the expression in his eyes. He waved. "That was for my wife and son," he said. "They're at home waiting for me. I can't wait to see them soon and hug them both."

I jumped up and switched off the set.

Benjie ran into the room wearing mis-matched pajamas and butter all over his face.

"Hey, you turned it off."

"It was a terrible program. Not for kids. You go on upstairs, son. Take the popcorn."

"C'un I stay up and play for fifteen minutes?"

"Uh-huh. I'll be up in a minute."

But my legs would not move. I sat frozen on the sofa. I sat there alone, all my strength gone, as the impact of what I had just seen crawled over me. Thank God Benjie missed it.

Mr. Dangerfield's surprise, though I knew his intention would never be to frighten us. He must have envisioned it as informative. What my mother would have endorsed as a solution for my life. Matt engineered it somehow, and he was right about her. This is what she always wanted, what she had always done. Whisked him away for help, hoping to bring him back to me transformed. Only this time Matt did it his way, out in the open at last, so laudable, and so threatening. Perhaps many of the people on that porch would go back to happy and productive lives, but not the man whose face I just saw. His demons lay deeper than drink. He knew I'd be watching. Mr. Dangerfield would surely have told him, all part of the happy news. For all these weeks, 14 of them, he was hundreds of miles away. Since the second week in June.

Then who …? Who had driven hunched over the wheel of our station wagon wearing Matt's hat? Who forced Benjie and me off the road on that terrifying wet summer night?

Who wrote the note that said Mr. Wells was coming to pick up his family in the hospital? Who drove the old blue wagon into the hospital parking lot? If not Matt, then who? And why?

Knowing where Matt was, seeing the look in his eyes on camera, made me even more frightened he would appear and try to grab Benjie. Did S.J. invent her sordid tale to make me forget about the book? Did I walk into the parlor like the unsuspecting fly? Was she a friend, or William's pawn?

What of William's fantasy? His talk of love? Did Harriet know, did she hate me, too? Would William admit it if the book was found, or would he order the children to keep silent?

I did not hear Harriet and William when they came home. For

once, I fell into a deep sleep from the sheer exhaustion, the heavy burden of endless questions like a thousand loose puzzle pieces I could not fit together.

24

When Benjie and I came down for breakfast in the morning, Harriet and William didn't seem to hear us. They were whispering, leaning together at the long kitchen windows, watching boats glide by on the bay. Her head on his shoulder, his arm around her waist. I thought I heard Harriet giggle, though that couldn't be. The sun was shining on her brass pots of pink geraniums. I smelled waffles baking. Could I have exaggerated S.J.'s grotesque, twisted story from last night?

Harriet wore a frilly apron tied over her slacks and blouse and her hair was loose, held back with a turquoise ribbon. She was glowing. Girlish. I had a feeling she did not need Benjie and me to spoil this moment.

I smiled at her in apology. "Ah, I think Benjie and I are going to get Skipper and go for a walk. We'll fix some breakfast later." I tried to steer Benjie back out into the hall.

"But I'm hungry," he said. "Can't I have some Sugarpops and then go?" If he was older, I would have elbowed him not too gently, but I knew he wouldn't understand.

"Of course," William said. "Come on in and sit in this chair, Sprout. It's just for you. Aunt Harriet's making a special treat. Maybe you'd rather have waffles and syrup."

I tried to catch Harriet's eye and signal my regret, but she ignored my glance. There was nothing to do but to join them and permit Benjie to be plied with butter, syrup and a plateful of waffles.

"How 'bout one more, Sprout? Could you handle it?" William grinned his sunny, beguiling grin.

"William, that child is swimming in syrup now." Harriet sounded stern, but her eyes were mellow.

"OK, Benj," I said, not wanting to spoil his fun. "I think this is breakfast and lunch all in one, don't you?"

He munched, licked his fingers, and studied us around the table. "Guess what," he said. He reached for his milk and swallowed a big gulp. "I saw the girl again last night."

Harriet dropped her fork. The three of us stared at him. The color and gaiety drained from William's face. I felt the rush of adrenaline I knew too well.

I tried to make my voice sound casual. "You must have been having a dream, sweetie. Remember, we decided about that before."

"Jake says she's a ghost," he said.

Harriet slapped her napkin on the table. "Enough. You should know better, young man," her voice shook, "than to listen to tales from a silly boy like Jake. There aren't any ghosts, Benjie. None. You know that. Ghosts are just made up in spooky stories. They are not real."

William rallied. "Come on, Sprout," he said, "you didn't see any ghost. Ghosts wear long white sheets and go, 'Whooo-whooo-whooo,' and they turn out to be somebody dressed up for Halloween. You didn't see anything like that, now, did you?"

Benjie frowned for a moment, then shook his head. "Well, no. Course not. I would've been too scared. But this wasn't a scary ghost. I woke up and she was there, then she just kinda went away and I went back to sleep. I wasn't scared. And, you know what?" He studied his plate, pushing more bites onto his fork. "She kinda looks like Mommy."

Harriet eyed William across the table before turning to Benjie again. "You see? You were just having a dream about your mother."

Benjie looked up at me. "But Mommy isn't a Indian," he said.

William pushed back his chair, knocking it over. It clattered to the floor where he let it lie. "This discussion's over." The look he leveled at me had nothing in it of love, as if the whole eerie, disturbing matter was my fault. "You had a dream, son, and we're not going to talk anymore about it. Come on, I'll walk you down to the stable myself."

"I'm sorry," I said to Harriet when they left. "You and William were having such a lovely time." I started clearing the table, taking our dishes to the sink.

She shrugged, rose, and began wiping batter from the waffle iron. "To be honest with you, Abby, I'm sorry you ever came here. All this business of stirring up stories of the past. It's pointless, and it's too late. But of course, we invited you, didn't we? Well, you'll be taking Benjie back to New York to start a normal life for him again soon." She folded the dishcloth on the counter and turned to me. Her arms were crossed, traces of girlishness wiped from her face. "What day are you leaving, Abby?"

"I should be hearing from Mr. Dangerfield any time now about the contract on my mother's house," I said. I was fencing that question off. "As soon as I get a check we'll be able to fly back. But, Harriet, you don't really believe, do you, that Benjie saw an apparition who appears when children are in danger?"

"I think he imagined it. I think those little roughneck Tomisons were trying to scare him and put the idea in his head from the tales they've heard around town."

Harriet stared straight at me, her lips clenched in a thin line. There was no mistaking the hostility in her eyes. "William despises that story, Abigail. Your father told it to him when he was a young, impressionable child, not much older than Benjie. People call it a charming old legend, but it didn't charm William. It frightened him. It was weird, the Indian girl who appeared, then vanished and was found floating near Broad Creek. Your father actually claimed to see her once, but he was delirious at the time."

"My father called her a gentle spirit." My voice quivered in defense of his benevolence. "I'm sure he didn't mean to frighten William. My father wasn't like that."

Harriet ignored my emotion because she was too full of her own to stop. "A Collington saw her the night before he fell off a pony and broke both his legs. The real story was, I heard it—and I lived with my family down the road at what used to be called the old Parker place, before that, you know. Well, the truth was the child didn't know how to ride. He was told not to get on that animal, but he did it anyway when nobody was around. So, after he fell, he made up the tale about seeing the girl as if his accident was some act of fate, and not caused by his disobedience."

"There are other old stories, but they all come down to the fact that nobody ever sees her except children or somebody already hysterical or superstitious." She took a deep breath, turned, and fixed her gaze beyond the windows to the rolling blue of the bay.

"A young guest, a teenager, was sleeping in the nursery at the time. One day William had a water-skiing accident. She woke up that morning, sobbing. She claimed she dreamed something awful happened to a child. But William was twenty years old then. He could hardly have qualified as a child."

"The guest went home, and her parents took her to a psychiatrist. She kept insisting she should have been able to warn William. I'm sure she thought she was in love with him, although William and I knew we'd marry someday, long before that."

"The girl was neurotic. You see, it's all somebody's nonsense. In a house as old as this, one tale leads to another and after a while it's hard to tell truth from legend, fact from fiction. But William doesn't like that story. He doesn't like it at all. He just has a strange, uncomfortable feeling about it."

"I think I can understand," I said.

The words of the eerie poem that gave me the shivers when I was a child came back to me in vivid, chilling detail.

Up the airy mountain,

Down the rushy glen,
We daren't go a-hunting
For fear of little men

That rainy afternoon was impossible to forget. I might have been six or seven. My mother was busy with errands. Daddy was working in his den, stopping to leaf through a book now and then, or tell me a story, when I ran out of ways to entertain myself. For no particular reason, certainly not to frighten me, perhaps just for the enchantment of it, he started reciting, and I started visualizing. The poem seemed to go on and on.

By the craggy hillside
Through the mosses bare,
They have planted thorn trees
For pleasure here and there.

They stole little Bridget
For seven years long;
When she came down again
Her friends were all gone.

"Daddy, stop," I cried. "Don't say that." I remembered putting my hands to my ears.

I experienced for the first time the power of imagination. Words painting pictures in my mind. The awesome terror of the mysterious unknown. He stopped of course and hugged me and picked up another book. Still, I never quite forgot that poem and that feeling.

The idea that William was also vulnerable to the inexplicable made me feel a new kind of kinship with this strangely complex man.

Harriet wedged the waffle iron back on its shelf. "I'll finish cleaning up," I said.

"Thanks, but you'd better go get Benjie. William has a meeting in Philadelphia today."

I was glad to head outside, anxious to have Benjie back in my sight. It was still warm enough for shorts though Benjie and I both wore sweaters.

"Keep an eye on that child, Abby," Harriet called after me. She made me feel more uneasy. It was as if she was saying, "It's not going to rain, but be sure to take an umbrella." I wasn't so sure about the rain.

Benjie and William were heading back from the stable with Skipper frisking in circles around them in the crisp morning. William ambled along, swinging Benjie's hand, enjoying the boy and the dog. He was whistling.

I was not prepared for a confrontation with William, but I could not afford to waste an opportunity to speak to him alone about the lost book. "William, we're going to walk down to the gatepost and back. Why don't you come along?"

"Well, what a splendid idea. I think I'll just do that." His reply was quick and pliant, but the glance he gave me was skeptical.

Benjie and Skipper sprang ahead of us. The boy's blond hair and the puppy's curly, russet coat riffled in the southwest breeze and glinted in the morning sunshine.

"We'll beat you," Benjie yelled. His arms were pumping and he was already panting. In his red sweater he seemed to scud along like the leaves from the oak trees that guarded the lane.

For a moment there was silence except for the crunching under our feet. "Well, Cousin Abigail," said William, "you see how things could be." He tried to take my arm and link it through his as we walked.

I side-stepped away and stuffed my hands in my pockets. "But it can't be, William. You must know that."

"It has to be. It will be. You and me and Benjie. A family." He quickened his pace and kicked at rocks in the rutted driveway. I had to take two steps to each of his to keep up, making me breathless, and this frustrating conversation even more impossible. It was clear we were out of step in every way.

"William." I trotted beside him. "You're a reasonable man. You don't mean any of this. I see that's what you really want. A family. I'm sorry it isn't that way for you and Harriet. Believe me, I am."

"I don't need an interpreter, thank you very much. I know what I want." He glanced at me. "You want it, too, Abby. Admit it."

"William, you helped me when I was desperate. You've been like a father to Benjie, and you've helped to bring me back to life again. I do admit it, and I'll always be grateful. But won't you face reality, please? We are cousins. That's where our relationship ends."

I tripped over a fallen branch but went on, determined to make him acknowledge the obvious. "I have a divorce to go through. I have to face a man who abused me, and fight for custody of my son. I know I'm getting stronger, but it'll be a long time before I marry again, if I ever do. And you have Harriet."

I paused but he didn't answer. Only started his tuneless whistling again. Benjie was almost to the gatepost. "What we really have to talk about," I blurted, "is Bay House. Harriet tells me you go to settlement right after the bazaar and the auction. But I'm still hoping," I looked up at him again, "and praying, that I can prove my ownership of half of it before then. Would you help me, for Benjie's sake, if you could?"

Skipper and Benjie reached the one remaining post. Benjie turned, grinned, threw his arms in the air. His tousled hair, pale corn silk in the sunshine, his cheeks almost matching the sweater and the leaves. "We beat," he yelled.

"We weren't half trying," William yelled back. "I'll race you home in a minute. I'll even give you a head start." He stopped, just out of earshot.

"That boy looks more like me than you," he said. "If I had a son like that, I'd do anything for him, anything at all. And yes, I'd help you if you had the slightest shadow of a reasonable claim. But, Abby, you're the one not facing reality. This whole place belongs to me. All that crap about Young Will Collington and Ellen Smalldeer and the *Marriage Book* turning up was in your father's head. Nobody in their right mind ever believed Will married that girl. If you ask me, he probably found her out in the woods after he got the baby home and did her in himself, so he wouldn't have to worry about her for the rest of his life. All that stuff about her drowning herself, or falling out of a canoe, nobody knows that for sure."

This had to be William play-acting again in yet another unfamiliar role. I was not joining in any kind of game, nor was I going to be part of his fantasies. Ever. We reached the one gatepost at the end of the lane. I started to protest but he shocked me again. "William. This is the last time I'm going to say this …"

"Hush. I mean it." He cut me off as if he did not hear a word I said. He stared at me. His eyes held no sparkle. They were deep empty holes. "You're changing, Abby," he said. "I don't want you to change. I've been wondering what it was. You're different. Benjie's right. You are beginning to look like her. Like the girl."

I reached up and felt my hair. It hadn't been trimmed or shaped since Helen cropped it off at the House of Grace. It fell to the tops of my shoulders now, long and straight. I was wearing khaki shorts and one of Harriet's old jackets. I looked down at my legs. They were tan as the khaki and shaped with muscle. *I had changed. No wonder. I just spent the better part of five months walking, running, swimming and playing outdoors with children. I did feel stronger. Freer. I'd be proud, I thought defiantly, to look like Ellen Smalldeer. Yet, how did William Buford, who did not believe my father's stories, know what she looked like?*

I stood immobile as William and Benjie turned and took off together in a race back to the house. Lost in confusion, I followed with slow, heavy steps.

Of course, William let Benjie win the race. Left him huffing and giggling at the front door and disappeared inside without a word. With relief, I remembered William's Philadelphia trip today, grateful to be free of tension for a long, quiet afternoon.

Benjie got busy chasing leaves. I stayed slumped in a chair near the drive, determined to compose myself. William reappeared, polished and shining in a beige linen business suit, ready to drive to Philadelphia.

"Take good care of my boy, Cousin," he said. The smile was back as if nothing happened. He stopped beside us again as he drove his car around the circle. "By the way, Abby," he said, "I meant to tell you the doctor's coming out today to give Benjie a final check-up. His nurse called this morning before you came downstairs."

I was instantly on the defensive and jumped up from the chair. "Which doctor?"

"Oh, it's Carpenter. Dr. Somerville's still in Bermuda. To tell you the truth, I think he must be enjoying the sailing down there."

"But Benjie's fine now."

"We can't be too careful with Benjie. If he needs a final check-up, he'd better have it. I'm just glad that stiff-necked Carpenter decided to break down and make a house call like I asked him. Well," he waved to Benjie, "so long, Sprout." He beeped his horn and was off down the driveway.

"What time, William?" I called after him, but he didn't hear me. I stood there, fuming.

Was I supposed to sit and wait all day for Peter the Great to arrive? I had planned to find a reason to be in the stable, seen or unseen, and search through those stacks of old books. It was frustrating, having to wait and wait while time ticked by.

It was Tuesday. Wednesday, the long-heralded St. Mark's Episcopal Church Bazaar was scheduled to begin. A luncheon would be served in the church hall, all the smaller hand-crafted items and homemade goods would be on sale there. On Friday, to complete A Day on the Bay festivities, Bay House would be open to the public, for a fee. Harriet's well-rehearsed guides would be on hand in colonial costumes with ruffled necklines and billowing skirts in every room.

The climax would be the auction on Friday afternoon after the hordes Harriet was hoping for had time to inspect the stable stalls and all the antiques on display. The auction was to last through the afternoon and into the twilight, if necessary, until everything was sold.

Saturday night, everyone, according to Harriet's friend, Vera, would be at the Yacht Club Gala, and on Sunday everyone would collapse.

What everyone did not know was that on Monday Harriet and William Buford were planning to meet with their lawyers and the corporation that was buying out all of Bay House, for final settlement.

Time, for me, was not only ticking by but running out.

25

"Tomorrow you and Benjie must disappear." Harriet was hauling plastic bags of frozen chickens from the house into her car. Benjie and I were helping her load the trunk. She sighed, sounding breathless. "Chicken and wild rice casserole. For the luncheon," she said.

She dropped into the driver's seat and looked at me through the window. "We can't have Benjie running around in the crowd on Friday. You realize that anyone," she raised her eyebrows, "can come in here that day and be absolutely anywhere, even on the third floor. This is the one thing I wanted to avoid."

She sighed again, her forehead creased and frowning. The skin of her fine-boned face sagged a bit below her eyes, although it was not yet noon. I could see a pale blue vein throbbing at her temple.

"Don't worry," I said. "You know I'll keep Benjie out of the way. I'll be glad for your sake when this is all over."

"Not as glad as I'll be. Next Tuesday I'm going to sleep all day. Well, bye-bye, Benjie. Take good care of him, Abigail."

She switched on the ignition and took off smoothly, but instead of leaving she wheeled the car around the circle and came back to stop beside me again. "Why don't you fly home tomorrow, Abby? I'll bet you could get tickets. I'll lend you the money. It seems to me that anyone with common sense would take the child and go."

I stepped closer to the car window so Benjie couldn't hear me. "You know I don't have a home, Harriet. I can't go back to that apartment. Just give me a few more days. Please."

"Well," she said. "It's up to you, then." This time she sped off, sending plumes of pebbles and dust in her wake.

When we were alone, I took Benjie into the study to play school. I was teaching him numbers and the alphabet, and he liked to draw and color if he had to be inside. We could watch through the long windows for Dr. Carpenter to come up the driveway.

The man was, of course, impossible. He was only coming to check Benjie. There was no logical reason, I told myself, for me to feel interested, beyond parenthood.

When he didn't arrive by lunchtime, we left a note on the door, got Skipper from the stable, determined it was padlocked on the outside, and took our sandwiches and hot chocolate down to the beach.

We were sitting on that long, bone-bare driftwood log when Skipper began a low, steady growl in between frantic barking. It was a warning. My heart lurched, as always, at the thought of Matt.

The doctor stomped down the steps. "I don't usually make house calls unless there's an emergency and I certainly didn't expect to make one on the damned beach." He looked harried and irate as usual. His navy suit was rumpled. His thick, dark shoes sank deep into the moist sand with every step.

Skipper barked with wild excitement, leaping, twisting, sending sand flying everywhere. Benjie shouted commands. "Down, boy. Down, boy."

The pup kept right on jumping.

Laughter spilled out of me. "I'm sorry." I grabbed Skipper's collar.

"Amusing isn't it." He was caustic, unsmiling. "Me, making a house call on the beach, covered in sand, looking so ..."

Together we said, "Unprofessional." Then his eyes crinkled, and we were both chuckling. I was amazed at the sudden ease I felt.

Maybe he was someone I could talk to, after all. Someone who might believe my hunch about the Marriage Book. A physician I could ask, what do you do when your child is sure he is seeing a ghost?

"Benjie," said Peter, brushing off his trousers. "Take this hound for a walk while I talk to your mother. I saw the shell of a huge fiddler crab further down the beach. You might want to check it out."

"Aren't you gonna 'zamin me?" asked Benjie. "I'm all better now."

"Yes, in a few minutes. I'll call you." Benjie and Skipper trotted off. Peter sat down on the log, and I did, too.

I hesitated. So many questions. How to begin? I started slowly, trying to ease into a discussion of the Bay House ghost without invoking his impatience again.

"Do you think, as a doctor, it's possible I would inherit a resemblance to Ellen Smalldeer, the Indian girl, after all these generations?" *By this time, I was so attuned with her story, our shared ancestry no longer seemed like a myth, but a fact.*

"Genetically, once chance in thousands. Not impossible, but extremely unlikely." He was not impatient or teasing. He was serious.

"But with your dark hair and light eyes, and all that tan, it could seem so. What do we know about her? Let's think. I remember your father's entire description. 'She spoke English in a soft, halting voice. She had long, shining black hair and eyes the color of the sky on a clear summer day.' I'll tell you, since you asked." Peter smiled and turned his face toward mine as we sat close together on the log. "The thought of a resemblance has crossed my mind."

Then quite naturally, as if there was nothing but tenderness between us, he took my face in his hands and kissed me. I closed my eyes. I could not move. *I didn't want to move. I kept my lips lifted to his, deaf to the cries of the gulls, the soft lapping of the water. Lost in this answer to the longing I hadn't known I felt.*

I heard Benjie in the distance. "Hey, Mom, lookit!"

I opened my eyes. Peter was gazing at me with the same lost, dazed expression that must have been on my face.

Far down the beach Benjie was pointing to Skipper. The puppy retrieved something from the water. It looked like a huge, dead fish.

"Way to go, Benj," Peter called. He sounded encouraging, even though it didn't make much sense.

We looked at each other, smiling. We couldn't seem to stop smiling. Peter leaned into me, rocked me back and forth with his arms around me on the log. "I've been wanting to do that ever since I saw you shivering on the table in my office."

"I thought you despised me. You were so furious."

"I was furious at anyone who would dare to hurt you. I was furious at life for letting these things happen. I was furious because you looked so forlorn, young, and so scared. You were hurt but you looked so damned appealing. You didn't even know you were being brave. You had to find that out yourself, and I couldn't tell you. So, yes. I was furious."

Peter stared out at the bay now, not at me. "Since then, every time we've met, I've bungled it. I wanted to help you. I mean, I wanted to see you help yourself, but I couldn't let it alone. I couldn't keep my own feelings out of it. Oh, hell. I'm no good at expressing myself, Abby. I'm not used to it."

This was the arrogant, abrasive Dr. Carpenter, bending his head so that his cheek rested against mine. I couldn't believe it and yet I think I always knew it could be like this.

"Peter, why do you build such a wall around yourself? Hold yourself back. Does it have something to do with growing up on an Indian reservation?"

He pulled away and turned to me, frowning. "How did you know that?"

My fingers reached up to brush back a wave of his hair, then lingered on his face. It felt so natural, yet so new, I kissed him again. "There. I've wanted to do that ever since you crashed Jake's birthday party with my father's papers. But your background, Peter. I think everyone knows. It's not supposed to be a secret, is it?"

"Of course not. I didn't think anybody'd give a damn, that's all. But it did make me different. My doctor dad was a true crusader. Even when

I was young, I was like him in a lot of ways. I sure wasn't what you'd call your typical be-bopping American teenager. The children of the other white agents were older or younger than I was. The only kids my age were Navaho."

A cluster of gulls soared and dipped above us through the clouds. There was a silent pause as Peter looked up and studied the sky.

"My best friend was named Wohali." He removed his glasses and, sighing, massaged his forehead. "I told you he died of polio. Well, that's a sad story for another day." *I remembered the heart-rending photo, the tribute. And the fact that he was already writing about his passion.* "I've published a few articles in some medical journals. A couple locally." He shook his head. "It's frustrating as hell but it's a start."

I took his hands in mine, started to tell him I saw his article, that unforgettable face, to ask about his childhood loss, and if he would show me all he'd written. But he cut me off with a rush of words that made me feel the depth of his pain.

"You have no idea of the poverty, the lack of modern medical care, the impossible limitations these people have had to endure. Things I saw and felt and never got over. I want to do something about it. There've been improvements, but not fast enough or good enough."

"When I first came here to Kent Island, I realized I was right at the heart of history. This is a place where Indians were living in their own way, and flourishing, when the Europeans came and discovered the so-called New World." He looked at me and shook his head. "Which just happened to be at least 20,000 years old to the natives."

Peter shifted his weight and leaned forward. He moved his arm but covered my hand with his as if there was already a comfortable wordless bond between us.

"So much more should be written about the little-known collaborative side of many early relationships between settlers and Indians. The great contributions Native Americans have made to our culture. It hit me like a brick since I lived in that world. I decided that's what I would do. Write those stories. Or my version, anyway."

I sat up straighter so I could still watch Benjie splashing down the beach.

"My dad." Peter went on, sitting up straighter, too. "He was a lot like Old Doc Sommerville. Everybody loved him, and that love killed him. He could never do enough, but he never stopped trying until his heart gave out. That's where we're quite different. I'm not going to be like that. I can't be everybody's buddy. I don't have time. First, I'm a physician. I practice medicine, not conversation. Second, I'm going to write a book. Maybe more. I see people ignoring things that are … inhumane. Without a drop of guilt. Cruelty. Discrimination. Abuse. Things that make me want to take some kind of action."

I felt the weight of his words. Suddenly I realized who this private, compassionate man of conviction reminded me of. The finest man I ever knew. My father.

Peter's eyes searched my face as if it held a mystery only I could solve.

"You have the strangest effect on me, Abby. I haven't talked so much at one straight shot since I took my oral exams, and I haven't even told you what I came to say."

He looked as if he was about to kiss me again. I jumped up and started to brush sand off my shorts. *I wanted to catapult myself into his embrace, but Benjie and Skipper were circling back toward us.*

"I have something to tell you, too," I said. *I almost forgot my certainty about the Marriage Book and the gatepost.* "You first."

"Well, I didn't come here just to please your cousin William." He crossed his arms and gave me a sidelong glance. "I do believe your boy is right as rain, and I have to get back to the office. I'll have to make it fast. It occurred to me, the day after you left the hospital, to go back to the front desk and see if your Mr. Wells came to pick up his family, as that note said he would. Nobody came, Abby. Nobody ever inquired whether you left. Nobody on the floor ever saw a Mr. Wells." A frown creased Peter's forehead. "What does that say to you?"

"He's still trying to frighten me, paying me back for leaving and taking Benjie, drawing out the agony, punishing me." *I knew this was the exact form of revenge Matt would attempt.*

"Haven't you thought of any other possibility?"

"What other possibility is there?"

"That it's somebody else trying to terrorize you. Somebody besides Matt, using your fear of your husband," Peter said.

I began to pace in circles. "That's impossible. We saw the car, remember? It was turning into the parking lot. Our old blue station wagon."

"You don't think there could be any other old blue station wagons around?"

My head was beginning to pound with each of Peter's questions. "I know that car. The paneling has faded since it was new, the paint, too. It almost has a grayish cast now. I'd always recognize it. Anyway, it was sent back to New York. The only way it could be back down here would be if Matt drove it."

"Suppose that car never got back to New York."

My feet felt buried. I could not move. "Then, who ..." I stopped. *I remembered the helpless terror of lurching off the road on that night in July as the wagon sped past. I remembered my glimpse of the driver out on the main road, under the light, hunched over the wheel, wearing that pork pie hat.*

"It was Matt. That awful night after the storm. I saw him."

"Then why don't we smoke him out?"

"What on earth are you talking about?"

"Stopping the game. You're hiding. He's hiding. Somebody has to come out first."

I looked at him in bewilderment. *I wasn't sure I heard him right.* "You mean legally? How can I start the divorce? I don't know where he is. I don't have the money yet."

"I'm not talking legal. I mean, you just appear. Here and now. If he's lurking around somewhere, watching every move you make, waiting to step on you like some scared little rabbit if you stick your nose out of a hole, challenge him. Go public. Show him you're not afraid of him."

Peter peered across the bay as if he was trying to see people walking on the streets of Annapolis. A land breeze stirred the reeds and grasses surrounding our little sanctuary. He slid his fingers into mine. "What I'm suggesting is that you go to the Gala with me on Saturday night. We'll be beyond reproach as far as the divorce goes. You can ride into town with William and Harriet."

All I could do was blink. "That's a very kind invitation Peter, but you must know it's simply not possible." *I felt dizzy, my thoughts blurred.* "Wait. What? Do you mean, a dance? A party?"

"Look," he said, "you're not visualizing the potential of this situation. I have to go to this shindig. Doc sent me his two tickets and I'm supposed to show up and put on a PR act for the community. Apparently, a lot of the locals already think I'm a social dud. They're probably right, of course." He shrugged and pulled his mouth in a droll, upside-down grin.

"Anyway, for once I'll turn up at a social function and be dancing, if you want to call it that, with a beautiful stranger from New York City, the guest of the almighty Bufords. What will every person on this island be talking about the next day? Won't Matt hear about it, wherever he's lurking? Won't he know that you're saying, 'Look, I'm a free person? I'm not hiding from you ever again?'"

"You know I couldn't possibly do that." My eyes were glued to my son as he skipped along the shore.

"Why not? One valid reason."

I sprang to my feet and pointed down the beach. "Benjie. I'm not leaving my child."

"I know several good women who'd be delighted to babysit. They'd be happy to make the money."

"No. I'm not leaving Benjie with any stranger. It's out of the question."

"Bring him along, then."

"With Harriet and William and the whole town? To a dance? You call that a valid suggestion?"

Peter stood up this time. He held my shoulders and gentled me down on the log. He faced me, his whole body leaning forward, his back to the bay. "What do you know about Lewis and Clark?"

Again, I was stunned into silence while my mind searched for an answer. "Um, their expedition opened up the American Northwest?"

"Yes. But did you know their main guide and interpreter was a young Shoshone girl of only fifteen or sixteen? Sacajawea. I'd love to write about her life. She was the only woman on the entire excursion. Plus, she was pregnant and had a baby boy along the way."

"Well, I guess I remember her from history class, but what connection …?"

Now Peter paced, his heavy shoes dug grooves in the sand. "Talk about strength. Talk about courage. Talk about alone. But she survived, flourished, so did her son. That's the connection. I'm hoping you'll break free. Be yourself. Come out of hiding."

I stared up at him. Blue sky faded to gray as mist rolled in from the channel.

I can't tell him, now, all my suspicions that the Marriage Book was found. That I can't leave Benjie anywhere, anytime, because I don't know who I can trust. Most of all I must never hint at William's bizarre obsessions. Peter will want to protect me. He'll insist that I leave, and I'm not about to do that. My caution is a fact he can accept, or not. Freedom, Abby. Find the courage to act alone.

"I am being myself," I said. "I'm taking care of Benjie."

"Huh," he said, in his old obnoxious way, fists balled at his hips. "I was hoping there might be a whole lot more gumption in you. I was sure of it after I saw you take off to scare those two deer from running into the road. But I guess you're not ready to be the heroine of your own story."

He picked up his bag. "If you call Benjie, I'll check him out. Then I've got to go."

Benjie trotted back to us and stood statue-still while Peter made his final exam. "He is fine." Peter spoke without looking at me. "I won't have to see him again." He frowned at Benjie. "Son, think what you're doing next time. Think before you act and stay off of tractors."

He was leaving, taking all my unanswered questions with him. I slumped down on the log again, too angry to care. Low clouds hid the sky. Lightning flashed across the horizon. Peter tramped up the steps. I lost sight of him as he started across the lawn.

As usual, Benjie popped to the other end of the log, the hollow end, to check for messages. "Lookit, Mom," he said. His voice rose and bubbled with amazement.

"That's nice, Benj." I was beyond frustrated. *Seething. I could not make myself inspect one more dead fish, stick or shell.*

Benjie insisted. "Look. It's a backpack or something."

I whirled around. "A backpack?"

Benjie held up a moldy, scarred leather pouch. It was tattered, ancient looking, and empty. *Shaped like those I had seen in my father's history books. Leather pouches used by soldiers during the Revolution, to hold ammunition and keep it dry. Exactly what Young Will Collington's emissary, Elijah, as Will's letter promised, might have used to protect the precious Marriage Book for safekeeping when he returned as bidden and hid it in the Bay House gatepost.*

Again, my mind slid into the past. I saw that children's hiding place. A gatepost. Cracked mortar, loose stones covered with vines, children on tiptoe, small hands secretly tucking treasures behind a loose brick. An Indian girl and an Englishman's son. Playmates whose friendship turned into love ending in tragedy. Will's last attempt to show his parents it was a good and righteous love, even as he marched off to war. I pictured Elijah's probing fingers finding the same loose brick, as Will surely instructed him to do.

Could I be right? Yes, oh yes. I feel it. I know it. My heart thundered in my chest. My hands flew to my face and felt heat. *I am right, I am right.*

I started to run, to catch Peter before he left. Then I stopped. *I would be myself. Show him I was a free person. I would handle this alone.*

Deep down, like buried treasure, I think Peter and I understood that one of life's generous, unexpected miracles had happened to us. But it was too new. We were not ready to deal with it yet.

I had to find that book. Before Matt found us. I was certain I knew exactly where to look.

26

"Gross, Mom. This thing is empty, and it stinks." Benjie wrinkled his nose and dangled the pouch from his outstretched arm. With horror I watched him trudge toward the bay. I knew he would wade up to his knees and fling it, Skipper bounding at his feet.

"Stop," I yelled much louder than I intended. "Sorry, Benj. Please. Give that to me."

"OK, OK. Yuk," he said. "Skipper wouldn't like it anyway. It's boring. He likes sticks better."

My mind picked over the obvious. Jake must have put the backpack in the log for Benjie as part of their hiding game. Was there something inside when Jake first found it? A tattered old ledger? From the rubble of the gatepost? Dear God, I prayed and wondered about the condition of something so ancient. If so, what did he do with it? Could the children have thrown it out with the trash? Or did some adult have it who forbade them to tell? Could it be Harriet? William? Noah? Their father, Burleigh? Or even Matt?

I was obsessed, of course. I had to know.

Would someone have hidden it in a place so obvious no one would think of looking there? Like that stall full of old books in the stable. The auction was just two days away. All the items were cataloged and labeled with price tags. The book could be safe and undisturbed until Friday. Why didn't I search in the stable? If I could get in the tack room and take the keys, I might be able to open the main stable door. Search through the books before Harriet returned. I might also be there when the Tomison children came through the cornfield on their way home.

On the wall of the tack room was a large rusty hook. On the hook was a ring full of keys. Rusty old wrought iron keys. Magical keys. I could see that ring in my mind, feel the rough weight of it between my fingers.

"Benjie, let's go back to the stable and get Skipper's leash."

"Aw, Mom, he doesn't need a leash. He likes to run. He won't get lost. He never runs away. And when he goes in the water, you know he always comes back to bring me stuff."

I was watching. Skipper paddled into shore as naturally as a fish, with a small tin can in his mouth. He came out of the water, delivered his prize to Benjie's feet, and shook himself, giving us a chilly shower.

The sky was clouding over. The breeze was sharpening from the northeast, ruffling the bay, draining it of color.

I shivered, even though I wore a jacket. But my child and his puppy were oblivious to the chill. "Come on, Benj. It's getting cold out here. You should dry Skipper off and start teaching him to heel. That means teaching him to stay close to us when he's not on his leash."

"Why does he have to heel?"

"We may be going to the city soon. There's a leash law there, you know. We can't just let him run everywhere."

"I thought we were never going back to the city. I don't want to go, Mommy. Skipper doesn't want to live in the city, either." He knelt in the sand shaking his head and nuzzled the puppy's face. "Do you, boy?" he said. He rubbed the puppy's ears.

"I didn't say we were going for sure. I just said we might have to go." I was frothing with impatience.

"Come on, Benj. We're getting his leash."

I must find a way to get in the stable and check those books.

Benjie scowled at me and threw another stick.

"Now," I said. *I stopped just short of swatting his bottom, determined to manage my son without physical punishment after what we had both been through with his father. But sometimes, like this moment, he almost wore through my resolve.* I turned angrily and started for the stable, the boy and the dog trudged along in silence.

I had an idea. My mind began creating a scenario with desperate clarity. The sudden thought of Peter's approval brought an inward smile, though his presence would have been even better. I longed to show off my bravery and feel his reassuring hand in mine. But this I would do alone. I pictured Benjie and me acting out my plan, step by step.

We go back to the tack room. While Benjie gets the leash and the puppy biscuits and the training manual, I examine the keys. One fits the lock to the inside door of the stable.

We go outside to the dirt lane that leads past the stable and the other outbuildings to the farmhouse. If anyone is watching, we are just innocent dog trainers.

We clip the leash on Skipper's collar. I start to show Benjie how the book says to give the puppy play on the leash. Then pull in firmly while you say, heel, and push him down on his haunches so he sits just behind you.

"Now, you, Benjie," I will say. "All by yourself. Don't let Skipper see me."

Then I duck inside. Unlock the inner door. Go out again to make sure the lesson is progressing. Go back in and start checking the books.

I keep this going, praying for Benjie's enthusiasm. There are plenty of things the puppy needs to learn. How to sit, how to stay. Raise his paw to shake.

I realize my scheme could really work. So, we are going to attempt it. Now.

The stable was dark and shadowy, even in the afternoon, but I could see the books through the chinks of light that came through the old boards. I heard Benjie chirping commands over the thumping of my heart.

Under normal circumstances the books would have fascinated me, as they most certainly would have intrigued my father. Some were yellowed and musty, rescued from somebody's attic, I fantasized. "Love to Robert, from Mother, Christmas, 1885." *Treasure Island, The Last of the Mohicans, Alice in Wonderland.* Some were more recently outgrown. Popular reads on sale for fifty cents. *Exodus, Michener's The Source. Up the Down Staircase. The Green Berets, In Cold Blood.* I shivered at that one.

I ran outside. Back in again. I would have to move faster.

I pulled the door almost shut behind me. Inside the door I paused. Somebody was moving the padlock on the outer stable door. It scraped across the wood. Not Benjie, I could still hear his voice outside. I had not seen anyone coming. I was too intent on running back and forth.

And then, of course, the entrance to the tack room was on the side of the stable, the side facing the main house.

I ducked into the nearest stall and crouched behind a pile of quilts. Light cut a swath through the shadows as the stable door creaked open. I peered between the wooden slats where I was hiding. A huge form loomed over the books on the other side of the aisle.

Burleigh. He picked through the stacked books as I had done, only faster and without care. Glance, throw it down. Glance, throw it down. His broad back was toward me, legs rooted to the ground like tree stumps, arms moving like pistons. His grin was wiped from my memory as his boots kicked and trampled the rough floor. *I knew he must not see me. I held my breath and shrank back into the darkness.*

Make noise, Benj, I prayed.

Skipper began barking. They were playing, scuffling. So much for training. I could hear Benjie's helpless, silly, peals of laughter. I crept out of the stall, slid through a narrow open door, a small, nimble shadow.

Burleigh lumbered out from the front of the stable and pulled the door closed behind him. As he clicked the padlock, I paced, commanding "Heel" in a loud, stern voice to that silly, floppy puppy, trying to get my heart to behave.

Burleigh looked flushed and angry but was civil enough when he spoke. "You've got your work cut out for you there," he said. He gave Benjie's head a casual little cuff, as was his way with children.

He ducked into the tack room. I just made it. The door was locked.

The key was on its rusty hook. A moment later he stomped out and gave me a long look. He said nothing more, just marched on toward the farmhouse.

I was exhausted. I would not try that plan again. If Burleigh was searching for the same thing I was, I was fairly certain he didn't find it.

It was at that moment that the Tomison children came charging through the cornfield. Josh first, as always, the oldest and the leader. Cindy was next. She saw us and her pixie face glowed with exertion and love. Jake ran toward Benjie, his grin wide, red curly mop bobbing, a happier little clone of his father.

"Yay, Skipper," Jess hollered, "greatest trick dog in the world."

Benjie was ecstatic, showing off for his friends, making Skipper jump shoulder high for a treat.

From down the lane Burleigh let out a shrill whistle. "You kids. Home. Now." He stood planted in the roadway, legs braced apart, jerking a thumb toward the farmhouse. The children wheeled and bolted for home. *There was nothing I could do but watch them go as my heart filled with sadness for my lonely little boy.*

Benjie dropped his arm. Skipper nipped the biscuit from his fingers. My son crumpled down in one of the dried ruts in the lane, cupped his grubby hands over his eyes, and sobbed. "It's not fair," he said. "Why can't they ever play with me anymore?"

His hands flopped to his lap. He peered up at me, cheeks blotched and tear-stained. "It's not fair," he said. "It's not fair, it's not fair."

I stooped, gathered him up and hugged him hard. "You're right, sweetheart, it's not fair. None of this is fair, but let's not give up hope. I'm trying my very best to make things fair for you. Come on, let's go make some cocoa. You can squirt the whipped cream." I kissed the tip of his nose. "Then I think we can find Superman on TV."

I put my hands under the thin heaving shoulders and pulled him to his feet. A small arm reached around my back and held on tight. Benjie and I wandered hand in hand to the big house through the raw and fading afternoon.

27

I awoke to the sound of wild geese honking above my third-floor roof, and loose branches scudding along the shingles. The house keened a little as it did on windy days. For a few minutes I drowsed, nestled in the coziness of my bed. Then anxiety leaped back into my mind like a fresh flame.

It was Wednesday morning. The beginning of the long-awaited church bazaar. On Friday, Bay House and all the grounds would be open and overrun with people. For the Bay House tour and later, the auction. Matt could drive right in and park in the field behind the stable with all the other cars. He could be anywhere in the crowd attending a public fund-raiser for the church.

Matt would be anonymous. No one here had ever seen him. What would he really do if he found us? Would he try to take Benjie away from me? Would he try to harm me, or anyone who tried to stop him? He did it before. I had no doubt he would do it again.

I didn't even have a picture of Matt to show William. I thought about Matt and how I could describe him in every physical detail, forever, with every shuddering memory of sound and smell and touch. I thought about the way he smiled while his eyes looked mean. A square-set, stocky young man in his early thirties, five nine, sandy brown hair, gray eyes and that over-indulged, rich-boy-jolly-good-fellow pudginess in his face going to jowl. On the whole an average-looking man, easy to lose in a crowd, not one you would suspect of violence. Not if he was sober.

William would be the auctioneer on Friday, of course. With his easy flow of banter, he was a natural crowd pleaser. He would want to be able to spot Matt amongst the sea of strangers.

But now there were too many disturbing thoughts about William. Could S.J.'s chilling warning have been real when she said, "William doesn't want you, he wants your son?" How could he even dream of separating us? Besides, it was sick, and a total delusion. I jumped up to make sure Benjie was safe in his bed.

Our doors were open to the third-floor hall. Loud voices eddied up the stairwell. William and Harriet were arguing. I went out to the top of the stairs. Harriet's voice was rising. "That Abby. She won't leave. She must be out of the house on Friday, but she won't take Benjie and go."

"That's out of the question. Period," William said.

"Then where are they supposed to be? We can't have Benjie running around outside all day. Really, William, this is just plain stupid, and I'm late. I must get into town, to the church. There's the luncheon to organize. But we have to settle this."

"I'll take 'em out all day on the boat."

"You know that's impossible. You're the auctioneer."

"Get somebody else to do that."

Harriet's voice softened a little. "Nobody else can do that job like you can, William. Last year we grossed over fifteen thousand dollars."

"Well, yeah." William nodded. *Good one, Harriet, I thought. The way to reach William was straight through his ego.*

"We'll send Noah, then," he said. "Let Noah take 'em off for the day."

"No William. She's afraid of Noah." *How did Harriet know that?*

"Now you're being stupid," William said. "I think Noah'd be more likely to be afraid of her."

"What on earth do you mean?"

"She's beginning to look like that damn ghost."

"Don't say that." Harriet's low, even voice shrilled. "Don't ever say that. You know you don't believe it." *I pictured her trying to collect herself. Smoothing her hair, stroking her pendant necklace.*

"Listen, I have to go now," she said. "But I just thought what to do. I'll call Vera and get her to take Abby and Benjie to her place in Annapolis." Her voice trailed off. *I couldn't think of anything worse than Benjie and me stuck with Vera's cigarettes and drama all day.*

A horn honked outside in the turnaround. I jumped. I had been lost in this appalling conversation.

The back screen door banged. Women's voices spiraled up the stairwell. Harriet's friends, all chattering at once. They were picking up the last of the baked goods from the cavernous kitchen pantry. Benjie wandered into the hall, warm and rumpled in his Superman pajamas. From the bathroom window we watched three women rush from the house, laden with trays and baskets. They filled a white van, which circled the turnaround and sped off. Harriet appeared, marching to her car with another load. We saw the top of her head, with her dark hair sleeked back into its perfect twist. Her car moved along the driveway and was gone. William emerged with his briefcase, brisk and dapper in a tailored charcoal suit, climbed into the Mercedes and wheeled off.

Benjie and I were alone. We went into the nursery to get Benjie dressed. As I sat him on my lap to tie his shoes, I hugged him tight for comfort. *I should have been furious or frightened by what I just overheard, but what I felt was deeper, different than anger or fear. It was sorrow. The nursery was full of sorrow, as I sensed it on the first day we arrived. Yet I knew we were safe here because, as well as the sorrow, there seemed to be a warmth, a presence, of infinite love. I couldn't bear the thought of leaving this little room, even to go downstairs.* I sat hugging Benjie until he grew restless and squirmed off my lap.

I had to get up and function. On Friday we were supposed to disappear. On Monday unless I could discover what the Tomison children found, my dream of Bay House would be over. Four more days, then. That was all.

The heaviness lifted a bit as we came downstairs for our morning ritual in the kitchen. I would have the telephone all to myself in this quiet house. *My mind raced down every possible avenue as I half-listened to Benjie's chatter. I would call S.J. I was not too proud to beg her to tell me what the children must know.*

And while I was throwing my pride away, should I call the opinionated Dr. Carpenter and ask him to help me? Since our intimate scene on the beach, he was always on my mind. Yet, I was conflicted by the need to be independent, and the need not to be.

First, I would call Mr. Dangerfield. He must know something about the sale of my mother's house by now, and I was in urgent need of money. Benjie and I could not be beholden to the Bufords forever.

The screen door banged again as the inner door shut. Benjie and I stared at each other. It pierced my heart to see fear fill his eyes. Then we heard Noah's low tuneless humming. I peered into the dining room. Noah, armed with the vacuum cleaner. He nodded, without looking up, and went on humming.

The telephone sat as always on the small table in the hall. *I looked at it with longing. Noah was the last person I wanted to overhear my conversations.*

I waited until he was busy in the study, then I grabbed Benjie's hand. "Come on, Benj. We're going to get some exercise." We were out of the house in seconds, dashing down the driveway toward the dirt road to the farmhouse.

Then I stopped, rooted to the ground, still gripping Benjie's hand. S.J.'s old green sedan was clattering down the dirt road. I caught a glimpse of Mindy in the car seat, wearing something pink, and S.J.'s bright ponytail. My one hope threw us a cheery wave and disappeared in a cloud of dust. Of course. She too, would be going to the church bazaar. All the women in town would be there.

The farmhouse would be empty now. Should I go there and search? I stood, torn, trying to think. Could I? Did I dare? What about Benjie?

Then I spotted Burleigh's big boots from beneath his pickup truck, parked just off the lane between the farmhouse and the stable. He crawled out, glanced our way without waving, opened the hood and went on tinkering.

Without S.J.'s presence I realized I was confused about Burleigh. Was he our protector? Our jailer? Or just the farm manager doing his work? No matter the answer, there was no way we could pass him unnoticed, enter and explore his house.

We gave up and went back inside. Noah was waxing the kitchen floor.

Benjie and I had our orders, too. Our third story rooms were to be clean and tidy, impersonal as a museum. All traces of us gone on Friday morning before the guides arrived. All the toys were to be stacked on the shelves as if long-deceased children had arranged them there. I was glad we had a job to do. It was going to be a long, anxious day. As we worked, I listened for Noah to leave so I could use the telephone.

At noon the porch door banged. I peered down from our high open window and saw Noah perched on the doorstep. He ate sandwiches he pulled from a paper bag, then lit his pipe. The scent of honey and tobacco wafted up and filled the storage room.

Harriet left that room unlocked for the few possessions I brought when I escaped from New York. I crouched among the dusty, dark-eyed Collingtons and checked again through trunks, photographs, and stacks of ancient volumes. Probably pointless, but of course, I was obsessed.

There was no *Marriage Book* written in the large, elaborate, script that would have belonged to the Reverend J. Russell Witherspoon.

I stared into the quiet eyes of my great-grandmother in her oval frame. The lady with the pearls. I had not worn those pearls since the night of my arrival, when I believed I had come home.

By 3:00 Noah clunked the vacuum cleaner up to the second floor and was doing the rugs, room by room. Benjie was so peevish and restless he was jumping on my freshly made bed. I couldn't blame him.

"Come on, sweetie." I had to rally a little for his sake. "Let's go down to the beach. It'll be fun. You can build an awesome sandcastle." The last one he would make here, I thought with infinite sadness. I gathered a few things for him to play with in his red bucket.

The wind had changed since morning. It gentled across the bay from the southwest and there was unseasonable warmth in this late November afternoon. The sinking sun started what Benjie and I called slanty time, lighting sparkles on the blue-green water. *It was impossible to believe there was pollution in this magic stuff of my old dreams. Someday I would join the work to save it.*

Benjie checked the secret hiding place. I waited, anxious with a last hope that S.J. might have let the children communicate, but there was nothing. Nothing. I slumped on the log and helped make a drawbridge for the moat that was to surround the awesome castle. I cut it out of cardboard. Benjie pulled two broken crayons from his pocket and colored it red and black. I felt his disappointment as he began a half-hearted attempt to dig in the sand several feet back from the reaches of high tide.

"Look, Benj." I dangled a broken necklace picked from the sand. "Here's a chain for the drawbridge." He grinned and, in a few minutes, he was very busy.

I just sat. *Too much time to think and feel. Time, precious wasted time. It dripped like honey from a bottle. I would out-wait Noah. At some point he would have to finish his chores and leave. Then I could make my calls. S.J. would be coming home soon.*

The days were getting shorter, though. Sunset came earlier. There was little wind and the water in front of me was mirror calm. A mile away across the bay the sun was a copper-colored ball at the horizon line. The whole western sky was becoming one vast glory of coral and gold and the water shimmered with pink and gold light. My mind's eye saw my father settling back to capture the poetic moment, pen in one hand, pipe in the other.

A flock of white swans rose from our creek and silhouetted themselves against the sunset in a procession, one by one, their wings wide and stately, their long necks arching.

"Let's go in," I said. "I can't take any more of this."

"OK. I'm starving, Mom. C'un we have SpaghettiOs and hot dogs for supper?"

I couldn't help a wistful laugh, gathering up our things. "Spoken like a hungry little boy. I guess you're not going to be a poet. Any time soon, that is."

"Huh?"

"Never mind, sweetie." We started up the steps.

"Tomorrow I'll come back and put flags all around the towers," Benjie said.

"Well, we'll see."

We drifted across the lawn toward the house. Noah sprawled on the back stoop, smoking his pipe. Taking a break from his work, or watching our every move?

Once we were indoors, Benjie raced upstairs, grabbed paper and crayons, and plopped down on the floor of the study to draw some colorful flags for his beach castle, but he wasn't quiet for long.

"Mommy, Mommy. Come quick." Benjie's little voice shrieked in excitement. He stood with his face and hands pressed to the long study window. "Lookit! There's a police car in the driveway."

I ran to look out over his head. Red and blue lights flashed in the dusk. William's car hurtled up the lane with Harriet's close behind. *Whatever happened, I made a mental note not to tell them my mother's house was sold, that I could leave now if I chose to go. Not until Monday.*

28

I had felt William's fury before. Once. The day of the bizarre island picnic. Though in a sly, sick, secret way. This time he aimed it at me again, but in full hurricane force, with nothing hidden.

He stormed into the front hall leading a uniformed policeman behind him. Harriet trailed in the background, pale and speechless.

"I've been at the station house again, Abby. There's news. Weird, inconclusive, one mess after another. I'm sick of our life being turned upside down ever since you came here." William slammed the front door, leaned against it with his arms folded across his chest. Harriet stayed silent in the shadows.

Does he expect me to apologize? I will not, under any circumstances. Not now, not ever. To cover the awkward silence, I introduced myself to the officer. "And this is my son, Benjie," I said, ruffling his hair.

The policeman's gaze was steady but kind as he handed me his card. Detective Hank Simpson, County Police Department, Investigative Branch. He was also, it turned out, a high school classmate of Harriet and William. He was sorry to trouble us at this hour of the evening, but a discovery was just made that was extremely puzzling. The station wagon was found in an unused barn on a farm on the fringes of town.

"Miss Lydia Uffleman's place, it was," the detective said. "Miss Lydia lives there alone in her old family home and doesn't get out much except to go to church."

"Get on with it, man. No one cares about the old lady." William's face was flushed. He was almost shouting.

I felt my son clutch my side. I looked down at him, staring wide-eyed at the policeman wearing a gun, and in shock at William's strange expression and scary new voice.

Harriet stepped from the shadows. "Benjie, let's you and I go feed Skipper. We'll make sure he has a blanket for tonight, and some treats." She took Benjie's hand and led him outside before I could think to mutter thank you.

The Detective removed his hat and settled into a wide stance. "Doin' my job, William. And Mrs. Wells here has a right to hear the details." He turned to look straight at me as he spoke. I hoped William noticed the authoritative shift of the man's shoulders.

"Anyway, back to the story. Seems Miss Lydia's conscience was plaguing her. She hadn't given a thing to the church for the auction. She remembered there should be a fine old saddle out in the barn, right on the wall where her father'd kept it. With her cane she hobbled all the way out to the old place. When she finally got the door open, she had quite a start. There sat this grayish-blue car she'd never laid eyes on before. Strangest thing of all, the keys were right there in it. She made it back to the house and called us and felt quite blessed she didn't have a stroke."

Of course, back at the station when Hank put the New York license plate number into the computer, he discovered the car theft report. They tried to contact a Mr. Matthew Wells in New York City but couldn't locate him. Then they discovered his wife and son on the national list of missing persons.

The detective remembered seeing that name, just recently, and it bothered him until he went and checked a copy of the newspaper still lying around the precinct, and there it was: "Mrs. Matthew Wells of New York, staying with the Bufords."

"It was just about then William called the station to check progress on the case. I was glad we had something to tell him. William got to the station soon as he could and told us all Mrs. Wells' side of the story. That was today, just a while ago."

Detective Simpson was perplexed. If the wagon was returned to its rightful owner in New York, and then that owner, Matthew Wells, was seen since driving it here on Kent Island, why would he abandon it and leave the keys? Miss Lydia's barn sure was a good hiding place. But where was Mr. Wells now?

The detective shuffled his feet and ran a hand over his crew cut. "Mrs. Wells, would you mind stepping outside to confirm identification of the car?"

"Damn it, Hank. Of course, it's her car. I've told you everything you need to know."

"It's procedure, William." Hank's mouth closed in a straight line as he shook his head. William yanked the door open and stomped out into the twilight.

"Thank you, ma'am." The detective stood aside as I slipped through the doorway. The sight of our old car, parked askew in the driveway, made me rigid with fear. *Now even Bay House, once our safe haven, seemed full of danger. We weren't secure anywhere anymore. Even here.*

Hank handed me the keys. "Mrs. Wells, would you get the registration papers out of the glove compartment?" He held a fist to his mouth to cover a short, embarrassed cough. "Don't worry about fingerprints. We checked. There are none."

I trembled as I opened the door to the passenger side. *There was the old clock, the worn steering wheel, the rear-view mirror that was my only defense that awful night of our escape from Matt. I had to block the fear that clutched at my heart, the memory of Benjie's ragged sobbing, his little voice in my head asking why his daddy hurt us.*

My fingers shook as I unlocked the glove compartment. I thought I saw a bit of cloth sticking out from under the front seat. I slid my hand beneath it. There was not much light in the gathering gloom, but I knew what I was feeling. I pulled out a hat, a pork-pie rain hat, and stuffed it into the waistband of my jeans. My hands would not stop shaking but my mind was clear. *Someday soon there will be a custody battle and I will have evidence. I will have Matt's hat. No way I will give it up now to the police.*

After I identified the car, we went back inside and stood in the hall. Hank scribbled notes on a pad he pulled from his pocket.

He stared at the floor, stared at the ceiling, and coughed behind his fist again.

"There's this matter of car theft and the matter of missing persons.

There's also the matter," he paused, studied his notes then looked up, "of domestic abuse."

William exploded. "I told you, Hank, that's why Mrs. Wells is here with her son. The child is only five years old. They're here in my charge and under my protection. Now, I don't know where this drunkard is, but I'll tell you where he ought to be. He ought to be in jail."

Hank turned to me like I was the only one in the room. "Tell you what." He nodded his head as if agreeing with himself. "Far as the missing persons alert goes, that's obviously no longer valid. I understand there hasn't been any decision about custodial rights, any legal decision, I mean. So you can take your boy anywhere you want." He glanced at William. "Some people don't know that's the law."

"Now the car theft charge is different. There could be a technicality involved in your taking your husband's car. Since this is a family law situation, that might give you some leeway. Still and all, your husband did have a warrant issued for your arrest in New York. I'm going to have to notify the state."

Hank looked as if he wanted to be anywhere in the world but here, yet he went on. "I'm also going to have to inform the FBI because the vehicle was transported across state lines. But if we're going to deal with first things first, we've got to locate Mr. Wells. He's the one who made the charges. So, if you please, Mrs. Wells, for safety's sake, just till then, don't leave this property. You or your little boy."

"They will not," William said. "I guarantee it."

"Well, then, I'll let you know as soon as I have anything to report."

"I'll expect something soon." There was a silent exchange between William and Hank, ending when Benjie banged through the front door with Harriet close behind.

They were both breathless, though only Benjie was laughing. "I beat," he said. I bent and scooped him into a hug. "Cartoons are on in the study if you hurry quick."

The Detective donned his hat, said goodnight, and left.

William turned to Harriet as if to vent his anger on his wife, but she darted past us up the stairs. He leveled his anger at me.

"So now," he said, as if this was my fault, "every big-mouthed Tom, Dick, and Harry in town including the whole damned police department's going to know that Benjie's worthless father is a wife-beater and a drunk."

"I don't care," I burst out, "as long as they find him. I can't stand this any longer. Worrying about what he's up to, what he'll do about Benjie. Trapped here and under suspicion like a prisoner, as if I didn't have a right to be here. You have no idea how I feel, William."

He glanced up at the empty stairs, then back to me. "No. I don't." His voice was a steely whisper, his eyes cold and hard. "I thought I did, you know, but apparently, I was wrong. In any case you and Benjie are to stay here tomorrow and Friday, no matter what. You understand me? I'll see that we have police protection. For both of you."

Out of the chaos in my mind, an idea surfaced. I lowered my eyes so

William wouldn't see any change in expression, or what I was calculating. "All right, William." I hoped I sounded meek and submissive. "On Friday I guess Benjie and I will just have to stay at the farmhouse with S.J.." I held my breath.

"You know how I feel about Benjie running around with that bunch of ruffians."

"The children will be in school all day. What else can we do?" I tried to keep my expression blank.

"Maybe they'll find your Matthew Wells in some bar or a ditch before then." *Tacit consent. I'm learning William is never willing to concede a point.*

In the study I found Benjie asleep on the sofa. As I carried him up the three flights of stairs my heart kept beating one last little note of hope. Friday. On Friday. I would have one more chance, maybe my very last chance, to search for proof.

I went to bed, but not to sleep. An hour later, I was up and pacing. Around my room, to the front dormer, across the hall to the other window, down the hall and back again.

Praying for Friday, when S.J. and I would be alone in the farmhouse except for Benjie and little Mindy. One thing I was sure of without a doubt. Her children had found what I needed so desperately in that ancient soldier's pouch. How could I get S.J. to tell me what happened to it if in fact she knew? She would have to know. I would trust her as my dear and only friend. I would ask her outright. Though, I remembered with a sinking heart, she already evaded my questions once. Maybe I shouldn't trust her. Maybe I would have to trick her into answering. But how?

Pacing, I tried to make the urgency of Friday keep thoughts of Matt out of my mind. Terrible thoughts came anyway, the kind that surface between midnight and dawn. I was powerless to stop them.

Would he have walked away from the car deliberately and left the keys? Was he lying somewhere in that overgrown field near Miss Lydia's barn unconscious, or injured? What if he was dead in that field? What if he was … dead? Would I be glad? I didn't want to be glad. I had loved Matt once and he was Benjie's father. I would not feel glad. I would feel guilty.

The Forces of Bay House. I longed for my father. He understood these forces, around us all and in us. If only I had someone I could talk to. Someone I could trust.

The creaking of Benjie's mattress interrupted my thoughts. The child thrashed about in his sleep and lay sideways on top of the covers. I snuggled him back under his quilt. The moonlight was not so bright now. I went to my own dormer window to search the sky. The first gray rim of daybreak was touching the horizon across the bay. I peered at the lawn down to the edge where it dropped off to the shoreline.

Images appeared in my mind. A rerun of Peter stalking up the steps from the beach after his examination of Benjie. Shoes soggy with wet sand, his suit full of Skipper's paw prints. His curt and furious old self, hiding the tender man he revealed as we kissed on the log. Not looking back. Not knowing I almost ran after him. And now, how I wished that I had.

I crawled into my narrow bed and lay there remembering the arc of his body as he pressed it to mine. My head nestled to his chest, feeling his heartbeats. The strength of his arms like a shield. It was him, of course. I would trust Peter.

I wanted his love, needed it, had it, and longed to be his in every way. I also knew his love would have a different meaning and melody from any I had shared with Matt. And no matter what happened, I would never be the same again. Still, it was very lonely, being brave and free.

The whole sky was graying and the birds in the treetops were singing when I was, at last, exhausted enough to sleep. For a long time, I slept. Blessed oblivion. It must have been almost ten when I opened my eyes to see bright morning light in the room and a strange woman staring at me from the doorway.

"Oh, my gosh," she said, "I'm so sorry. I didn't know anyone was up here." I sat up and tried to collect myself, pushing my hair from my face.

"I was just checking, you know," she went on apologizing. "Seeing what to do about flowers up here. I know you must need your rest, you poor child. Please don't mind me. I'll come back later." She backed out of the doorway, her footsteps fading quickly down the hall.

This woman knew about me and my plight. The whole island must know, this morning, I was that poor child waiting to hear about my vicious, infamous missing husband. *Oh, Mother, you would be so humiliated.* Ten minutes later Benjie and I walked down the steps. I held my head high.

We passed a pretty young volunteer arranging gold and crimson dahlias on a table in the second-floor landing. Music drifted up from a radio downstairs. She was humming, concentrating on the flowers as if the perfection of that bouquet was the most important matter on earth. She stopped, surprised, nodded at us, then bent back to her work.

We went into the kitchen. Four women, girls to grandmothers, bustled about with cutting sheers and buckets of blooms. Sprays of chrysanthemums, marigolds, hothouse daisies, black-eyed Susans and frothy white Queen Anne's Lace, my favorite, spilled from vases of every size. Everyone stopped chattering.

"Good morning. I'm Abby Wells and this is Benjie." I was determined to smile if only my lips would cooperate.

They muttered introductions and went back to work. Conversation was pleasant but strained and full of pauses. Sunlight poured in the long kitchen windows, gilding the copper pans that hung on the wall. The radio pulsed with soft, hummable, danceable tunes. I felt like an alien from another planet.

I smelled the overpowering scent of flowers blended with the honey and tobacco aroma of Noah's pipe. Benjie and I made our usual rounds. The stable to get Skipper. To the beach and the sandcastle and the long, bleached log, the empty hiding place. Then to the study for books and games and too much television. We didn't always see Noah, but we never escaped the scent of that pipe.

I waited for the phone to ring, dreading Matt would be found, dreading he would not be found. That night Hank Simpson finally called. There was nothing to report. No trace of Matt, despite a county-wide search.

Bay House was burnished and glowing and blossoming in every room, ready for Friday.

29

Friday morning. The day of our exile, and my last chance to search for proof. It was early when Benjie and I started down the lane and turned off to the farmhouse. Harriet and William, like anxious parents, stood outside and watched us go. Earlier, we saw the Tomison children crossing the field, and the bright yellow top of the school bus rolling along the main road beyond the corn shocks, toward town. Benjie trudged along beside me, quiet, pale and sleepy.

I wore one of the few dresses found in my closet, but my hair still hung to my shoulders. *If the length and shade of it identified me with Ellen Smalldeer, so much the better. She was real once, a woman like me, and she loved her tiny son as I love mine. I want to feel close to her. Thinking about her made me feel stronger and more determined to claim what was truly ours if there was any chance left at all. I tried to believe I was ready for whatever lay ahead, yet I was compelled to glance behind every bush and tree we passed as if Matt could be lurking there.*

A few cars were already parked behind the stable. One was an empty police car. Hopefully, its occupants were staked out about the property in plain clothes, as Hank Simpson promised. We put Skipper in his pen, temporarily moved behind the barn. The main double doors of the stable were propped open beneath its flowery horseshoe. We could see the volunteers bustling inside on duty in the stalls, awaiting the first wave of buyers, arranging and rearranging their goods, heard their excited chatter. The scents of sea salt and sunshine on the cool morning breeze mixed with the sounds of voices and laughter. Balloons floated from the weathervane on the stable roof. At the edge of the cornfield, a golf cart waited, trimmed with red and gold crepe paper streamers. William would be using it later in the afternoon to drive among the crowd, weave among the larger items for sale and start the bidding. Now the wind freshened, still from the southwest, making the streamers dance. The sky hinted of blue skies and a fair day to come.

"Hey, Mom," Benjie was wide awake now, catching the carnival spirit. "C'un I ride in the cart?"

"No, Benjie. That's for William when he's the auctioneer."

"Well, William would let me ride with him. I know he would."

"No, Benj, I'm sorry. We'll be at S.J.'s house all day."

Benjie scowled, planted his feet, his eyes searched through the crowd toward Bay House. "I'm gonna ask William. He'll let me do it."

"No." I grabbed his hand. "I said no. Come on, son, right this minute."

We moved on past the stable, Benjie hanging back with stumbling steps. "I can't never do anything," said Benjie, kicking pebbles in the lane.

"That is absolutely ridiculous." My voice was angry and abrupt because I was so nervous. "We're going to have a wonderful time today."

Benjie mumbled, sounding older than his five years. "Yeah, right."

I said no more since we reached the farmhouse. I knocked on the door. There was no answer. The door was usually unlocked. I gave it a little push but it didn't budge. I knocked again.

S.J. cracked the door open. All I could see was a sliver of her forehead and the freckles dotting her red nose.

She did not resemble my upbeat friend. Her hair was matted out of its pretty flyaway tangle as if she hadn't brushed it. Her eyes were red and puffy, her creamy complexion was blotched. I knew she had been crying.

"S.J., what on earth is wrong?" She shook her head as if to silence me and didn't answer, just stood aside and motioned us in.

The kitchen was, if possible, more cluttered than usual. Burleigh sprawled at the table surrounded by bowls, cereal boxes, milk cartons, newspapers, stuffed animals, small metal cars, and leftovers from making school lunches. He gulped coffee from a large mug painted with a bright orange crab.

"Mornin'." His voice boomed, deep and gruff. It seemed to match his giant frame. He scowled at us and avoided looking at his wife.

No one said anything else. The tension in the room was tangible. I assumed Burleigh would be outside somewhere and I'd have my chance to be alone with S.J. Instead, here I was intruding on some family crisis.

I had to say something to ease the strain. "I'm sorry we came so early. William insisted, you know."

S.J. scraped her hair from her eyes with her fingers. "Sure," she said. "He told us you'd be here all day. Sit down, Abby. I'll get you some hot coffee."

Because there was nothing else to do, I obeyed. Benjie plunked onto the chair next to mine and reached for small a small red truck. Burleigh stood and stalked out of the room. For a moment I felt some hope until I heard him hammering nearby.

"He's mending the porch railing," S.J. said. She handed me a cup and sat down with her own, not meeting my gaze but staring through the window. "It's been needing it for more'n a year."

So then, like Noah at the big house, he was to remain on guard here. I would have to take advantage of the banging and hammering to talk to S.J. There might not be a better chance for privacy.

I sipped from my cup. I wanted to squeeze her hand, help her, find out what was wrong. "S.J., I can see there's something going on between you and Burleigh and I probably shouldn't even be here, and I'm really sorry. But there's something I must ask you while we're by ourselves."

She arched her eyebrows and nodded in Benjie's direction. "Little pitchers," she said, with tight lips. "Kids pick up more'n you think, Abby."

"That's just what I want to talk to you about," I said. "Benj, you can go ... Where can he go, S.J.? I don't dare send him outside today and I know you don't want him in the parlor. Can he go upstairs in the boys' room?"

"OK, I guess," she said, not too willingly. "But, Benjie, don't let Mindy see you. She's still in her crib with a bottle waiting for me to get her up. If she sees you, she'll holler."

When he was upstairs, I leaned forward and put my hand on S.J.'s. "The other day I asked you if your kids found a book, and you didn't really answer me. I think they did. I think they found the old *Marriage Book* that proves my ancestor married the Indian girl you told me about.

I think they found it when the tractor hit the gatepost, and if that's true, I must have that book now. S.J., won't you help me? Please."

She pulled her hand from mine. Before she looked away, I thought I saw tears starting in her eyes. "I can't talk right now, Abby. I've got to get Mindy. Can't leave that child in her bed all mornin'." With that, she left the table and clattered up the stairs from the kitchen to the baby's room.

I stayed at the table and finished my coffee. The hammering on the porch continued. S.J. was gone much longer than seemed necessary to dress one small toddler.

I got up as if to move only to the stove to pour another cup and peered into S.J.'s prim little parlor. If the book was in this house, I must try to find it. The shades were halfway down. The lace curtains were drawn but I could see it was not a room of books or easy hiding places. The glass-front china cabinet held only S.J.'s mother's precious plates and cups plus her collection of antique figurines. On the small table in front of the Victorian sofa was one large volume. A thick Bible with a red leather cover embossed in gold letters.

The hammering stopped. Burleigh poked his head in the door, looked around, frowning, and shut the door again.

Back in the kitchen I tried to read. The newspaper in my hand was from Sunday, five days before. It was impossible to concentrate. The precious morning was dwindling away. "S.J.," I called, "I'm coming up to check on Benjie."

He was sprawled on the floor of the boys' room pushing a wooden train around a wooden track and making little choo-chooing sounds. There were three unmade beds, two oak bureaus, mounds of clothes and pajamas on the floor beside more toys, and a bookshelf. On the shelf some books were stacked, others had tumbled off. My heart actually raced. I felt it pumping.

"Gosh, look at all these neat books." I rifled through the lot of them as fast as I could. Benjie kept playing with the train as I slid my hands under the mattresses, feeling like a lunatic but unable to stop myself.

We tramped back downstairs to the kitchen. S.J. had Mindy on one hip and began stirring baby cereal with her free hand. "I'll take her," I said. *I loved the feel of Mindy.*

"Just put her in the highchair. I'll have this ready in a minute." S.J.'s voice was casual, but her eyes kept darting to the porch door. She had washed her face, used lipstick and combed her hair. *I was not fooled. She was in some kind of torment.*

Burleigh opened the door again and stared at his wife. He pointed to the clock on the wall. It was 9:30. "One more hour," he said. "That's it." He slammed the door shut.

I lowered Mindy into her chair while she wiggled like a little fish. I kissed her head. "S.J., what is going on?" I couldn't help asking.

"Here, I'll do it," she said. She stood in front of me, bending over so I couldn't see her face. She fumbled with the strap that held Mindy's chubby body in the highchair. This one had seen lots of use and was still too big for Mindy. So, as usual, she was propped on a nest of papers and magazines and whatever made a makeshift perch. S.J. couldn't pretend she didn't hear me. I was standing three feet away.

"S.J., please. You haven't answered either of my questions."

She swung around and faced me. We were standing so close she looked directly into my eyes. I could see the tiny red veins from her tears. "I can't," she said. "Stop asking."

We spent the next hour in a kind of stalemate. We hardly spoke at all. Anyone looking in the window would have simply seen two mothers taking care of two children. S.J. washed the dishes. I dried. Benjie sat at the table coloring, slurping a bowl of cereal. Mindy smeared bits of banana and toast on her tray. S.J. and I drank orange juice. She kept looking at the clock.

At 10:30 the door banged open. Burleigh stared at S.J. but did not enter. She went on scrubbing the frying pan. He slammed the door shut. She stopped scrubbing and turned paler. We heard the revving of a motor outside.

I peered through the window. Burleigh backed the pickup truck all the way to the porch's bottom step. Again, the door banged open. Burleigh stomped past us, looking neither left nor right, straight through to the parlor. He came out carrying the loveseat as easily as if it was a toy, his face flaming the color of his hair. He marched down the steps and hoisted it into the truck. S.J. said nothing, but her hand went to her heart.

Burleigh tramped through again. This time it was the rocking chair. Into the pickup truck. Next the oval rug with the cabbage roses rolled up on Burleigh's shoulder like a baby blanket. He was emptying the parlor and everything in it.

I could only stand in stunned silence, watching the anguish on my friend's face.

Burleigh came in a fourth time, carrying a large cardboard box.

S.J. stepped in front of her husband, waving her hands in the air. "No, Burleigh. Not the china. You never packed dishes in your life. It'll break before you get it down the steps and what's the use of that?"

He pushed past her, opened the cabinet and scooped up a load that clinked and clattered into the box. He stalked in silence back through the kitchen and out the door. This time S.J. screamed. "Not my mother's china." She ran after him, slamming the door behind her.

Benjie gaped at this bizarre behavior of the grownups. "Mommy, why is Jake's daddy taking everything if S.J. doesn't want him to?"

"I wish I could tell you, Benj."

Mindy was frightened and crying, twisting and kicking in her highchair. "Benjie, play with Mindy. Keep her quiet. I need to hear what's happening."

I raised the kitchen window, hoping S.J. and Burleigh wouldn't hear its scraping sound. They were behind the truck so intent on their argument they didn't even look around. Burleigh paced, arms waving like branches. S.J.'s head whipped back and forth and she was crying.

I could see the line of cars moving down the lane turning toward the stable. From the farmhouse window I saw a crowd of people milling around. The auction. I had forgotten the auction.

S.J. was struggling to lift the box of china from the truck but it was too heavy. Burleigh stood facing her and held up his hand. I saw him jerk his head toward the auction. I could see her face. She was angry beyond caution. I heard her plead, "You can't do this."

Burleigh jabbed his finger toward the cornfields and swung his body around, flailing his arms as if to include the house, the trees, the yard, creek, and the sky above it. I backed out of sight.

"You're a fool," he yelled. "You're a stubborn, do-gooder fool. Who do you think's got a right to this place? Who do you think's kept it going, night and day, winter and summer, with almost nothin' but sweat?"

"You think it was William Buford, strutting around like some big-assed rooster, running back and forth to the city in his fancy Mercedes? You think it was Mrs. Hoity-Toity Fran Collington all those years ago? Too good for this place, wasn't she? Did she ever give a damn about it? And that worthless dreamer she married. Ben Collington. What did he do other than float around scribbling in his journals? Absolutely god damned nothing–that's what."

With a jolt I realized those were my parents he was talking about. I couldn't hear S.J.'s answer but tears ran down her cheeks. Mine, too. *No wonder I felt such ambivalence for this man. How long and deeply he resented me from the start, I could only guess.*

Then Burleigh's voice again, lower, slower, trembling with rage. "Can't you get it into your head? We won't have this house. This house won't even be here. It'll be bulldozed, right into the ground. And I'm going to shove that book right up William Buford's ass, so if he goes through with his big deal, and takes my job and my kids' home, he's going to pay me for it. And you're going to tell me where that damned book is, or this truckload goes right down that road to the auction."

I eased the window shut. I didn't need to know any more. All I needed was strength and more time. Oh, bless you, S.J. But, where?

Now Mindy was whining and kicking in her highchair. "Come on, Mommy, she wants to get down," Benjie said.

"OK. But you'll have to watch her. I have to think hard right now and very fast."

Mindy raised her chubby little arms. "Uppie."

I tried to move her but the strap was twisted and her little nest was falling apart. I wrenched the strap out of the buckle, lifted her and settled her on the floor. A corner of paper stuck out of the haphazard pile. There was handwriting on it. Large, elaborate script in faded brownish ink. It said, *Spoon.*

I stared, still bent over, my eyes level with that bit of paper projecting from the rickety stack where the child had been sitting. *Spoon. The word was so random, so out of place. Yet why did it seem so familiar? Then I knew what was in front of my eyes, but I couldn't believe it.*

I forced myself to act. I straightened, and with trembling fingers slid that loose page out slowly, carefully, so it wouldn't tear, holding my breath, tensed for the moment when Burleigh would burst through the kitchen door. Now I could see the remainder of the word and the florid signature it was part of. *J. Russell Witherspoon.*

The entire *Marriage Book* was there, cover to cover, aged and ragged, but right there, amid that small tower of trash. I laughed out loud as my tears fell. I rocked back and forth clutching the book to my heart. *Who else in this world but my crazy, wise, blessed, fearless, friend S.J. would hide such a treasure by letting her baby sit on it?*

I sank into the nearest chair, gripped the book as if it was the *Guttenberg Bible. Common sense told me to take the book and run, but I was transfixed. My fingers were numb as I turned to the last page, and I stopped breathing. I had to see. Touch. Believe. I gave thanks to God, and my father.*

30

I do not know and I may never know whether what happened next was accidental or deliberate. Perhaps it was a combination of both. I heard the sound of a crash outside the kitchen door. Staccato cracks of dishes breaking, and a high-pitched scream of pain. Still clutching the book in my hand, I rushed to the open door. Benjie and little Mindy jostled with me in the doorway, drawn by the strange and frightening sounds.

S.J. knelt on the bottom step, her left knee smashed into the wood. Her right knee was buried in the box of shattered china, her lower leg and foot bent up and backward behind her. She stared at us, wide-eyed with shock and pain.

"Abby, grab Mindy," she shrieked. I looked down and realized the toddler was holding out her arms to her mother, about to plunge off the top step. I swung her up in front of me and the book in my right hand swung with her.

For not more than a second, Burleigh saw and comprehended. His face went blank, his eyes darted from the book to the highchair. Then he was bending his huge bulk over his wife. He put his hand into the box. S.J. threw back her head and grimaced. When he brought out his hand it was bloody. He wiped it on the side of the box. He moved with surprising speed and tenderness, carrying S.J. to her old sedan, parked there on the grass.

"Abby, ice and lots of towels. Quick," he said, over his shoulder. My brave friend lay stretched out in the back seat with her right leg elevated.

Through the gaping red gash in her knee, I could see the white of bone. Her ankle was a purple balloon.

Burleigh shouted orders, working with the towels and ice and his large fingers as if he was a surgeon. "She's gotta have stitches. Old Doc's back. Call him and tell him we're coming."

S.J. grimaced but managed to blow kisses to Mindy. "Baby, stay with Abby. The doctor's gonna make me all well. Mommy loves you." The car skidded off through the yard and onto the lane in a cloud of dust.

"Benjie, Mindy, quick. Let's go back inside," I said. "I have to call the doctor. Then we'll see if we can find some cookies." I was jabbering, behaving like a robot, all the while on fire to stop the world and pour over the *Marriage Book. Did I truly find it? Was it really real?*

We circled around the forgotten pickup truck loaded with the contents of S.J.'s parlor. Went up the steps, past the box of bloody, broken china, into the silent kitchen. The *Marriage Book*, its scarred leather cover crumbling and battered, lay on the counter. By the refrigerator, where I left it in my rush to get ice. It could have been a loaf of bread or a carton of eggs. *At least I hadn't been hallucinating.*

Benjie brought me back to the present crisis. "Mom, you said you were gonna find some cookies. Is S.J. gonna be all right?"

"Sure, honey. She'll be just fine." I heard, more than felt, myself speak.

I picked Mindy up and dialed the doctor's number that was taped on the telephone, smudged and ragged from many years of use. A brisk feminine voice took my message. Dr. Sommerville was indeed back on duty. He would be ready for the Tomisons.

In answer to what must have seemed an irrelevant question, the voice said, "No, Dr. Carpenter won't be in his office today. Dr. Sommerville will be taking all calls for the weekend."

I put down the phone and started rummaging for cookies. There was not much logic in the way S.J. stashed things. I finally found gingersnaps, put Mindy back in her chair, and sat down at the table by Benjie. Powerless, I watched him dump out half of the box and stack cookie towers which he then demolished with his usual sound effects.

At last, with infinite care and, holding my breath, I opened the book. As I did, edges of the cover turned to powder. I turned the fragile yellowed pages as quickly as I dared. There were lists, by years, of the parishioners, their births, deaths, marriages. I skipped long columns of names, though some still-local surnames jumped out at me. I knew our story well and craved only the last page.

There it was. The last entry. There it miraculously, unbelievably, was. William Henry Collington, II, married to Ellen Smalldeer—April 27, 1770, by the Reverend J. Russell Witherspoon, Kent Island Parish, witnessed by Emma Elizabeth Hollins.

I sat, stunned, awe-stricken, drained of emotion. *Where was the jubilation? Where was the wild, exultant high? The kind Young Will felt when he went down on his knees among the dusty, tattered wreckage of that old tobacco barrel?*

I steeled myself as I poured over each word. Immobilized by the weight of all the grief and all the fury and all the pain that could have been avoided by knowledge of the simple truth, or by simple trust. *Young Will and Ellen, another unwilling, tragic Romeo and Juliet. They were my flesh and blood ancestors. Not figures of fiction. The first Henry Collingtons, heartbroken by the son they loved and lost but couldn't bring themselves to believe. Will's sister, Mercy, jealously fighting a ghost, and all the divided Collingtons and Bufords ever since. My father, Ben Collington, and my mother, Fran ... if they had known the truth and she had chosen to stay here with him, and me. My own long, anguished search.*

Burleigh, a good man, my father would have said, lost in the classic struggle. So in love with this place, so in need of it, so a part of it he was willing to steal Benjie's birthright and use it to blackmail William, except for S.J. and her mother's broken china.

What now for Harriet and William and Bay House Manor Estates?

If only my father was here to share the victory. I couldn't imagine him a grandfather. I saw him still dark-haired, dark-eyed and vigorous, all-powerful, a confident visionary. It's your home, Abby-girl. Someday I'm going to take you there. "Well, you were right," I said out loud. "You did believe, and you were right."

"What, Mom?" said Benjie. Mindy was fussing to get down.

It was a long, strange afternoon. I read stories, invented stories. We played games and made a fort with the kitchen chairs. It was not easy to occupy children aged five and one at the same time and also contain my monumental fear and joy. *I silently thanked the Lord for Benjie and me, but I kept wishing for someone to yell and shout with, dance on a table and drink champagne and blow trumpets. I didn't feel like that, but I wanted to.*

Down by the stable the auction was in full swing. We could hear blasts of recorded calliope music playing as people poured over the goods displayed. There was laughter, people enjoying A Day at the Bay. It sounded more like a circus than a church bazaar. Even when the music stopped, Benjie and I could hear the singsong of William's voice chanting like an auctioneer. I kept watch through all the downstairs windows.

The plainclothes policemen were assigned to monitor the crowd for anyone resembling the description I gave them of Matt. *Burleigh, I was sure, was instructed to guard the farmhouse. His pickup truck was still parked at the front of the steps. Would anyone have seen him roar off in the green sedan?*

On the creek side, all was stillness except for the wild geese and gulls that roved the sky. In the fields beside the farmhouse and in front, nothing moved but the stirring of the wind. Dying leaves drifted down from the trees. The soybean fields were bare but loose fronds from shocks in the cornfield fluttered now and then, drawing my eye, making me wonder. *Did something move behind those stalks? Something, or someone?*

The older Tomison children would be coming home from school soon. And S.J. and Burleigh back from town. *How long would it take to stitch that pitiful knee?*

"Come on, Mom, open the window." Benjie was pleading. "Why is William yelling in that funny voice? What's he saying, anyway? I want to hear it better."

We opened the window and listened, leaning together with our elbows on the sill. I tried to explain to Benjie what happens at an auction. Then I slammed the window shut. There was an unmistakable drifting scent of honey and tobacco. Noah. Of course. *I was still afraid of Noah, although now I was more afraid of what would happen when Burleigh came back.*

I turned into the shadowy kitchen, wrapped the *Marriage Book* in Benjie's extra tee shirt and buried it in the toy bag I brought, longing to escape to the sanctuary of our third floor in the big house. The afternoon was waning. *The house tour must be over by now and William and Harriet, I realized with floods of joy, were innocent of Burleigh's scheme. They couldn't even know that the book was found. Yet there was no way I could leave little Mindy, who had finally gone down for her nap, sleeping in an empty house.*

"Yay," yelled Benjie, peering through the window. He jumped up and down so hard the farmhouse floors shook. "The kids are home from school."

I heard that special coughing of S.J.'s car. The Tomisons were arriving all at once. Josh, Jess and Jake and Cindy encircled it with noses pressed against the windows. They moved in a cluster, Burleigh in the center carrying S.J., whose knee and ankle bulged with gauze and white tape. The children babbled questions all at once. S.J., looking ashen, was trying to answer. Nobody paid the slightest attention to Benjie and me.

Burleigh carried his wife into their bedroom, just off the kitchen, which S.J. once explained, had been the farmhouse dining room. He settled her gently on the bed.

"Take care of your mother," he said to their hovering brood. "She needs ice packs and a cup of hot tea."

I stood in the kitchen feeling my heart hammer as I clutched the toy bag to my chest, ready to protect it from Burleigh with all the strength in me. *Like David vs. Goliath. No match, said my common sense. My own righteous anger was diluted with fear, while rage only seemed to increase Burleigh's strength. Yet he brushed past me without looking or speaking.*

He hoisted the sofa from the truck, carried it up the steps and into the parlor. It seemed to be heavier now. His steps were slow, his back stooped. He shuffled as he went back outside.

I moved to the door of S.J.'s room. The older boys were gingerly putting pillows under her injured knee. Jake patted her shoulder. Cindy held her hand. S.J. opened her eyes and looked at me. She winced but managed a hidden wink. Then that wide unstoppable grin belonging to nobody in the world but S.J. spread across her face.

Burleigh tramped through the kitchen again, the parlor rocking chair on one arm, the rug rolled up on his opposite shoulder. Hardly in a position to protest, he hung his head in the bedroom doorway. "I'll have that room put back together in no time, darlin'. I'm so sorry. I was real wrong about your mother's china, but I swear I'll find a way to make it up to you." This he promised his wife as she squeezed her eyes shut again and lay back, grimacing, into the pillows. A helpless sufferer buried in ice packs.

The classic struggle. S.J. had won this round for me.

31

I grabbed Benjie's hand, pressed the precious bag to my chest, and was out the door before Burleigh could stop us. Benjie complained all the way. He hated to leave the kids and all the excitement.

Out on the lane, I ran as fast as I could, almost dragging him. *I wanted no part of Burleigh just then though I knew, and he knew, he was supposed to protect us from Matt.* Down by the stable, the crowd was thinning out. *There was no place to hide.*

William saw us coming. He bounced toward us in the cart. *I was both glad and sorry. I wasn't ready to face another furious male.* "What the hell do you think you're doing? Where's Burleigh? Here, get in."

Benjie was thrilled. Life could be great, after all. "That stupid ox isn't supposed to let you out of his sight. Where is he?"

"It's such a long story, William. You'll never believe it." *I was feeling, I must admit, a bit smug and not a little triumphant. It seemed as if the Marriage Book had to be shining through the bag I still clutched in my arms.*

William fumed. "They haven't turned up a single damned trace of you-know-who, that cowardly bastard. Nothing from town or from Simpson. Nothing here today. So, what's with Burleigh?"

"Never mind Burleigh, William. Listen to me." *I was dying to tell somebody. And who would be more appreciative than my cousin?*

"Hold it." His hand shot up. Someone was waving William back to the stable.

"Damn. We've still got a couple more of those white elephants to unload," he said. "Then we're almost done," he said with a sly smile. "People are starting to leave but I see there're a few more suckers to snag."

He drove us back through the thinning crowd to the grassy area where a roll-top desk, a fancy white wicker dressing table, and a beautiful, delicately carved antique harp were gathered. A soft-eyed woman in a long lavender skirt sat playing it. *If only I could stay and hear her heavenly serenade it would be celebration enough for my miracle. I wished Benjie could pluck those magic strings and see how they felt.*

Benjie, I thought with sudden panic. He and I were exposed to every danger, perched in William's golf cart. My eyes searched the thinning crowd. I could see Matt was not in any of the groups still standing about. Shoppers trudged back to the parking spot behind the stable carrying their purchases. Cars were already moving down the lane. The sun slanted in its golden time across the bay. For the first time in days the band around my ribs released and I let myself relax.

William aimed his charm and his auctioneer's spiel on those who lingered. Harriet rushed from the stable, surprised to see us in the cart. She waved to Benjie and was soon organizing a crew to help carry off the harp. When the other two items were sold and the buyers out of earshot, William let out a loud "Hooray."

"Hang on Benjie. We're going for a ride," he hollered. He flew us back to the big house as fast as the cart would go, bumping on purpose over the lawn.

"That was cool," said Benjie as we reached the turnaround. "Let's do it again."

"Not now, son. Your mother has something to tell me." He turned to gaze at me. His blue-green eyes burned into mine. "So, what happened at the Tomisons?"

I was bursting with my good news. Logical or not, I couldn't contain myself any longer. "I found the book, William. The *Marriage Book.* It's here." My words tumbled out, my voice loud and breathless.

I eased it from the bag and the whole story poured out with it. I remembered the day we walked to the gateposts. How, despite the fantasies he continued to spin, I boldly asked if he would help me prove my ownership if he could. How he shrugged, frowning and skeptical, but said, "Yes. If you had a reasonable claim." Now, he was looking at it.

William listened without saying a word. Benjie listened, too, squeezed between us in the cart. His eyes were round and solemn. When I finished, William was silent, staring, unblinking, at Bay House. Gulls soared above the bay, shoppers shouted goodbyes as car doors slammed shut.

The eyes he turned on me had lost their shine. "Well, Abby, you won, didn't you? I always half believed that story about Will and the Indian girl. I fought it, but I've known somewhere in my bones it was true. Harriet never believed it, but then she's not born of the flesh and blood of this place like we are." He put his arms around Benjie. "That Burleigh's a fool. I wouldn't have gone along with any blackmail scheme of his to deprive this boy."

"Harriet's going to be disappointed," he went on. "Mightily disappointed. We're going to have to work out a new plan. That's right, isn't it?"

Said the spider to the fly? "William, you know I'd never sell Bay House. Not my half of it and Benjie's. He'll have to decide that for himself someday."

"Well, yes," William's voice was sharp-edged. "But let's not tell Harriet 'til morning. She's riding a big wave right now. Sure, she's exhausted, but she and her cronies have made more money for this church than anybody's ever made at any of these shindigs. She's not ready for a devastating let-down, and she's not going to take it lightly."

He looked at me again, his eyes narrowed. "Who are you, anyway, Blue Eyes? I always thought that Indian girl would come back someday to haunt me." Then he was grinning his teasing grin again, eyes flashing inches from my face.

Up the airy mountain
Down the rushy glen

Why should I feel uneasy? He was only kidding. Actually, for a man about to lose half a fortune, he was being extremely understanding. Still, I shivered, anxious to get inside, and glad when he paused the cart near the house.

"Race you in the door, Benj," I said. "I think Superman's on if there's no one in the study." We leaped from our seats and Benjie beat me, of course. I prayed William wouldn't follow us, but he wheeled off in a sudden cloud of pebbles and dust.

Peter. I had to tell Peter. I trusted him with my child, my heart, now I would trust him with the truth. My fingers shook as I dialed his number and ducked into the shadows of the dining room. Hiding was still automatic. I hated the feeling. Why would secrecy matter now?

"Peter. Yes, hi. Wait. Listen. I found the *Marriage Book*. You won't believe where. I'll tell you the details later." I was breathless, pacing, my heart hammering in my chest. "I'm holding it in my hands."

"Hold on. Slow down before you faint." I heard the pride and tenderness in Peter's voice, even though he chuckled. "You're amazing, Abby Wells. You're the real treasure of Bay House, and I love you. Welcome to your new old home."

I finished my conversation with Peter, and still giddy, I called Mr. Dangerfield. Before we could even exchange pleasantries, I blurted, "I have the most amazing news."

"Oh, how wonderful. Have you been in touch with Matthew?" *My mother's old ally still held out hope of a reconciliation.*

"No, that's not going to happen. I called to tell you I found proof I have a valid claim to Bay House."

Mr. Dangerfield sucked in his breath but recovered his composure. "What evidence could you possibly have?"

I gave him the essential details of finding the will in my father's papers as well as the miraculously discovered *Marriage Book*, which proved the union between Young Will Collington and Ellen Smalldeer was legitimate. He was silent as I repeated the story of little Mindy's highchair perch. "So, now what do we do?"

"Abigail, this is extraordinary." Mr. Dangerfield's voice rose in excitement. "Make copies of the will and the page from the *Marriage Book* and send them to me right away. This could take some time, but I have a colleague in Annapolis who can help us get this before a probate judge. I am cautiously optimistic that we will get a favorable ruling."

In bed later that night, I tossed and turned, pondering more questions than answers. When could I borrow S.J.'s car to make copies? What would Harriet's response be when she found out they can't sell Bay House? How long would it take to resolve my inheritance? And what if the judge doesn't believe my claim?

32

Saturday morning. I awoke feeling chilled to the bone, haunted by fading bits of dreams I couldn't piece together. I fell asleep in happiness even as more questions formed. But I couldn't rid my mind of William's eerie stare.

The telephone shrilled below. Harriet hoo-hoo'd up the stairwell. Detective Simpson wanted to talk to me.

The body of a 28-year-old white male, no name or address, was waiting for identification in the morgue in Baltimore. Description somewhat similar to that of Matthew Wells, with the exception of a small skull tattoo on the inside of his left ankle.

I shuddered, putting down the telephone. *Not Matt, but the thought of finding him in a morgue was unbearable. I forced that image out of my mind. There was no question the Matt Wells I lived with and knew was still waiting somewhere, plotting to repossess his son, his wife, and to punish me for daring to escape. His own ego depended on that.*

"Hey, Cousin Abigail, not so fast." William burst out of the kitchen as I started back upstairs. He was wrapped in a white terrycloth robe with his monogram in blue on the pocket. His bright eyes were shining, his cheeks were flushed, his energy infectious.

"Go get the Sprout and come on down for breakfast," he said. "The weather's turned chilly and we've got the first fire of the year going in that old fireplace in there. We need some company."

My hands went to my hair, and I started to protest. I had thrown on the faded flowered caftan that hung in my closet.

"Oh, come on," he said. "It's just family. You don't need to get all gussied up."

I smiled a little at that. *I would hardly have been gussied up in my usual jeans and tee shirt, but I needed warmth right then, of any kind, after discussing a corpse that could've been my husband. And maybe this was William's way of smoothing over yesterday's lapse in consistency about the Indian girl's story.*

"Fine, that would be nice. Of course, we'll join you. But first, William, seriously. What about Harriet? Does she know about the *Marriage Book*?"

"That woman is remarkable. She's taking it like an absolute trooper. Come see for yourself."

When the four of us were eating bacon and scrambled eggs, cozy with the fire leaping and crackling, I tried to decide how Harriet was taking it. And William's cheerfulness, was it an act? I wondered if William ever guessed how much of a trooper Harriet always managed to be. She looked even more tired than she seemed during the week. The fragile skin beneath her brown eyes was more shadowed. Small lines were distinct on either side of her pursed lips.

"Well, the book really belongs to the church, doesn't it?" she said. "I'm sure there are many families besides ours who'll be fascinated with those old records."

"How 'bout some of Aunt Harriet's strawberry jam for your toast, Sprout?" William bent over Benjie to spoon the jam out for him. Their blond heads matched in every way but size.

Harriet's eyes were full of distress as well as fatigue as she watched. She raised her chin and got up for more coffee when she saw I noticed.

"Abby, I never dreamed, of course, that there was even a grain of truth in that old tale about Will Collington's marriage. My word, the whole story was so bizarre, and then it's been compounded through the years with all the nonsense about a ghost."

William held out his cup for a refill. "I'm not so sure that it's nonsense. Maybe the girl had a part in everything that's happened. Doesn't it seem more than accidental that the *Marriage Book* turned up here, after 200 years, just as we're about to sell off property that should come to this boy who belongs here as surely as God made the earth?"

"Benjie," I said, "when you finish your milk, you can run out and see if any cartoons are on."

"Please," I said when he was gone. "Let's not talk about the girl in front of Benjie. She's far too real to him as it is."

"She's always real," said William, "to children."

"Oh, William, stop." Harriet sat down again with her second cup. "You're acting like a child yourself, and you're going to frighten Abby with that kind of talk." She tucked some loose strands from the nape of her neck into her French twist. "Besides, we're about to be mobbed again with people coming to clear out the stable and take inventory for next year. Then we have to be ready for the Gala tonight. But we must get down to business here as a family." She pushed her cup aside, clasped her hands and leaned forward. "It seems we own this place together after all. What are we going to do next week? In case anyone could possibly have forgotten, we're supposed to go to settlement. The legal complications here are unbelievable, but, Abby, the years of worry about expenses have been far worse."

Her expression remained stoic. Here was the trooper. *I wanted to give her some of my hope. William was perfectly rational this morning, and all three of us needed some positivity.*

She pushed her chair back. "Sorry, I didn't realize the time. We've got to dash up and dress. We'll continue this later. Coming, dear?" she said to William.

The fire was dying but the kitchen was warm and bright. I sat where I was, listening to the faint creakings settling throughout the house like contented sighs, thinking of generations of a family linked through time by this beautiful place. Gazing out the long windows I watched the moody, gray-blue bay flowing beyond the terrace, the lawn a dormant brown, clouds racing across the gray-blue sky studded with flocks of gulls. How could anyone not love this place? How could anyone bear to leave it or give it up? Could what I was feeling be happiness, belonging, at last?

I was eager and impatient to get on with the divorce and start to live my life again, with Peter in it. Everything was different now. I was an owner—as William reminded Harriet. I just hadn't taken it in. The impossible dream was true. Now I needed to make it legal, with documentation and … what else? I would have to rely on Mr. Dangerfield again. I was ready to face Matt and be free.

Irritated with myself for not demanding more details earlier, I went to the telephone in the hall and dialed the police station. I had a right to ask questions and be answered.

Detective Simpson was not there. The officer on duty had nothing new to tell me about the search for Matthew Wells. Everything possible was being done. As soon as there was any break at all, I would be notified.

I hung up the phone and wandered, frustrated, into the study to check on Benjie. He was content, stacking several teetering walls of blocks, cartoons on in the background. I looked out all the windows on the first floor. Noah was on the tractor at the edge of the soybean field. A circle of robins, in no hurry to go south for the winter, pecked in the grass. Leaves were changing from green to gold. I could hear the voices of clammers, whose boat was anchored just off our shore. Nothing but ordinary, safe sights and sounds, prolonging suspense, making it more impossible to bear.

There was another phone call I was dying to make. I went back to the telephone and settled into the chair beside it.

I picked up the receiver, stared at it, put it down again. Picked it up once more and this time I dialed Peter's office. I knew he was on call this weekend. Please answer. I longed to hear his voice. To be with him.

Tonight was the Gala, but I had been firm in refusing to attend, leaving Benjie with an unknown woman to watch him, alone in Bay House. For a tiny second I pictured myself flaunting a new dress and my great-grandmother's pearls, twirling on the dance floor for the whole town to see.

"This is Dr. Carpenter," Peter's message announced on his new answering machine. "Please leave your name and number and a brief message. I'll be in touch with you as soon as possible."

He had explained how the machine worked. I just hoped I could use it correctly, though when the beep sounded my mind went blank. What should I say? How should I say it? I closed my eyes and tried to sound like an adult. I failed, half laughing as I spoke.

"Peter, it's Sacagawea." Then he would know. "I'd like to come out of hiding. And I have to finish telling you my incredible story. Please call me back. I'll be right here … um … OK … great … thanks … um … bye." An impressive message if ever there was one, I thought, feeling the smile fade from my face.

As I put the phone down the front door swung open. "Hoo-hoo. Harriet?" I ducked into the study with Benjie. Harriet's friends trooped into the hall.

"Down in a minute," Harriet called. They stood in the hallway, chatting, admiring the paintings, the old, wide, polished wood floors, the hues of the fringed hall rug.

I recognized some of the voices, could connect voices with faces. I longed to be like them. To be one of them. "I don't think I've ever been so tired."

"Tell me about it. I thought that auction would never end."

"Well, we served 86 lunches more than we planned. I was up at 5:30 yesterday morning stewing chicken. Dave said, 'Grace, you must be out of your mind.' So of course, I said, 'Never again.'"

"She says that every year."

"And Dave says that every year."

Little gusts of laughter. "We couldn't do it without you, Grace."

"It was fun, though, wasn't it?" This fresh voice I recognized as that of Kate Weston, the perky little librarian.

"It always is, in a wild kind of a way." I knew this voice, too. It belonged to a matronly-looking woman about my mother's age.

"But I'm grateful it's over and we made a big profit and now we can relax and enjoy tonight if we have the strength."

"Oh, I can't wait," said Kate. "What's everybody going to wear?" There was a flurried discussion of dresses and fabrics, colors and hem lengths, all voices chattering at once.

Listening from the study, I caught a sense of their holiday spirit now that their task was done. *My own spirit lifted as it hadn't in forever. Why did I scuttle away into hiding like a non-person? The curtain was about to rise on the best part of my life and Peter was waiting for me center stage. He cherished and believed in me. I felt him holding me, touching me, his lips warm and real on mine. I was done with hiding.*

There was an explosion of laughter in the hall. "Well, I mean it. I think he's kind of cute," Kate said.

Harriet must be coming down the stairs. "What am I missing? Kate Weston, who is so cute?" Her voice had a playful, chummy sort of tone unfamiliar to me.

Somebody said, "You may not believe this, but she's talking about the new doctor, Peter Carpenter. She's vowing she'll get him dancing tonight. He's the cute one."

"No, I don't believe it. I really don't," Harriet said.

"You'll see," Kate said with a giggle. They drifted out the door on ripples of laughter.

Loneliness hit me. I felt like a hollowed-out tree, knocked to the ground. Benjie's blocks tumbled to the floor as I bent down and hauled him into my arms.

"Mommy, you wrecked my fort. You're squishing me. Why are you crying?"

"Cause I … I love you so much." I buried my face against his neck. "Sorry, sweetie. I just really, really, need to hug you."

This was no game, and I was no desperate ingénue. Peter would hear my message and understand it. I would hold on, stay calm and get to Peter tomorrow in peace when today's dramas had passed. What difference could one more night make?

33

The day dragged on. Benjie and I spent the afternoon in search of diversion. We checked the crab pots off the dock. Counted jellyfish bobbing in billowing clusters around the pilings. We gave Skipper a run on the beach where Benjie had a romp in the sand. He had a loud, bubbly bath followed by his favorite tomato soup and grilled cheese sandwich for supper. Then he scurried back to the study and his stacks of blocks.

It grew dark very early. There was no sunset. The sky was heavy with low-hanging clouds. A northeast wind gusted across the bay, flinging waves that made a constant shushing sound like the ocean surf against our shoreline. Over and over, the foghorn at Bloody Point Light sounded its one mournful note.

I wandered onto the terrace, huddled in a sweater, wishing I could take a walk along the lane, down to the stable, anywhere. I needed to do something to take up time, to ease the endless suspense of hiding, and wondering, and waiting. There was still no news of Matt.

Harriet peered through the screen door. "Abby, you'll catch your death. I think we were granted a special dispensation of the weather. If it had turned cold one day earlier, our auction would have been a disaster."

I came inside, following her voice into the front hall, unprepared for the resplendent new Harriet shining before me. She was gorgeous. Stunning. Aristocratic. Dressed for the Gala.

Benjie wandered into the hall from the study. He was wearing white fleecy pajamas donated by S.J., and Superman socks.

"Wow," he said. His eyes and mouth were as round as they'd been the moment William popped Skipper into his arms.

Harriet smiled and looked more gorgeous. Such a compliment from Benjie was touching. She stooped and gave Benjie's cheek a tender kiss.

William bounded down the stairs, burnished, glowing, every bit the king in his kingdom, dressed and primed for the celebration. They looked beautiful, standing together. A pair of matched thoroughbreds.

Harriet's black gown was simple and elegant. It was classically timeless and molded gently to her tall frame. It bared one tanned square shoulder, gathered in soft folds to the narrow waist, and flowed in a straight graceful line down the length of her long legs to her ankles. Her hair was twisted into its own perfect figure eight. The tanned skin of her face was brushed on cheeks and lips with apricot blush and gloss and the new lines and under-eye smudges had disappeared. She wore no jewelry except long, slender, glittering earrings.

William seemed to light up the hall. His dark tuxedo, perfectly fitted shirt and diamond studs were a perfect complement to his chiseled good looks, the brilliant blue-green of his eyes. His blond hair was still a little damp and curly from the shower.

"We'll probably be late, Abby," Harriet said. "But thank heaven we can sleep in, in the morning." She was addressing me but stared up into William's eyes as she spoke.

The couple floated together, arm in arm, to the front door. "Lock up behind us," William said, over his shoulder. Then they were gone. I heard his Mercedes start up in the drive and pull away.

The house was silent in their wake, a brief magic gone from the air.

The foghorn in the bay sounded its one plaintive, lonely note in the stillness. Grief and longing swept over me. It gripped my heart, this forgotten force, this muted memory of love shared with a loving man. The burning need not only to receive it but to give it.

I jumped when the telephone rang. Silly of me, I told myself, as I went to answer. Detective Simpson was calling to say there was still nothing new about Matt, but there would be an officer patrolling tonight as long as necessary. Hank was thoughtful beyond the call of duty. I felt safer for it. I would not torture myself worrying about Matt tonight.

As for the naive librarian who used a word for Peter like cute, I would give her no further thought, either. She was young, a flirt, as distant from his world as an unnamed galaxy. What Peter and I shared was a connection as real, as natural, as the waves to the shore. Besides, he had admitted to being the worst possible candidate for any dance floor.

I wouldn't even allow myself to wonder how William and Harriet could act so, I groped for the word, so detached. As if the bazaar and the Gala and the usual daily details of their lives were all that mattered, that nothing else was happening, or was just some sort of fantasy.

Benjie, I thought in a panic. How long had he been off on his own in this house of shadows and secrets?

I raced up the stairs. He was playing with the cars, making little rumbling sounds. He was safe. I squeezed him with all my might. Perhaps I seemed somewhat demented, but Benjie was used to my random strangleholds.

I looked out the window. The police car that was in front of the house all day was gone. In an instant I knew why. The Detective, and everyone in the department, was on high alert for information regarding Matt. Monitoring the radio, news broadcasts, anything related to missing persons due to mental illness, addiction, foul play. Naturally, they thought I was safe. So, no more need to patrol the grounds.

"Benj, you can stay up and play a few more minutes."

I had to think. Someone forced Benjie and me off the road in the dark, but I saw that driver under the streetlight wearing Matt's hat. I was so sure then that it was Matt.

The hat. The feel of it. I remembered pulling it from under the seat the night the detective brought the car to the house. No one saw me in the dark when I hid it, my evidence, in the waistband of my jeans. Matt never parted with that old pork pie. How could it have been in the car if Matt hadn't worn it?

I pushed aside the few possessions on my closet shelf and pulled out the folded and crumpled hat. Opened it, spread it out. It looked the same as always, an old tan golfer's pork pie rain hat. With one difference. Sewn inside the back was a small label. The label had three woven initials on it. HPB. Harriet Parker Buford.

Harriet. Her athletic shoulders, square like a man's, huddled over the steering wheel, her own rain hat on her head with her hair stuffed under, chasing me relentlessly that terrible night. Harriet?

What kind of dangerous passionate woman lived behind the facade of that disciplined, perfect trooper? She never wanted me here. I had felt it, known it, but denied it all along.

There was no time for shocked disbelief. I would have to take my son and go, now, before Harriet and William came home.

Running. Again. But not for long. And this time it was on my terms. This time I knew exactly where I was going and who would be waiting.

I felt a sudden calm. Perhaps like a soldier who defies the fear of death when battle begins. I would call Hank Simpson, ask him to come get us. We would go to the police station, stay all night while he drove to find Peter at the dance, or at his apartment above his office.

"Benjie, put your clothes on. We're going on an adventure. I'm going to run downstairs and use the phone."

I picked up the receiver. Silence. I jiggled it. Put it down. Lifted it again. There was no dial tone. The phone was dead.

I cracked open the front door and peered out to the turnaround. The sky was leaden, starless. There was no police car there, or anywhere along the lane. Only Harriet's sedan. There were no lights at the farmhouse. I remembered the Tomisons were at Burleigh's mother's place for a family reunion until tomorrow and doubted S.J.'s injuries would have stopped them from going. My heart began a slow thudding beat. Vapors from across the bay drifted on the chilly northwest wind. That one note from the foghorn droned its sad sound. I slammed the door and bolted it.

I raced to the kitchen. Harriet kept her car keys on a brass hook near the stove. The keys were gone. I searched the counter, telephone table, rummaged through the desk in the study. I bolted upstairs to the master bedroom, groped through the bedside stands, the bureaus and drawers I would never have otherwise dreamt of invading.

No keys. We were trapped then, until morning. I didn't dare take Benjie and plunge out into the dark on foot.

Upstairs, he lay asleep on the floor in his jeans and pajama top. I picked him up and put him in bed. It did not take long to pack a few things in the bag we brought from New York.

I was still in my jeans and dark sweater. I laid out Benjie's jacket and sneakers next to my shoes and coat. Then I sat down in the rocking chair in my room to wait until dawn. The light was off, so William and Harriet—mainly this new, horrifying, secret Harriet—would think all was normal when they returned, that I was sleeping and unsuspicious.

Danger seemed to stimulate my brain. I planned quickly as if I already knew what to do. Tomorrow morning at first light I'd wake Benjie. We would creep down the steps and out along the lane. We would hide in the woods by the road, long before anyone else was up, and meet the paper boy delivering William's *New York Times.* This was our ride to town, straight to Peter. If only, I thought, reviewing the plan in my mind, if only the stairs don't creak. I tried to remember each step, which one would betray us, which one was safe. I wished I had thought to bring up a thermos of coffee.

I must not fall asleep.

34

"Abby-girl," a voice whispered in my ear. "Abby-girl." A sound so familiar, so beloved, yet lost to me through time. "You can do it. You can." Through the mist of memory my father held out his hand to lead me over the stream's steppingstones. The current clawed at my feet as they slipped on the rocks and the churning water was freezing cold.

The rocking chair creaked as I thrashed in my sleep and woke up, chilled to the bone. I was not aware of the moment when, obsessing about the stairs, exhaustion overcame my willpower. The voice I heard was only in my head, only the remnant of a dream. The room held shadows and deeper shadows. A force, a gentle but all-pervading force, seemed to have entered my body, alerting each one of my senses to danger.

I stumbled in the dark to the long window with the bedside clock in one hand. In the pale moonlight I saw it was near midnight, and everything felt wrong. Now, suddenly, I was wide awake, the hair on the back of my neck bristled like antennas of warning.

From somewhere below came two terrible sounds. Skipper, who should have been locked in his pen in the stable, barking and whining. Benjie's frightened little voice in the distance calling, "Mommy, Mommy." Anyone who has ever loved a child will know the emotions that fired through me at that second.

I was on the stairs before I knew what I was doing, never thinking of caution much less putting on my shoes. "Benjie, Benjie," I screamed, "I'm coming." At the end of the first flight down, his cries were louder.

William and Harriet's room. Their door was open. The curtains were drawn, the room was in darkness. The only faint light came through the unbolted, gaping inner door that guarded the deep drop into the Old Cabin. I could see just enough to know the bedroom was empty.

"Mom-meee." It was a terrified wail, high and thin and close. I caught myself half-falling as I leaned into the darkness beyond and below the open door to the Old Cabin in my blind rush toward that sound. Dank, cold air emanating upward shocked my senses. There was an instant awareness in me, deeper than thought, of the presence of evil beyond all the foreboding of it I had in this place. I tried not to gasp, although I felt short of breath.

Two small windows far below let in dim patches of moonless light. That was all.

"Where are you, Benjie?" I fought to keep my voice steady. "Keep talking."

"I'm here. In the middle. And I'm scared." Skipper whimpered somewhere beyond Benjie, as if he, too, sensed danger.

My eyes were adjusting. I was beginning to see a long, narrow strip of something darker than the air. It stretched from the doorway all across the height of the gutted cabin and disappeared into shadows. About two-thirds of the way along crouched a little shape. I forced my mind to focus.

From below, when I last stood there with William, I knew the doorway where I now clung was a small, vulnerable entrance to nothing.

The flooring of the loft on this side had all been ripped away. Only an edge of the loft remained on the opposite side above the fireplace.

So, what …? How …? I sat, warm and content, listening to William's rousing speech this morning, a hundred years ago, about the reconstruction. The work was starting today, he announced, his face glowing with pride and pleasure. He had paced, back and forth, back and forth, speaking faster and louder …

"Mommy, where are you?"

My heart banged in my chest. "I'm here. I'm coming."

I stuck out my bare foot and felt something solid. Wooden. Like a log, but not as round. William said a catwalk would precede construction, supported by scaffolding. Pointing my toes, I felt further, to one side then the other. My son was on this catwalk between the opening where I stood and the wrecked flooring on the other side. For some inexplicable reason the puppy was trapped there in the loft.

"Benjie, don't look down." My mouth formed words though I'll never know how.

"Mommy, I think there's somebody down there." His voice was not much more than a whisper.

"No, sweetheart. Listen to me. There's nobody down there. Nobody's here but us. Just stay very still. I'm coming to help you."

"I heard Skipper barking. You were asleep. I thought I could just go and get him. But it's dark, and it's so high."

"It's all right, sweetie. Just. Don't. Move." I started across the boards, testing the width of them with my feet, telling myself not to look down, willing my heartbeat to ease so I could breathe.

The boards shifted, swayed a fraction of an inch. There was, from somewhere along the catwalk, a slight cracking sound. *Oh, God. This thing probably isn't strong enough to hold Benjie with me on it. I inched backward, six steps to the doorway.*

"Benjie, you're almost to the other side. You're down on your knees holding on, aren't you?"

"I'm too scared to stand up." His little voice from the dark was shaky but held no tears.

"That's OK. You're being very brave. Don't stand up. Feel the sides of the boards with your hands, one on each side. Can you feel them?"

"I am feeling them. They're right here."

"Now crawl forward. Keep touching the sides so you can go straight ahead. Keep going. You'll get to a part of a room that has a floor, kind of. Like a little ledge. But that's all."

Dear God, please help this child. I tried not to think about the piles of huge, jagged flagstones laying below.

Skipper's yelping crescendoed. I couldn't hear any other sounds, but I could make out the small form in a pale pajama top creeping along the dark boards in the middle of nothing.

"Son, when you get there, don't let Skipper jump on you. Don't let him jump. There isn't any railing on that part. Stay back along the wall." Silent seconds while my heart hammered in my chest. Then scuffling, and the puppy's soft yipping, like the contented sound he made in Benjie's lap. "Benj, where are you now? I can't see you."

"I'm here, Mom. I'm over where this floor is and Skipper's here and I'm not scared now."

"Don't let him jump. Don't let him push you to the edge of the floor."

"He can't, Mom. He's tied."

Tied. The dog is tied. Then someone tied him. Someone who wanted Benjie and me to try to cross these high and narrow planks in the dark. The presence of evil is pressing upon me as if, in the yawning cavern below, lighted only by those two eerie patches of foggy gray, old tragedies wait to happen again.

I had to get to Benjie. There was nothing to keep him from falling off the edge of the loft. Now Skipper was whining, starting to bark. I could picture Benjie crouching with his arms around the young dog's neck. *What if the puppy pulls loose?*

"Son. Stay back against the wall." I prayed my voice signaled a command. "I'm coming over. Don't let Skipper get excited." I started forward using pure instinct. Shot out both of my arms for balance like a tightrope walker.

I did not look down. Kept my eyes riveted as far as I could into the darkness of the loft at the other end. Far ahead I could see a blob of white and a shaggy shadow. I inched forward, arms still groping like antennae, feeling my way with my toes. Not letting myself think about anything but the width of the boards and the safety of each step, though my whole being wanted to go faster.

The slower I went, the more accustomed I became to the dark. Like an animal, I began to distinguish objects from space. I perceived I was getting close to the midway point where I knew the largest jagged flagstone loomed below. It was then that the boards under my feet swayed again, more sharply this time. I paused for balance. The catwalk shuddered. I looked down. Dropped to my knees and clutched the wood with both hands.

Someone tall, wearing black that was darker than the night, stood directly below me, next to the scaffolding that supported the narrow perch where I knelt. Something sparkled, impossibly, in the inky black.

My fingers clawed into the boards as I stared down in horror, dreading to see what I expected to see. I knelt there, trapped and clutching, for what may have been seconds but seemed a long, slow lifetime, waiting for this figure to look up. It seemed especially terrible to me that her long earrings might glitter.

In the faint luminous dark, the face that raised itself to look at me was not Harriet's. It seemed almost that of a stranger.

"This is when you disappear, Ellen," said William. William, in his black tux and diamond studs. His casual tone was more frightening than anything that had gone before.

"William, please listen. I'm Abby, Abby Wells. I'm not Ellen Smalldeer. She died long ago."

"No," he said. I could make out his hands moving along the

scaffolding that supported the catwalk. "You were never really Abby Wells. You were always Ellen. You even found that goddamned *Marriage Book*. Now you disappear and the boy stays here and grows up as my son. You know that. And we won't ever have to sell Bay House. You have to fall now and everyone will think it was an accident. That's how I make you disappear forever."

He was beginning to rock the base of the scaffolding. There was no time to think. I had to act. In a macabre way, William and I understood each other.

"Watch, William!" I yelled. He paused and stared upward. "Don't you remember?" He stood transfixed.

"I was Will Collington's legal wife. I didn't fall down and disappear. I ran away to give our child a chance at a good life. But I'm not leaving now."

I stood up, somehow keeping my balance, straight and proud in my dark jeans and sweater with my long black hair streaming about my face. I turned and skimmed along the last half of the catwalk to the loft where Skipper and Benjie waited in the dark.

There was a sudden blast of light as the cabin's outer door burst open. "William, stop. Stop!" Harriet screamed as I had never heard her. "It's me, William. It's Harriet. There is no Ellen. Dr. Carpenter is here. He's going to help you."

Headlights beamed across the jagged stones to William's frenzied face and wild stare. He turned, lunged toward the light, but tripped in the debris. He sprawled onto the floor, motionless.

"Harriet, stay back. I have to move fast," Peter said. "I think he's only stunned, but not for long. I'm giving him an injection. Thorazine, a sedative. It'll kick in shortly, then we can deal with him. Detective Simpson's here. Noah's checking the house."

I was shaking, incapable of speech. My bones seemed to melt in reaction to my surge of strength and daring. I crumpled in the loft crushing Benjie to my chest. Skipper jumped on both of us, frantic with excitement, yanking on his rope.

There were more voices below. Lights flicked on in the bedroom across the catwalk. I could see what lay below, and what might have been. Someone was putting a ladder up to us in the loft. I watched as fear, relief, and wonder played across Peter's face as he reached the top. *I felt the world of love that awaited as his arms encircled us. I knew that all my questions at last would have answers and that all the answers led to him.*

35

Peter gripped a squirming puppy and shouldered Benjie. He supported me, with my bloodied, splintered feet and fingers. Dazed, mute, my screams still echoing in my head. I only know his touch turned my terror into a sense of safety and a longing to live wrapped in his arms for the rest of my life.

Of course, I was in shock. Now I know many things happened I only half remember. William, crumpled, gray, wasted, slumped like a rag doll on the floor. Hank Simpson speaking in slow motion to Peter, "I can arrest him or not, Doc, it's up to you." Peter shaking his head, his voice loud and hollow. "This man needs psychiatric help." Harriet's blanched, tearful face as she begged me not to press charges. Someone leading me, edging us around the stones until my feet touched grass, and the Old Cabin door swung shut with a crash.

No stars, only a sliver of moon. Crickets chirped. Waves slapped against the shoreline. I remember Noah's tobacco smoke mixed with crisp fall air. Peter holding Benjie, his voice sounding far away, repeating, "He's all right, he's all right, he's all right." Squealing tires, headlights bouncing down our lane, a car door slamming. Burleigh's eyes as they swam into focus. His strong arms as he said, "Abby, you and Benjie are comin' with me." Then a bed, a quilt, my child and me tucked inside. After that, nothing.

Until now. I blinked open my eyes to see S.J. perched on the bed, holding out a steaming mug of coffee. The warm spot in the nest of blankets beside me was empty. I panicked. "Benjie, where's Benjie?"

"He's fine. He's OK, I promise. He's downstairs with my kids eating donuts." She squeezed my hand. "Peter's here, Abby. He's been pacing in the kitchen all morning. He wants to see you right away."

A memory tugged at my heart. We were given donuts and shelter at the House of Grace in our far-off other lifetime, five months ago. Now S.J.'s coffee smelled so good, so normal. I needed normal, and Peter was here. Still, everything felt so hazy. I struggled to sit up on my elbows. Golden light poured through the window, but like a wave, the horrors of last night flooded back.

"S.J., Abby, I'm coming up." Peter's footsteps pounded on the stairs as S.J. moved to the window, opening it to the clean November air. Then Peter filled the doorway. Rumpled dress shirt and rolled-up sleeves, half pulled from his navy trousers, silver striped tie stuffed in a pocket. Flushed cheeks, dark circled eyes smiling into mine, dark wave of hair tumbling across his forehead. *How did I ever think this man was unremarkable?* He crossed the room in two steps, kissed my hands, my eyes, my mouth. He wrapped me in his arms and began to talk.

"Thank God you and Benj are all right. Thank God I left the Gala when I did and followed William home. I'll never forgive myself for what I didn't see." When he sat up, he blinked back tears. "You were in danger here. But after all that fear, all that hiding, it was never from Matt." He dropped his head in his hands. "It was from William."

S.J. laid her hand on Peter's shoulder. "I'll leave so you two can be alone."

"No," he said, looking up. "What I have to say you both should hear. You've been a wonderful friend and Abby and Benjie are going to need the support of your whole family."

Somehow, I managed a faint whisper. "Go on, Peter. Please." His eyes bore deep into mine. *I felt his physician's skill, his intellect, his analytical training shining light through murky waters.*

"Abby, William is mentally ill, and he's become delusional. He suffered a complete psychotic break. All this time I felt something was wrong, but not as wrong as this. He was good at masking his illness, with his glib nonchalance, the shining exterior. Last night I saw him start to lose control. He and Harriet were on the dance floor. He began twirling her faster and faster. She stumbled. I think he tripped her. But he let her fall. I saw the panic on her face. Then he laughed. Left her there on the floor and disappeared."

I shivered, thinking of this dangerous, mercurial man who had posed as my rescuer. His bizarre behavior, changeable as the tides. The sexual innuendos, lapses into fantasy and threat.

"I got to her fast. She was shaken but unhurt. She kept saying William insisted he had to check the renovations. It was so strange I called Detective Simpson, then Harriet and I drove straight here." He rubbed his eyes with the palms of his hands, massaged his temples. "But his obsession with you—and Ellen Smalldeer—and his fanatic insistence that Bay House belonged to him were clues he hid. Narcissism like his is fueled by a sense of entitlement, a constant need for power. Plus, with Harriet to shield him, unknowingly, I believe, he was able to glide along in the life he loved. His violent tendencies stayed hidden."

"And then I found the *Marriage Book.*"

Peter nodded. "Finally, your presence was so threatening it pushed him over the edge into violence and aggression."

"Where … where is he now?"

"He's in the hospital in Annapolis. He was admitted to the psychiatric unit. I'll be responsible for getting him into treatment, although that's probably going to be a long road."

"Then … you took him there. So he wouldn't be arrested."

"Yes, and with Detective Simpson's help. We don't charge patients like William. He's far too mentally incompetent. We went straight there after Burleigh came for you and Benjie. Harriet rode in the police car with us. She would not leave William's side even when we got him to the Emergency Room. He was still sedated and silent. She was … very vocal … demanding a private room for him with a meal. But by this time it was almost three a.m. and Harriet was in shock herself, still in her black gown."

"And you've been up all night."

Peter leaned forward, wrapped my cold hands in his warm ones. "It's not the first time," he said, with a shrug.

My mind formed the words I could barely speak but could not blot out. "William … lured me … with my own child." Tears streamed down my face, my heart hammered at my ribs. I was choking on my words.

"How can a child … survive such a trauma?"

Peter pulled me close. "Because he's the child you taught to be brave." My arms reached up to hold him. Our lips met. Time stopped. There was nothing more to say.

36

In the days that followed, Peter ordered quiet and constant care for Benjie and me. For a week while I floated in and out of reality, S.J. was guardian and nurse. She fed us, plumped our pillows, regulated long naps. Benjie and I slept or cuddled with books until the rosy shine was back in his cheeks and his eyes lost their fearful hollow look. In a vague, disconnected way, I was aware of her bandaged knee and ankle. I worried about her limp, her endless trips up and down the stairs. When I managed to murmur my concern, she waved it away.

"Doesn't that hurt?" I said.

"Nope. I've got ice packs." She winked at Benjie and helped prop us up in bed. "Now both of you eat your soup while it's nice and hot." On our tray next to the steaming bowls were a Superman comic book and a small pitcher of holly with shiny red berries.

Autumn, with its glorious leaves of scarlet and gold, seemed to have vanished overnight. It was the first week of December, unusually cold, I gathered from the look of the bare frosty branches outside our window and S.J.'s layers of sweaters and vests. One windy afternoon the Tomison crew tiptoed up to peek in our door with Skipper in tow, bundled in flannel shirts and scarves up to their noses. The puppy leaped onto the bed, tail swooping, licking Benjie's face as he shrieked with joy.

"Mom, Skipper needs a walk." So did Benjie. So did I. It was time to get back to my life, whatever it was meant to be. He pulled me to the doorway and hopped down the steps two at a time. I followed him, wrapped in an afghan, feeling stronger with each step, shedding my fears like a set of old clothes. *I was grateful for each blanket, each hug, each sheltering moment in the Tomisons' care. But my heart knew it was time to return to Bay House. My home, my world, waiting just a quick walk down the lane under an azure sky. Benjie and I would take that walk today.*

In the kitchen S.J. held out a plate of warm cookies. Melted chocolate perfumed the air.

"Well, welcome back to the world, sweet girl. I was just comin' up to check on you." She cleared newspapers from the rocking chair. "We just lit the fire. Have a seat and stay warm."

She studied my face with a knowing smile as I munched a cookie and studied hers.

The fire leaped and crackled, sending a shower of sparks onto the hearth. I stopped rocking, took a deep breath, shrugging the afghan from my shoulders. "It's time to go home," I said.

S. J. threw her arms in the air. "I knew it. Yeah, it's time and you're ready. Grab Benjie, and fly." Then came her throaty laugh. "Call me when you get there ... in about a minute. Remember, no more hiding, ever again."

"Come on, Benj," I said. "It's time to go home, take Skipper and, I'm pretty sure, find something fun in the attic. And later Jake can be our first visitor." The boys raced upstairs and returned to the kitchen with our few possessions stuffed in a grocery bag, babbling about what the attic might hold. I ducked into S.J.'s bedroom and changed into jeans and a sweatshirt. All the Tomisons gathered around as we said our goodbyes and blew kisses. As Benjie skipped down the lane I watched gulls soar, listened to the tide foaming onto the beach, and remembered my promise to myself.

I lay in my safe haven in S.J.'s guestroom and thought about nothing but my first mission as an owner. The instant Benjie and I got the deed to Bay House I would hire a crew to clean, paint and carpet the Old Cabin, and with that, erase the scene of our harrowing episode. I'd restore the upper loft and complete the flooring to span its entire width. Add a solid half-wall and sturdy railing. No more scaffolding, no more lethal jagged stone. Finally, I would wall up the little inside door with that yawning drop into thin air. From now on the only entrance would be through exterior, reinforced, double padlocked doors. Later I might make it an office. For now, it could hold William and Harriet's belongings until they sent for them. The transition would be done quickly, without fanfare or a big proclamation. And my ownership would stay private for now.

Then, suddenly, we were standing at the massive front door. My hand trembled as I reached out to turn the knob, thankful that Burleigh gave me the spare key.

"We're going to live here now, Benj, and your friends can come whenever you like," I said, as we entered the hall. The fresh lemon scent was more fragrant than ever. The rug more plush, the colors more regal. Sunlight danced on the crystal fixtures, and beyond the long windows the bay was bathed in gold.

"We're never leaving here again." I leaned on those magic words, never and again. I knelt to kiss his soft cheeks. "I promise."

Benjie stared at me, confusion flickered in his eyes. "But Mom. I don't understand. Aren't we gonna live at S.J.'s anymore? Why are we gonna live here now? I don't think I like this place very much."

No wonder. How could he? I thought. Nestled at the Tomisons' I had, at Peter's prompting, spoken in quiet, reassuring words about the trauma we suffered in the Old Cabin. Now I pulled him into my lap, rocked him, held him close. I pushed the hair from his forehead, my eyes locked on his. "Sweetie, remember how we talked about that scary night? And everything that happened? But now it's all over. And, what's more important to think about is how brave you were. You saved yourself and Skipper, too, and Peter called you Superman."

He gave a little half smile and nodded. "Yeah, I remember that made me not be scared anymore."

I closed my eyes and bowed my head. *Oh, how I adored Peter, kind, wise, and unfailing, for loving us the way he did.*

It was time for my promised surprise. "I'll race you to the third floor." Benjie's eyes grew huge and round. I took a deep breath, my teeth chattering, thinking how cold I was from just my short walk. Winter seemed to be descending along the Chesapeake Bay.

In the attic was an ancient wind-up toy train sitting askew on a circle of rusty track. I discovered it one day on one of my endless searches and hid it under a pile of old and faded children's clothing. I plunked down next to him in the dust, beside the photo of my young father with his arm around his grandmother's shoulders. She was looking up, smiling at him, her face lit with pride. And wearing her pearls. My pearls. The only possession I stuffed in my bag with our disguises the day we fled from New York. Those pearls were my birthright, as they had been hers.

While Benjie knelt inside the circle, choo-chooing through crashes and derailments, I began to talk. "I'm going to tell you a fantastic story. Are you listening?" This would be a challenge with competition from the train. I scooted closer and put my hand across the track. Before Benjie could complain I lowered my voice and whispered, "It's about me and you and a long-lost treasure."

His eyes popped wide as I unwound the tale of the English boy who married the Indian girl, and what the word ancestors meant. "It really, truly happened and was written down in a great big book so everyone who read it would know it was real. Not a made-up story like *Winnie the Pooh* or *Peter Pan*. It was called the *Marriage Book*. But then, guess what happened?" I was thrilled when Benjie didn't even blink. "It got lost, like a pirate's chest. For years and years. Until I found it at the Tomisons' house when Mindy was sitting on it. Remember?" He nodded as I held his little hands in mine. A cold draft was stirring the attic dust and he was beginning to sneeze.

"Here's the best part of the story," I said. "The *Marriage Book*, now that it's been found, proves that I own Bay House. And someday, so will you. So that's why we're going to live here from now on. Just us, by ourselves. William and Harriet are far away in Annapolis now, across the Bay." The relief in his eyes was unmistakable. And my heart twisted again with sorrow and grief at the memory of what my child endured in his young life. First from his father, then from William.

Then a stark, impossible realization struck me like a lightning bolt. *We both suffered threats, terror and abuse from the same two men. The same two patriarchs we depended on the most for love and protection. Yet we had more than endured. More than survived. We were free, on our own. Trusting. Thriving. Living in a limitless present, seeing a shining future.*

My gratitude for this new reality went far deeper than the fear and desperation that drove my search. But it was also exhausting, keeping hope alive, chasing a dream that was true all along, surpassing William's illness. Though I was weary, peace, joy and contentment filled my soul, sitting sheltered under the ancient eaves of Bay House with my son, surrounded by a gallery of Collingtons to bear witness to our miracle.

37

Warm and contented as I'd been, a frigid wind whistled through the drafty attic and my teeth started to chatter. Benjie was coughing and sneezing, and I realized my fingers were numb. I felt the collected Collingtons watching us with silent approval. The loving care of Bay House passed to me. This wasn't my job, it was my life. The life my father promised, and I searched for but thought would never be mine. I had a long mental to-do list and was anxious to begin taking charge as Benjie and I clambered down the stairs. I couldn't wait to begin the transformation of the Old Cabin I spent so much time imagining. But, I had to wait. For that, and everything else, including Christmas. I had no money.

The teetering stack of mail on the hall table seemed an obvious place to start learning. It was a heap of bills from sources all foreign to me. I sent Benjie into the study to find cartoons before I began sorting.

Grayson's Feed and Grain. Johnstone's Fencing, Inc. Tires to Go. Joe's Bait and Tackle. Again, I gave silent thanks for Burleigh's presence, his skills and dedication to the maintenance of the house, buildings and farm. I was baffled about priorities. Once I was officially named the owner I was confident he could teach me all I needed to know to be at least an informed partner. I was already intrigued with the harvesting of our corn, growing tomatoes, and determined to drive the tractor. I began to smile as I tried to picture our tutorials.

Then as I eyed the bills again, I worried, not for the first time, where the money to pay for the upkeep of the farm was going to come from. My stomach roiled with a wave of nausea. For the moment nothing needed to change, Burleigh assured me, since up until two weeks ago William and Harriet managed Bay House as they always had. All these months I was only a guest, not privy to their financial affairs. Until the night of the Gala when William's mind splintered and dissolved, and with it the cool, orderly world of Bay House. Nothing would be the same again, and now I would have to right that world. Could I do it? Yes, without doubt I knew I could. The question was, how?

When the phone rang, I jumped. "Yes, ah, hello?" I said.

"Abby. It's Harriet calling." *I was almost too stunned to speak, as if my musings conjured her forth through the telephone.*

I stuttered, making no sense. "Well, um, hello also. Harriet?" *Of course, it was her. How could I forget that icy voice?*

"I wonder if I might come get some personal belongings … and my car." Her tone was flat, almost bored, as if we were discussing the weather. "Vera will bring me, then I'll follow her back home. To Annapolis, that is. Would Wednesday the eighth be convenient, let's say about 11:00? We won't be staying for lunch."

An imperial command, as usual. Though it shocked me, since the last time I saw her she was undone. Fine. The fewer reminders of William and Harriet the better. And something to cross off my list.

"No, actually nine would be preferable. I have an appointment at ten and am busy the rest of the week. But Noah can help you load your things and see you out." *And Benjie will be nowhere in sight.* Before she could respond I said, "Goodbye, then." And I hung up.

I was glad to be busy while I waited for my visitors. S.J. and I went Christmas shopping together. That is, I looked, she shopped, then often hid her gifts at Bay House. I helped her wrap presents to put under their tree and prayed silent prayers for the existence of a real Santa Claus.

On Wednesday the eighth, promptly at 9:00, I heard the rumble of Vera's sports car coming up the lane in a cloud of dust and the ping of pebbles. I went out to greet them with a thin smile. Vera parked in the circle near Harriet's sedan, her long legs emerging, then a hand waving her silver cigarette holder with its plumes of smoke as she stood and slammed her door. Her eyes swept the lawn, the bay and up the steps to the massive doorway with its shiny brass hardware.

"Nice," she said.

This was the droll movie star-architect I remembered from two months ago when Harriet introduced us and Vera's big master plan for the selling and renovation of Bay House.

"Yes, isn't it?" I said.

Then I turned to Harriet, who still sat motionless in the passenger seat. I leaned down and spoke through her lowered window. "Harriet, we meet again. Come in. There's coffee or tea. Noah's waiting with boxes, ready to help you." I opened her door and reached out my hand to steady her. I couldn't help noticing her halting gait. She gazed around, her eyes glassy and unfocused.

I realized after watching her what she was looking for. She stopped and stared, with her hands clasped over her mouth. Her sight fixed upon the Old Cabin and tears streamed down her cheeks.

"Harriet, do sit down a moment," I said.

Vera wedged a lawn chair behind her friend, her bored demeanor replaced with concern, but not surprise. *Suddenly I guessed the situation. It was not only William who faced mental decline.* "Harriet, no one has been in your bedroom or disturbed anything of yours or William's. Noah already has put a lot away for safekeeping, and there's no need to hurry today. I'll sit with you while he and Vera bring out what's been packed, and you can rest a bit and then go home."

Noah approached with a thermos of coffee on a tray and a thick shawl to wrap around her shoulders. "I'll drive your car back to Annapolis, Miss Harriet, and come back here by bus." He looked at Vera, who nodded gratefully, then glanced at me with a shy smile. "It's early yet, not even 10:00. Won't be a bit of trouble at all." *I knew this was his way of apologizing for his subservience to William, lending support now that he was gone.*

Harriet sipped hot coffee and watched the seagulls dip and soar, seemingly unaware of where she was. Vera explained this new behavior which came in unpredictable waves, and how William's doctors were helping her cope with it. She promised to keep me informed of Harriet's progress. "Don't worry, Abby. Plenty of days she's still the same old Harry." Then she smiled.

Noah loaded large cartons into Harriet's sedan. Suitcases and carryalls went into the back and trunk of Vera's car. I laid several garment bags across them.

"Please do let me know about Harriet. I'll tell Peter and we'll get his opinion about her condition as well. And you can come back for William's car another time. We'll work out a plan."

Noah helped Harriet into her car, still wrapped in the shawl. He got into the driver's seat and with a wave of his hand, followed Vera off down the lane in the wake of her rumble and dust.

I felt a wave of fatigue, not at all the outcome I expected from this morning's visit. I shuffled into Bay House, chilled to the bone. There, lying on the hall table, was the damning initialed pork pie hat I planned to present to Harriet as a reminder of the secrets I once thought I understood. Now, what would be the point? I picked it up, walked to the kitchen and tossed it with all the other inconsequential waste into the bin under the sink.

It was another gray day, blustery and raw. Through the frosted windows I watched the bay foaming in the wind as if it was boiling, though the terrace thermometer read 34 degrees. I had to get Benjie back from the Tomisons' where S.J. was keeping him hidden during Harriet's visit. I was to call when the coast was clear and she would send him dashing down the lane. Then we would … do what, I wondered? Light a fire in the study, watch cartoons, read stories, play with his blocks. I would not look at farm bills or fantasize about renovating the Old Cabin.

This morning's encounter took all the pleasure from any thoughts of transforming that horrid place. I would not worry about money and, most important of all, I would not agonize over Christmas.

I made myself pick up the phone and call S.J. "Hi, it's me. You can send Benjie back. Thanks for keeping him. Everybody's gone." I sighed, frustrated and distressed at the memories Harriet's presence rekindled.

"Sorry," S.J. said. "You don't sound real happy. I thought you'd be relieved."

"It didn't exactly go as I expected but at least it's over." I slumped where I sat and stifled a yawn. I was exhausted after such an emotional morning. "How did the kids do? Did Benjie behave? I know he won't want to leave but we have some chores to do and he needs to pick up his room." *Half true, but I really needed him home so I could curl up in the study and take a nap with him nearby. I would tell S.J. the details later. But at the moment Bay House felt bleak and forlorn. Benjie would keep me from being alone.*

"OK. Give me a couple minutes to bundle him up and I'll call you when he's out the door." Which meant S.J. was also packing us a fresh batch of cookies or brownies, which I was in the mood to make our only meal for the day.

Benjie banged through the front door with snowy footprints on the rug and wet mittens from snowballs, I guessed. I wrapped him in my arms until he squirmed to be set free. "What's wrong, Mom?" he said. "You look weird. Oh, here's the stuff we made." I could smell the chocolate through the bag. I helped him out of his jacket and boots and found Captain Kangaroo on TV.

Later in the afternoon when the phone rang I snatched up the receiver thinking it was S.J. again. "So. How much sugar did you feed my child?" I couldn't help a little chuckle. But all I got in return was silence. No guffaw or denial from S.J. Nothing but a dead phone. *Oh, no. Power outages from the weather already?*

As I jiggled the buttons, ready to hang up, I heard a mild, shy, unmistakable cough. *My spirits soared. There was a Santa. And he made phone calls.*

"Abigail, dear child, is that you?" said Mr. Dangerfield. "I'm so delighted I found you. Mrs. Tomison just assured me of yours and Benjamin's recovery from your ordeal and that you are now living at Bay House." His voice rose and quickened. "At last I'm able to give you the news you've been waiting for so long. A gift from your dear mother, you might say."

The chair fell over as I sprang to my feet. My heartbeats pounded like drums. I felt the forces of my mother's spirit reaching out through her old friend and ally. She loved me and here was the proof. Mr. Dangerfield was speaking his usual legalese and delivering his real estate expertise. I tried to keep up with his tutorial and scribble notes on the pad by the telephone. But I couldn't grip the pen. There was only one word that mattered. Only one word I recognized.

"Sold!" *My mother's house was sold.* I wrote it over and over, feigning attention as Mr. Dangerfield spouted details. He told me the house sold for more than he anticipated and he would send me a check overnight. I thanked and thanked him and didn't really remember hanging up. I wasn't rude, I was numb.

I called Peter. He was astounded at my news and elated the house sold for so much. As we spoke, the shock subsided, and a plan formed in my head. Something I would do all on my own.

The next day the check arrived as promised. My only thoughts were leaving Benjie at S.J.'s, borrowing her car once again and getting that check to the bank. "You've more than earned this," S.J. said. She handed me the keys at her door, her usual grin lighting her face. "Take as long as you need and enjoy yourself for once."

Chesapeake Savings and Loan was an unfamiliar trip to Stevensville though I drove straight to it as if guided by unseen hands. I filled out the simple new account details, in my name only, then the deposit slip. When the teller cashed my first check I wanted to hug her. How different my life is now. So free, so full of promise. So distant from memories of those painful, hopeless forms required at the women's shelter that long ago day when I made my escape.

Now that my mission was accomplished, I almost skipped through the parking lot. I breathed in the cold clean air as I rolled down the window and pulled out into traffic. Noticed the roads dotted with Christmas tree lots, colored lights in store windows announcing the season of giving. Remembered S.J. telling me to take my time.

My former fear of Christmas melted away with my new identity. I cranked on the radio. "Jingle Bells" was blaring, and I joined in at the top of my lungs. Pulled my shopping list from my purse and instead of heading for home, took the main highway to the nearby cluster of shops. I was going to buy gifts, by myself, with my own money. And Benjie's big present would be first.

When I whispered my idea to S.J. her eyes popped. "Yes, yes." She clapped her hands together. "He'll be thrilled and totally surprised." She told me the exact store to go to. "And they sell all the outdoor kids' stuff you're talking about, too. Good thing I emptied my trunk, but I hope it all fits."

I found a toy store with perfect gifts for the Tomison children. Then a luggage shop where I chose something elegant for Mr. Dangerfield and left it to be engraved with his initials. I already knew the huge surprise awaiting S.J. and Burleigh, but that would come Christmas night at the end of the gift-giving.

Just one thing was missing. Something special to wear. I spotted it on a mannequin in a store window. Shimmery red taffeta, tied at the waist with a wide, flouncy bow, and a price tag I could more than afford. With money that was my own. I couldn't wait to wear it for Peter. I barely remembered driving home.

When I stopped to return S.J.'s car, she eyed the bulging bags with approval and offered to keep them hidden, as I kept hers in the Bay House attics.

"Guess what, Benjie?" I said. We were walking hand in hand, swinging our arms, up the lane from the Tomison's. "We're going to have a party. And Peter's coming for dinner. I'm going to call him right now."

"Yay. I like Peter. He can share the cookies we made."

"Uh-huh. I like him, too. And we're going to celebrate." I gave Benjie a brief explanation of the occasion.

I spent the late afternoon making S.J.'s recipe for meatloaf and mashed potatoes. When Peter's car arrived he bounded up the steps. I opened the door to a wide grin that lit his eyes like candles as he leaned in to kiss me.

He stooped down to hug Benjie. "Hey, buddy," he said. "I'm really glad to see you. Your Mom says we're going to have a special party, just us three. It's a great number, don't you think?

Benjie shrugged. "I guess so. Then maybe we can walk Skipper. Mommy sold a house or something, but I don't know what that means."

I pictured the bank, the beautiful dress in my closet, the blessings that had brought me to this moment.

Peter circled his arms around Benjie and me as if he never wanted to let go. The fireplace snapped and crackled spreading warmth throughout the study. Peter nodded and smiled as the wave of his hair dipped across his forehead. "It means, Merry Christmas, Benj. That's what it means."

38

"Mommy, how do you spell Santa?" Benjie's voice was muffled, and he coughed as he spoke.

We were in the study clearing his toys from every surface, nook and cranny, though I wasn't getting much help. Every inch mattered. The sofas had to be pushed back to create a wide, empty corner space—today. I looked up from the clutter, my mind racing with so much to do in not much time. But what I saw stopped me in my tracks. And turned my frown into a grin.

At the fireplace Benjie was crouched on all fours. His hands coated in ashes, his neck and head craned so high up the chimney they disappeared.

"What on earth are you doing? Quick. Close your eyes and don't talk." I dropped down beside him, reaching up to help him back himself onto the hearth. When he emerged, he was covered in soot with a giggling mouthful of white teeth. "You silly goose," I said. I chuckled and brushed ash from his face so he could see. "You look like a raccoon." While I wiped him clean with a damp cloth, I asked him what he was doing with his head in the chimney. *Why did I neglect to make this a forbidden activity? Like going on the dock without an adult, or riding on the back of a tractor?*

"I just wanted to see if Santa would fit," he explained with the simple logic of a five-year-old. "And Jake said they already wrote letters to Santa but I don't know how to spell so you have to help me write my list. It goes in the chimney, too."

I let out a long, contented sigh and tried to rock my child in my arms. But he could not be still. Christmas was ten days away. *His very first Christmas outside a cramped New York apartment, where a small mini treetop dragged through street sludge and up an elevator was the only decoration he'd ever known. And a fireplace did not exist. No wonder he was exploring and full of questions.*

So was I. Though I knew in my soul we belonged here, the practicalities of producing a holiday celebration worthy of Bay House's grandeur were daunting. However, I'd learned lessons from watching its festive transformation for the house tour and auction only a month ago. I decided just the downstairs would matter—the hall, study, and dining room. But I would make them magical.

"Mom, lookit. It's snowing." Benjie sprang to the windows to watch huge heavy snowflakes swirling down through a slate-gray sky. "Frosty the Snowman" was playing from the radio on the mantle, his little feet were marching in time with the music. "Quick, come look before they melt. I hope they do, so Burleigh can take us to cut down our tree. He's going to pull us on the tractor, remember? And we get to put it up tonight."

And Peter was coming for the grand occasion and a dinner I hadn't begun to concoct yet, except for the huge pot of beef stew I made last week thawing in the kitchen. I wasn't the cook Harriet was but I was experimenting with simple recipes. Benjie wasn't the only excited one. I wanted to dance, too. And sing, and shout. I could barely think straight, and sleep was impossible.

"Sweetie, sometimes snowflakes freeze and stack up high where they land. And the radio says we're in for super cold weather these next few weeks." *I hoped the snow would stop so today's plan could work. In keeping with tradition, Burleigh would hook his tractor to one of the farm carts, pile his kids in, minus baby Cindy, and add Benjie. "Our newest elf," he called him. And off they'd rumble into the thickest pine grove on the property to cut down the perfect tree. With vast relief I realized this promised high adventure for Benjie. The fear and threat from his accident at the gatepost had vanished.*

Now the study was getting chilly. In fact, the whole house felt cold, with wind gusts blowing through Bay House's many windows, rattling the old panes. All I could think about was lighting the fire and warmer clothes. And hoping we'd cleared enough space to accommodate Burleigh's towering choice. He tended to do things in a big way when given a task.

"Burleigh's like a kid himself at Christmas, so get ready for a tree-trimming you've probably never seen before." S.J. warned me during one of our many phone calls. I needed constant advice and assurance, and she gave it with her usual competency mixed with humor. "Who do you think's been helping our kids cut and glue paper chains? I had to hide the popcorn when we ran out of room to store all the strands. He must have strung at least fifteen feet. He wouldn't let the kids touch a needle and thread. Can you picture him stitching popcorn?"

I shook my head and slowed my voice as I answered her. "I can hardly picture Benjie and I are here. And what a difference a month makes. I'll never forget being at your house, recovering in what felt like a safe, warm bubble, while the rest of the world went on without us. It was Thanksgiving, I came down in my bathrobe. I remember a lovely meal I couldn't taste, Benjie tackling a giant drumstick. And your children around us were sweetly quiet. Mostly I felt profound gratitude for our being alive. The prayers you offered were answered …"

S.J. finished my sentence. "And then you were ready to start your life at Bay House."

Carols floated into the hall from the radio in the study. "Angels we have heard on high, sweetly singing o'er the plains …"

There was a pause while I gripped the phone and tried to speak. "I don't know how I can ever thank you."

"Let me bring yeast rolls and gingerbread men tonight," she said. "Burleigh, me, you and Peter can use the sofas and eat on our laps with trays. The kids can sit on the floor. I can't wait to watch Peter and Burleigh deal with the tree and the lights. Then the pandemonium after with five of Santa's helpers and a toddler arguing over which balls go where. Cindy is very opinionated and has no trouble speaking her mind to her brothers. Ha! I wonder who she gets that from? Mindy will head for my lap when it gets rowdy. So us girls can just sit and watch the show." *I felt brighter as S.J.'s laughter traveled up my spine.*

The snowstorm let go of its grip in time for Burleigh to load the children in the cart and bump them off to the woods where the perfect tree awaited. By lunchtime they returned, chilled to the bone but thrilled with the classic white spruce they chose. Burleigh, Jess and Josh carried it into the study and fitted it into a sturdy stand, even wiring it to the baseboards for extra stability. Its wide graceful branches of soft green fringe formed the perfect point nearly touching the ceiling, with plenty of room for lights, decorations and an angel on top. The pungent pine fragrance alone announced the holidays like a trumpet's blare.

Everyone gulped the hot chocolate I passed around, but before the Tomisons were loaded in the cart Benjie was fast asleep under the tree. He no doubt needed a nap, so I wedged a pillow under his head, tucked him under a quilt and headed to the kitchen to think about dinner. Beef stew and S.J.'s additions seemed easy enough, even for me, though food was the last thing on my mind.

My divorce, the *Marriage Book*, my inheritance, and Peter occupied my every thought and heartbeat. Now our tree was up, child-approved, and with more snow on the way to keep them busy I could concentrate on the business of becoming the legal owner of Bay House. One person held the key to documenting my legitimacy. Mr. Dangerfield, with his contacts and connections to expert D.C. lawyers and probate judges. When I invited him to our first Bay House Christmas, he was thrilled to be our special guest and to receive the treasured *Marriage Book*, plus a copy of my father's journal containing both critical wills, in person.

"I'll take the train and arrive on the 23rd, dear girl," Mr. Dangerfield confirmed. I could hear the pride in his voice. "I will be so happy to help with the legalities." Then his voice was more somber. "However, I must warn you this process will be a long one. You must be patient."

But at last it would begin. I was so overjoyed I wanted to hug someone. Benjie. Peter. I'd been standing in the shallows of life so long, now I wanted to jump in the waves.

Of course, I told Peter the incredible tale about finding the *Marriage Book* stacked in Mindy's highchair the day of the auction. Also, I showed it to William that very day. I knew the time to celebrate would come in its own way and time. Now I couldn't wait to see him again.

39

I opened my eyes to dawn breaking through bare, glistening trees and a luminous sky promising sunshine. My mind was racing, though Bay House was peaceful, for the moment, at least. Any minute Benjie would wake up, leap onto my bed and beg to go see if Santa came. I pulled on my robe, ran a brush through my hair and crept downstairs.

First, I turned on the tree lights and started the model train on its slow chugging journey around the track underneath. Thrilled when smoke emerged from the locomotive in acrid, oily little puffs. I switched on the radio, lit the fire to "Deck the Halls." Sat back on my heels admiring our handiwork. Benjie's bulging stocking hung from the mantle next to Skipper's. The train construction was Peter's creation last night after I put Benjie to bed.

"Dear girl, Merry Christmas to you. Is there anything you haven't thought of?" Surprised at his early appearance, I looked up at Mr. Dangerfield, neatly dressed in a red sweater and gray slacks. His hair parted and combed just so. He smiled and pointed at Skipper's stocking. Then at the train with its coal car, timber loader, cattle car and caboose. "Abigail, I so enjoyed my journey on the train. I remember my train collection was my favorite toy growing up." His eyes had a wistful, faraway look.

I realized I knew nothing of his life beyond the work he faithfully provided as my family's attorney. And once again he came at my request to help settle the most critical legal issue of my life.

"I'm delighted you made the trip to join us. You've always been so kind to me, and now I can finally thank you properly. Let me get us some coffee before the mayhem begins." *I laughed at this understatement. The quiet couldn't last too much longer. Benjie spent yesterday sledding through new-fallen snow and was worn out by bedtime, though I regretted that driving conditions kept us from the local Christmas Eve service.*

When I returned with two steaming mugs Mr. Dangerfield and I sat enjoying the fire. "Tomorrow I'll give you the *Marriage Book* after the dust settles. Wait 'til you see …"

"Mommy, where are you?" Benjie's footsteps pounded down the steps and through the hall. He was giggling. "Did Santa come? What's that sound …?" He froze, wide-eyed, when he entered the study, saw the tree lights blazing, and his train.

Then Benjie was on his knees, his nose nearly on the track. "Here's the switch that turns it on and controls the speed. And the button for the horn," I said. In one loop around, two cars flipped sideways before he could manage the switches, though the locomotive chugged on with its puffs of smoke filling the air.

"Lookit, Mom. I'm giving everything a ride." His eyes were shining through a huge grin. He stacked candy canes on the coal car and perched a tiny angel on the caboose.

"Benjamin, my boy," said Mr. Dangerfield, "I believe it's time you open this." He ruffled Benjie's hair as he bent to hand him a large box tied with a huge red bow.

Benjie tore into the paper, muttering "thank you," then held up his gift with a quizzical smile. "Wow. It's a cow," he said.

Suddenly, with a spry leap of which I hadn't thought him capable, Mr. Dangerfield knelt down, his fingers weaving wires over and under the track. "Here's more fun for your train set. "The Cow on the Track" is what it's called. When I get it set up, you'll see how the cow jumps in front of the train, and the button that moves him off just in time."

"Sweetie," I said. I blew Mr. Dangerfield a kiss. "I think Santa Claus left you something else. Better have a look around." It was the top request on Benjie's list but too large for wrapping. I pulled it out of hiding and leaned it behind the sofa. A new wooden sled with shiny red runners and a red-painted handlebar. Next to it was a pair of black and red ice skates with gleaming silver blades. These I wrapped clumsily in green paper, knowing paper-tearing was part of the fun. Santa's elves had a reputation for being fast workers.

The phone rang as Benjie leaped on his sled, trying to tie Skipper's collar to the handlebar. The pup was with us in the house since the stable was so brutally cold, even for him.

"Merry Christmas to Bay House!" It was S.J. firing off a list of logistics, reminding me I had more to do than sit and watch Benjie's train. We needed some breakfast. Dinnertime was 4:00, a long way away. "The turkey is in the oven," said S.J. "and I have extra stuffing in a casserole dish. I'm about to peel the potatoes, mash and keep 'em warm in the oven. I'll make the gravy here when the bird's done. There's no sense in making that mess at your house. Then all we have to do is keep it hot." She paused to take a breath. "You remembered the green bean casserole, the sweet potatoes and the marshmallows, right?"

S.J. was still directing, saying something about her pies. "Burleigh's on his way with them along with Mindy's highchair if that's OK. Have you heard the weather report? They're calling for heavy snow all day. A couple years ago there was a blizzard you wouldn't know about. But I remember Burleigh used a chain saw to cut the boats out of the water when the bay started to freeze."

Could that be true? It sounded impossible. Though I was glad I would see Burleigh and review instructions for cooking a goose—my secret contribution as the crowning touch to a Chesapeake Bay Christmas feast.

Burleigh made his deliveries, stomping snow from his boots, pointing to the sky I did not notice had turned from blue to white. "I'm nervous about the goose," I admitted. *It was a long way from stew and meatloaf.*

"Aww, it's nothin'. I've done a hundred of 'em." He gave a quick, low chuckle. "You just roast it wrapped in bacon and tin foil, keep basting it, and don't forget the Cumberland Sauce."

That, I memorized. A simmered blend of red currant jelly, dry mustard, egg yolk and white wine, of course. I had all the ingredients, now just needed courage.

I lit the fire in the kitchen where Benjie, Mr. Dangerfield and I devoured warm cinnamon buns and scrambled eggs. Skipper thumped his tail at Benjie's feet. I was shocked when I saw it was past eleven. Benjie was yawning and Mr. Dangerfield's eyes had a glassy, sleepy look. "Abigail, I believe I'll be more help to you later if I have a quick nap." I carried Benjie upstairs and tucked him in bed, with Mr. Dangerfield following behind.

As I came down the steps, the phone rang again. It was Peter. His voice was tender and loving. "Is everything on schedule for the Tomisons arriving at fourish? You told me Noah will be at his sister's. Is there anything else you need? Conditions are icy in town, with rumors of downed telephone poles." Then almost as an afterthought he added, "How's your supply of firewood?"

"Fine. We're fine. I just need you." *I pictured the chic crimson A-line I'd be wearing when he arrived. And how his kiss would feel when he greeted me under the mistletoe I hung in the hall.*

"Don't worry. I'm coming early with the wine. I think you're going to need extra hands." I heard the smile in his voice. *Not a command. The reassurance of a first mate.*

From then on, time raced. I was delighted to be alone in the kitchen. Now I had to concentrate on green beans, sweet potatoes, and a goose. Everything was in the oven or bubbling on the stove.

Benjie shuffled into the kitchen from his nap while I was lost in basting the goose. "When does the party start, Mom?"

I glanced at the clock, horrified at the time. "Any minute. Quick, we've got to go up and get dressed." In his room I helped him into long pants and a snowman sweater.

I went to my closet, slid my red dress over my head and dashed on lipstick to match, along with my great-grandmother's pearls. There was no sky outside my windows. Only billowing, driving snow that made time seem irrelevant.

Suddenly the Tomisons were trooping in the door, shedding coats, boots and gloves. Peter's car crept up the drive and skidded around the circle. He bounded up the steps, swooped me in his arms and kissed me.

Benjie jumped up and down in the hallway, bursting with excitement. "Hey, everybody," he shouted. "Come see what Mr. Dangerfield brought me. And Santa, too. All the way down the chimney." He grabbed our lawyer's hand and led everyone but S.J. and me into the study.

S.J. looked at me as if she was reading a script. "It's kitchen time, my friend." She let out a husky laugh. "Time for the show."

Where else would it be? I smiled to myself as our hands flew over the stove, pulled dishes from the oven. I could smell the fresh thyme in S.J.'s stuffing, the onion rings browning on the green beans, the aroma of the bacon roasting with the goose. And the Cumberland sauce, sweet and tangy, simmering on its burner.

Peter appeared at the kitchen door, rubbing his hands together in anticipation. "What a team you two are. Everything smells fantastic and

S.J., that turkey is a sight to behold. How can I help?"

"Thank you, ahead of time," I said. *I felt a smile spread across my face. It was a bit silly, but I was proud of every morsel.* "Can you and Burleigh corral everyone and get them into their seats, please?"

I heard Peter's voice in the study. "Abby and S.J. prepared a very special feast for us, and it's time to eat. Let's all gather in the dining room and find a spot. I'll pour the wine, Burleigh, and help with the chairs if you'll serve the plates."

Yesterday I set the table with silver and china, crystal candlesticks, fresh pine and holly berries for a centerpiece. There were places for eleven, including a linen napkin and a little spoon in front of Mindy's highchair. *It was fragrant. It was family. I was thrilled.*

Jake was the first to sit. "Wow. Everything's so … shiny," I heard him say. Then everyone took their places. Our cue to fill the plates so Burleigh could serve them. All the food was hot and steaming, even the gravy.

"Yes, indeed," said Mr. Dangerfield. "What a splendid room this is, Abigail." Burleigh had already sliced my epic roasted goose. When I entered carrying the platter and warm sauce, "Hooray, Abby," and applause around the table confirmed my success. *For one moment of pure satisfaction, I gazed at the faces around the lovely old dining room table. Young and old joined together, celebrating joyfully. The new family I never dared dreamed could be … with Peter carving the turkey, his eyes warm and shining into mine.* Until the lights where we sat, and in the hall, and the study, and on the Christmas tree, all flickered at once. And went out.

There was a stunned silence. No one moved in their seat. Not even a child.

"Ah, Abigail dear. What a lovely touch. I've always been fond of dinner by candlelight." Everyone turned toward Mr. Dangerfield in the soft glow of the dining room's firelight. "I believe I'll have some more of that excellent goose," he said. "This seems to be the perfect occasion to have a gas oven."

"Exactly right," said Peter. He stood, pushed back his chair and began lighting candles all over the room, through the hallway and into the kitchen. Once again S.J. and I replenished plates, spooned out second helpings of our deliciously hot, miracle meal. "It seems our adventure has turned this unlikely group of kids into silent saints." Peter chuckled. "Maybe they've forgotten when we're finished eating, presents are next, even if mostly in the dark." With that, all six children including little Mindy on Burleigh's lap, began to clap and cheer and giggle. Peter led us into the study, lit more candles and brought out flashlights from a drawer.

"Silent Night," playing on the radio, was interrupted by a public service announcement stating that the power outage would continue until tomorrow morning at the earliest.

"Brrr," said Benjie. "It's getting cold in here, Mommy."

Burleigh piled more logs onto the fire. But the wind still rattled the windows and the snow continued to pour down in icy sheets we could hear as they hit the glass. Gift-giving had to begin so the Tomisons could stumble home through the rising drifts.

S.J. jumped into action first, giving Benjie a long thin package wrapped in Rudolph paper. "Mommy, lookit," he said. "Yay. It's Superman." He held up a huge kite with a double red tail. "I bet he could fly in a blizzard."

"Now, Peter," said S.J. "Here's a little something for you." She handed him a large round tin I knew held her famous rum-soaked fruitcake. "You, too, Mr. Dangerfield. So you won't have to share with anyone here. I hope you like, ah … rum."

"OK, now it's my turn." I smiled at the Tomison boys. "For Jess, Josh, and Jake. I can see you three now, playing with these on your steps at home." They each got a bag with a fat wire Slinky and a chocolate Santa. "Competing, too, I'm sure. Maybe something fun to do inside when it's too cold to go outside."

I had to sort through another pile for the two Raggedy Ann dolls I popped into Cindy's and Mindy's laps. As I leaned down to kiss their cheeks they stared at me, wide-eyed and beaming with surprise.

"Mr. Dangerfield, you're next." He sat, shy and quiet, near the fire. I passed him a box covered in silver paper, touched as he removed the ribbon with careful precision. When he lifted out the shiny leather briefcase with his initials in gold, he was speechless. "Abigail, dear, how elegant. How can I thank you?"

"Now, Abby. I've been waiting for this." S.J. turned to me with her pixie smile and laid something soft and bulky across my arms. "Sorry there's no box and only Rudolph paper, but we ran out of everything." Her voice grew soft and halting. "Abby, you are so … I hope this is special enough ..."

I felt tears swell as all eyes watched me open the Rudolph wrapping to reveal a breathtaking hand-stitched quilt. Just like the ones S.J. bundled Benjie and me in while she nursed us through our crisis. Every shade of blue that existed was there, as in the skies above Bay House and the water below. Incapable of speech, I merely draped it around her shoulders and mine. "Yes, yes, yes," was all I could whisper. When I could speak again, I stepped to the mantle and pulled the hidden paper scroll from the pine.

"This," I said to S.J. and Burleigh, "is from me to you both. I have searched my heart and wracked my brain to think of a gift that could express my love and gratitude to you and your precious children," I paused to smile at them, gaping at my speech in wonder, "for being the friends you are. To me, to Benjie, even to Skipper. You are more than friends. You're our family. You've helped make Bay House feel like home to us." I paused and looked at Peter, who smiled and nodded. "So, from our home to yours, Merry Christmas." I reached out and handed the ribboned scroll to Burleigh." I laughed and hugged him. "You'll understand why this is only a replica. The bona fide documents are coming soon. Signed and sealed. When I receive the deed to Bay House you'll get the deed to your farmhouse. Minus the bow, of course."

He was reading, holding the page so S.J. could read with him. His face was blank but his eyes were dancing. I could see he was trying to grasp the meaning of the scroll as a promissory gift. He began to bellow along with the radio, his deep clear baritone ringing out every beautiful word of "Joy to the World." There was nothing else to do but belt out the song along with him. Even the children joined in while Skipper sat near the windows and barked.

Benjie grinned as he knelt to hug his dog and ruffle his fur. "He's singing with us. And I think he wants to play in the snow." Benjie's face was pressed against the windowpane. He paused, staring at the glass. "Mommy, guess what?" he said. "I can't see out anymore." The singing stopped.

S.J. ran to open the front door. "Kids, Burleigh, Abby, Benjie's right. I hate to end this, but we've got to get home while we still can. I can barely make out Peter's tire tracks but with flashlights we'll be OK for such a short distance if we go now."

"Of course," I said. "Leave everything where it is. We're not touching the dishes. It's so cold in the kitchen I'm not even worrying about the leftovers."

The Tomison boys were ready, dressed in their coats and boots. "Dad," said Jess, "why don't we use Benjie's sled to take the girls home on? We can shine the lights with Mom so you can pull the sled."

Benjie pulled his sled into the hall. "Here, Jess. This'll go really fast 'cause Santa's elves made it."

Burleigh chuckled. "Great idea, son. Another adventure for the books, I guess. Thank you, thank you all for ..." he shook his head and looked at me. "Everything."

"Well, it appears I'll be here for the night," said Peter. "In the morning we'll see what's happening next. Over breakfast, if we're lucky. Remember, we've got a gas stove."

To me, he murmured, "I took most of the plates and silverware to the kitchen. Now I'm going out for more firewood. Why don't you check every room and blow out the candles? Then check again. We don't want any emergencies on a night like this. And then get all the blankets you can carry, and some pillows, too."

"But, why? What do you mean?" I said.

He laughed out loud. "Because we're going to have an old-fashioned sleepover. That's why. Benjie's nearly passed out on one couch, Mr. Dangerfield on the other. And I can't go anywhere, not that I want to." He paused, brushed the hair from my face and kissed me. "The study's pretty warm at the moment but it won't be for long. It's important to stay warm with blankets and bedspreads since we have to let the fire go out.

"Oh, no, Peter. We'll freeze." *I hadn't thought about the danger of an all-night fire while we slept.*

I made two trips upstairs for blankets, pillows and more flashlights. Peter loaded firewood in the kitchen, the hall and all over the study. Finally, with Benjie bundled and Skipper at his feet, Mr. Dangerfield, Peter and I sat covered in comforters with the fire turning to embers, enjoying the last of the warmth. I was filled with contentment, despite the cold, and the sudden fatigue of the long-awaited and surprising Christmas day.

Mr. Dangerfield yawned but stood and handed me a slim, square package. "Perhaps this small token will show you a happy time you may not remember. And may help you remember this one, forever."

When I pulled back the paper, the present slipped away. A framed photo, one I had not seen, showed my young, laughing father and mother, leaning together against a Bay House gatepost. In my father's arms was a little girl with a bow in her dark hair. Me. Leaning toward my mother's cheek with arms outstretched as the camera caught my kiss and the beautiful welcoming tilt of her face at the moment we touched. *My mind opened to the essence of her. The scent of roses, her velvet skin. My mind opened, and with it, a heart full of love for my mother.*

Mr. Dangerfield covered himself on the sofa and said no more.

Peter scattered the ashes and embers until the fireplace was still and lifeless. He pulled me down on a pallet of blankets, wrapped me in his arms, whispered, "You did it." And fell asleep.

Our plan to exchange our own presents would have to wait until tomorrow ... this was my last thought as I reached out for S.J.'s quilt and draped it over us both.

40

"We're in luck this morning, the power's back on," Peter said.

I blinked open my eyes and stared at the tree lights.

"The coffee's ready if anyone's interested. And, Benjie, I bet you could use some hot chocolate."

Peter was in the kitchen. I heard cabinets and drawers opening as he looked for cups and spoons. I kicked off layers of blankets, struggled to sit up, warm but stiff from sleeping on the floor.

Benjie rubbed his eyes and peered around him in surprise. "Mommy, why am I on the couch? Did we have a spend-the-night?" He giggled. "I'm all twisted up. But if the lights are on that means I can play with my train, right? Where's Peter? Where're my skates? I'm hungry."

"I see you slept well, Benjamin," said Mr. Dangerfield, "with your energy fully restored." He was awake, smiling, sitting on the sofa. He smoothed his hair and sweater, folded his blankets into a neat pile.

Peter appeared, laid fresh logs on the fire and lit it to a crackling blaze. "The house is still chilly, as big as it is, but there's a fire going in the kitchen, too. The rest will warm up soon enough. Meanwhile, breakfast sounds like a great idea. Ah. Here's our hostess, good as new," he chuckled.

"Hardly." I laughed and fluffed my hair with my fingers. My silky red dress was tossed on my bed upstairs where I rushed to change into jeans and a wool sweater, warm socks and sneakers. "But thank you. And I have the perfect menu. It's Benjie's favorite thing." He knelt by his train, attempting to run it backward. "Benj, can you guess? One part's bacon, the other part is …"

His hands flew into the air. "Happy face pancakes."

"That's right, sweetie, and you can add the faces. I think we have some chocolate chips," I said.

"And whipped cream, too?"

"Why not? Mr. Dangerfield, Peter, follow us and we'll give you a real treat."

We trooped into the kitchen. Peter started the bacon while Mr. Dangerfield sat at the table sipping his coffee. Benjie perched on the counter helping to stir the batter, sneaking chocolate chips while I pretended not to notice. Soon we were eating large mouthfuls of pancakes. Mr. Dangerfield even asked for whipped cream in his coffee cup.

"When breakfast is over I'll take Benjie up for a change of clothes. I'm afraid a hot shower won't be possible quite yet, I'm sorry. But please, take your time cleaning up, resting, whatever you'd like to do. The bath next to your room will have plenty of water, it'll just be cold." Mr. Dangerfield nodded his thanks and started up the stairs.

"Hey, Benj. Hey, buddy." Peter gave Benjie a hug. "I was so proud of you for offering your sled last night."

I watched Benjie's eyes grow round and solemn. He seemed to be thinking hard about what he would say next. "Peter, you know what?" He sounded shy, but sure. "You're my best friend."

Peter looked stunned, although his eyes filled with delight. "What? I thought Jake was your best friend. Or Skipper."

"Nope." Benjie shook his head, quite sure of himself. "You're first, they're second. Can we please go outside now?"

"Well, you're my first best Benjie, always. And we'll go to the Tomisons' in just a minute. Can you check on the locomotive while I talk to your mom?"

"Abby, my medicine bag is in my car, with a toothbrush and razor," Peter said, turning to me. "Along with a change of clothes I always keep there out of habit. You never know when you'll be stuck in a blizzard." He winked and shrugged his shoulders. "After I change I'll take Benjie out for some exercise and give you and Mr. Dangerfield time to do what he came to do. Discuss your inheritance and get all those documents he needs. I know you're anxious to give him the *Marriage Book* … although I'm sure anxious doesn't come close to the right word."

Who is this amazing man who knows what I am thinking and feeling?

Peter was pacing, his fingers rubbing his forehead. "I thought of something else. They're clearing the major roads today but it's still going to be tricky driving here. I'll have to dig my car out and get Burleigh and his kids to help. Ha. That's my exercise plan for me and Benjie this afternoon. Shoveling, and possibly a snowman or two. But by tomorrow I think everything will be clear even here, over the Bay Bridge and into Annapolis. Which is where Mr. Dangerfield has to meet his probate attorney friend for advice regarding your claim." Peter stopped pacing and looked at me. "So, I'll take him. It won't be a problem and I have the time since Dr. Sommerville is in town."

I shook my head. "No, Peter. It's too much. I couldn't let you."

"Abby, love." He held both my hands. His voice was deep, intense. "This is your miracle. It's the least I can do to help get this final piece signed, sealed and delivered." A sheepish grin crept across his face. "Besides, Mr. Dangerfield agrees. We've, um, already discussed it. He'll take a car service afterward into D. C. and catch the train back to New York from Union Station."

"Peter, can we go outside now?" Benjie stood in the hall trying to zip his jacket.

"Absolutely." Peter was dressed for the snow in an instant. "Bye, Abby. We'll be back later. Good luck with your mission. Enjoy it."

I thought about Peter's plan, could see the sense in it even if it meant overnight guests one more time. We had heat, more than enough room, and we had each other. Plus, we had all the leftovers. The time to talk to Mr. Dangerfield was this minute.

He was in the kitchen getting more coffee. I joined him, refilled my cup and suggested we sit by the fire in the study. "We'll have some quiet time to discuss my inheritance." I felt my smile light my whole face. "And I'll give you the *Marriage Book*." I turned to face him, on the edge of my seat. "You won't believe what it looks like. How it feels. The cover's scarred, so soft and crumbled at the edges it hardly looks like leather.

The pages are as thin as tissue paper and the ink is faded but legible. The script is beautiful, bold in some places, with delicate flourishes in others. Reverend Witherspoon's signature has been verified multiple times. It's truly a piece of art. Luckily, I have photographs of it before it was wrapped." I pulled three from my pocket and laid them in his lap. Mr. Dangerfield looked down, took my hand, and was speechless.

"I was advised about storing and handling by an archivist at the Smithsonian." The ancient, fragile book and my father's journal with the two wills were wrapped inside thick, unsealed plastic bags so they could breathe. Then boxed in an acid-free container. "Anyone examining them should wear gloves."

"My colleague is an expert on ancient estate claims such as yours and will treat it accordingly. And pass it to the proper authorities. It will be up to a probate judge to render the formalities, which I must warn you may be a long process. However, I am certain that your documents will be more than sufficient to support your claim. The *Marriage Book* is living proof, as you so vividly and eloquently describe."

I reached under the couch and lifted out a plain, sturdy cardboard box, adorned only with an address label. I handed it to Mr. Dangerfield. "Here it is," I said.

Mr. Dangerfield held the box to his heart "Dear girl. Nothing will give me greater pleasure than to accomplish this task for you at long last, starting tomorrow. I will call you when I'm back in New York and tell you everything that happens and explain every word. I promise you will have your deed and title in the new year."

41

January came with more snow and a thick manilla envelope by special delivery. I stared at the package. Arthur L. Dangerfield, Esq., 113 E. 39th St., N.Y., N.Y. was the return address. It was heavy, official-looking. My heartbeats quickened.

"The inheritance issue is still being examined, Abigail. Have patience." Mr. Dangerfield was calm and reassuring by phone, although I thought about it every day. So, what now? Maybe more paperwork dealing with the sale of my mother's house? I sat down on a dining room chair and ripped open the envelope. Ready or not, I knew the contents were essential to my life.

Or rather, the end of one life and the start of a new one.

Mr. Dangerfields's cover letter slipped to the floor. I stared at the seal of the great state of New York, with the words, "Uniform Uncontested Divorce Packet Forms" underneath. I picked up the packet and read what I prayed about so often in the dazed hours under S.J.'s quilts. But here was the impossible. Matt had contacted him and asked to start divorce proceedings. Making a clean sweep of everything, including our child. He wanted nothing. No part of custody or the fiction of fatherhood. Slate cleaned. No apologies, no remorse. Just goodbye.

According to our lawyer all I had to do was respond in kind and he would file the petition. Proceedings would end with Mr. Dangerfield appearing in my stead in New York, our legal residence, and with several signatures my marriage to Matt would be over. All the terror, all the abuse, suspense, self-doubt. Perhaps this was the best way to ensure Benjie's safety, an ultimate act of love. I did not know what Matt's life was or where he was living it, and I no longer cared. I tried to remember the exact shade of his eyes and, with a grateful sigh, realized I couldn't.

Furthermore, Matt transferred the title to our station wagon to me. It was all included in the envelope. Now, suddenly, I had a car, and, very soon, would have my freedom. I pictured Peter's face hearing this long-awaited news.

My fingers were dialing his number before I knew it. He answered on the second ring.

"This is Dr. Carpenter speaking," he said.

I stifled a laugh. "This is Abigail-almost-not-Wells-anymore." I waited for him to reply while my heartbeats kicked up again.

"Abby. What?" Peter said. His voice rose. "Say that again, please. What do you mean?"

I was thrilled at his eagerness. "I mean Mr. Dangerfield sent uncontested divorce papers I can sign and he can execute for me in New York. Plus, in the process, Matt gave me our car. I don't know why, except to think all this compliance is driven by guilt. That, and his wish to wash his hands of me, Benjie, and anything to do with his former life." *The thought of us, especially his son, being so dispensable brought a speck of sorrow for the waste it all it was. Except for our child … the joy of my life, the burden of his. But the regret was fleeting, like a cloud passing over the sun.*

"On top of the inheritance proceedings this just doesn't seem possible. I never thought Matt would give us up so easily. Or willingly. Especially Benjie. A long ugly custody battle is what I expected." *I had denied pieces of myself for so long it was hard to know what was real, what was a fantasy.* But the bay sparkled through the windows as if it was studded with diamonds. The sky shone bright and blue at the horizon, as real as could be. *My spirits soared with the gulls.*

"Peter, come to dinner tonight and we'll celebrate. Come help convince me this is really going to happen. Benjie will be thrilled. And wait 'til you see his kite-flying skills. Burleigh's cleaned off the drive so it's like he has a private runway."

"You're sure? You don't need some time to process ..."

"No. Just come straight from work." *I didn't need anything but Peter.* "We'll be waiting for you, even Skipper." *I knew I must sound ridiculous and tried not to laugh. Somehow it didn't matter.*

Peter arrived at five-thirty, with velvety, fragrant red roses I put in a vase on the dining room table. We had pot roast and fresh buttery yeast rolls that neither of us had much interest in beyond random bites. Mostly, we listened to Benjie's chatter and shared glances at each other.

"I hope the flowers weren't too much," Peter said. "I, uh, don't want to rush you. Or scare you."

"Rush me, scare me?" I shook my head, almost too confused to answer. "You saved me."

"Not true," Peter said. "You saved yourself because you never gave up."

I laid my fork on my plate. "No. I was numb, terrified. I doubted every decision."

"But you followed your instinct to leave, months ago, even when that's all you had to go on. I can't imagine the courage that took." He reached across the table and took my hands. "And look where you are now."

"Mommy, what's for dessert?" Of course, it was Benjie being a five-year-old, though his eyes lingered on my hands clasped in Peter's.

Ice cream and a cookie came fast. So did Benjie's bedtime. He was sleepy and snuggled into bed in an instant.

When I came downstairs Peter had a fire going in the study. He held out his arms to me and I walked into them.

"Abby, I'm so in love with you. It seems now I can finally say it, though I never thought this would happen to me." His dark wave of hair brushed his forehead. "It feels like a medical condition I hope never to recover from. I want to love you as you deserve. Make up for all you've suffered. And you must know I want to adopt Benjie and be his legal father. As soon as the time is right."

We sat entwined on the couch with the fire snapping and leaping. Peter stroked my cheek, my hair. He kissed me long and deep. His warmth filled all my empty crannies, my hollow places.

I wrapped my arms around him, pulled his lips to mine, kissed the old goodbye, and embraced the new.

42

Winter deepened, bringing more things new and miraculous, owl and eagle aeries on display through the leafless landscape. Nesting swans like white clouds afloat near the shoreline. The creek where we skated amidst snow-capped trees with trunks that shone like crystal. I learned about oysters. How to eat them when they were plentiful in months spelled with an R. It was February, and Burleigh brought them to us by the bushel.

Once again, I owned a car. While having it serviced, I decided to further erase what memories I could and had it painted a warm, creamy beige. The tan side panels were a nice blend and our old station wagon seemed almost brand new.

"It looks like a vanilla ice cream cone," said Benjie. He crawled all through it, played with the steering wheel. He showed not the slightest bit of remembered fear from our terrifying hours disguised in it. His recovery was another miracle, a constant relief. I never forgot Peter's insistence that my child's bravery reflected my own.

Throughout the holidays Benjie, Jess, Josh and Jake skated, sledded, and held epic snowball fights. But when school resumed for the older Tomisons, Benjie and Jake spent hours after half-day kindergarten sharing conductor's hats, blowing carved wooden whistles under our tree, racing, de-railing and crashing the train. When Peter and I dismantled the Christmas tree after New Year's Day the study seemed empty, diminished.

"Mom, please can we leave my train up?" He pointed at his blocks and books and antique attic toys with a mopey face. "There's nothin' else fun to play with." *I had to admit these were poor substitutes for the chug of the locomotive, the smell of the smoke, cars rattling around the track.*

In the weeks that passed the train track grew, with Peter's help, from an oval to a figure eight. A bridge appeared, and the cargo load changed daily. Toy soldiers rode on the coal car, marbles in the cattle car, the log car carried crayons. "The angel's still my favorite," Benjie said, "on the caboose. She watches to make sure everything's OK. And she likes it 'cause it's red."

One frigid day we were in the kitchen eating vegetable soup and cheese toast while Benjie practiced writing the alphabet letters he learned that week. When the front door knocker banged, he grinned, jumped up and ran to answer it. "That's Jake, Mom. And he said he was bringing cookies."

There was a pause and a deep, unfamiliar murmur. Then Benjie called out for me. "Mommy, it's the mailman." I was already behind Benjie at the door.

"Hi, there, Ma'am. I have a certified letter for you, Mrs. Matthew Wells? It requires your signature, if you please."

That's when I stopped breathing, though I watched my hand sign a form and reach for the letter. I read it, leaning against the door. I leafed through pages of legal terms, names I recognized and some I did not. But the first page, written to me by Mr. Dangerfield in simple letter form explained all I needed to know.

He confirmed that the *Marriage Book* proved my ancestor's legitimacy.

But it was further study of obscure historical documents that sealed my entitlement. A little-known fact was unearthed about Mercy Collington Buford, a great-great-granddaughter of Young Will's devoted sister, Mercy. I read and re-read the unexpected accounts dating back to the Civil War, wishing I could reach back in time to know and thank this woman.

As Buford descendants she and her only son were the owners of Bay House as stipulated in the first William Collington's will. Together with her husband they loved farming the land that was "kissed by the bay," as she described their life. Until their son, just nineteen, left to do his duty and died in the Battle of Bull Run in 1861. In a remarkable show of strength and resolve Mercy had her own will changed. Upon her death, ownership would convey to a descendant of her beloved brother's legitimate son, little Benjamin Collington. And so on, through time, to me. Next, the deed followed, with seals and dates and signatures in black and white. Finally, I felt myself breathe.

The Tomisons' deed and title were formally bound together and addressed to them. And lastly, an explanation of William and Harriet's entitlement to 125 acres. This information, Mr. Dangerfield assured me, would be sent to Harriet and clarified by him personally if need be. I felt the forces of my mother's spirit reaching out through her old friend and ally. A final blessing, since she had loved me and, once, my father, whose life's purpose and passion was the legacy of Bay House.

"Mommy, the phone's ringing." Benjie stood beside me, tugging on my sweater. Skipper was barking and the train was clacking around the track. I picked it up in a daze but forgot to say "hello."

"Abby ... are you there? Are you alright?" Peter sounded more amused than worried.

"Wow. I hear the dog, the train, and Benjie wailing on that whistle. What's going on over there?"

"Sorry," I said. "I'm trying to bring myself back from a dream. Except it's not a dream. It's real, like the paper in my hands." *I was coming back to life with my heart beating like a locomotive.* "The mail came. The Tomisons' title, Harriet's documents ... and ..." *It was hard to speak.*

"And what?" cried Peter.

"The deed to Bay House. It's here. It's real. It's mine."

"Well, what are you doing right this minute?"

"I, ah, don't really know. I don't even know what day it is."

"Darling Abby, it's a celebration day. I'm coming right over." I had just enough time to brush my hair and redo my lipstick. Then Peter filled the hallway with outstretched arms and a bottle of champagne.

"It's February, remember?" I stared at him blankly. "You still haven't figured it out, have you?"

"I'll tell you what. I've got to fix something on Benjie's caboose. It'll only take a minute. So why don't you get us three champagne glasses? Benjie can have chocolate milk. Then come right back and we'll have the toast of the century."

While I searched for the champagne flutes I heard whispering and giggling from the study. "OK, you can come in now, Mommy." Benjie couldn't stop giggling. They were on their knees handling the caboose. They both stood while Peter poured champagne and raised his arm in a toast. "To Abby, Benjie and Bay House, at long last."

"Mom, you should see how we fixed the caboose." His eyes danced as he put his hand over his mouth to stifle a laugh.

"Yes," Peter said. "By all means check out the angel."

"Untie her, Mommy." My fingers trembled, on my knees I leaned forward and pulled the bow at her feet.

A lovely clink hit the tracks. I put my fingers out to find where the sound landed. And what it could be. It was small, round, like a ring. A gorgeous, glistening, diamond ring. I looked up into Peter's eyes. "Happy Valentine's Day," he said. "Will you please, please marry me?"

43

"So, which one do you like? Scarlet or Geranium?" S.J. tilted her head back and forth, holding up two paint swatches, squinting against the sun. "For the front door, I mean. As long as we're putting on a new roof, we may as well give the whole place a facelift. It'll be charcoal, and Burleigh's going to paint the house dove gray." She let out a raspy laugh and pointed to another swatch. "Doesn't sound much like Burleigh, does it? The man is on fire with all the fixups now that we're owners, especially with your wedding coming up. And I talked him into putting a pretty white railing around the porch. A red door seems cheery and welcoming, and a good match, don't you think?" S.J. turned to me and studied my face. "You're awfully quiet for a bride-to-be."

I was lost, gazing at the ring on my left hand sparkling in the sunlight. It was early morning. The children just climbed onto the school bus at the end of our lane. S.J. and I were sitting with coffee on the terrace watching the bay, lists in hand, scribbling notes, plans and duties. "Then you like my idea for the ceremony?"

"Yes, it's perfect, and absolutely you. And I promise not to tell a soul. And not a word about the food or the guest list, either. My lips are sealed." S.J. swiped a hand across her mouth. "But, Abby, we have got to go shopping. Remember? We've got to find you a wedding dress. For April thirtieth. Today's the middle of March, you know. That only gives us about six weeks."

"Yes, I, well … of course I remember." All I could do was nod. "It's the last Saturday in April and spring will be here and the grass will be green and the flowers blooming … and Bay House will be magical." I sighed. "Like the house in my dream."

S.J.'s voice rose with delight. "It is the house in your dream. It's yours and your handsome groom's. And everything will be perfect, I promise. Even the weather. *The Farmer's Almanac* says we're in for a warm, early spring. Burleigh swears that's our reward for the freezing winter we had. The snow's gone, and the slush. Days are longer and I can't remember this much March sunshine in forever. Take a look." S.J. pointed to the ground. "The new shoots are already starting to show."

"OK. I'll stop worrying about the weather." *I was coming back to reality, picturing my endless to-do list, vowing to cross that one off.*

"Aren't you glad you started the renovations of the Old Cabin when you did?" The question caught me off guard but was natural coming from S.J. We were sharing builders for both of our remodeling projects.

I'm not convinced anything a construction crew could do would transform the ancient cabin. Would it always smell of ash and fear? Would removing the treacherous board Benjie and I crossed erase the terror we endured? It would always be a part of Bay House just as Bay House was part of me. My inheritance includes everything on the property. My task is to revive what was past and renew it for the next generations to come.

"Yes. That's another reason I asked you over. It's finished. You've got to see it. I promised myself I would do it but honestly, it's amazingly different now. It's full of light, the carpet's in, and they're done painting. The fireplace is brand-new, and I'm thrilled. You've already seen how they walled up that horrible door in the master bedroom when they enlarged it and re-did the master bath."

"Of course, you're thrilled. And relieved. I know it's weighed on your mind. But now it's done." A slow grin spread across her face. "And I think we should celebrate with a wedding dress. I've got a feeling we might get lucky today and find it. It's still early and we can shop 'til we do. Burleigh will be around all day. He'll get Jake and Benjie from the bus at noon, give 'em lunch, and be here for everybody else after school and later if we need to stay gone."

"How sweet of him," I said. "I'd love to see him reading to Jake and Benjie and practicing their rhyming words with them. *The Cat in the Hat* is Benjie's favorite. Cat, hat, sat, rat, pat. Such little words coming from such a big man … they'll love it." I couldn't hold back a laugh.

S.J. stood and reached for my coffee cup. She held the screen door for me as we entered the kitchen. "I've got a few places in mind to look. I know you don't want a traditional gown but there are a lot of stores in Stevensville. I've been asking around about formal wear," she chuckled, "since I'm not exactly a fashion plate. But I'm gonna splurge and get a new dress, too. There are some vintage places closer to Easton and St. Michaels that might have more choices. Of styles and, uh, colors."

I shook my head. "Right," I said. "No white."

"Got it. Meet you in my driveway at 9:15." Twenty minutes later we were on our way. We were both quiet until the road opened up to two lanes and shopping centers began to appear. I stared at my ring, tried to picture myself marrying anyone, much less a man as wonderful, kind and loving as Peter.

My heart beat faster, my palms were clammy. "S.J.," I whispered. "I just realized I'm nervous."

She stole a quick look at me, wide-eyed, and covered my hand with hers. "Me, too, I'm surprised to say. But we're going to be calm and have a great adventure. And find your dress. OK?"

"OK. If you say so." *Joy and freedom and happiness in such huge doses were making me numb on top of nervous. Then I remembered Peter convincing me again and again of my courage. I didn't feel it but maybe I could pretend until it returned.*

We drove through parking lots, wound around shopping centers I had never even seen. *I was reminded of how safe and secure I felt at Bay House, miles away from this suburban hustle and bustle. Stores and restaurants we could always visit, but return to peace and beauty where we lived.*

"Abby, look at the clothes in that window." S.J. pulled into a parking spot and we both got out. There were dresses and gowns of every color, length, and style. Simple, sequined, feathered, flowing. We were surprised to be alone in the shop except for a young teenage girl who appeared to be the sole employee. She flashed a half smile, stumbling over her words as she offered to direct us. When I said, "Wedding dresses, please," she balked.

"I'm new," she said. "We're taking inventory. We're low on those, of any kind. Sizes, styles, or fabrics. We don't have any veils, and we have nothing in white."

"Well, that's just perfect," said S.J. with a bright smile. "We're looking for color. Maybe something long, and in silk?" I had to turn away to keep from laughing at S.J.'s speech.

While the salesgirl continued to stammer apologies, S.J. started a slow loop around every rack. She pulled out frocks with yellow daisies, pink and white dotted Swiss, purple taffeta with sleeves like balloons, black satin, off-shoulder, slinky numbers she pushed aside without hesitation. I wandered around, listening to the sound of hangers sliding back and forth, feeling strange and disconnected from this process. Until, from the corner of my eye, I caught a sliver of blue that made me stop and look twice. A scalloped hemline dappled with crystals just peeking out between a thick crush of skirts. On the one rack in my size.

It was pale blue, like the sky in spring. Made of softest silk, with a long skirt that flared and flowed. The *V* neckline, too, was edged with crystals. S.J. stopped pacing and stared at me as I held the dress up to my shoulders. Her hands flew to her face. "Go put it on," she said.

When I stepped out of the dressing room, I knew this was my gown. It was like wearing a cloud. The fit was uncanny, like my own skin, only better. Other shoppers who had entered stopped chatting. Someone blurted, "Absolutely stunning." All eyes were on me.

"I don't believe this," said S.J. "It's perfect. It's the exact color of your eyes."

She turned to the salesgirl, applauded, waved her hands in the air. "She'll take it."

How could something so hard be so simple? I remembered my list, thinking nothing would ever feel unsurmountable again.

S.J. squeezed my hand when we got into the car, with my gorgeous blue gown laid carefully in the back seat. "I'm feeling so emotional suddenly, and it isn't even my wedding. I just keep seeing you the day we met on the path in our woods. You were terrified. Beaten black and blue. Forced to run without knowing where to go, and no one to love you and Benjie." She flicked away tears from her eyes.

"And now we have all of you, and a storybook home … and Peter." I felt my own eyes fill with joyful tears of disbelief.

"Plus," S.J. said. "You learned how to cook a goose." We laughed and cried all the way home to Bay House.

44

Peter and I were married on the lawn facing the bay, at slanty-time, in a soft spring breeze with the setting sun warm on our faces, sparkling the bay to liquid gold. Bay House was decked for the occasion like a stately dowager in fancy dress. Her ageless brick walls were aglow, rouged by sunset. Her windows seemed to catch fire, as glittery as diamond buttons on a gown of rose velvet. Towering evergreens perfumed the air, forming an arch as if loving arms, cloaked in emerald, were raised in perpetual benediction.

"Sweetie, I know you're excited. Me too." I bent to kiss Benjie's cheeks, his hair, his hands, for what felt like the hundredth time. "But please stop fidgeting."

"Mom, I can't see through these trees. Why are we hiding in here?"

My smile felt glued in place from ear to ear. "We're not hiding. We're waiting. Stand a little closer and peek through the branches. There. Now, what do you see?"

"Um, chairs kinda lined up with people in 'em, and ribbons blowing everywhere. Wow. It's S.J. and the kids. All dressed up. And that nice nurse from the hospital. And over there," he pointed to the terrace, "is Noah with Skipper on his leash." *I prayed he wouldn't start clapping and call out to his puppy.*

"OK. Keep looking a little farther. See anybody else?" I wondered if he noticed the harp nestled near the arched trellis of greens and a rainbow of April buds and blossoms. The lady in lavender from the auction day was delighted when we asked her to provide music for our ceremony. Now I could hear her melodies floating on the air.

Benjie glanced up at me, eyes round and shining. "Peter. I see Peter. He's standing under a bunch of flowers like a tunnel or something. Next to a man in a long black robe. They're laughing and Peter's looking at people and waving. And, Mommy." Benjie tugged at my arm. "Here comes our friend you said is gonna walk with us."

A dapper little man in a navy striped suit appeared from behind more branches. He stood between us, offered Benjie his hand, and me, his arm. "Dearest girl," he whispered. "I am so proud of you."

The music swelled, the guests' voices hushed. Our trio stepped out together into the sunlight as Mr. Dangerfield escorted us down the grassy carpet of jade. The rest was a haze. I saw only Peter.

My sky-blue dress floated around me. For a moment Peter seemed too stunned to move. "It's just like your eyes," he said as his lips sealed mine with a forever kiss. The silk and crystals rippled at my ankles, my dark hair brushed my shoulders, clipped behind one ear with a cluster of ivory tea roses. My great-grandmother's pearls were my only jewelry.

Benjie stood between us, clutching our hands. When the minister pronounced us man and wife he leaped into Peter's arms. "And now you're my daddy," he shouted. His little voice rang out like bells from a steeple.

Everyone rose and applauded. S.J., in flowing coral lace matching her hair, sprang in front of the crowd, waving her arms for attention. In her easy, carefree, only-S.J. way, she invited our guests into Bay House for the reception.

Gulls sky-danced as we drifted from the lawn into Bay House. Benjie and the Tomison children led the way, skipping through the sweet new-cut grass. Then the fragrant lemon-scented entry hall, the glorious rug with furnishings aglow, and views of the bay in all its majesty. Hugs and handshakes from Dr. Sommerville and Peter's grinning staff. Peter's editor from his articles in *The Kent Island Chronicle*, a photographer at his side. Later, somehow, Hank Simpson bouncing Benjie on his knee.

Kisses from the church ladies, whose warmth turned to friendship when I asked to join their dedicated group. I knew they staged my entrance from the pines, created the arbor, placed the chairs, tied them with ribbon bouquets, and designed every magical view to face the shimmering bay. They radiated love even as I stumbled over introductions, mixing up their names.

Noah was busy in his starched white jacket. He passed a tray of champagne glasses, then banged through the kitchen door bearing platters heaped with delicacies. As I circled the buffet I caught his eye and mouthed, "Thank you," remembering his cantaloupe and fried chicken, our first meal as fugitives to Bay House. It was impossible to forget his fierce protection of Benjie after his fall from the tractor.

Now I marveled at the delicious display arranged on the dining room table. Mounds of peeled shrimp with cocktail and remoulade sauce. Stuffed mushroom caps straight from the oven, a colorful fruit and cheese board. Chilled marinated asparagus and a tray piled with golden crab cakes. Noah carving prime rib or slicing glazed ham beside a huge bubbly casserole of potatoes au gratin. Then, of course, hot rolls. And finally, my favorite. Crab imperial. Served in shell-shaped ramekins, creamy and rich and full of sweet lump meat. I knew I couldn't taste a morsel, but I smelled the enticing blend of aromas and felt my new reality filling me up like haute cuisine after starvation.

There were two faces I would never forget. Sister Florence Katherine and the intrepid Helen, from the House of Grace. I invited them as special guests, thrilled to be surprising them with a large check. I could never repay their kindness, but I could help provide a children's daycare center so needed at their women's shelter.

Peter took their hands in his and thanked them for protecting his wife and son. I was so befuddled it took a moment to register that this was me and Benjie. *And of course I knew he meant it in every way, including adoption. It seemed a lifetime ago, the loneliness, terror, pain. Now, all over and in the past, with the future beckoning like a cloudless sky.*

Mr. Dangerfield stood in the doorway, coughed behind his hand, lifted his champagne flute and gave it several taps. Peter joined him, happy and handsome, his face aglow.

"Ladies, gentlemen, and beloved friends of Abigail, Benjamín and Peter … Carpenter," our lawyer stuttered with a shy smile. "I've been asked to make an announcement. Although it is really the bride's news to share. Abigail, dear, will you please come forward?"

All heads turned as I wove through the room, pressing a large bundle close to my heart. I smiled as Peter leaned forward to kiss me.

My pulse began to race and I fought back tears. "Peter, will you help me with this?" As he held out his arms, I laid the *Marriage Book* across them, opening the crumbling cover to reveal the last page. The room fell silent.

"We've kept this a secret, but now it's time for a double celebration," I said. My words flowed loud and strong. I hooked my arm through Mr. Dangerfield's. "With Arthur's help, my legitimacy as heir to Bay House was recently proven beyond doubt. Everything my father told me was true. So now Benjie and I are home to stay." I glanced up at Peter and laughed. "Sorry. And Peter, too. We give our thanks to you and to God for the blessings of your love and support, even during the worst of this journey." *Matt's cruelty, Harriet's manipulations, William's terrifying mental decline, and the nightmare Benjie and I survived. It might take more than time to erase my sad story.*

"Cheers," cried S.J. Glasses clinked, applause broke out, and everyone talked at once.

The *Chronicle* photographer flashed his camera throughout the dining room, the hall and study, scribbling names for the news story that would be in print the next day.

S.J. waved her glass. "It's time for cake. My kids insisted on helping me bake. Don't worry, Abby," she said and winked at me. "I made two."

Peter closed the book with tender care. "The *Marriage Book* will be in the study across the hall. It's a piece of living history for everyone to enjoy. Our friend in the gloves will be happy to turn the pages for you. Later it will be on permanent display. Possibly in the Smithsonian Archives, open to the remaining legible page from 1770, where the marriage proof was recorded. Now, please," he said. "Come enjoy more cake and champagne."

"Dr. Carpenter," a woman's voice rang out. I recognized Benjie's favorite hospital nurse. "Where are you going for your honeymoon? Someplace exotic and very far away, we hope. We need some time off." Laughter bounced around the room.

Burleigh stood with a plate of food teetering on one huge hand. "According to S.J., he's movin' from town into Bay House. That's the honeymoon trip. Pretty big one, of course. Seven miles, maybe? With yours truly drivin' the truck." He let out a belly laugh, raised his glass as bubbles and fizz spilled down his fingers.

Benjie turned to me, giggling and breathless. "And I get to go stay at the Tomisons' and play in the creek and play in the woods with all the kids and go fishin' with worms and catch frogs and pound crabs and even take Skipper, too. Don't I, Mom?"

"Yes, Sweetie, you do. And I can't think of anything more perfect."

45

The last vestige of my old life was Harriet. She declined her invitation to the wedding, so I went to see her several weeks after in Vera's Annapolis townhouse. There she occupied the entire third floor and, she wrote, was helping Vera with "bookkeeping and client matters." And the hospital was a quick walk down an old brick street. I knew her life would always be wherever William was.

Vera ushered me into her gleaming chrome and leather living room with a wave of her cigarette holder and a sympathetic shake of her head. "She's not the same Harry," she said. Then she disappeared and left Harriet and me alone with our memories.

Harriet sat stiff and unmoving on the edge of a chair and recited a valiant myth about William's recovery. How they lounged together in the lovely day room, enjoying the books she brought him. How any day now the doctors would invite her to join his therapy sessions and William would know her name. She thanked me, unnecessarily, for allowing her the future proceeds from the sale of their portion of land for her expenses and William's treatment. I held out our wedding photos, but she stood and turned to the window, as remote as the first day I met her.

I pictured their boxed-up belongings waiting in a corner of the new Old Cabin. "Shall I have them stored for safekeeping, or delivered to you?"

"Maybe … someday …" Harriet said. She continued to stare out of the window.

It was clear this was the end of everything we shared, or escaped, from life at Bay House. As I thanked Vera for her hospitality, she shrugged and blew a long plume of smoke. "You tried," she said.

Yes. I tried, and it brought me peace. Despite Harriet's threats and deceptions, I knew she only wanted us gone, not harmed. In a way she was just another victim caught in William's tangled web. Finally, I was ready to put the past behind me, but close the door gently.

I was not the woman I used to be. Alone, frightened, displaced. Now Peter and I strolled with Benjie between us, along the sparkling shores of home. Bay House. This was no child's dim and distant dream. This was real. This was my life. And I was pregnant.

I thought of my father, his father, and his. Centuries peeled back, no longer leading only to the past, but lighting a path to the future. I remembered the Indian girl playing in the forest, the English boy who grew up loving her. The gnarled and broken chain of events, a simple marriage, a covenant of love destroyed by hate. Good and evil, the enduring forces around and within us. I pictured Ellen Smalldeer, whose story started mine. The young mother whose life was cut short for selfless devotion to a child. The woman I so resembled, whose ancestors once thrived on this land.

We were on our beach enjoying the morning's ships and sails parade up the bay. It was hot. End-of-summer, August hot. Benjie was surrounded by his usual buckets and shovels, throwing sticks for Skipper to retrieve. He kicked up plumes of sand and ran in circles with Skipper barking at his heels. Peter nestled beside me on the hollow log. Gulls soared above us in a cloudless sky that promised sun.

"So," Peter said. He tilted his head. The salty breeze ruffled the hair dipping onto his forehead. "What should we name the baby? I wonder what the big brother thinks?"

He jumped up, waving his arms like antennae. "Hey, Benj. Hey, buddy." He hollered down the beach, repeating the question.

Benjie stood stock-still and turned to face us. "My sister, you mean? Gosh, Peter, Mommy already knows her name."

Peter's grin lit his whole face. I felt the baby flutter deep inside. I sat up, straight and tall as a tree. "So…what is it?" he said.

"Well, it's more a question of *who* is it." In my heart I knew he guessed this long ago. Possibly even ahead of me.

"And?"

"It's Ellen. It's time to bring her out of the shadow of history and give her life again."

"Well of course," he said, as his lips brushed mine. "Who else could she be?"

"Absolutely no one." I gave him a playful smile and squeezed his hands. "Just remember and be prepared. I think she's going to have sky blue eyes."

Acknowledgements

"The art of making art ...
is putting it together."

~ Stephen Sondheim

This creation took more than a village. It took the help and dedication of an entire tribe.

My thanks to Lynn Skapyak Harlin, editor, mentor, teacher and friend, for her tireless efforts over many years to bring out the best in each facet of this book. Her astute contributions enabled me to produce a product far beyond my expectations. She guided me through the potential choppy waters of co-writing with my deceased mother so our story flows like ripples in the same pond.

Also, my praise and appreciation for Amy Cherie Copeland's professional services. She is a teacher, writing consultant, indefatigable proofreader gifted with laser focus, and is herself a co-author with an eagle eye for hidden flaws. She tackled this project with microscopic detail while maintaining optimism and good cheer. Lynn and Amy were a perfect team and this book would not exist without them.

Thanks to author and poet Paula R. Hilton for her perceptive, experienced commentary as a beta reader, and her beautiful back cover blurb. Along with Amy, also a beta reader, both sets of eyes gave the manuscript added depth and vitality. Lynne Radcliffe's blurb rounded out the story's essence and her countless read-throughs offered invaluable feedback.

Special thanks to artist and graphic designer Oscar Senn for his contributions from front to back and in between. When he agreed to paint an original cover, design the back, plus do the inside formatting, I was thrilled. His brush captured the essence of the story so well, and I'll always love Abby's intensely blue eyes.

Thanks to Elizabeth Pampalone of Absolute Marketing for her social media skills and website creation. And to Ericca Harvey for technical and administrative support. These talented experts made life glued to my computer not only bearable, but possible.

To all my dear friends far and wide my thanks for your love, support, critiques, enthusiasm, faith, and when I doubted myself, always saying, "Of course you can." And to my fairy-god-sisters, Clarissa, Lynne and Vivien, who helped keep the magic alive when I ran out of juice.

Thanks to my sons, Taylor and Chase, who always encouraged me, albeit impatiently, to finish each re-write which I swore was the last. And to the rest of my big, loving family, huge hugs for cheering me on.

Again and forever, I thank my mother for dreaming up this wonderful story and entrusting it to me at the end of her life. It's still hard to believe all of this really happened. I only know the journey was worth every step.

About the Authors

Bess Paterson Shipe (*1919–2015)* was a born writer with a collection of over 200 poems written from ages eight through twelve, gathered by her father and titled, *Fallen Petals*. One of them became the core of the novel she began 50 years later. A native of Baltimore, she graduated from the University of Maryland in 1940. She was a war bride, an English teacher and prolific author. She had a gift for ideas portrayed in fluid, linear order with beautiful imagery and lyrical style. She and her husband lived in Potomac, Maryland, enjoyed large, close-knit families, lifelong friends, their church and community. They raised three daughters with grands and great-grands they cherished.

During her long life, Bess continued to create poetry, also writing in every genre possible, on subjects too varied to list. Writing for children was a favorite. *Country School Boy,* 1976, Historic Medley District, Inc., tells about one room schoolhouses through the misadventures of Jerimiah Allby, a real-life rascally seven-year-old boy in 1875. *The Mysterious Tail of a Charleston Cat,* 1996, Sandlapper Publishing Co., Inc, co-written with her sister, Ruth Paterson Chappell, reflects her flair for mystery and history. She was an antique buff drawn to the mystique of old houses, as displayed in one of her earlier articles, "A House with a Past", June 1980, Chesapeake Bay Magazine. In 1974 she began *The Forces of Bay House* and continued creating it up until her death.

Bess loved learning for learning's sake, excelled at research, and spent hours lost in the stacks of the Library of Congress following her intellectual curiosity on countless topics. She treasured her book clubs, always with work in hand for critiquing. "What if?" was her favorite question. Her answer was always, "Why not?"

Susan Shipe Calfee was hooked on words with a rhyme published in second grade. "I love sketty, can't wait till it's retty," lit her interest in writing for school newspapers and publications. She later became a Speech Communications major at the University of Maryland, her home state. Susan lives in Ponte Vedra Beach, Florida, where she joined the local Shantyboat Writer's Workshop, learning craft techniques and developing her skills. In 2013 she published her award-winning children's book, *St. Augustine A to Z–A Young Reader's Guide to America's Oldest City.* Still popular today, it's the subject of school visits where Susan introduces children to the magic of language.

Her second passion is singing. She performed in show groups at Busch Gardens, Tampa, and Disney World in Orlando. Susan produced a Christmas CD in 2000 and performed with the Jacksonville Symphony Chorus for 16 years. She still enjoys membership in numerous vocal ensembles. Susan plans to write and sing as long as she can hold a pencil and a piece of music.

While volunteering at Baptist Medical Center, 2004–2013, her passions merged. She served on the Auxiliary Board of Directors as editor of its publication. Her work with Body & Soul–The Art of Healing, gave her the privilege of escorting musicians to patients' rooms for bedside concerts. The highlight of her service was chronicling the miraculous transformative power of music.

Childhood summers on and around the Chesapeake Bay planted a love and affinity for the region. In 2017 she began revisions to *The Forces of Bay House*, the novel her mother could not finish before her death. Susan has two adventurous sons and is the grandmother of two little whirlwinds. She is proud to be among many authors in her family. This is her first novel.

How This Book Came to Be

In 2014, my mother, Bess Paterson Shipe, age 95, left her home in the Washington area and came to live with me in the Florida warmth and sunshine. I was thrilled my best friend, best writing pal, best everything, was also going to be my roommate. I knew that along with the responsibility of helping her navigate her final years would come some care givers, but moreover, a parade of family, friends, and fun. There was much more adventure than adversity resulting, and no regrets.

I set up a little writing nook for her in my office and when the household got hectic, Mom would shrug and smile. "Let's work on the book," she'd say. And we'd slip off to our legal pads and close the door. She was loving and kind, gracious and wise, savvy, selfless and funny.

A prolific and accomplished writer all her life, her notes, files, publications and works-in-progress came with her. Boxes of them, plus World War II love letters from my father, deceased. Last off the moving truck was a heavy trunk with a tiny label marked, "Forces."

Inside were 14 notebooks with versions of this novel atop piles of loose random pages. She'd been writing it as long as I could remember, but I knew nothing yet of its potential. Since I too, was studying the craft and had published a children's book, I thought, "Hmm. Here're some lessons ahead." In that trunk like a treasure chest was her life's literary dream. Little did I know it was soon to become mine.

She penned a wonderful story of 34 chapters which my own editor read and urged her to polish, but first those stacks of pages had to be made digital and brought into the computer age. Narrative and sentence structure needed an update. Beats and dialogue tags were missing. Her beautiful, lyrical prose was unique, descriptions captivating. Her characters had great bones, though they needed more flesh. What was too elusive for her was the wrap-up and ending. When she asked for my input, I was honored, delighted. I promised to help finish what she could not, never dreaming I would have to make good on my pledge, as a solo act. Before we could begin our collaboration, she passed away in November of 2015.

My decision to tackle the revisions and completion came in 2017. I rounded out the story, growing it to 45 suspenseful, fast-moving chapters. The foremost challenge was keeping her voice, characters, conflicts and resolutions so congruent, additions so seamless, they would appear as if two hands held the same pen. The work, with life often getting in the way, took seven years. Though at first I fought the feeling of being a thief, taking credit for what was originally my mother's creation, I finally added my name to the title page. I wasn't stealing it. I was saving it. From another box, another trunk. Fulfilling my promise with pride, gratitude and awe, and both our dreams at once.

This novel is many things. A wish, a fluke, a miracle and a compelling, complex saga. How it came to be? That's just a simple love story.

~ Susan Shipe Calfee

Made in the USA
Middletown, DE
27 November 2024

65585368R00265